TITLES BY DELAS HERAS

The Intergalactic Interloper
Foxman and the Cat Burglar
The Nine Lives of Bianca Moon

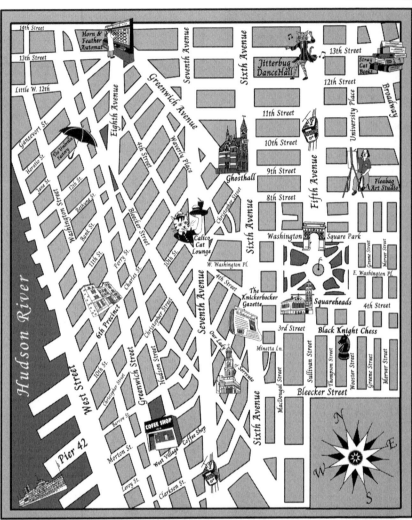

14th Street

Horn & Feather Automat

13th Street

Little W. 12th

Gansevoort St.

Horatio St.

Jane St.

Bethune St.

11th St.

Perry St.

Charles St.

10th St.

Bank St.

Washington Street

Eighth Avenue

4th Street

Bleecker Street

Greenwich Avenue

Seventh Avenue

Sixth Avenue

Jitterbug DanceHall

13th Street

Stray Cat Books

12th Street

University Place

Broadway

11th Street

10th Street

9th Street

8th Street

Fifth Avenue

Fleabag Art Studio

Waverly Place

Ghosthall

Christopher Street

Calico Cat Lounge

W. Washington Pl.

Washington Square Park

E. Washington Pl.

Greene Street

Mercer Street

Sixth Avenue

The Knickerbocker Gazette

Squareheads

4th Street

6th Precinct

10th St.

Christopher Street

Greenwich Street

Hudson Street

Perry St.

Seventh Avenue

4th Street

Our Lady of Sorrento

3rd Street

Minetta Ln.

Black Knight Chess

Sullivan Street

Thompson Street

Wooster Street

Greene Street

Mercer Street

Hudson River

West Street

Barrow St.

Morton St.

Leroy St.

Greenwich Street

COFFEE SHOP

West Village Coffee Shop

Clarkson St.

MacDougal Street

Sixth Avenue

Bleecker Street

Pier 42

N
E
S
W

Greenwich Village

The Nine Lives of Bianca Moon

Morton Digby #1

Delas Heras

DOUBLE SIX BOOKS | NEW YORK

DOUBLE SIX BOOKS
New York, New York

ISBN 978-1-7353175-5-7 (trade paperback)
ISBN 978-1-7353175-4-0 (ebook)

To Mom and Dad,
who shared their lifelong love of books with me

1 · Junior Detective Morton Digby: A New Partner

Tuesday

It was the summer of 1954 and the noonday sun was stopped dead in the sky high above the City. Its rays beat down mercilessly on Junior Detective Morton Digby, who was standing outside the precinct by the food cart on the corner. He was a border collie mix. An average-sized dog with a thick black coat and a white belly, neck, and ruff. His ears were fully dropped, his eyes were icy blue, and a characteristic white strip ran down the middle of his face spreading out across his snout. He had on a threadbare tan jacket that hung loosely over a white linen shirt and a navy-blue tie.

Morton tugged at the brim of his battered trilby, shading his eyes from the sun's glare as he turned to face his partner. "And this is Frankie's Frankfurters," Morton said, snapping his fingers and pointing finger guns at the food stand. "I can vouch for the number one, which comes topped with sauerkraut and mustard."

It was his partner's first day on the job and Morton was giving him the lay of the land. Senior Detective J.B. Puddleworth eyed the food cart dubiously. "Don't tell me you eat this junk for lunch every day?" he asked much too loudly.

"Just about," Morton replied, casting an uneasy glance

at the dachshund in the baseball cap who was poised at the ready in the shade of the cart's umbrella.

"I suppose it won't kill me to eat a little street food," his partner muttered. Detective Puddleworth was a Scottish terrier with a wiry black coat, a stubby tail, and a long, bearded face. A short dog, the tips of his bat ears reached only to Morton's shoulder. The Scottie had arrived for his first day decked out in a gray pinstripe suit with a paisley kerchief folded into his breast pocket, a dotted tie twisted just so, and a felt fedora set at a rakish tilt.

Morton stepped up to the cart. "Hiya, Frankie. I'll take the usual. And a bag of salt-and-vinegar potato chips." The dachshund handed him a wrapped-up frankfurter and a bag of chips, and Morton pocketed his change. Detective Puddleworth ordered the same for himself with the air of someone throwing caution to the wind.

Morton was just getting acquainted with his new partner. A framed photograph of a dog in a pink hat had already landed on Detective Puddleworth's desk, and when Morton had asked about it he'd learned that the Scottish terrier and his wife had just moved from a stand-alone house in Staten Island to an apartment on the Upper East Side. His partner had proudly revealed another morsel of personal history when he'd declared—in front of all their gathered colleagues, mind you—that he could trace his ancestry back to a twelfth-century Highland chieftain. Muted laughter had rippled through the bullpen, and Morton had spotted one patroldog making a finger-twirling motion near his temple.

With their lunch in hand, Morton turned west in the

direction of the nearby river, and said: "Our best bet is to grab a bench over by the water."

Detective Puddleworth went all pop-eyed. "You can't be serious, Morton! I'm going to melt if we stay outdoors a minute longer." To prove his point, he began to pant heavily and mop his brow theatrically with his pocket square. "Come along, Morton. Let's get out of this heat." Without waiting for a reply, the Scottie turned and marched back toward the precinct.

Morton stared after his partner, wondering if he was expected to follow. The knock on short dogs was that they were often bossy, and while Morton didn't want to pigeon-hole his partner unfairly, he was worried that Detective Puddleworth might prove overbearing. They were ostensibly equals, but it wasn't unheard of for senior detectives to treat a junior detective partner more like an assistant.

Reluctantly, Morton turned and followed the Scottie up the steps and past the granite columns that flanked the police station's main entrance. He was desperate for their partner-ship to work. He had been without a proper partner since he'd been promoted to detective at the start of the year.

The West Village's 6th Precinct was based out of a five-story building on Charles Street only a few blocks from the Hudson. It had an attached garage fashioned from a con-verted stable, and a small jail capable of holding up to twen-ty-five prisoners in a pinch. Inside, a cavernous first-floor hall served as the bullpen for detectives and uniformed officers alike. It was a dreary wood-paneled room, unevenly lit by brass pendant lamps.

Like most police precincts around the city, the 6th remained something of a boys' club for dogs. In recent years a wave of female personnel had joined the force, but for now the fairer sex were relegated to desk work and not permitted out on patrol. The changes opening up the force also meant that plenty of cats had earned their badges. Most notable among the felines at the 6th were two huge Maine coon littermates who alternated shifts at the front desk. This brother and sister duo boasted mitts the size of bear paws and claws to match. Nobody messed with those two cats. But the bulk of the uniformed officers and detectives at the 6th were the usual lads—male canines who started out as flatfoots and worked their way up the ranks. There were a handful of terriers, bull-dogs, and mutts. The rest were mostly hounds: bloodhounds, basset hounds, coonhounds, foxhounds, greyhounds—and anything and everything in between.

The two detectives found the break room empty. It was a windowless space adjacent to the bullpen with sickly green walls and a lingering smell of burnt coffee. There was a small fridge, an electric percolator resting on the narrow counter, and a row of vending machines along the back wall.

Detective Puddleworth grabbed a paper cup and filled it with water from the small sink, slurping it down in a few gulps. "Ahh. I needed that. You know what this precinct could use? Air conditioners!"

"Don't hold your breath, J.B.," Morton observed dryly. Detective Puddleworth frowned and patted his whiskers with a small napkin. Morton went up to the bright red Cleo Cola machine and dropped two nickels into the slot. They both caught on the first try and he gave the chrome knob a twist until it clicked, allowing him to remove a chilled glass bottle. After popping the cap, he sat down at one of the room's two round Formica tables. Tearing open the bag of potato chips with his teeth, he popped a handful in his mouth. Then he took a bite of his frankfurter and chewed thoughtfully.

Detective Puddleworth sat down across from him, his short legs dangling from the wooden chair. The Scottish terrier took a dainty nibble from his frankfurter, and then another. "Not bad," he conceded.

Conversation centered on Detective Puddleworth's recent move. Adapting to apartment-style living was proving to be a big adjustment for the Scottie and his wife, especially as they had a family of Saint Bernards living directly above them. Morton reckoned Detective Puddleworth was perhaps seven years older than him—but as he listened to the Scottie talk, he was struck by how little resemblance his partner's life bore to his own carefree bachelor existence.

"I wish I'd thought to ask for ketchup on my frank-furter," the Scottie griped. Morton would never think to ruin a perfectly good frankfurter with ketchup. Nevertheless he hopped to his feet and went over to the fridge, returning with a half-full bottle of the red condiment. "Fabulous!" the Scottie exclaimed, unscrewing the cap. "Now tell me, Morton, what made you join the force? Not many border collies go into police work, do they?"

"I am something of an anomaly around here," Morton admitted. "Border collies generally prefer country life, and we lack that fierce pack-dog mentality that draws so many canines to law enforcement. Of course I'm not one hundred percent border collie," Morton added, not wanting to make a secret of his mixed heritage. "My grandmother ran off with a stray, returning home alone two months later to give birth to a litter of five. It was a big scandal in its day." Morton scrutinized the Scottie's face for any hint of disapproval, and saw none. Even though most cats and dogs nowadays held open-minded views on the subject of purebreds, the police force drew more than its fair share of troglodytes. "My two older brothers run a wool factory up in Maine," Morton went on. "They expected me to join them and were upset when I packed my bags and left for the City Police Academy. I remember my brother Petey saying, only half-jokingly, *You'll be back soon enough with your tail between your legs! Herding dogs need fresh air and open horizons!* But I had a foolish notion that by joining the force I could help make this city a little safer."

Morton was startled when Detective Puddleworth banged on the table with his fist, causing the ketchup bottle to jump half an inch into the air. "Horsefeathers!" cried the Scottie. "There's nothing foolish about it! This town is overrun with dangerous criminals, and it's up to us to catch them. I'm itching to roll up my sleeves and dive into some big-city police work! At my former precinct we were lucky to get the occasional burglary. I got out of bed one day and told myself that I needed to go where the action was if I expected to make a difference. So here I am, for the exact same reasons as you! I may not have much practical experience with major crimes, but I've read every criminology book on the shelf. I know all there is to know about conducting crime scene investigations. But my real forte is the psychology of the criminal mind. I just finished reading *Think Like a Crook* by Wanda Squirlcatcher. It was a revelation."

Morton cocked his head to one side and gave his partner a curious look. "Can books really help much with police work?"

"Oh yes. Very much so. Surprisingly I've learned almost as much from reading murder mysteries as I have from textbooks." The Scottie dropped his voice: "I'm addicted to dime-store crime novels. They are a reliable source of crime-fighting tips. All the great detectives combine keen powers of observation with a deep insight into animal psychology. It's not enough to have a great sniffer, the modern-day detective must employ deductive reasoning to pinpoint the villain!"

Morton got a sinking feeling in the pit of his stomach as he listened to Detective Puddleworth ramble on about his favorite fictional sleuths. When the Scottish terrier finally paused to take another bite of his frankfurter, Morton couldn't resist throwing cold water on his partner's dreams of crime-solving glory. "I hate to break it to you, J.B., but I doubt they're gonna hand us any big cases. There's a pecking order around here and currently we rank dead last. We're looking at mostly shoplifters, pickpockets, and drunk tank duty."

Now it was Detective Puddleworth's turn to stare at him in dismay. "I didn't sell my home and move into a cramped apartment to be put on pickpocket duty! Didn't you and your former partner ever work on any interesting cases?"

"Actually, you're my first partner since I made junior detective," Morton confessed, leaving unsaid the fact that no one there had wanted to team up with a herding dog. Morton blotted at his chin with a paper napkin to rid himself of a stray dab of mustard and took a swig of soda as a brief silence descended between them. Morton had no desire to go into detail about how tough the past few months had been at the 6th Precinct.

The Scottie gulped down some more water and then changed the subject: "Looks like we picked the right lunch spot."

"I suppose," Morton conceded. "But the break room isn't always this quiet. As often as not it's full of rowdy dogs telling crude jokes and playing juvenile pranks."

The Scottie raised his bushy eyebrows. "That explains your reluctance to eat inside. Lucky for us there's nary a scoundrel in sight!"

The words were barely out of his mouth when Sergeant Doyle wandered into the break room in search of a fresh cup of java. The sergeant was a barrel-chested bulldog with a smushed nose and an unfortunate propensity to drool. He was wearing his usual crisp navy uniform with two columns of brass buttons going down the front.

"Sergeant," the two detectives grunted in unison, acknowledging their superior officer with a nod.

"Well, well. What do we have here?" sneered the bulldog. "If it isn't dingbat Digby and his new partner Detective Puddlenuts!" The sergeant guffawed at his own lousy joke and a stream of spittle shot out and smeared against one of the lower cabinets.

Detective Puddleworth's lip pulled back in a snarl, but thankfully this passed unnoticed by the sarge, who had shuffled over to the counter. Cursed with short arms and legs, the bulldog needed to stretch to reach the coffeepot. He unscrewed the cap, filled his mug with the sludgy brown liquid, and then turned to face the detectives. "Did you two hear the news? Buckley and Callaway finally collared that arsonist. They're doing a victory lap around the station as we speak. The captain is happy as a pig in mud!" The bulldog chugged his coffee as he circled their table. "You're new around here, Puddleworth, so let me clue you in. Buckley and Callaway are the top dogs on our team. They can follow a week-old scent blindfolded over bridges and through tunnels until they close in on their target. Of course, they're both hounds. You could say they've got a nose for the job, unlike some other detectives I know." The bulldog hooted and slapped Morton on the back. Then the sarge's eye landed on the ketchup bottle sitting mid-table. "Hey! Leave some ketchup for the rest of us! Is there even any left?" Grabbing the glass bottle, the bulldog gave it a shake. The cap must have been loose because it flew off, along with a spurt of ketchup that caught Morton right in the face. "Oops. Sorry about that, pal! Geez, I really nailed ya!" The bulldog snickered. Then he smacked the ketchup bottle back down on the table and sauntered off, chuckling heartily.

Without saying a word Detective Puddleworth held some napkins out to Morton, who did his best to wipe the splatter off his fur. Feeling miserable, he got up and went over to the sink to rinse his muzzle. When he was done, he patted himself dry with a dish towel.

The Scottie regarded him sympathetically. "Looks like that bench would have been a better lunch spot after all."

"It's just a bit of ketchup. I'll live."

Detective Puddleworth shook his head in disgust. "I don't think I can put up with that sort of thing day in and day out. He's lucky I didn't pop him in the snout!"

Morton grinned. "I doubt punching the sarge on your first day would go over well."

"Please tell me he's not in charge of assignments?"

"I'm afraid so."

The Scottie looked crestfallen.

Morton now regretted dampening his partner's enthusiasm on his first day. Detective Puddleworth might be a bit of a loon, and a major food snob, but he also seemed like an honest dog whose heart was in the right place. "You know what, J.B.? Let's just take it one case at a time. With hard work and a little luck, we're bound to catch a break."

"That's the spirit!" cried the Scottie, beaming. "Every dog has its day! Our luck could change in a flash! Who knows? We might even land a murder case before summer's end."

2 · Flint Lockford: The Piano

Flint Lockford was an Irish wolfhound with a scruffy gray coat and glowing amber eyes. He was seated at his desk with the sleeves of his checkered shirt rolled up past his elbows and his furry fingers tapping out a steady beat on the keys of his Underwood SX. Flint worked as a newshound for the *Knickerbocker Gazette*, where his turf was mostly crime, vice, and stories that dealt with the mob. The *Gazette*'s headquarters were located in a flatiron-style building in the heart of Greenwich Village. Its busy thirteenth-floor newsroom was filled with a veritable flotilla of desks, with Flint's jammed in the northeast corner, affording him a small sliver of a window looking out onto a busy Sixth Avenue intersection and the West 4th Street basketball courts across the way.

When the typewriter dinged, Flint slid the carriage over and picked up his staccato rhythm right where he'd left off. But moments later he stopped mid-sentence when the telephone on his desk leapt out of its cradle with a loud jangle. Wondering if this might be the call he'd been waiting for, he grabbed for the receiver.

"Good morning, sir. This is Thompson Jewelers," a curt female voice on the other end of the line informed him. "Your ring has been sized and polished, and is ready to be picked up."

"Thank you. I'll be right over," he replied, biting back what he really wanted to say, which was that it was about darn time. He had a dinner reservation for two tonight at Bertolotti's, and the jewelers had cut things mighty close.

Hanging up the phone, he glanced at the Timex on his wrist and saw that the hands were converging at the top of the dial. Flint rubbed his chin as he contemplated the complex logistics of stopping at Thompson Jewelers during his lunch hour while still meeting his deadline. The *Gazette* liked to keep its reporters busy, and Flint always had several irons in the fire. He was currently working on a piece dealing with corporate malfeasance at a blue-list Wall Street firm, as well as another article about the mob's efforts to infiltrate the police force. But it was his muckraking exposé of the deputy mayor—whose scandalous backroom deals had become a real headache for city hall—that was due on his editor's desk for initial review by three o'clock.

Over the years Flint's daily routine had settled into well-worn grooves. He was a dog who knew where his bones were buried, and he faithfully returned to his favorite haunts whenever possible, never feeling the need to stray far from the beaten path. On weekdays he typically ate lunch by himself at the Ritz Diner on the corner of Waverly and Grove, where he sat on the same stool around the bend of the counter, and without fail ordered the egg and cheese sandwich on a roll with cheddar, chasing it with a root beer. His next stop was always Claudette's Bakery on Bleecker, just to end on a sweet note. Then he would be back at his desk by quarter to one. With his extra errand today, Flint knew he would have to up his tempo to double time.

With some misgivings he set aside his typewriter, slid his jacket off the back of his chair, grabbed his hat from the rack, and strode briskly toward the exit. He would just have to type a little faster when he got back. Right now what he needed to do was get his paws on that ring.

The editor-in-chief, Mr. Boswell, was standing in his usual spot, surveying the busy newsroom. He was a gray-ing tortoiseshell with owlish eyes and thick bristly whiskers, impeccably dressed as always in a chestnut brown suit. As Flint walked past him, Mr. Boswell tugged discreetly on the chain of the pocket watch tucked into his vest and his round eyes grew curious. No doubt he was wondering why Flint was jumping the lunch gun when he had a deadline looming.

Boswell was a no-nonsense army veteran who had served as a captain during the war, where he took part in the D-Day invasion. In peacetime, he had swapped out his platoon of soldiers for a platoon of journalists. Plenty of cats and dogs in the newsroom's staff had their own war stories, although they almost never talked about them. Flint was no exception, having served as a seadog aboard a submarine hunter in the Atlantic, where his ship got torpedoed about a month before the end of hostilities. With a gaping hole below the waterline the vessel soon capsized and sank, and Flint was one of only a handful of survivors.

He stepped off the elevator in the lobby and was spun out through revolving doors onto the street where he was met by a wall of heat. Suspended high in the sky the blinding summer sun beat down on the concrete and asphalt, which in turn soaked up the sun's rays and spit them back up with a ven-geance. Heedless of the soaring temperatures, the Greenwich

Village sidewalks were bustling with the usual mix of too-cool-for-school cats and dogs. The long-haired breeds were all showing off clipped summer looks, with many of the lads sporting Bermuda shorts paired with colorful socks, while the dames opted for A-line skirts that hit just below the knee. And who could blame them in this weather? Flint chose to keep his shaggy appearance year-round, coping with the heat mainly by panting. And because Mr. Boswell was a stickler for office dress codes, no one on the newsroom staff was permitted to ditch the jacket and tie during the warmer months.

Flint bounded through the door of the Ritz Diner and claimed his stool, tipping his hat to Margie, the tabby in the pink gingham apron who was standing behind the counter.

"You're early today," said Margie.

"Yeah, I wanted to beat the lunch rush."

"The usual?"

"You betcha."

His food arrived promptly. Flint wolfed down his sandwich and drained his soda in half his usual time, then he hopped up to pay his tab at the register.

"And you're off like a shot!" Margie quipped as she handed him his change. "What gives? You working a hot story?"

"Nope. I'll tell you all about it tomorrow, depending on how it goes." Flint gave her a wink and slapped a quarter down on the counter by way of a tip. Margie watched him with a bemused smile as he flew out the door in a whirlwind.

Flint set off for Thompson Jewelers at a brisk pace, still licking his chops and brushing crumbs from his whiskers. The store was nearly twelve blocks away, and he was huffing and puffing by the time he got there. He disappeared inside for all of five minutes, and when he came out he had a velvet box weighing down the pocket of his tweed sport coat. Inside said box was a modest diamond engagement ring that he hoped would do the trick. It was all he could afford on a journalist's salary, and it had left his bank account as empty as an old tin can.

But what do I need money for? he asked himself. *I have good friends, a job that means something, and the most amazing girl in the whole world.* Flint wasn't sure what he had done to deserve Bianca, but he wasn't about to question his good fortune. Flint glanced at his watch again and was pleased to note that he was back on schedule, which meant he had time to swing by Claudette's and still make it back to his desk under the unofficial lunch wire. The bakery was a daily ritual that he hated to skip. He had a real weakness for peanut butter cookies.

Whistling an airy tune, he strolled east on Bleecker's scant sidewalks. Despite being little more than a narrow one-way street, Bleecker had evolved into a bustling main drag as the neighborhood had grown into a magnet for artists, writers, musicians, and free-spirits of all kinds. The street's many cafés and music clubs were getting set to throw open their doors and welcome crowds that would linger well past midnight.

Flint soon found himself standing in front of the small pastry shop, its name stenciled in gold leaf on the tinted window. Before heading inside, Flint stopped to check his reflection in the glass—as he always did—taking a moment to straighten his striped tie and set his hat at a jaunty angle.

Six stories above his head, an upright piano began to fall silently through the air. Flint never saw it coming. One minute he was standing there, eyeing himself in the darkened glass, the thought of the still-warm peanut butter cookie making his mouth drool. And the next a four-hundred-pound piano clobbered him with irrevocable finality, the ear-splitting clang ringing out through the neighborhood, punctuating his death with the dissonant sound of every possible chord played simultaneously. The plate-glass windows of his favorite bakery frosted over with a web of cracks.

Later on, the crash of the piano would become a doleful topic of conversation for anyone who happened to find themselves within a ten-block radius at the time. These ear-witnesses would shake their heads sadly and point out how unlucky it was that the poor pooch happened to be standing right in that spot at that moment. And did you hear that he had a ring in his pocket?

Flint's ghost, released from its corporeal anchor, hovered three inches off the ground, contemplating the mangled figure that was himself, lying prone under the smashed piano. The busted strings were still reverberating in the air around him and it looked for all the world as if the instrument had expired as well.

Flint instantly grasped the gist of the situation—he was dead. There could be no doubt about that. He held up a transparent paw and stared right through it at the checkered yellow cab coasting past him on the street. He gazed upward, curious as to where this unanticipated piano had come from. Up on the rooftop he saw a rope and pulley, and next to it stood a figure—the silhouetted head of a dog—peering down in his direction. A moment later the mystery dog ducked out of sight, but not before a flash of silver caught the sunlight, drawing Flint's attention to the knife gripped in the dog's hand.

Flint blinked in disbelief. This couldn't possibly be what it looked like, could it? Had he just been murdered with a piano? It seemed the most plausible explanation considering the knife and the way the sinister figure had stared down at him.

Horrified passersby were beginning to gather. Cats and dogs ran out of nearby shops and gawked at the grisly scene. Blood was oozing out from under the piano's busted frame, and Flint felt oddly embarrassed that his body was at the center of it all. Not that there was anything he could do about it.

Once the reality of the moment sank in, Flint's thoughts turned to sweet Bianca and the life they had planned together. Their whole future had just gone up in smoke: No more getting married. No more honeymoon in Rome. No more adopting pups and kits together. He wondered what would become of Bianca without him? Flint hovered on the sidewalk, not knowing which way to turn. Everyone pouring out onto the street looked right through him. He was utterly invisible. A frizzy white dog rushed out of the bakery, and Flint recognized the bichon frise as the eponymous Claudette. She moved toward him, and before he could react, she had walked right through him as if he wasn't even there. Flint shuddered—it was a most peculiar sensation.

Wanting to put some distance between himself and the growing number of onlookers, Flint drifted into the shadows of an open space by the stairwell of the neighboring record store. His feet weren't actually making contact with the ground, and near as he could tell, locomotion was mostly a matter of leaning forward and willing himself to move.

He was still astounded by how suddenly his life had been

snuffed out. Although, perhaps he shouldn't be so shocked. Just the other night, while out on a date with Bianca, they had stopped to have their fortunes told at Louisa's Psychic Parlor over on Christopher Street. Louisa, a melodramatic Russian blue with a towering turban and hoop earrings, had peered closely into her crystal ball and frowned in confusion. "Your future appears unusually clouded."

"What's that?" he'd said.

"I see your upcoming week clearly but then it fades. I'd watch my step if I were you. Don't take any needless risks. And steer clear of musical instruments!" Flint and Bianca had been mystified by Louisa's cryptic prognostication, but they had simply laughed it off. After all, who took something as silly as a crystal ball reading seriously? Of course, he would've taken Louisa's warnings more to heart if he'd thought for one second that pianos would be falling from the sky.

3 · Tatiana Val: The Getaway

Businessdog was one of Tatiana Valova's favorite disguises. She was wearing an oxford-blue shirt, gray slacks, and a striped tie, such that at a glance anyone would mistake her for a working stiff. A beat-up leather satchel and thick square glasses with clear lenses completed the look. Standing up on the roof, five stories above the bakery, Valova braced herself for the loud crash of the piano after she cut the rope. But she was still taken aback by the resonating boom that spread out across the neighborhood. She poked her nose over the ledge and peered down at her handiwork—a perfect bulls-eye. Crushed beneath the busted piano, the wolfhound lay motionless. She flipped the knife closed—it was time to make herself scarce.

Valova, who usually went by Val, was an Afghan hound. She was tall and slender with combed cream-colored locks and a pointy snout. Her great-grandmother had been the grand-niece of a Bulgarian tsar—if family lore was to be believed—and from a young age Val had held her chin up a little higher than all the other pups in her mountain village.

As a teenager Val had immigrated to America along with her family, settling on the border of the City's rapidly expanding neighborhood of Siamese Town. Her father found work at a coffin manufacturer while her mother did women's wear piecework. Val was in her twenties when the war broke out. She enlisted as a Bulgarian translator for the Office of Strategic Services, and from there it was a short jump to field operative, as female agents were prized for their ability to pass unnoticed behind enemy lines. She had been schooled in the dark art of espionage, which included all manner of weapons training, after which she'd taken a primary role in various covert operations involving the elimination of high-profile targets.

After the war, Val had returned home an unsung hero, only to find that a series of foolish investments, combined with the shenanigans of a crooked accountant (now deceased) had left her family destitute. To save her family from ruin she had fallen back on her wartime training and set herself up as an independent contractor. She didn't like killing, but she had become inured to it, and more importantly—she was good at it.

Val took off at a light jog across the rooftop, the piano's strings still humming in the muggy West Village air. She easily hopped over a low double wall onto a neighboring roof and kept going. On reaching the next building over she leapt effortlessly across a three-yard gap—heedless of the five-story drop. Sprinting over to the hutch, she yanked on the stairway door. It wouldn't budge. Undeterred, she picked the lock in seconds and stepped into the murky stairwell. There she paused, letting her eyes adjust to the light and listening intently, her curved tail held still and alert as she assured herself that all was quiet.

One floor down Val located a garbage chute, conveniently tucked away in a small nook. Opening her leather satchel she removed a gray dress with a houndstooth pattern and a pair of matching flats. She peeled off her disguise, shoved it into the satchel, and tossed it down the shaft. Then she slipped on the belted dress and shook out her blond tresses, and the transformation was complete. Val proceeded down the stairs at a leisurely pace.

On the third floor she smiled nonchalantly at a housecat carrying a heaping laundry basket up the stairs. The housecat peered at her curiously. "Excuse me, miss, but did you hear that strange noise moments ago?" the cat asked her.

Val responded without slowing her pace: "Yes, it was very odd, don't you think?"

"It shook the whole building!"

"Maybe it was some sort of truck crash on the street?"

"That's what I was thinking!" said the housecat.

Val reached the next floor, turned, and passed out of the cat's orbit. Reaching the lobby, she walked out through double doors and back into the sunlight, emerging behind the ring of rubberneckers that had formed around the lurid scene outside the bakery. Fighting the urge to take a closer look, she turned in the opposite direction, swimming against the tide, as more cats and dogs were drawn to the commotion. She continued east on Bleecker, crossing Sixth Avenue, the tumult receding behind her.

Confident that she wasn't being followed, and a firm believer that the best place to hide was always in plain sight, Val stopped at a lively soda shop on MacDougal. The soda jerk behind the counter was a chipper young mutt in a white paper cap and a red bow tie. She ordered an ice-cream soda and watched as he poured milk into a tall glass, stirred in the chocolate syrup, added two scoops of vanilla ice cream, and filled the glass up the rest of the way with soda water. He slid it over to her with a straw, a long spoon, and a congenial "Here you go, miss." She flipped a nickel into the tip jar.

Val was pleased with herself. Today's job had been just the sort of plum contract she'd needed to leave this sordid life behind. She could finally afford that California beach house she'd been dreaming of. The plan was to move out west with her elderly mother and start a new life. The minute the second half of her payment for today's job was wired to her account, she would kiss this lousy city goodbye. Her client, Mister X, had specified that she needed to make it look like an accident, and surely there could be no complaints on that score.

She had gone out with a bang, pulling off an unprecedented hit that was sure to be written up in the papers. The idea for the piano drop had come to her while she was tailing Flint around town, learning his obligingly predictable routine. When the wolfhound had stopped outside the bakery after lunch for the third day in a row, Val's gaze had wandered upward to the APARTMENT FOR RENT sign in the fifth-floor window directly above the pastry shop. That's when it hit her. If she dropped something heavy out of that window, it would land right where Flint took a beat each day to adjust his tie in the glass.

Later that night Val had been given a tour of the vacant apartment by the building's super. Val had stuck her head out of the large French windows and peered down at the ground below, her mind whirring as a plan began to take shape. All she needed was something lethally heavy. Turning around, her gaze settled on a dusty old upright piano pushed into a nook of the living room.

"Does that piano come with the apartment?" she asked the super, a slovenly gray cat in a stained T-shirt.

"The last tenant left it behind," he replied. "That busted piece of junk ain't worth a dime. I was gonna put it by the curb but it's all yours if you want it."

The piano drop idea was so outlandish that Val was immediately taken with it. She rented the place on the spot, putting her deposit down in cash. It took her half the night to jerry-rig a rope and pulley to the frame of the water tower directly above her on the roof. Then she leaned a ramp against the windowsill and slid the piano along it, hooking it to the pulley with a canvas strap.

After that it had been a simple matter to hoist it into place shortly before Flint Lockford's arrival. And sure enough, the next day at 12:25 the piano was dangling high above the ground with the rope securely tied to a radiator. Val went up to the roof, ready to cut it loose in a flash. The minutes ticked by as she stood there out in the open, completely exposed. Where was that darned wolfhound, she grumbled. Just as she was getting set to bail on her plan, she spotted him walking down the block, approaching from an unexpected direction. The brim of his hat was pulled low to keep the sun out of his eyes, but she recognized him from his loping gait, his shaggy outline, and his tweed jacket.

The rest was history. The cops would likely file away the whole affair as a bizarre accident. There was nothing to suggest otherwise. Nothing, that is, except for the queen of spades playing card she had threaded brazenly between the piano strings. She delighted in leaving her calling card hidden at the scene of the crime, a telltale clue meant to torment whatever hapless investigators were charged with solving the case.

Val carried her ice-cream soda over to a free stool at the counter by the window and tucked into her treat, savoring each sugary spoonful. The bell on the door kept dinging as dogs and cats came in looking for icy relief from the heat. The stool to her left was taken over at one point by a college pup in torn jeans and a baseball cap, who tossed his backpack on the floor. Val paid him no mind, but five minutes later when he was joined by a university friend, her ears twitched in their direction. The new arrival was a tubby young cat with an equally overloaded backpack. "Hey, Jimmy, get this!" he exclaimed. "Some poor wolfhound got flattened by a falling piano just a few blocks from here. It was some kind of freak accident!"

"Geez! That must've been that sound I heard!"

"I bet it was. I was several blocks away when I heard it, and by the time I got there a bunch of cops were blocking off the scene and pushing everyone back. But I managed to catch a glimpse from a distance!"

"Was the dog badly hurt?"

"Hurt? A piano landed on him. He's dead as a doornail!"

The other cat let out a slow whistle. "Unbelievable."

"Talk about being in the wrong place at the wrong time. Can you imagine having that kind of rotten luck! And to top it off, someone saw the cops pull an engagement ring from the dead dog's pocket. He must've been about to propose to his sweetheart!"

Val stole a sideways glance at the two students who were shaking their heads sadly. *Now I know why he was late to the bakery*, she thought to herself, unsettled by this unexpected information. When she had tailed Flint around town, she had seen him with his feline girlfriend, but she hadn't thought their relationship serious. The timing of the hit made her feel suddenly queasy.

Hers was an ugly business, she was under no illusions about that. Being a hitdog meant getting your hands dirty in the worst possible ways. Still, she always stuck by her own moral code. For one—she refused to kill cats. She had nothing against cats. Besides which, with up to nine lives each, cat assassination was infamously problematic. She also never targeted female dogs. On the rare occasion when jobs like that came on the market, she took a pass. Nope, it was only male canines for her, and it was rare for her conscience to tweak her on that score. Val had a low opinion of your typical male dog. She considered them belligerent, unimaginative, and foul-smelling creatures. All the evils of the world could be traced back to them. Of course there were exceptions, but as a rule the dogs who ended up on hit lists in this town were real lowlifes.

It occurred to her now that in her zeal to leave this seamy underworld behind her she had not done her due diligence on this job. Was it possible she had just killed a kind and decent dog? Val slurped down the last bit of her ice-cream soda, a troubled look on her face. *What's done is done*, she told herself. There was no point in tormenting herself about it. It was time to clear out her bank accounts and get the hell out of Dodge.

4 · Junior Detective Morton Digby: The Investigation

The din made by the smashed piano petered out before reaching the 6th Precinct, which meant Morton and his partner knew nothing of the incident until the sarge collared them after lunch. "Look alive, fellas! Your day just got a whole lot more interesting. A crazy call just came through to dispatch—a ten fifty-two. You're not going to believe this! Some dog just got flattened by a falling piano! The word from the captain's office is that I should hand the assignment off to the two of you. You're not the team I would've picked, but hey, the big dog must have his reasons."

"We're on it!" said Detective Puddleworth, taking the pink dispatch slip from the sergeant. The two detectives grabbed their hats and made a beeline for the door. Morton got behind the wheel of a black-and-white patrol car while the Scottie sat beside him in the passenger seat. They turned on the siren and the lights and took off down the street, followed closely by another squad car full of patroldogs. They made a left on 10th, the wheels of the cruiser squealing on the blacktop, and then a right on Bleecker. Not two minutes later they screeched to a stop behind a small crowd of onlookers.

"Police! Coming through!" The two detectives pushed their way past the crowd of cats and dogs gathered in front of the bakery. An unsettling sight came into view. The busted upright piano had flattened the poor Irish wolfhound like a pancake. As they edged closer to the body, the two detectives exchanged a look and Morton saw his own revulsion mirrored in the Scottish terrier's eyes. It was a sobering thing to see a dead dog lying there in the street like that.

"Everybody, step back!" barked Detective Puddleworth, taking charge of the scene. He directed the patroldogs to rope off the area and to press back the ring of cats and dogs. A fire truck pulled up, sirens blaring, as well as a box truck ambulance. A keen-eyed journalist flashed her press ID and slipped under the police rope. She was a chic gray tabby, her white blouse tucked into a pencil skirt with a split hem. She was already scribbling away furiously in her notebook. Directly behind her came a lumbering Saint Bernard with his press card stuck in the band of his hat. A head taller than his colleague and three times as wide, he stepped over the rope that the tabby had ducked under. A large camera with an attached flash hung from his neck, and, raising it to his eye, he set about documenting the grisly incident.

The firedogs were barging onto the scene, and Morton took a step to his left to let them pass. He shivered, feeling a sudden chill, as if he had just walked into a meat locker. It was a darn peculiar sensation, at odds with the scorching temperatures on the street, but it was gone as quickly as it came, and Morton chalked it up to a delayed reaction to the mangled body.

In a short time, Detective Puddleworth managed to impose a semblance of order on the chaos churning around them, after which he joined Morton, who was examining the dead dog. "That poor wolfhound didn't stand a chance," the Scottie lamented. "He really got clobbered by that piano. Looks like an open-and-shut accidental death case to me."

Morton cocked his head. "Let's not jump to conclusions."

Puddleworth shot him a quizzical look. "Jump? It's barely a hop. I mean, just look at him! Still, we'd better find whoever was moving that piano. My guess is they're looking at dog-slaughter charges."

"Something is bothering me about this business. But I can't quite put my finger on it," muttered Morton. "This whole scene feels oddly theatrical."

"Theatrical? This is the City, Morton! Crazy stuff no one would ever believe happens every darn day!"

Morton squinted up at the building and saw a thick rope dangling from a hoist attached to the water tower on the roof. He pulled off his hat and scratched the patch of white fur on his forehead. "That's true enough as far as it goes, J.B. But it won't hurt to poke around for a few minutes and make sure it all adds up."

Detective Puddleworth fanned himself with his fedora. "There's no harm in being thorough if it will set your mind at ease. I'll tell the firedogs not to move the busted piano until we give them the okay."

Then the two detectives set about interviewing bystanders in search of any direct witnesses to the incident. They talked to a few cats and dogs in the front rows of onlookers, but no one seemed to have been looking that way at the precise moment it happened. They were about to give up when Morton spotted a snowy bichon frise in a white apron poking her head out the door of the bakery, looking distraught. "Hey, what about her? Let's see if she knows anything," Morton suggested, jerking his head in her direction.

"I'm Detective Puddleworth, and this is my partner, Detective Digby," said the Scottie. "Do you work here?"

The bichon peered at their gold badges. "Yes. I mean— this is my bakery. I'm Claudette."

"Be sure you write all this down," the Scottie whispered to Morton. Addressing the baker, he asked: "Did you know the victim?"

"Not by name, but he's one of my regulars. He came into the shop every day at half past twelve, like clockwork, and he always stopped to straighten his tie in the window. He was a big fan of our peanut butter cookies."

"Did you see what happened?"

"No. There was a huge crash! It shook the whole store and scared the living daylights out of me. I looked over and saw the window filled with cracks. It wasn't until we opened the door and looked outside that we realized what had happened." She stared at the ground. "What terrible luck."

When they were done questioning the baker, the two detectives moved on to a close-up examination of the victim. The first thing that struck Morton was that the piano had not slipped loose from the canvas sling wrapped around it, but rather it was the thick rope holding up the sling that had given way. Morton traced the meandering path of the rope on the sidewalk until he located the loose end, squatting down to inspect it closely. "That's odd," he said. "It looks like a clean cut."

The Scottish terrier frowned as he too scrutinized the severed rope. "That *is* strange. You'd think it would be frayed.

But still, in and of itself this doesn't tell us that much. I'd say it's time to let the firedogs haul that piano off him. Then we can go through the victim's pockets."

They had just finished communicating this to the fire chief when Sergeant Doyle appeared at their side. "Hey, fellas! I figured I'd stop by and see this with my own eyes. What a gruesome sight!" he said gleefully. The bulldog glanced down at Morton's notes and looked puzzled. "What's with all the notetaking? What happened here isn't much of a mystery."

"We just figured we'd do this by the book," said the Scottie.

"Suit yourselves," said the bulldog with a shrug.

The three of them watched as the firedogs—Dalmatians in domed metal helmets—lifted the busted piano off the wolfhound and lugged it over to the curb. Three Siamese cat paramedics maneuvered the crumpled form of the wolfhound onto a stretcher. Morton cringed. There was nothing dignified about being scooped up off the sidewalk.

With the wolfhound rolled over onto his back, the photographer took two steps closer to the stretcher and a look of horror spread across his features. The two detectives converged on him. "Hey, you with the camera! Do you know the victim?" Detective Puddleworth demanded.

The Saint Bernard removed his hat and nodded glumly. "Do I ever. It's my pal Flint! I can't believe it. We worked together at the *Gazette*. He was a buddy of mine, and a top-notch journalist. We often played pool together after work. I can't believe it's actually him." The Saint Bernard hung his head, his droopy eyes welling with tears.

Detective Puddleworth peered up at the press card tucked

into the reporter's hat. "Mr. Otis Hubbard, is it?" The Saint Bernard nodded. "Morton, be sure to take down this dog's name and phone number."

Morton dutifully recorded the dog's contact information in his notes, even as he chafed at his partner's commanding tone. The feline reporter had been interviewing the baker, but seeing the look of distress on her colleague's face, she rushed over. Glancing down at the dead dog, her eyes went wide as saucers. "Oh no! It's Flint! How awful!" She put a hand to her mouth, squeezed her eyes shut and stood there, stunned.

"And your name is?" Detective Puddleworth inquired delicately.

The tabby opened her eyes and took a deep breath. "Penelope Flick, field reporter for the *Knickerbocker Gazette*," she replied in a trembling voice. Morton scribbled her name in his notes as well.

They found several items on the dead dog's person: a scuffed leather wallet with a press ID card in the flap that confirmed the dog's identity, a spiral notebook full of hard-to-decipher shorthand, a shiny ballpoint pen, and a wristwatch with a cracked dial, the hands stopped at 12:34.

"That gives us a pretty good time of death," Detective Puddleworth noted matter-of-factly. They placed the items carefully into a canvas evidence bag. Patting down the wolfhound's jacket, Morton discovered one last thing. He peered curiously at the small ring box. Detective Puddleworth took it from him and opened it to reveal a diamond ring glinting in the sunlight.

The Saint Bernard hung his head morosely. "Flint told me the other day that he was planning to propose. You've never seen a cat and dog more in love than Flint and Bianca."

The gray tabby stared at the ring, aghast. "Poor Bianca! She is going to be devastated."

"Tell me about this Bianca," said Detective Puddleworth, nudging Morton in the ribs so that he would get his pen ready.

"She works as a bartender over at the Calico Cat Lounge," Penelope informed them. "She's as close as you're gonna get to a next of kin within city limits."

Morton looked up from his notes to see the sergeant looming over them again. "Let me see that ring!" demanded the bulldog, stretching out a meaty paw.

Detective Puddleworth handed him the box.

The bulldog tsked. "That's one unlucky son of a gun. I guess I'd better go break the bad news to this waitress, before she finds out some other way."

"I can take it if you like," Morton said quickly.

"No, no! I'll do it myself," said the bulldog, sucking back a stream of drool that had dipped below his chin. "You need tact for this kind of thing!"

"Perhaps we should let Bianca keep the ring?" Detective Puddleworth suggested kindly. Morton cast an appreciative glance at the Scottie. He approved wholeheartedly of this notion.

The bulldog shrugged. "Sure, why not? No point in having this little gem sit in an evidence locker gathering dust. Just make sure to leave it off your report so our good deed doesn't bite us in the ass! I'll see you two bozos back at the station." The sergeant stomped off, barreling his way through a wall of rubberneckers.

The two detectives watched solemnly as the paramedics

covered up the wolfhound with a white sheet and slid the stretcher into the back of the ambulance. The gathered crowd around them began to dissipate as it drove away.

Detective Puddleworth leaned against a nearby lamp-post. "Are you ready to conclude it was an accident, Morton? I'm sure there's some logical explanation for the way the rope broke. We can't be grasping at straws."

"Why don't we take a closer look at that piano?" Morton suggested, pointing at the busted instrument sitting in the gutter. He had to admit it did indeed seem like a tragic accident, but having done little more than follow the Scottie's orders since they'd arrived on the scene, Morton relished the opportunity to direct the investigation for a few minutes, even if it turned out to be a waste of time.

They circled the piano, examining the stray copper wires jutting out from the frame and the disjointed ivory keys. Morton reached out and lifted the piano's splintered lid, peering down at the tangled mess of strings inside. His eye snagged on something out of place. Reaching down, he worked a playing card free from between the strings, holding it carefully by the edges. The Scottie peered eagerly over his shoulder as he flipped it around and they both stared down at the queen of spades.

Detective Puddleworth let out a slow whistle. "I don't believe it! It's the calling card for the Queen of Spades! The notorious hitdog!"

Morton leaned in and gave the card a sniff. "It's been sprayed with perfume. Some kind of citrus floral fragrance."

The Scottie's nose quivered above the card. "You know what, Morton? This playing card changes everything!"

5 · Bianca Moon: The Broken Heart

In the moments before the piano came crashing down to earth, Bianca Moon was standing outside the Calico Cat Lounge, patiently waiting for the boss to arrive and open up shop. The lounge was a snazzy West Village hangout, set at the unlikely intersection of Fourth Street and Tenth Street in the topsy-turvy geometry of the West Village, with Seventh Avenue making up the third edge of a triangular plot.

Bianca had silky white fur, a plumed tail, and eyes like large green marbles. She looked resplendent in a periwinkle keyhole dress with a ribboned collar and a matching pillbox hat. Bianca was a Turkish Angora. That is to say she was an Angora on both sides, and stashed somewhere in her closet she had the papers to prove it. Not that she put much stock in that kind of thing.

Two other employees were waiting alongside her. A few paces to Bianca's left stood Gerald the janitor, a grubby mutt who was always mumbling unintelligibly to himself. He seemed to go through life in a state of perpetual drowsiness. At this very moment his head was drooped beneath his baseball cap, and Bianca could make out the telltale sound of snoring, even though he was standing upright on the sidewalk. Bianca suspected the only reason Gerald managed to hold on to his job was because he was a whiz at fixing the finicky bowling pin machines in the lounge's basement game room.

And to Bianca's right was Roxy, an alley cat who had recently been brought on as a waitress. She was sprawled unladylike along the metal steps that led up to the back entrance on the second floor. Dressed in a battered denim jacket and matching denim pants, she kept her eyes hidden behind wayfarer sunglasses. Roxy's fur was a mottled red and black tortoiseshell pattern that suited her hard-boiled personality.

Bianca flicked her wrist and stared at the dial of a square silver watch. Her eyebrows twitched. Normally by twelve thirty they'd already be inside setting up. With a sigh she pressed herself back into the little sliver of shade afforded by the building's overhang. The sidewalk was crowded with a mix of fast-walking locals and slow-moving tourists. Snippets of conversations drifted to her sharp ears, mixed with the occasional rumble of a passing truck and the background hum of the city.

"Broonnggg!" A loud jarring clang cut through the air, echoing throughout the neighborhood. There was a momentary glitch in the pedestrians' steps as they looked around, ears perked, trying to locate the source of the booming noise.

Bianca froze. "What the heck was that?" she asked, her tail already puffed up to twice its normal size as a shiver ran through her.

"Beats me," Roxy replied. "Some kind of church bell gone wrong?"

Gerald pushed his hat off his face and blinked sleepily before letting out a noncommittal grunt.

The last echoes of the mysterious ringing faded away. "It was too jangly to be a bell," Bianca pointed out.

"Look at you with your hackles raised, acting all spooked! You're such a scaredy-cat! You gotta learn to play it cool in this town, Princess." The alley cat unsheathed her claws and studiously examined her needle-sharp nails.

"Don't call me 'Princess'!" Bianca snapped, rankled as always by the nickname Roxy had cooked up for her. "And I'm not a scaredy-cat. That sound just gave me a strange feeling is all."

"I know a scaredy-cat when I see one," Roxy insisted. Gerald let out another grunt, this one managing to get across the sense that he agreed with the alley cat. Roxy peered at Bianca over the top of her sunglasses. "You won't last long around here if you hit the roof every time someone turns on a vacuum. Get a grip, Princess."

Bianca scowled at her.

As the normal noises of the city reasserted themselves, and with no repetition of the eerie sound, Bianca began to wonder why she was so jumpy. She hated looking like a wuss in front of the alley cat. Roxy was chewing gum, making the occasional loud pop whenever a large pink bubble collapsed. But her gum must have been losing its flavor because she unexpectedly spit it out of her mouth, sending it flying over the sidewalk and into the gutter.

Bianca cringed. "Did you have to do that?"

The alley cat shot her a *What?* look. "Did you want me to swallow it?"

"There's a garbage can right on the corner."

"Yeah. Key word in that sentence—*corner*. We can't all be as ladylike as you, Princess."

Bianca gritted her teeth.

"Hey, did you write any pretty poems this morning?" Roxy asked her teasingly.

"So what if I did?" Bianca replied curtly, regretting the day she had mentioned her writing ambitions in front of the alley cat. When Bianca had packed her bags and traded a cloistered suburban life for the excitement of the big city, her goal had been to become a published poet. But writing poetry wasn't going to pay the bills anytime soon, which was why most of her evenings were spent behind the bar at the Calico Cat Lounge.

"Just making conversation," said the alley cat. "Don't get your knickers in a twist."

Bianca groaned inwardly. Talking to Roxy was pointless. The alley cat only poked fun at her ambitions because she didn't have any of her own. *We aren't friends and we will never be friends*, Bianca told herself, not for the first time. Roxy had taken an instant dislike to her when they first met. The alley cat had pegged her right out of the gate as a stuck-up rich girl, even though Bianca would never dream of looking down her nose at anyone. At least Roxy hadn't caught on yet that she was a college girl, because if she ever found out about that she would have a field day. They said cats were crueler than dogs, and while Bianca had never allowed herself to believe it, Roxy had just about changed her mind. The alley cat liked to push her buttons, and there were moments when Bianca felt the urge to lunge at her and scratch her eyes out. But she always took a deep breath and counted to ten, giving herself time to cool off.

Roxy was a born-and-raised city girl, and she had been

a regular at the lounge long before Bianca arrived in town. Roxy had a posse of alley cat pals who liked to crowd around and watch her play pinball. She was known for being able to squeeze twenty minutes' worth of fun from a single nickel on any of the pinball machines. And thank goodness for that because she was always strapped for cash. Bianca had a hunch that Roxy had been just one paw away from living out of a garbage can when Tabatha hired her. The skinny around the lounge was that years of living on the street had left Roxy with only four lives to burn.

Bianca didn't doubt that her own life had been easier than the alley cat's. But easier did not mean easy. Orphaned as a kitten, and with no close relatives to take her in, Bianca had been lucky to be adopted by a well-to-do couple who raised her as their own on a large estate in Scatsdale. The Stewarts were Angoras like herself, and they had been her only family for most of her life. She loved them both dearly.

Looking up, Bianca saw Tabatha hurrying up the street in their direction. Her boss was dressed simply but elegantly in a form-fitting purple dress, accessorized with a chunky set of pearls and a floppy hat. Fishing the keys out of her purse, the buxom calico went up the steps. "Did you guys hear that weird boom?" she asked. "It gave me such a fright! I wonder what it was?"

Bianca smirked at Roxy.

"We heard it too, Boss!" replied the alley cat. "I'm sure it's nothing to worry about!"

Tabatha set about unlocking the back entrance. A widow, she had opened this joint herself after the war and it had quickly become a home away from home for a lively mix of

hepcats and dapper dogs from the neighborhood, and transformed Tabatha into a doyenne of Village nightlife. Bianca
adored her boss—even though she knew that hidden behind
the calico's broad smile was a hard-nosed businesscat. Bianca
knew Tabatha had taken a chance when she'd given her a job
without any experience, and she was determined not to let
her down. She relished having a front row seat to the nightly
dramas of West Village life and took great pride in her work.
Bianca never forgot a regular's name or drink, and was known
for crafting smooth and well-balanced mocktails, such as a
virgin Sea Breeze, which had quickly become a popular hit
with customers.

Tabatha pushed the door open with a grunt and they all
piled inside. Bianca was the last one through the door and she
cast an uneasy glance over her shoulder before stepping into
the stuffy interior. She made her way up to the bar, which
occupied a long stretch on the mezzanine level overlooking
the snack room on the ground floor. Down below, in the
basement, was the main draw: the popular game room. It
boasted two bowling lanes, three pool tables, a long wall of
flashing pinball machines, and a soda counter.

Bianca hustled about behind the empty bar in an effort
to get things up and running. The lounge opened daily at
two, which meant she had just over an hour to wipe everything down, clean the hoses on the tap, set up a fresh keg, fill
the beer-nut bowls and the ice bin, make sure the glasses were
all spotless, and complete a million other niggling tasks.

She was only working a half shift today since Flint was
taking her out for a fancy dinner at Bertolotti's tonight.
Tabatha had been surprisingly accommodating about this

request, further raising Bianca's suspicions that tonight was *the* night. She was sure Flint was getting set to pop the question over spaghetti and meatballs. A few weeks ago he had casually inquired about her ring size, doing his best to pass it off as idle curiosity. She knew a thing or two about curiosity, being a cat, and had seen right through him.

They'd first met right here in the lounge. Flint was an avid pool player and after work he liked to shoot nine ball with his pals, at a nickel per ball sunk, with a juicy quarter going to the game winner. It was a harmless bit of gambling between friends, with bragging rights changing nightly.

Flint was rakishly handsome, with shaggy gray fur and bushy eyebrows. A journalist by day, he always looked dapper in tweed jackets that fit his lanky frame. He was considered something of a square by most of the lounge's clientele, but he never took offense to being dubbed a *Clyde*. Kind by nature, he never had a bad word to say about anyone. Class—in the true sense of the word—was the one quality Bianca considered essential in a life partner, and Flint had it in spades.

They had taken things slow at the start. Bianca had not dated much in school, having no interest in casual flirtations. She had always been sensible when it came to romance, unlike Roxy and her alley cat friends, who swooned over every good-looking hound or tomcat who wandered through the doors. But Flint had slowly won her over, until one day she woke up and realized that her first thoughts each morning and her last thoughts each night were for him. In the span of a year, she had fallen hopelessly in love with that shaggy gray dog.

Flint's salary as a journalist was barely enough to make ends meet in the City. But even if he gave her the world's smallest diamond her answer would be an elated yes. Flint was the bee's knees as far as she was concerned, and the thought of spending the rest of her life by his side filled her with unimaginable joy.

Bianca was cutting up some lemon wedges when she heard the pulse of the back door buzzer. She turned, expecting to see the mailcat or the icedog coming in. But no, it was Otis, the burly Saint Bernard who was one of Flint's pals from the *Gazette*. A photographer, he often came to play pool with Flint in the evenings. Seeing him, Bianca frowned. What was he doing here at this hour? And why was he out of breath?

"Hiya, Otis! We're not open yet!" she called out.

"Yeah, I know," he replied, giving her an odd look. Then he turned and hurried down the stairs, muttering something about needing to talk to Tabatha. Baffled, she watched him tramp into the empty snack bar one level down and disappear through the swinging kitchen door. No sooner had he vanished from sight than two more unexpected guests came careening through the back door. She recognized them as two of Roxy's alley cat friends. Pam and Jan were littermates, salt-and-pepper tabbies who looked so much alike that Bianca was always hard-pressed to tell them apart.

"We're closed!" Bianca declared loudly, a feeling of déjà vu overtaking her.

"Yeah, we know," they replied, giving Bianca the exact same look that Otis had shot her moments ago. Following in his footsteps, the two sisters scrambled down the stairs and disappeared through the still swinging kitchen door.

There had been alarm, sorrow, and even pity etched in their faces, Bianca was sure of it. An unnatural stillness descended on the lounge. Nerves prickling, Bianca set down the glass she was polishing and walked around to the customer side of the bar. Hopping up on a stool, she propped her elbows on her knees and put her chin in her hands. The West Village was like a small town in some ways. Word always got around fast among the locals.

Bianca had only nebulous memories of life as a small child when her biological parents were still alive. Her first really sharp memory from her childhood was of a black Labrador in a crisp blue uniform showing up at her home late one rainy night, water trickling from his five-pointed cap. He had spluttered something incomprehensible about a train derailment in New Jersey. About a storm washing debris onto a grade crossing. About a desperate search for survivors. Having lived through the atrocities of the war and a dangerous transatlantic voyage, both her parents had been down to their very last lives.

Bianca's breaths grew shallow as a trickle of other cats and dogs appeared. She watched the growing crowd of regulars gather in the snack room, one level down, many of them sneaking glances in her direction. A grim-faced Tabatha emerged from the kitchen with Roxy trailing, just as a police-dog showed up. He was a thickset bulldog with sergeant stripes on the shoulder of his uniform. He marched down the steps and conferred momentarily with Tabatha, who subtly jerked her head up toward the bar area.

The police sergeant, his hat in his hand, climbed back up the stairs in her direction, followed by Tabatha, Roxy, Otis, and everyone else.

"Miss Bianca Moon?" the police sergeant asked.

"That's me," Bianca replied in a hoarse whisper.

"My name is Sergeant Doyle. I'm afraid I have some bad news. I hear that you and a Mister Flint Lockford were in a serious relationship?"

"Very much so. Wait—what do you mean *were*?"

"There's been an unfortunate accident," the bulldog replied. "And I'm awful sorry to say that Mister Lockford didn't make it."

Bianca would have fallen off the stool if not for the steadying hands of Tabatha and Roxy, one cat on each side of her. "There must be some mistake," she said softly.

"I'm afraid there isn't any doubt, miss. He was pronounced dead by the ambulance crew. Several cats and dogs have come forward to identify him, including Mr. Hubbard here." He pointed to Otis. "So there's no need for you to burden yourself with that unpleasant task."

"It's true, Bianca," said Otis, his voice raw and ragged. "I saw him with my own eyes. It was definitely Flint. It happened outside the bakery he goes to after lunch."

"What happened? Was he hit by a car?" she asked, barely trusting her own voice. She found the words and sentences directed at her almost impossible to comprehend. It couldn't be true that her Flint—always so vibrant and full of life—had left this world behind. Tears streamed down the white fur on her face, catching on her whiskers.

The police sergeant cleared his throat. "No. It was a freak accident. He was struck by a falling piano that was being hoisted up to a fifth-floor window."

"A piano?"

"Yes, miss. I'm truly sorry."

"That sound earlier—it was a falling piano? It was Flint?"

"That's quite possible, Miss Moon. Apparently, it made quite a racket throughout the whole neighborhood." The police sergeant dug into his jacket pocket. "Mister Lockford was carrying a personal item that we believe was intended for you. We're bending the rules, but we thought you should have it." Sergeant Doyle held out a small velvet box to her.

Bianca stared at the box, aghast. The ring. The ring she had been daydreaming about for months had suddenly appeared. And it was too horrible. Like some grotesque parody of what a proposal should look like. She snatched the box from the policedog's paws. Holding her breath, she cracked it open and stared down at a beautiful silver band set with a modest-sized emerald-cut diamond. It was perfect in every way. Bianca's breath caught in her throat. This had to be some crazy prank. She looked around, sure that Flint would leap out from behind the jukebox and tell her it was all a joke, but he was nowhere to be seen.

Reaching down in a daze, she plucked the ring free of the cushion it was nestled in. Placing the case down on the bar, she slipped the diamond onto her finger. It fit perfectly. She gazed down at her splayed fingers in disbelief. Flint might not be here, but the ring itself was a question that demanded an answer, and answer it she did. "Yes, Flint. Of course I will marry you," she said quietly. "You make me the happiest cat in the whole world." She choked back a sob.

When she looked up, she saw a chorus of horrified expressions around her. Bianca almost laughed through her tears. She was engaged to a dead dog. Of all the crazy stories she'd heard since arriving in the City, this one took the cake.

Getting to her feet, she tested her weight on jelly-like legs. Turning to Tabatha, she said in a strangled voice: "If you don't mind, Boss, I think I'm going to take the rest of the day off."

"Of course, hon. Take as much time as you need. But you shouldn't be alone right now. Who can I call? Friends? Family?"

Bianca shook her head. She had never gotten around to telling her parents about Flint, sure they would disapprove. They'd always talked about her meeting a nice cat with a good job, preferably an Angora. Bianca had been waiting until her engagement was official before breaking the news to them that she had fallen in love with a dog. Squaring her shoulders, she fixed Tabatha with a blank stare. "I think I need to be alone."

Tabatha frowned and said nothing, but the calico's firm grip on her arm didn't loosen.

Then Roxy spoke up. "I'll take her home, Boss. Settle her down and stay with her." Bianca was taken aback by this offer. Roxy was the last cat on earth she expected any help from, and the last cat she wanted any help from. But with no strength to dissuade her and with Tabatha insisting on an escort, Bianca didn't protest further. The crowd parted as Bianca walked toward the exit with Roxy by her side, the alley cat's fingers entwined with her own.

6 · Flint Lockford: A Ghost

The ghost of Flint Lockford sat on the stone threshold in front of the bakery entrance. That is to say, his backside hovered about an inch above it, never actually making contact with the gray stone. He held his face in his hands as he stared glumly through his fingers at the sidewalk. A long patch of shadow had engulfed the south side of the street now that the sun was no longer directly overhead. Behind him, Claudette's had gone dark, a CLOSED sign showing in the door. Befuddled customers came along repeatedly and rattled the locked door handle, passing right through the spectral wolfhound. Irritating as this was, Flint couldn't be bothered to move.

Life on Bleecker Street was quickly returning to normal. The emergency vehicles had driven off, including the ambulance containing his dead body. Only one squad car was left, and the two detectives who it belonged to had disappeared inside the building. To their credit, they seemed to have figured out they were dealing with a murder, but Flint suspected his killer must be miles away by now.

So far he didn't much care for being a ghost. It was being invisible that bothered him the most. Earlier, he had waved his arms about and hopped up and down like a mad dog in front of his friends Otis and Penelope, and they had stared right through him as if he weren't even there. Then, Flint had become incensed when the detectives had gotten their mitts on the engagement ring—Bianca's ring! He'd tried to snatch the box from the Scottish terrier's paws, but it had been like trying to grab hold of thin air. That was when it really sank in: he could still see and hear everything going on around him but it was strictly a one-way street.

Flint hung his head. "I'm a ghost," he muttered, incredulous. "I'm an actual ghost. That's all there is to it." As he said this, he became dimly aware of a puffy Old English sheepdog crossing the street and walking in his direction. This dog stopped and seemed to look directly at him. Flint glanced over his shoulder, confused—no one else was nearby. Dressed in a checkered yellow sport coat, the sheepdog's large tongue lolled to one side of his mouth. He had a thick coat of fluffed-up white and gray hair that fell down over his eyes and a feathered tail that poked out through the tail hole of blue balloon pants. It wagged back and forth in the universal gesture of canine goodwill.

Leaning casually on a furled umbrella, the sheepdog tipped his hat and said: "Excuse me, sir, but you look like you could use some help," seemingly addressing Flint. There was something peculiar about him. It wasn't until a truck drove past on the street that the penny finally dropped—this dog was transparent and his feet weren't touching the ground!

Flint jumped up and stood face-to-face with the sheepdog and said: "Can you see me?"

"Of course I can see you!" he replied. "We're both ghosts!"

"So you're a ghost too!" Flint exclaimed in amazement.

"Certainly."

"And you really can see me and hear me?"

"Oh absolutely!" He chuckled. "You're coming in loud and clear. You're looking a little washed-out perhaps, but aren't we all. Allow me to introduce myself. My name is Professor Chumley." The sheepdog stuck out a paw.

"Flint Lockford." Tentatively, Flint reached out and grasped the sheepdog's hand, giving it a shake. He half expected his own hand to pass right through the other dog's paw. Instead, Flint was delighted to find the sheepdog's hand felt solid enough, albeit with a faint prickly sensation.

"I confess I've been watching you surreptitiously for a little while," said the sheepdog. "And I can tell you're having a rough time of it."

"You can say that again," Flint replied. "But I suppose you've been through something similar yourself. How long have *you* been dead?"

"Me? Oh, I've been floating around for ages. I kicked the bucket back in twenty-nine. I'm what you might call an old-timer. Most ghosts don't stick around very long—typically just a few hours—but not me. Why, my twentieth ghostiversary is come and gone! Of course, you do occasionally run into a spook who has been rattling about for centuries, and they make *me* look like a rookie. But by golly, those ghosts are rare."

The sheepdog's words filled Flint with amazement. "What do you mean when you say ghosts don't stick around? Where do they go?"

"Ah, well. We're not too sure about that. As ghosts, we are stuck in the in-between. A limbo of sorts. But none of us has a clue about what happens when we cross over for good. Some ghosts describe it as walking into the light when they fade away. Others—disturbingly—say they feel they are being enveloped by shadows. But whether these are references to some immortal realm, well, your guess is as good as mine."

"I see." Flint had never spent much time worrying about his immortal soul before, but the topic was taking on a new urgency in his mind. "What makes some ghosts stick around?"

"There's always some unfinished business. As soon as that gets resolved—bam! They disappear into the ether! It might take a day, or a week, or sometimes years."

"Or decades, like yourself."

"Exactly. A lot of the time it's the haunters who linger. But you don't seem like the haunting type to me. Accidental deaths almost never make ghosts vengeful."

"My death was no accident," Flint clarified.

"Really? Didn't you have a piano fall on you?"

"Yes, but someone deliberately cut the rope. I saw them up on the rooftop afterward holding a knife."

Professor Chumley smiled sympathetically. "Foul play is surprisingly common in the spirit world. Still, using a piano as a murder weapon is unheard of!"

"Were you murdered as well?"

"After a fashion. I met my demise at the Central Park Menagerie, but it's a bit of a long story, I'm afraid, so I'll save it for a later date."

"It's such a relief to talk to someone, Professor. I was beginning to think I was all alone."

"I remember when I croaked," said the sheepdog. "I ended up wandering the park for hours without bumping into another soul. Spirits are nocturnal by nature, you see. So they avoid the outdoors during the day."

"Why are you out and about at this hour, then?"

"As a matter of fact, I am on the prowl for newly minted ghosts. My job is to muster up new lodgers for Ghosthall. That's what we call the abandoned courthouse up on Tenth Street that a bunch of us neighborhood spooks call home. Maybe you'd be interested?"

"Wait. Are you asking me to join you?"

"That's right. What do you say? Do you want to come back to Ghosthall with me and meet the gang? Your death will be the talk of the cantina tonight!"

Flint hesitated. This sheepdog was a chummy sort, but they had only just met. Besides that, Flint felt strangely rooted to the spot. "I don't know, Professor. I feel like I have some things to sort out here first."

"It's not unusual for spirits to become linked to their immediate surroundings when they pass. But ask yourself this: Do you really want to wind up as the bakery phantom? It would be a lonely experience. Back at Ghosthall you'll find plenty of camaraderie."

Flint stared into the sheepdog's earnest eyes. He prided himself on being a good judge of character, and the professor felt like a dog he could trust. Besides—he didn't *really* have a good reason for sticking around. "All right, Professor, lead on. I'll put myself in your paws." As he said it, he felt immediately relieved at the prospect of putting this place behind him.

"Marvelous!" The sheepdog popped open his blue umbrella. "Stick close to me on the street. It's best if we stay out of direct sunlight."

"Why's that?"

"A stray patch of sun here and there is harmless enough,

but if you get caught out in direct sunlight for too long then you'll burn up. You'll start to sizzle and then—poof! You're vaporized! Whether you've wrapped up your business or not."

"No midday strolls on the beach, then. Got it." It occurred to Flint that he had been hugging the shadows instinctively.

"We'll catch a cab over on Sixth Ave. That'll keep us out of the sun."

"Can we still take cabs?"

"Oh absolutely, and they're free! It's one of the many perks of being dead. You just need to time it right and slip in at a red light. Doesn't even have to be a taxi. Any old car or trolley will do."

Flint stuck close to the professor as they drifted down the sidewalk sharing the shade of the sheepdog's umbrella. Flint stuck his hand out experimentally into direct sunlight. Sure enough it made for an uncomfortable stinging sensation, and his already translucent hand faded almost to the point of invisibility. He quickly yanked it back into the shade.

They stood on the corner of Carmine and Sixth Avenue waiting for the stoplight to turn red. When it did, Professor Chumley dove into the empty back seat of a large seafoam green Studebaker, passing right through the closed car door. Flint took a deep breath, closed his eyes, and plunged in after him. When he opened his eyes, he saw they were both ensconced in an otherwise empty back seat. A beefy tomcat in a striped T-shirt was sitting behind the wheel, humming along to a Beach Dogs tune on the radio. The driver frowned and glanced over his shoulder into the back seat, but seeing nothing, he returned his attention to the road. The light turned green and they sped north along Sixth Avenue.

"It's not far," said the sheepdog. "We'll hop out when we get close to Tenth Street. Don't worry if the car is still moving, just link your arm to mine." Two minutes later Professor Chumley hooked his elbow around Flint's, stuck his other arm right through the roof, and popped open his umbrella. As the umbrella caught the wind it yanked both of them right out of the still cruising car. Flint felt a rush of wind, only the wind was both pushing against him and surging through him. They drifted slowly down to the ground. Flint experienced a brief moment of terror as a street trolley barreled toward them on the car-filled avenue. He squeezed his eyes shut, bracing himself for impact, but when he opened them moments later, he realized the trolley had passed right through him.

Chumley pulled him along and they were soon standing in a patch of sunlight outside the entrance to the old courthouse. The professor angled his umbrella so that it bore the brunt of the sun's glare. Flint had long admired this exemplary piece of Gothic architecture, with its red brick walls, steeply pitched roofs, and decorative stone pinnacles. The main turret soared above the neighborhood rooftops, encircled midway up by a wrought iron balcony, and culminated in a magnificent clock tower. The clock hands on all four sides were stuck permanently at five past nine.

"And this is Ghosthall!" the professor declared excitedly.

"I've walked by here a million times," said Flint. "This place has been boarded up for years."

"We moved in right after the living abandoned the joint. We have the run of the place, apart from Gerald, the mutt who lives upstairs and acts as the building's custodian. Ready to head inside?" The professor arched his bushy eyebrows.

Flint set his jaw firmly. "Let's do it."

"Great. My umbrella can't take much more of this sunlight!"

Flint looked up at the umbrella through slitted eyelids. It seemed to be smoking.

"The building doors are thick so just keep moving forward."

Flint followed the sheepdog up the steps, drifting through a barred gate and pressing himself into the heavy wooden doors. His movement slowed and he was momentarily worried that he would get stuck in the dense wood. Then, suddenly, he was through to the other side. Flint found himself in a stone entrance hall lit by a hanging lantern. He had been expecting a dilapidated ruin, but the place looked in good repair apart from a few cobwebs and a layer of dust. Chumley was staring with dismay at the partially disintegrated canopy of his umbrella. With a shrug, he thrust his arm out and tossed it back through the door. "The sun will burn up what's left of it. There's no such thing as littering in the ghost world!"

The hall was bare except for a semi-transparent mahogany desk by the far wall. Floating behind the desk was a red-and-white corgi in a checkered pullover shirt with a wide collar. His large head was drooping to one side, his eyes were closed, and his breath was emerging in deep sawlike rasps. Professor Chumley led Flint over to the desk and rapped on it with his knuckles. The stocky dog snorted and opened his eyes.

"Wake up, Albert!" cried Chumley. "We have a new lodger."

"Another inmate for the asylum," grumbled the corgi,

peering at Flint. "How long are you planning on sticking around?"

"I don't know yet. I just got here."

"You probably won't like it. It's dark and gloomy, and full of crackpots. I bet the professor didn't mention that in his pitch. Did he tell you the dormitory is down in the basement in the courtroom's old holding cells? It's like a dungeon down there."

Professor Chumley waved his arm dismissively. "Don't listen to Albert! He gets grouchy when he's working the day shift."

"I do not!" protested the corgi. "I'm just not annoyingly cheerful like some other dogs I won't mention. But who knows, maybe he'll like it here! Stranger things have happened." With a sigh, the corgi flipped open the leather journal on the desk in front of him and uncapped a nearby fountain pen. Flint's perplexity showed in his furrowed brow.

"It's a ghost book and a ghost pen," said the corgi gruffly. "Try to keep up."

Professor Chumley explained: "When a ghost slips the mortal coil, anything they're touching or have on their person passes into our realm and we can make use of it. Them's the rules!"

"Like our clothes?"

"Exactly."

"Save the ghost tutorials for later, Chumley. Time to get down to business. Name?" the corgi asked, poised and ready with his pen.

"Flint Lockford."

The corgi scribbled a line in his book. "Age at time of death?"

"Thirty-one."

"And you died today?"

"Yep."

"Breed?"

"Irish wolfhound."

"Haunting status?"

Professor Chumley fielded this one: "Undetermined."

"Right," said the corgi. "I've assigned you to cell number one-oh-two. Your roommate is a pooch named Paco. Don't even think about asking me for a key, that joke went out of style last century. Now—empty out your pockets for me."

Flint glanced at Chumley, who nodded reassuringly.

"It's just for inventory reasons," added the corgi. "We like to keep track of any items ghosts bring in with them, as a way to discourage petty theft."

Having come this far, Flint complied with the request. He pulled his wallet from his right pocket, and his keys and a handful of pocket change from his left. When he chucked the coins and keys on the table, they fell with a strangely muted jingle. From the inside of his jacket, he pulled a pen and a small notebook and placed those on the desk too. It was reassuring to think that he might still be able to use his notebook.

The corgi poked through it all with a bored expression, counting his money and flipping through the cards in his wallet. He made careful note of everything.

"Nice watch," said the corgi, glancing at the wolfhound's wrist.

"Nothing special, really. It's just a Timex," Flint volunteered. "But I'd swear it was cracked and broken when I saw it on my actual wrist earlier. On dead me's wrist, I mean."

Flint held the watch up to his ear. "Yet somehow this ghostly version is still ticking."

"You must've passed on an instant before the watch got cracked," pointed out Chumley. "So the link between the ghost watch and the earthly watch was severed right before it broke. Pretty lucky."

"I don't feel lucky," Flint said matter-of-factly.

"Anything else?" asked the corgi.

Flint hesitated. "I do have one more thing." He pulled the ring box out of his jacket pocket and opened it up for Albert and Chumley to see. But he didn't put it down on the table.

"Well, will you look at that," said Albert. "Looks like you were getting set to pop the question."

Flint nodded.

"Tough break, pal." The corgi printed another line in his book—*One diamond ring in a box. Emerald cut.* "Right. You're all set, then, Flint. Grab your things. Like I said—room one-oh-two. Sleeping hours in Ghosthall run from nine in the morning to six in the evening at this time of year. No screeching, howling, or rattling is permitted during those hours. The professor here can fill you in on the rest of Ghosthall's rules. Break enough of them and you'll get booted to the curb."

"Thanks, Albert, we'll let you get back to your siesta." Professor Chumley pulled Flint toward the winding tower stairs to their right. "I'll give you the grand tour later," said the professor as they descended to the lower level. The sheepdog stifled a yawn. "Dang, this daytime jaunt always catches up with me. I could do with some shut-eye. Your first night is bound to be a long one so you should try and grab a few z's yourself."

The basement level turned out to be a cramped cellar with arched brick ceilings. Weak sconces on the walls lit the way as they proceeded through a series of corridors with gunmetal prisoner doors on either side. Flint reckoned Albert had not been far off in his description—the place had a distinctly crypt-like aura.

The professor gestured toward the doors, his voice a low whisper. "They're not luxurious digs, to be sure. But you get your own little space to hang your hat during the day where no one will bother you. And it's a nice clean mattress. We have plenty of those. Ah. Here we go. Number one-oh-two." Chumley peered at the number etched into the metal. Then he put a finger to his lips and stuck his head through the door. Seconds later he was back. "Right, Paco is fast asleep in the bunk on the left. Which means the one on the right is all yours."

"Is it pitch-black on the other side of that door?" Flint asked, making an effort to keep his voice steady.

"Don't worry, there's no such thing as pitch-black for us. You'll see what I mean. I'll come back and get you in a few hours and we can head up to the cantina to meet the rest of the gang. This place really comes alive—so to speak—after sundown. Sit tight until then? There's a good dog!"

Cantina? How was that gonna work? Flint wondered. He watched Chumley wander down the corridor and disappear from sight, leaving Flint all alone in the underground cell block. What had he gotten himself into? It hardly seemed like an improvement over the bakery steps, but at least it had distracted him from his troubles, and he had picked up some useful tips.

I've got nothing left to lose, he told himself, and, taking a deep breath, he glided through the closed door and into the penumbra of the cell room beyond. It was dark, as he'd anticipated, except for a faint greenish glow enveloping a bunk to his left, and for a similar phosphorescent glow that was coming from—of all places—himself. Flint held up a luminous hand and stared at it in amazement. It was just enough light for him to find his way around the room. He floated over to a narrow cot along the right wall and sat down. Leaning back, he felt no contact with the mattress, but somehow it felt more comforting to be lying above a bed.

Flint's thoughts drifted back to Bianca. He wondered whether she had heard about his death yet. He desperately wanted to go and see her, but at the same time he was terrified of what that might be like. If he couldn't hold her in his arms, or tell her everything he needed to say, then being around her would be torture.

7 · Junior Detective Morton Digby: The Big Barracuda

Morton couldn't quite believe that he'd found that ominous playing card hidden inside the wrecked piano. Murder. It was like a jolt of adrenaline, but mixed with it came a heavy dose of the jitters. If his previous cases had felt like splashing around in the kiddie pool, this one was more like diving into shark-infested waters.

Detective Puddleworth did not seem troubled by any pangs of self-doubt. He launched himself enthusiastically into the hunt. First he located the building superintendent loitering nearby, a scruffy-looking middle-aged tom with whiskey on his breath and a toothpick dangling from the corner of his mouth. Detective Puddleworth asked him where he was when the piano hit and the scraggly tom said he'd been playing poker with his buddies down in the basement when their game was interrupted by a big booming sound.

"Any idea who dropped this piano?" asked Morton.

"I got some idea," replied the super, smiling thinly. "That's the piano from apartment 5A. It was inside that unit when I rented it out yesterday to an Afghan hound. She said she wanted to keep the piano, so it beats me why she would chuck it out the window!"

"Does this tenant have a name?" the Scottish terrier asked the super. Morton's pen hovered over his notes.

"As it happens, we didn't get around to doing the paper-work last night."

"Can you describe her?" Morton asked.

"Late twenties. Tall. Not a bad-looking pooch, with light cream-colored fur. Claimed to be a secretary at an ad firm and I had no reason to doubt it. She paid her deposit in cash."

Morton pulled Detective Puddleworth aside and whispered: "What are the chances this Afghan hound could be the Queen of Spades?"

Detective Puddleworth stroked his beard. "I was wondering the same thing. We'd better go take a look upstairs."

They followed the super into the building and wound their way up a creaky staircase to the fifth floor. The super unlocked the door to apartment 5A for them when there was no answer to their knocks. Stepping into the bare one-bedroom apartment they found it deserted. They immediately took note of a wooden ramp leading up to the window and the rope knotted around the steam radiator. They were clearly in the right place.

"This whole place reeks of that same perfume!" exclaimed Morton. "She must've sprayed it everywhere to cover her tracks."

"It looks like this Afghan hound has flown the coop," said the Scottie, throwing open closet doors. "We'd better put out an all-points bulletin immediately, before the trail goes cold!"

They hurried back downstairs to the squad car, while the super gravitated back to his basement poker game.

"I think they expect us to consult with a superior officer before putting out an APB," said Morton.

"That will only slow things down." Detective Puddleworth pressed the button on the radio's mic and barked out instructions to the dispatcher: "That's right. A female Afghan hound. Cream-colored coat, late twenties. Yes—she should be considered *armed and dangerous*."

When he was done, he turned to Morton and said: "Don't worry. I'll take the heat if there's any pushback. I'm the senior detective here."

Morton bristled. "We're in this together, J.B."

The Scottie beamed and clapped him on the back. "That's the spirit, Morton. You're absolutely right. We're in this together!"

For the next twenty minutes, Detective Puddleworth traipsed up and down the stairs from the rooftop to the empty apartment on the fifth floor and back again, crawling about on his hands and knees with a magnifying glass as he sniffed out every possible clue. Every time he found so much as a stray dog's hair, he cried "Eureka!" and used tweezers to place it into a corked vial. This included one wiry black hair that Morton suspected belonged to the Scottie himself.

"Take my word for it, Morton. Forensics is where the future of criminology is headed. Something as pedestrian as a shoe print can crack a case wide open!"

Morton offered to help but the Scottie waved him off. "No, no, stand aside, Morton. You'll only contaminate the scene."

Finally, Detective Puddleworth's whirlwind of activity came to an abrupt halt. "I think we're done here," he said. "Let's head back to the precinct."

"We should enlist the superintendent's help to make a

sketch of the suspect," suggested Morton, who had spent the last twenty minutes brainstorming.

"Capital idea! We'll bring him along."

The super proved uncooperative until they threatened to initiate an investigation into the illegal gambling den in his building. Muttering curses under his breath, he followed them outside and climbed into the back seat of their squad car.

A hush fell over the crowded bullpen when the two detectives arrived at the precinct. Detective Puddleworth marched the recalcitrant super downstairs to an interrogation room, while Morton proceeded to his desk, ignoring his colleagues' stares. He put in a call to police headquarters, and they promised to send over a sketch artist right away. Finished with his phone call, Morton looked up to find Buckley and Callaway sneering down at him. The two hounds were similar in size and build but Buckley's markings were standard black and tan, while Callaway had the speckled coat of a coonhound. They both wore dark suits with white button-down shirts.

Buckley fiddled with Morton's stapler, squeezing it repeatedly and shooting staples out into the air. "Are you and Detective Puddlenuts for real? Did you really peg this piano case as a *murder*?"

"And you put out an APB on the Queen of Spades, no less!" exclaimed Callaway. "What a bunch of hogwash!"

"We're just doing our jobs," Morton replied coolly.

Buckley smirked. "We figured you fellas would be desperate for a real case, but we didn't expect you to just manufacture one out of thin air."

"Don't you two have a bank robber to catch?" Morton

snapped. "I heard you've been chasing that cat around town for months."

Callaway leaned in and dropped his voice. "Oh, we're gonna catch that son of a gun any day now, you better believe it."

"That's right!" snapped Buckley. "We're closing in on him. Just you wait and see!"

Morton gritted his teeth. These two hounds delighted in making his life miserable. Like all bullies, they had a sixth sense for weakness and they had zeroed in on Morton from the start. A good City detective had to be tough and fearless— like them—and Buckley and Callaway didn't think Morton made the cut. The worst part was that deep down, Morton wasn't too sure about it himself.

Detective Puddleworth appeared moments later and let out a low rumble when he caught sight of the two hounds loitering by his desk.

"Who do you think you're growling at?" Callaway snarled, and things might have gotten ugly if Sergeant Doyle hadn't come tromping down the aisle, causing Buckley and Callaway to scatter.

"Right. You two. Follow me!" grunted the sarge, pointing at Morton and the Scottie. "The captain wants to see you upstairs! Bring any evidence you've collected with you."

The bulldog berated them nonstop as they made their way up to the second floor: "It was a simple accident case but you two had to turn it into something big! When this thing backfires the two of you are gonna wind up directing trolleys around the Washington Square arch!"

As they neared the captain's office they heard the

clickety-clack of his secretary's typewriter. She soon came into view, perched at her own small desk, pecking away at the keys with her delicate fingers. She was a mild-mannered papillon named Shirley, with tufted ears and a wispy tail that resembled a feather duster. She instructed them to wait while the captain finished up a phone call. Proximity to power had bestowed on this humble secretary an out-sized role in the daily affairs of the precinct. It was common knowledge that the captain's memory was slipping as he neared retirement, and he relied heavily on Shirley to help keep things straight.

Through the open doorway Morton could see Captain Maddox seated at his desk. He was a hefty mastiff with a fawn coat and a black mask across his face. Gold banded cuffs on his uniform proclaimed his authority. He was a dog with a formidable temper, and even the smallest bit of bad news would send him into a fit of rage, causing him to pound his desk with his meaty fists and let loose with thun-derous bellows that echoed throughout every corner of the precinct. In between these daily outbursts he behaved like a kindly father figure, happy to take you under his wing and share his hard-earned wisdom. And that was the trouble— you could never be sure which captain you were going to get. Shirley had an uncanny ability to read her boss's moods. She always seemed to know when one of his volcanic erup-tions was imminent. Judging from the pitying look she was casting their way, Morton reckoned the current forecast was not good.

Morton's pulse was racing. He had never been called to the captain's office before, or been on the receiving end of the captain's wrath. The mastiff ended his phone call with a series of grunts, slammed down the receiver, and waved them in. He had a spacious office, with two tall windows behind his desk that cast him in a dark silhouette. Morton, Puddleworth, and the sarge came to a halt in the wide carpeted space in the middle of the room. There were no chairs to sit on, or hide behind.

The big dog leaned back and put his arms behind his head. "Let's hear it, fellas," he growled. "Explain to me how this bizarre mishap turned into a murder investigation?"

Detective Puddleworth pulled the queen of spades playing card out of the evidence bag and held it up for the captain to see. "We found this threaded through the piano's strings."

The sarge was incredulous. "Any fool could've shoved that card in there! Without a bullet wound or a knife wound in the victim it doesn't mean a thing!"

"Put a sock in it, Sergeant," snarled the captain. "I'm talking to our detectives."

"Yes, sir!"

The captain motioned for the Scottish terrier to come closer. "Let's have a sniff." Puddleworth held out the playing card and the captain's large nostrils quivered above it briefly. "Have you identified this perfume yet?"

"It's a popular scent called *Mellifluous*," Morton replied. "It's sprayed over most of the evidence connected to the suspect. It's the same scent that was found on all the playing cards from earlier Queen of Spades crime scenes."

The captain scratched his bristly chin. "That stuff makes things practically impossible to track, no matter how good your nose is. Okay, I can see how you might've gotten this cockamamie idea into your heads. But it's still a big stretch, considering the manner in which this pooch died."

Next, Detective Puddleworth showed him the cleanly cut rope. And he explained how the Afghan hound who had rented apartment 5A above the crime scene was nowhere to be found.

"Let's say there *is* something fishy about this," conceded the captain. "It was still premature to put out an APB. I mean, do you guys really think this female hound could be the notorious Queen of Spades?"

"Not a chance!" snorted the sarge. "Most of the Queen of Spades's victims were killed by sniper shots! And there's no such thing as a female sniper!" The captain gave his sergeant a withering stare and the bulldog clammed up again.

Detective Puddleworth's bushy eyebrows knit together. "There were plenty of female secret agents kicking about during the war and I imagine they had weapons training."

The captain looked doubtful. "So your theory is that the Queen of Spades was some sort of Mata Hari spy? And now that she's back on home soil she's gone rogue?"

Detective Puddleworth held the captain's gaze. "That's our theory in a nutshell."

Morton cringed at his partner's poor choice of words and quickly pulled Flint Lockford's notebook from the bag. "We also have a lead on who could be behind the hit. The victim was a journalist for the *Knickerbocker Gazette*, and we found this notebook in his pocket. There are a lot of prominent names scribbled in here, including this one that he circled."

Morton handed the open notebook to the captain, who

put on his half-moon eyeglasses and peered down at the page. "Osvaldo Delgatto," grunted the mastiff. "The mobster? So you think this journalist pissed off the mob and they had him rubbed out?"

"It's a reasonable hypothesis," Detective Puddleworth said defensively.

The mastiff regarded them in silence for a long minute. "Who even put you two dogs on this case to begin with?"

They all turned to look at the sarge, who looked perplexed. He replied with considerable trepidation: "Er, I thought you did, sir?"

A momentary cloud passed over the mastiff's face. "Hmm. Yes, of course. It must've just slipped my mind. Anyway, the point is I think the two of you have gone out on a limb here. You put out that APB without consulting your superior officers first, and now that it has reached all the transport hubs, we can't take it back without looking like fools! Do that again and I guarantee you'll be sorry you ever joined the force." The captain drummed his fingers on his desk. "But . . . you've caught me in a magnanimous mood. I'm gonna give you a shot at making your case. You have one week to dig up something solid to support these wild conjectures, and not a minute more. I'm talking hard evidence. And if you strike out . . ." The captain trailed off.

Morton smiled nervously. "We won't let you down, Captain."

"You can count on us," echoed Detective Puddleworth.

"Dismissed!" The captain reached for the phone and began to dial a new number, but he stopped with a finger partway around the dial. "And fellas?" His tone was suddenly menacing. The two detectives had made it halfway to the door, but they froze and turned to face the captain once more. "Don't do anything to damage this precinct's reputation," he growled. They nodded and backed out the door.

The sketch artist pulled a drawing pad from his satchel and sat down opposite the superintendent at a bare metal table, a naked yellow bulb dangling from the ceiling above them. Morton and his partner stepped outside, keeping an eye on things through the door's wire mesh window. The two detectives could still hear the superintendent's nonstop bellyaching. The sketch artist had been delayed for over an hour, and the super was fed up with the wait. Now he was insisting that once you'd seen one Afghan hound, you'd seen them all. But after much poking and prodding, the sketch artist came out of the room with a surprisingly detailed portrait of an attractive blond dog. She was conservatively dressed in a spiffy jacket, with a buttoned-up blouse that closed with a brooch, a shell-shaped cap, and cat-eye glasses. The two detectives released the resentful super and returned to their desks, drawing in hand.

"I hope this sketch helps," said Morton. "Otherwise our first dogicide case may be our last."

"Don't worry," the Scottie assured him. "We'll track down this hired killer and book her a room at Sing Sing!"

"It might be worth showing the sketch to this contact I have," said Morton. "He's a small-time crook whose turf includes the stretch of Bleecker where the murder went down. He's the kind of dog who keeps his ear close to the ground, so if there's any chatter going around, he'll have heard it. It's a long shot, but if we get lucky we might gain a toehold in this investigation."

"It's worth a try. Do you have a way to reach him?" asked the Scottie.

"When he's not picking pockets, he likes to hang out at the chess studio over on Sullivan Street. I'll give him a call there."

"Perfect!" The Scottie looked thoughtful. "I think we should work the spy angle too. If the Queen of Spades *is* some sort of ex-CIA agent, then there must be some record of her in government files somewhere."

"Sure. But you're talking about classified documents that will be under lock and key down in the capital," Morton pointed out. "How are we supposed to get our paws on them?"

"An old buddy of mine works for the CIA. I'm gonna give him a ring and see what he can find out about any female Afghan hound operatives during the war. You'd better run this sketch through the ditto machine so we can send him a copy."

Morton looked at his partner, impressed. "He must be a really good pal if you expect him to root around through classified files."

"You were too young to get drafted, weren't you, Morton?"

"I turned eighteen during the final year of the conflict. I had just finished basic training when suddenly it was all over."

"Count yourself lucky. I was in the Signal Corps. A communication specialist."

"You mean like a radio guy?" Morton couldn't help wondering if the Scottie had seen any real action.

"No, nothing as glamorous as that. I was a Pigeoneer. I was in charge of sending and receiving classified messages via homing pigeons."

"Pigeons? I didn't know we still used pigeons during the war!"

"Sure, and the messages those birds carried saved thousands of lives. One of my pigeons was even awarded a medal after the war!"

"No kidding?"

"During the conflict I was in frequent contact with numerous agents from the Office of Strategic Services. My pigeons helped to keep some of them alive."

Morton grinned. "So you're saying this friend of yours owes you a favor."

"Like you said, we're good pals. Let's leave it at that." Detective Puddleworth took out a small black address book from the top drawer of his desk and thumbed through the alphabetical listings until he found the name he was searching for. He dialed the number and Morton listened as a lively back-and-forth followed.

When the Scottish terrier hung up, Morton looked at him expectantly. "What did he say?"

"He promised to do some digging for me and cut through all the red tape. He's gonna get back to us with some names as soon as he can."

"Great!"

"What's great?" asked Sergeant Doyle, who had sidled up to them again—he could be surprisingly stealthy for such a burly dog.

"We're just waiting for a phone call from a source who might provide us with a lead," Morton replied vaguely.

"I hope you're not gonna sit around waiting for the phone to ring? You heard the captain. Time to get cracking!"

"No, of course not," said Morton. "I was just about to reach out to Zachary Fishpupper. We'll show him the sketch and see if he's heard anything."

"That two-bit crook won't be any help!" the bulldog said dismissively. "Murder is well above his pay grade. If Fishpupper is your best shot for working your way into this case I'd be worried."

"And we need to have a chat with Flint Lockford's lady friend, Bianca Moon," added the Scottie. "She may have some idea about who wanted to kill him."

"Ah yes, the Angora," said the bulldog. "I broke the tragic news to that cat earlier. When I gave her the ring, I swear she went batshit crazy! She put it on her finger and acted like she was engaged to a dead dog! Can you believe it?"

"Poor girl," sighed Detective Puddleworth. "I expect that finding out he was murdered will come as another shock to her."

The bulldog stuck his thumbs in his belt and rocked back and forth on his heels, eyeing them skeptically. "Yeah. Murder, you say. I'm still not convinced. I've got a feeling you two boneheads are barking up the wrong tree!" With this last retort, the sarge spun around and shuffled off down the aisle.

Zachary Fishpupper agreed to meet them at the Horn and Feather automat at a quarter to four, lured by the promise of a free meal. The two detectives drove up in their squad car and found a parking spot under a leafy tree on Thirteenth Street, half a block from their destination.

"Do you trust this dog?" Detective Puddleworth asked Morton.

"For an incorrigible pickpocket he's not a bad sort. He's nuts about the game of chess. Picking pockets is just his way of paying the rent so he can spend the rest of his time staring at a chessboard."

Situated on the corner of Eighth Avenue and 14th Street, the Horn and Feather occupied a stately building that in earlier days had been a bank. It was an impressive setting for a restaurant, with lofty ceilings, brass fixtures, and marble tables, all of which belied the automat's cheap fare. Pushing through bronze doors, the detectives handed the nickel lady at the counter a quarter each and she pinched five coins for them in return.

"This place is a step up from Frankie's," Detective Puddleworth noted approvingly.

"Yeah, I love it here. A slice of pie is just five cents. Same for the coffee. Hot food is a dime, but I'm guessing you'll have a warm meal waiting for you later at home."

"Actually the missus took the ferry to Staten Island today to finish packing up our things. But it's too early for dinner anyway."

"You're right," replied Morton. "It's snack time!" He wandered over to the dessert corner and peered into the little food windows, dropping his nickel into a promising slot and lifting the glass to extract a chocolate frosted donut. A second nickel filled his mug with coffee and cream. He managed to snag a quiet table in the back and parked himself in a bistro chair. Detective Puddleworth appeared moments later with a slice of cheesecake and a glass of milk.

Morton took a bite of his donut. "So, J.B., don't take this the wrong way, but I wouldn't mention the whole pigeoneer thing to any of our colleagues if I were you. I don't mean to make light of your service, but it's the kind of thing Buckley and Callaway would needle you about for months."

"Don't worry, Morton, I've heard it all before. Birdbrain! Lamebrain! None of it bothers me. If they want to stoop to juvenile name-calling it's no fur off my back."

Morton took a second bite of his donut and munched thoughtfully. Then he noticed a skinny figure slinking up to their table. In spite of the greyhound's efforts to conceal his identity, Morton had no trouble recognizing Zachary Fishpupper with his narrow snout, beady eyes, and rat-like tail. He was wearing rose-colored glasses and had on a rather obvious wig of brown curls that put Morton in mind of a dead gerbil. A jean jacket with a flipped-up collar and various beaded necklaces completed his disguise.

"Can we help you?" Morton asked, pretending not to recognize him.

"It's me, Zachary!" hissed the greyhound, pulling down his sunglasses to give him a wink. "I'm going incognito. I can't afford to be seen talking to coppers!"

"Is that really you, Zachary?" Morton asked, playing along.

"Shh. Don't say my name! Just call me Joe. I'm just a regular West Village beatnik."

"Glad you could make it, Joe the Beatnik," said Morton, suppressing a laugh. "This is J.B. My new partner. Go ahead and pull up a chair."

Fishpupper sat himself down between them, casting wary glances to his left and right. "We gotta make this quick. I'm putting all my cred on the line by agreeing to meet with you fellas."

Morton fished around in his pocket and pushed two shiny quarters over to the skinny dog. "Here you go, Joe. Get yourself something tasty on us."

The greyhound pocketed the coins in a flash. "I'll eat when we're done talking. What kind of info are you looking for? You were very vague on the phone earlier. You're not looking into that dead piano fella, are you?"

"That's our case, all right," said Detective Puddleworth.

"I'm guessing you figured out that it was no accident?" said the greyhound.

"Yes. We got that far," said Morton. "What do you know about it, Joe?"

"I've heard some things."

Morton gave him a sharp look. "Like what exactly?"

"The only thing I know for sure is that the Queen of Spades was involved. Word is she's going to ground for good. That this hit may have been her swan song."

"We're wise to her already too, but it's good to get confirmation," said Morton.

"Well, that's all I got," said the greyhound, shrugging his shoulders in a way that made the beads around his neck rustle.

"You must've heard something else?" Morton prodded.

"Well, there is a rumor going around. But I don't know how much truth there is to it."

"Grapevine rumors are all we're expecting from you. Just let us decide if it's important or not," said Morton.

"Okay, okay! Don't push me!" whined the greyhound. "What I heard is that one of Osvaldo Delgatto's deputies went off script and ordered the hit without the boss's authorization. Apparently, he's furious about it!"

"How curious," said Morton. "Now why would someone do that?"

"To save their own bacon," said the greyhound. "It's the only reason anyone would do something stupid like piss off Delgatto! But that's it. I don't know anything more."

"Fair enough. I reckon you've earned your fifty cents."

The greyhound peered at Detective Puddleworth's dessert plate. "Hey, pal, how's the cheesecake here?"

"Like a little slice of heaven," the Scottish terrier replied.

"Right, I'm gonna grab myself some of that before I skedaddle." The greyhound pushed back his chair, but Morton reached out a paw and caught hold of his arm. "Hold on. Do you know where we can find him?"

"Find who?"

"Delgatto."

The greyhound's nose trembled. "Trust me—you don't want to find that dog."

"Let's just say we do," Morton insisted.

The greyhound's eyes darted left and right to make sure no one was close by. "Mama Leone's. Dinnertime. Five nights a week. And that info alone is worth more than your measly fifty cents."

"Thanks, Joe. Pleasure doing business with you," said Morton, releasing his hold on the greyhound. Zachary Fishpupper scurried away as fast as his skinny chicken legs would take him. Morton turned to his partner. "What do you think?"

"This just confirms the mob angle," said the Scottish terrier. "Lockford circled Delgatto's name in his notebook for a reason."

"When I talked to the editor-in-chief at the *Gazette* earlier, he told me there's a long list of cats and dogs who might be nursing a grudge against Lockford."

"Sure," replied the Scottie. "But no one hates seeing their name in the paper more than a mob boss. It ruins the image they've cultivated for themselves as respectable businessdogs."

"Zachary says Delgatto may not have actually ordered the hit."

"Which is exactly the sort of rumor Delgatto might spread to confuse us."

"I don't know, J.B.," said Morton. "Delgatto is a nasty customer. We may need more than just Fishpupper's scuttlebutt to go after him."

"He's the biggest mob boss in town," the Scottie conceded. "All the other mobsters are afraid of him. But that doesn't mean we should be too scared to do our jobs. He's clearly implicated in our murder investigation." The Scottie scraped up the last crumbs of his cheesecake with his fork. It seemed like his mind was made up.

"Then I guess I'll make a dinner reservation for two at Mama Leone's." Morton had to admit that life with a new partner was far from boring. It was only the Scottie's first day, and so far Puddleworth had put out an APB on a wanted hit-dog, stood up to Captain Maddox, and was ready to launch an investigation into the city's most notorious crime boss. No one could accuse him of lacking courage.

Looked at another way, Morton supposed his partner could also be viewed as harebrained and impetuous. The City was a precarious place: stabbings were the main worry for beat cops, who had only a billy club to defend themselves with. But the mob had access to firearms, which made them dangerous on another level.

Back on the family farm in Maine, Morton's brothers read the metro section of the *Gazette* over breakfast every morning with great horror. They were routincly shocked by the daily list of big-city crimes. When Morton had announced his intention to become a City cop, his brothers' biggest fear was that Morton would end up as just another horrifying news item in their morning paper. He had assured his siblings that he would play it safe. Yet here he was now, going after the City's biggest crime boss. Morton sure hoped the Scottie knew what he was doing, because he had no desire for the both of them to end up dead.

8 · Flint Lockford: The Party

Muffled sounds of shouting and laughter roused Flint from a deep sleep, cutting short a remarkably vivid and strange dream—murdered and turned into a ghost! He opened his eyes to find himself in darkness. Sitting up he stretched and attempted to rub his eyes, but his movements felt oddly indistinct, as if his arms weighed nothing at all. He looked down at his peculiarly luminous hands and was filled with a sudden sense of dread.

A voice called out: "You must be my new roommate." To his right a glowing Chihuahua with pointy ears was sitting on a bunk along the opposite wall. Everything clicked into place for Flint. He was dead. He was a ghost. The things he'd dreamt were all too real.

"Welcome to Ghosthall. Did you die today, my friend?" asked the Chihuahua, waving his hand through a nearby lamp. The yellow light bulb lit up. He was wearing a white dress shirt and tight-fitting black pants. His coat was a deep chocolate brown.

Flint did his best to marshal his wits. "Yes, I did. In sensational fashion. I was squashed on the street by a falling piano."

"What a way to meet your maker!" exclaimed the Chihuahua.

"It certainly caught me off guard."

"You are lucky to have had such a spectacular death!"

"If you say so."

"I do," insisted the Chihuahua. "Me? I choked on a piece of popcorn. A humiliating and ridiculous way to die!"

"I take it no one was around to pound you on the back?"

"Not a soul. I was working as a projectionist over at the Third Street Cinema, and I was all alone up in the booth."

"I know that place," said Flint. "I've been there on dates a bunch of times."

Their conversation was interrupted by a jovial voice coming from the hallway. "Knock, knock! Are you lads up?" Chumley's head pushed through the door. "Ah, Paco, I see you've met Flint. Excellent! Hustle up, fellas. We'll kick off the night with a drink at the cantina!" Chumley's head vanished back through the door.

Flint hopped off the bed and was once again surprised when his feet didn't hit the ground. The Chihuahua—Paco—jumped up too. He looked around four feet tall, and only came up to about Flint's chest. Paco drifted over to a wall mirror and dexterously looped a skinny tie around his collar. When he was done, he settled a panama hat on his head and grabbed a compact umbrella from a hook on the wall. He gestured with it toward the door. "After you, my friend."

The hallway was bustling. Dozens of jovial ghosts were flitting by, all of them carrying furled umbrellas and all of them headed for the stairs. Flint joined the stream of jostling spooks. Reaching the ground floor, they poured into a spacious old courtroom with arched stained glass windows along the back wall. Seemingly untouched since the building was shuttered, the room had rows of benches and a low wooden fence with a gate separating the gallery from a judge's bench and a jury box. Stacked against the judge's bench were half a dozen transparent wooden barrels, and a long line of ghosts had formed leading up to them. Each ghost held an empty mug, and once they got to the front of the line, they held them under a tap gushing with a peculiar frothy substance. Chumley handed Flint and Paco mugs and they took their place in the back of the queue.

The jury box at the far end of the room had been taken over by a musical act. A tall and curvy marmalade cat was singing a moody ballad into a mic, her hips gyrating rhythmically in time with the music. Flint listened to her transfixed as she serenaded the audience in low tremulous tones, switching unexpectedly to a higher register for the refrain. She was wearing a low-cut sequin dress, and her face was made up with sparkling silver circles around her eyes and purple stripes running across her cheeks and bare arms.

"That's Tiger! Isn't she something!" Professor Chumley said proudly. "She's one of the gang, so you'll get to meet her soon. She used to be a target girl in a knife-throwing cabaret act. Don't mention knives around her—she's still a bit sensitive."

"I'll try to remember," said Flint. "Seems like the kind of gig you would quit before getting down to your last life."

"That was her plan," explained the sheepdog, "only her parents never told her about the time she died as a baby, so she miscounted. It happens more often than you'd think!"

Flint looked around the room. There had to be over a hundred ghosts gathered around him. "I imagine every cat and dog here has some tragic story," he said.

"Not me!" grunted Paco. "My great tragedy is that I died in an absurd manner!"

"And don't mention popcorn around Paco," Professor Chumley said in a pretend whisper, earning himself a poke in the ribs from the Chihuahua's umbrella.

"I'm surprised at how many cat ghosts there are," said Flint. "I always thought most cats died peacefully in old age?"

Chumley nodded. "That's true, but the cats who do die young are more likely to stick around. One popular theory is that they have less forgiving natures. It's also true that the more lives you have the more careless you are with them. You'd be surprised at how many cats work their way through all nine. Take Benny over there." Chumley gestured to the plump brown tomcat standing alongside the singer in the jury box. He was plucking the strings of a standing double bass with zeal, his deft fingers hitting every note even as he twirled the bass in circles every few bars. "Benny was a race car driver in his youth," Chumley went on. "He burned through several lives a year trying to climb the ranks in the racing circuit, but was forced into early retirement when he was down to his last life. Then he was run over in the street by an old rival looking for payback." The sheepdog seemed to catch himself. "Sorry, Flint, I shouldn't be dishing out everyone's death stories! Not exactly the most cheerful introduction to Ghosthall!"

Flint shrugged. "I get the feeling death must be a common subject of conversation around here."

"You're right about that!" The professor chuckled.

"Hey, what is that stuff anyway?" Flint asked, pointing over at the barrels. "It's not beer, I can tell that much from here."

"We call it Spume," said Paco. "I hope you take a liking

to it because it's pretty much the one thing ghosts can drink."

"But what is it?" Flint asked again.

Chumley launched into full professor mode. "Have you ever wondered where the beer foam bubbles disappear to in your lager? Well, centuries ago, some enterprising phantasms stuck their noses in a beer mug and realized they could taste the beer foam as it evaporated. They recruited a brilliant chemist who figured out how to collect the vaporized froth and store it in ghost barrels."

"So it's made from actual beer?"

"You can think of it as condensed evaporated beer molecules if that helps," said the sheepdog.

"Er . . . I hate to ask," Flint said hesitantly. "But where does it go after ghosts drink it?"

Paco grinned. "Ha ha, that's everyone's first question. Spume is more of a gas than a liquid, so it just dissipates into the ether. But it has a pleasant effervescent sensation going down, with just a hint of malt. The afterlife can be very bland, so even the slightest taste is considered a treat for ghosts. Keep in mind it's ten cents a mug," he added.

"But your first drink is on me!" Chumley dropped two ghost nickels into Flint's hand. "Spume is the main economic engine in the spirit world. Without it, there would be little motivation for ghosts to do anything productive."

"Does that mean you all have jobs?" Flint asked with surprise.

"In a manner of speaking, but a couple hours of work a week is all it takes for most ghosts to scrape together enough dimes for a week's worth of Spume. So we're not exactly toiling away in the coal mines. Most spooks find they like keeping busy."

"What's your job?" Flint asked the sheepdog.

"My job, you'll be surprised to hear, is to go out into the world and introduce myself to promising new lodgers." Chumley tipped his hat to Flint with a wink. "Other ghosts are performers." Chumley pointed to the band with his umbrella. "But the most popular gig is plain old finder, like Paco here."

"What do finders do?" asked Flint.

The Chihuahua was happy to explain: "We go out and look for useful ghost items, bring them back to the hall, and turn them in to the Trading Post upstairs for a fee. Matches are always popular items, as are sheets, blankets, books, and records."

"And umbrellas, I take it," said Flint.

"Actually, umbrellas are hard to find," Chumley replied. "Except for the occasional pedestrian accident, few cats and dogs kick the bucket while holding one. But some enterprising ghosts about a hundred years back took it upon themselves to manufacture umbrellas from ghostly materials. The largest umbrella factory on the East Coast is up on Jane Street, not far from here. It's run by about fifty ghosts, and they do amazing work. Of course they charge a pretty penny for their products, since they've got something of a lock on the market for new umbrellas. Umbrella factory ghosts are some of the flushest spooks you'll ever meet!"

"You got that right," Paco piped up. "Those bigwig factory owners practically run this town!"

The collie standing behind the Chihuahua poked her thin snout up to Professor Chumley's ear and whispered loudly: "And who's this handsome fella?" She fixed Flint with a piercing stare. Dressed in a puffy blouse and a mustard colored skirt, she had a mane of luxurious white and tan hair. Her right hand was gripping a neatly furled parasol.

"Sophie, doll," said Chumley brightly. "Allow me to introduce my new friend Flint Lockford."

"The piano guy?" she exclaimed. "Holy smokes! I can't wait to hear your story!"

"Drinks first!" Chumley said firmly. They were approaching the head of the line. Moments later Flint handed his ten cents to a bored-looking shorthair cat parked on a stool. This cat dropped the change into a slotted wooden box and indicated for him to hold his mug under the tap. Flint, Paco, and Sophie followed Chumley over to an empty bench, gingerly carrying mugs full of the bubbly pinkish froth. They were soon joined by grumpy Albert, the corgi from reception, as well as the singer and the bass player, who were taking a break from their set. Chumley introduced Flint to Benny and Tiger respectively and they looked pleased when Flint mentioned how much he had enjoyed the music.

"So Flint, what do you think of the Spume?" Albert the corgi asked him.

"I haven't tasted it yet!" Flint raised the mug to his lips and took a cautious sip of the foam. He felt a strange effervescent feeling as it trickled down his throat, with barely a passing hint of hoppy flavor. "It doesn't exactly pack a punch," he said cagily.

"Spoken like the freshly dead!" Sophie giggled. "Give it a few weeks and you won't be able to get enough of the stuff. Now, Flint, don't keep us in suspense a moment longer. We want to hear all about your tragic encounter with a piano, and don't skimp on the gory details!"

Flint told his story from start to finish to a rapt audience. When he got to the part about how he'd glimpsed a figure up on the roof holding a knife, both Sophie and Tiger gasped. He finished his account by mentioning how the two detectives found the playing card stuck inside the piano.

"Another murdered ghost," said Albert. "What a shocker. No wonder you're sticking around!"

"Dollars to donuts you'll end up a haunter," said Benny.

"Now, don't go putting ideas in his head," Chumley snapped. "Just because he was bumped off doesn't mean he's headed down that road. He could have other reasons for sticking around."

"So why are you lingering, then, Flint?" Tiger asked, hitting him with a piercing stare. "Are you secretly out for revenge?"

Flint took another sip of Spume, buying himself time to untangle his jumbled thoughts, then he said: "I'd love to know who killed me and why. But the thought of trying to even the score hasn't crossed my mind. What's done is done. What I'm really worried about is Bianca."

"Who's Bianca?" asked Sophie. "Don't tell me you were *married*? I don't see a wedding ring on your finger! You haven't traded your ring in already, have you? It makes me sick when cats and dogs ditch their rings the minute they drop dead. 'Til death do us part, they always say, as if that excuse makes it remotely okay!"

"Sophie, please let the dog speak," Paco snapped.

"No, I wasn't married," Flint clarified. "Not yet, anyway. But I was about to propose. Bianca and I were supposed to be having dinner at Bertolotti's this very night, and I was gonna pop the question over dessert." Flint felt his eyes begin to well up.

"How awful!" Tiger said sympathetically.

"I keep wondering what will become of her now that I'm gone," Flint went on. "I desperately want to go and find her, but at the same time I'm terrified of being near her when she won't even know I'm there."

The ghosts around him exchanged glances. "You know, Flint, there are actually ways to communicate with the living," said Professor Chumley.

Flint gawked at the sheepdog. "Don't kid me about this, Professor."

Chumley put a hand on his heart. "It's perfectly true, there are ways to make contact with the living."

"But first you need to be sure about who you want to communicate with," said Sophie. The other ghosts all nodded.

Flint sat in stunned silence, blindsided by the sudden revelation that he might be able to talk to Bianca. Then he drained his mug and jumped to his feet. "I need to find her right away."

Professor Chumley stood up as well. "I'll come with you. You may need my help."

"Why don't we all go!" exclaimed Tiger, clasping her hands together gleefully. "It's been ages since we went on a proper field trip." The rest of the gang warmed quickly to this idea, and drained what was left of their drinks. Only Albert seemed unenthusiastic, grumbling something about a fool's errand.

Paco eyed Flint stonily. "But before we go, we need to get you an umbrella, my friend."

"Darn straight," said Benny. "None of us wants to be seen around town hanging out with an umbrella-less spook!" This sparked giggles from Tiger and Sophie, who hooked elbows with Flint, one on either side of him, and marched him toward the staircase.

Up on the second floor the layout was similar, only instead of a cantina there was a general goods store that sold items like hats, watches, and books. In the back of the shop, a wide rack spanned the breadth of the store, displaying umbrellas of every color and pattern imaginable.

"Wow, that's quite an impressive collection!" Flint exclaimed.

He reached for a sleek black umbrella with a bamboo handle but Sophie steered him away. "You should pick one from the used bin over here. They're banged up, but they work fine, and new ghosts always wind up ruining their first few umbrellas anyway."

Chumley nodded. "That's a good tip. You're better off starting with a bargain umbrella. Especially if you're planning to go out during daylight hours like me."

Flint was mystified by the umbrella mania the ghosts all displayed, but he took their advice and selected a slightly beat-up umbrella, paying fifty cents for it at the register. A jar at the counter was full of round patches with the tower clock embroidered on it, and the word *Ghosthall* spelled out underneath. Chumley plucked one out. "You're gonna need one of these too since you're one of us now! It's just a nickel." The professor pointed to an identical badge sewn to his own jacket lapel. Benny showed off his badge on the side of his bowler hat, and Tiger and Sophie both flashed neck scarves with the same Ghosthall patch fixed on a corner. The collie whipped out a ghost needle and thread and set to work sewing Flint's patch to the shoulder of his jacket, while Flint fidgeted impatiently.

Chumley used the opportunity to explain the basics on communicating with mortals. "The most important thing to keep in mind about communicating with the living is that you can only ever speak to one specific mortal, and whoever you pick is the only one who will ever be able to hear your voice. So you need to be sure."

"I choose Bianca," Flint stated matter-of-factly. "So what do I do?"

"It's easy," said Chumley. "You just need to speak right into her ear. The first mortal who hears your voice right up close becomes linked to you permanently."

"But no one else will be able to hear me speak?"

"Nope. And it can't be undone," the professor warned.

"*I* picked a local medium as my mortal to talk to," Benny confided. "Psychics are used to communicating with ghosts and they're typically happy to pass on messages to friends or relatives."

"I need to speak to Bianca directly," Flint said firmly.

"You should also be aware," said Albert, "that not all mortals handle the initial interaction well. As likely as not they will think they've gone mad."

Flint frowned. He had no desire to add to Bianca's distress.

Chumley did his best to reassure him. "That said, plenty

of ghosts successfully communicate with their loved ones to say their piece. Of course, once they do they usually vaporize!"

"I see," said Flint. "So you might be wasting time sewing on that patch, then, Sophie."

The collie flashed him an alluring smile. "I have a feeling you're going to stick around for a while, Flint." He watched as she tied a knot in the thread, pulled it tight, and snipped the end clean with a pair of ghost scissors.

9 · Bianca Moon: The Knock at the Door

Bianca lived at 81 Perry Street, a six-story building on a pretty tree-lined block not far from the Calico Cat Lounge. It had an ivory brick facade, arched windows, and an elaborate wrought iron fire escape. Bianca's apartment was at ground level, reached via a sunken entrance tucked under the stoop. Bianca thanked Roxy for walking her home, but the alley cat refused to take the hint, insisting on coming inside to make her some tea.

Three hours later, Bianca found herself slumped on the velvet settee in her small living room, mindlessly sipping lukewarm tea from a chipped cup and staring blankly out into space. Her sharp ears picked out Roxy's movements in the kitchen where she was busy refreshing the teapot: the sound of running water, the clank of the kettle hitting the stovetop, followed by the rasp of a match and the faint whoosh of the burner. Bianca sighed. It was clear Roxy wasn't leaving anytime soon.

Bianca had been drinking tea all afternoon, and she was sick to the teeth of it. The alley cat soon reappeared, cradling the blue teapot in both hands. Roxy poured them each a fresh cup of orange pekoe, adding a lump of sugar and a splash of milk. "There you go, Princess," she said, giving it a stir with a small spoon and nudging the cup and saucer in her direction. Bianca took a sip—it was bitter, just like all the previous cups. She gave Roxy a dark look.

The alley cat cast aside the *Life* magazine that had occupied her most of the afternoon and began to poke around Bianca's living room with an unabashed curiosity that in Bianca's mind bordered on nosiness. Her railroad apartment was boxy and small, but Bianca had cozied it up with plush red drapes, wool rugs, decorative mirrors, and a pair of antique lamps with amber glass shades that she had positioned on either side of the living room window. Bianca made no objection when Roxy riffled through her record collection, but when the alley cat picked up one of the papers piled next to her typewriter Bianca snapped: "Those are private!" Roxy put it down and backed away with her hands in the air. Unfazed, the alley cat proceeded to the bookcase in the corner, where she ran her fingers over the dusty spines of Bianca's poetry collection before leaning in to examine a silver framed photograph.

"Oh look, a Moon family portrait!" The alley cat picked up a photograph of a teenage Bianca sitting on the porch with her parents.

Bianca wasn't sure why she bothered to correct her, but she did. "It's not a Moon family portrait," she said. "My parents are the Stewarts, actually."

"Say what?" Roxy looked confused.

"The Stewarts. They adopted me. My birth parents died in a train crash when I was six."

"You're an orphan?" The alley cat's eyes went wide.

"Yes."

"Me too."

"I guess we have something in common after all."

"Why didn't you ever say anything?" Roxy asked her.

Bianca shrugged. "Do you go around telling everyone you're an orphan?"

"Nope. I sure don't."

"Besides, I was lucky. My adoptive parents gave me a wonderful home."

"That reminds me. Why haven't you called them yet?"

"Well—I never told them about Flint. They're kind of old-fashioned in some ways."

"I take it they wouldn't be keen on you marrying a dog?"

"Not exactly. I mean, they're fine with it for others, just not so much for their daughter. Also, if I tell my mom about what happened, I know she'll drive right into town and whisk me back to Scatsdale."

"And that would be the end of your big city adventure."

"And the worst part is I don't think I'd put up much of a fight."

"Well, you're only putting off the inevitable. You have to call them sooner or later." Roxy's next stop on her living room tour was a narrow table along the wall, on top of which was a large birdcage made out of carved wood, with thin metal bars and a curved roof. Inside, a small green parrot was perched on a wooden branch. The alley cat peered at it with rapt attention.

"What did you say his name was?"

Bianca sighed. "That's Rupert."

"Do you ever let him out of the cage?"

"Yes, I let him out daily so he can fly around and stretch his wings."

"He's adorable. Although I must confess, I can't look at him without wondering if parrots taste anything like chicken."

"Don't be crass, Roxy. That's my pet you're talking about."

"Sorry. That was thoughtless of me. I take it you never look at him and think what if . . . ?"

"No. I don't. I don't eat birds for a start. I'm a pescatarian."

Roxy grimaced. "I should've guessed."

The parrot stared back at the alley cat and bobbed his head up and down. "Bad kitty!" he squawked.

"He talks!" Roxy clapped her hands together in delight.

"He knows a few words. He can be quite funny when he wants to be."

"What else does he say?"

"When you sneeze, he sometimes says 'bless you.'"

The alley cat promptly faked a sneeze. "Bless you!" squawked Rupert.

"That's hilarious!"

Rupert let out a fake laugh and then said once again: "Bad kitty!"

"You might as well feed him for me," said Bianca. "If you think you can control your predatory impulses, that is. The birdseed tin is in the table drawer. Just put one level teaspoon in his dish."

Roxy followed her directions, and the happy parrot squawked his appreciation.

Bianca set down her teacup. "Thanks for all your help, Roxy, but I think it's time for me to go rest in bed."

"Good idea. I'll help you get set up. We can put your teacup on your bedside table."

"Seriously, Roxy, you don't need to babysit me!" cried Bianca.

"The thing is, Princess, I can't just leave you like this. You look so very . . . not okay."

"I never claimed to be okay. I'm not the least bit okay. I feel like all the hope and joy has been sucked out of the world. It's the same feeling I had when my parents died all those years ago, only this time I don't think I'll ever really recover. But I'm not about to throw myself off the Brooklyn Bridge, if that's what you're worried about."

"It wouldn't do you much good if you did. You'd just get *rekindled*."

"I know."

"You'd have to do it over again nine times for it to really count, and *that* would get tedious. Trust me, I know. I was rekindled five times during my youth."

"What happened?" asked Bianca.

"As a kitten I caught flea-borne typhus, then as a teenager I got knifed three times—I grew up on the Lower East Side, near the docks, and knife fights were a weekly thing. And the last time I got my head split open with a brick. One of the stabbings still gives me nightmares. You should count yourself lucky to have all nine lives."

Bianca quickly disabused her of this notion. "Actually, I've died twice."

"Really? You're full of surprises, aren't you, Princess? All right, your turn, let's hear it."

"I wasn't stabbed or anything. As a young kitten I was in the back seat of my parents' car one night when we hit a patch of ice and spun out. My mom was behind the wheel and she couldn't stop us from crashing into an oak tree. All three of us were killed. I still think about that one because if it weren't for that ice patch my parents would have had a life to burn when their train crashed."

"And the second time?"

"The second time I died was as a teenager. I was playing tennis back home—"

"At your adoptive parents' country club?" Roxy interrupted, a hint of glee in her voice.

"*Yes*. At my parents' country club." Bianca rolled her eyes. "And I was locked in an exciting match with my best friend from high school when a storm rolled in. Did you know that most lightning strikes occur on the edges of the storm?"

"I'll take your word for it."

"I was serving for the match when—Bam!—I got fried by a direct hit."

"Wow! Smoked by a thunderbolt. Who knew country clubs could be so risky? I never would have pegged you for being down to seven. Where did you get rekindled?"

"City Hospital, in midtown, where I was born."

"Ahh, that's why you're a city girl at heart."

Bianca took another tiny sip of tea and pushed away her cup. "Well, Roxy, thanks for the tea and the scintillating conversation. I promise to tell Tabatha that you took great care of me."

Roxy looked pained. "I'm not here to score points with Tabatha. Can't you see that I genuinely want to help?"

"Well, it's weird—seeing as how you've always despised me."

"I know I've been hard on you sometimes," Roxy replied, her brow furrowed.

"That's putting it mildly. You and your friends have done your very best to make my life miserable."

Roxy bit her lip and fiddled with one of the zippers of her

cropped denim jacket. "About that. I have a small confession to make." The alley cat sat down next to her on the edge of the settee and took a deep breath. "Did you know that before you started working at the lounge Flint used to come over to the pinball machines and watch me play whenever things got quiet?"

"Really?" Bianca said, perplexed.

"He would nurse a bottle of ginger beer while I worked my pinball magic, and we would chat for hours about life in the City—just the two of us."

Bianca gave her a sharp look. "I never saw him go anywhere near the pinball machines, or say more than two words to you."

"That's because since the day you turned up, he only ever had eyes for you, Princess."

Bianca's mind was reeling. "Hold on a minute. Do you mean . . . are you telling me you had a crush on my Flint?"

Roxy avoided her gaze. "I know it's nuts. A respectable dog like him and an alley cat like me. It would never have worked. But you know how charming he could be. It's possible I may have gotten a touch sore when he suddenly forgot I even existed."

Bianca bit her lip. "I wish Flint had told me about it."

"There was nothing to tell."

Bianca stared down at the amber specks swirling around in the depths of her teacup. This made a lot of sense. She finally understood why Roxy had always acted so spiteful toward her. Bianca turned to face the alley cat. Roxy's light blue eyes held none of the usual rancor. Instead they were filled with a deep sadness that mirrored her own. The alley cat reached out and pulled her in for a hug. Bianca was taken aback at first, but soon found herself lingering in the embrace of this cat who she had loathed up until about two minutes ago. Her eyes flooded with tears.

"It just doesn't seem real that he's gone," Bianca murmured. "How can this be happening?"

"It doesn't make a lick of sense. But that's dogs for you— they only get the one life."

After a minute or two they pulled apart, wiping at their eyes with their tea napkins. Roxy topped up Bianca's cup and they began to share stories about Flint, chatting like old friends.

"When did you first know he was the one?" Roxy asked her.

"There was this one day when we took a rowboat out on the lake in Central Park. It was an unseasonably warm spring day and I was wearing a tight-fitting purple dress that I wasn't sure I could pull off, but Flint insisted I looked beautiful. We made our way across the lake with Flint at the oars, having a lovely time. Then, as we passed under a bridge, some young dogs in a nearby boat made some crude comments about my figure, loud enough for us both to hear. I was mortified, but Flint didn't miss a beat. When he pushed the oars forward on his next stroke, he caught the surface of the water with one oar and splashed a huge curtain of murky water right at their boat, soaking them! He feigned an apology and with the next pull of the oars carried us twenty feet past them. I remember being impressed with how smoothly Flint handled things and thinking that he was a real marvel."

Roxy listened with a wide smile. She started asking Bianca another question but they were interrupted by the ding of the doorbell. Rupert squawked in alarm at the sound.

The alley cat sprang to her feet. "I'll go see who it is." She scurried down the hall and put her eye up to the peephole. With a scowl she undid the locks and stepped outside. Bianca heard the sound of muffled voices. Roxy returned moments later with a puzzled look on her face. "There are two police detectives outside. They stopped by the lounge looking to talk to you, and Tabatha gave them your address."

"What do they want?" asked Bianca.

"They wouldn't say. They're an odd-looking pair of coppers if you ask me, but their badges are legit."

Bianca swung her feet down to the rug and smoothed her skirt, hugging her knees with her long white tail. "I suppose you'd better let them in."

The alley cat led a short Scottish terrier in a pinstripe suit into the living room, followed closely by a border collie in a rumpled brown jacket. Both dogs were holding their hats in their hands.

"Miss Bianca Moon?" the Scottish terrier asked gently.

"Yes."

"My name is Detective J.B. Puddleworth, and this is my partner, Junior Detective Digby. I'm told you've already heard the terrible news about Flint Lockford?" His gaze met her own and then dropped to the diamond ring glistening on her finger.

Bianca nodded grimly.

The detective raked a paw through the black hair on his forehead. "I'm truly sorry. It's an awful business. I take it that you and Mr. Lockford meant a lot to each other."

"Flint was the love of my life," Bianca stated in a hoarse whisper.

"I hate to trouble you at such a sensitive time, Miss Moon," said the Scottish terrier. "But we were hoping you might be able to help us with some questions related to our investigation."

Bianca's brows knitted together. "Into the accident, you mean?"

Detective Puddleworth sat down opposite her on the edge of a small armchair so that their faces were level. He massaged the back of his neck with his paw. "Perhaps we could speak privately?"

Bianca looked up at Roxy uncertainly. The alley cat plopped herself down next to Bianca, taking her hand once more. "No dice, Officer." The alley cat's mouth set in a hard line. "Whatever you have to say, you can say it in front of me." She gave Bianca's hand a squeeze.

The two detectives exchanged a rueful glance. "Speaking plainly, Miss Moon, we're concerned that Flint Lockford's death may not have been an accident. There are indications that someone intentionally cut the rope securing the piano at the precise moment when Flint was standing underneath it."

Both cats gasped and Bianca's eyes went wide. "You don't think . . . ? You're not saying—he was murdered?"

The border collie, who had been silent until now, said: "We also found a queen of spades playing card entwined between the piano's strings, which happens to be the calling card for one of the City's most notorious hitdogs."

Bianca sat there with her mouth agape. A minute ago she wouldn't have believed that things could get any more bleak, but it was as if the sharp pain in her chest had just been ratcheted up in intensity. *Please don't let this be true*, she thought.

The Scottie held her gaze. "I realize it's a lot to take in, but from what we've gathered, your, er . . ." The detective glanced at her hand once more. "Your *fiancé* was very regular in his habits. It's possible someone used that against him to concoct an unusual dogicide. Do you know if Flint had any enemies?"

"Everyone loved Flint," Bianca answered. She stole a sideways glance at Roxy, whose grip on her hand tightened. The alley cat was visibly shaken.

"We talked to Flint's boss on the phone earlier," said the border collie.

"Mr. Boswell?" asked Bianca.

"Yes, at the *Knickerbocker Gazette*," said the border collie. "He told us that Flint had received a number of death threats in recent weeks as a result of some articles he wrote. Particularly after one recent exposé where Mr. Lockford took on the mob, suggesting that they were behind the rash of bodies found floating in the Gowanus Canal."

The Scottish terrier nodded. "Mr. Lockford was bold enough to mention the infamous crime boss Osvaldo Delgatto, hinting that he would have been arrested if investigators hadn't conveniently misplaced critical evidence."

Bianca squeezed her eyes shut and took a few slow breaths. A truck rumbled by in the street. She could feel rage bubbling up inside of her. She had always been an even-tempered cat, and this wave of murderous fury overtaking her felt entirely unfamiliar. Bianca heard herself speak in what sounded like a faraway voice. "If that gangster murdered my Flint, I will rip him to shreds with my bare claws."

10 · Flint Lockford: The Voice

Darkening skies overhead were quickly blotting out the last hints of daylight. A somber Flint hastened down the street while around him his new ghost friends bobbed and weaved, excited to be out on the prowl. When they drew close to Bianca's building, Flint was surprised to see two dogs emerging from her ground floor entrance. Then he recognized the border collie and the Scottish terrier as the two detectives he had seen earlier at Claudette's Bakery. He watched them climb into the squad car parked out front and drive off.

Flint swooped through Bianca's front door and into her parlor, along with the other ghosts. Bianca was seated on the sofa in her living room, looking beautiful as ever in a satin periwinkle dress with a ribboned collar, except that she was sitting stiffly and her eyes had a strange faraway look. He drifted closer until he was floating directly in front of her. She stared right through him. He wanted to lean in and whisper in her ear then and there, but she was in mid-conversation with Roxy. What was the alley cat even doing here? Flint wondered. Bianca and Roxy had always bristled in one another's company.

"Wait until you can catch her alone," the professor advised him, tugging gently at his elbow.

Flint stood there mutely, eavesdropping on the conversation between the two cats. Bianca sat motionless on the settee while Roxy paced in circles around the living room. This was in many ways everything Flint had feared—here he was, trapped on the outside looking in. He wished the Ghosthall gang weren't witnessing his anguish. The only one he didn't mind having close by was Professor Chumley.

Flint was forced to retreat when Roxy wheeled around in his direction. He floated back through the armchair as she charged past him, her arms waving madly in the air as she cried: "Who would have thought things could get any worse?"

"Do you think it's true?" asked Bianca, her voice quavering. "Do you think Flint was really murdered?"

Roxy froze. Then her head swiveled to meet Bianca's gaze. The alley cat swallowed hard. "It sure sounds like he pissed off the wrong dog. That Delgatto character is bad news. My friend Eleanor used to wait tables at a restaurant over on Mulberry Street, and Delgatto would eat dinner there every night. He would sit in the back twirling forkfuls of linguine with clams, night after night, barely saying boo to anyone. She was terrified every time she had to wait on him."

"What restaurant was this?"

"I can't remember. Mama something or other. Wait— Mama Leone's? Yes, that's right." Roxy eyed Bianca suspiciously. "Hold on a darn second. You're not *actually* thinking about confronting this guy, are you? Because if you are, you need to put that idea right out of your head!"

Flint stared at Bianca with concern. Her expression was unreadable. He certainly hoped she wasn't planning on going down there. You couldn't go around accusing mafia dogs of murder without landing in serious trouble.

"What are you worried about, Roxy?" Bianca asked. "I've got seven lives left, remember?"

"That doesn't mean you should throw any away on mad revenge schemes," the alley cat replied. "Trust me, Princess, you need to steer clear of that scumbag."

"All I want to do is look him in his eyes and ask him if he killed my Flint."

"That's a one-way ticket to Deadsville. Those criminals don't bat an eye when it comes to killing cats. Everyone knows the cops won't do a thing about it. They already have their paws full just with dog murders in this town."

"Unless it's a cat's ninth life. Then they're looking at real trouble."

"How often does that happen?" the alley cat scoffed. "Just forget about Delgatto and let the cops do their jobs."

"Do you really think those detectives are up to the task? You want me to sit tight and not worry my pretty little head about it? Just let the dogs get on with their fancy investigating?"

Roxy hesitated. "I admit I would feel a lot better if it had been two teeth-gnashing hounds who knocked on your door. The meaner the better. But still, we should give them a chance."

Flint watched Bianca dig her nails into the settee, piercing the plush purple fabric. He had never seen her like this. After an extended silence Bianca let out a long, slow breath. "I guess you're right, Roxy. There's not much we can do. I feel so drained all of a sudden. Like I could sleep for days." She stood up and walked down the hallway in the direction of her bedroom.

The professor put a hand on Flint's shoulder. "That's a relief. I was worried she might do something rash!"

"You and me both," said Sophie. "I could've sworn she was about to go on a citywide rampage!"

Roxy trailed Bianca down the narrow hallway, and Flint and the other ghosts followed as well. At the kitchen doorway Bianca stopped short. "Could you check the fridge for me, Roxy? I think I might be out of eggs and milk. I'll need something for breakfast tomorrow."

"No problem. Do you want me to pop out to the store and pick up a few things?"

"That would be a huge help. Here, let me give you some cash." Bianca took a five-dollar bill from her wallet and pressed it into Roxy's outstretched paw, along with a front door key.

"I know this is a fancy part of town but surely eggs and milk don't cost this much?" said the alley cat.

"Stock up on some pantry essentials so I won't have to think about food for a few days."

"Good idea. I'll make sure you're set for groceries. You go lie down."

Bianca disappeared into her bedroom, leaving the door ajar. Flint and the other ghosts stopped outside the threshold. Through the cracked doorway he glimpsed Bianca unbuttoning her dress and he quickly backpedaled, arms outstretched to either side.

Tiger and Sophie both giggled. "You're such a gentledog,

Flint," said Sophie, giving his nose a playful tap with her fingertip. "It's so refreshing. You have no idea how many ghosts become Peeping Toms after they pass. It's appalling! Why don't you guys go wait in the kitchen? Tiger and I will let you know when she's decent." Flint retreated down the hallway along with Chumley, Paco, Benny, and Albert. They found Roxy poking around in the fridge, and Flint was stunned to see she wasn't alone. A face was protruding from Bianca's pantry—the graying ghost of a springer spaniel. Chumley wandered over to introduce himself to this stranger and apologize for barging into her home. Reassured by the sheepdog's friendly demeanor, the old lady, whose name turned out to be Gertrude, timidly emerged from her hideaway. "I know you," she said, peering at Flint. "You're that fellow Bianca has been smitten with for the past year."

Flint blinked at the ghost, unsure of how to respond. The thought that Gertrude had been lurking in this apartment the whole time he'd known Bianca was unsettling. Professor Chumley picked up the conversational slack and was soon chatting away with the elderly ghost. She readily shared her story, telling them that she'd been murdered in that very kitchen by her own niece, who had struck her in the head with a frying pan with an eye to speeding along her inheritance. She'd gotten away with it too. Flint grimaced as he pictured the poor spaniel lying dead on the checkered tile floor next to the stove. Thankfully Sophie and Tiger reappeared just then and gave them the all-clear to proceed to Bianca's bedroom.

Flint found her sitting on a stool facing her vanity mirror, brushing her white fur in long sweeping strokes. She was wearing ruby red pajamas—a two-piece set with a collared shirt and loose-fitting pants.

"Hey Flint, watch this!" said Benny. The bass player went out through the window and then came rushing back in, rustling the curtains by the window and fluttering the pages of Bianca's journal on the bedside table. Bianca's eyebrows knit together, puzzled by the unexpected breeze.

Flint was equally mystified until Professor Chumley explained: "We can move extremely light objects if we work up sufficient momentum. But only enough to affect things like feathers, leaves, or papers."

Sophie peered closely at Bianca. "Why do I get the feeling your girlfriend is plotting something?"

"Bianca is a sensible girl," Flint demurred, even though he had also noticed an unusual intensity in Bianca's eyes. He really needed to talk to her.

Flint glanced at Chumley, who seemed to read his mind. "Go ahead, this is as good a time as any to reach out. Just don't expect too much too soon." The professor turned to the other ghosts. "C'mon, guys, let's give Flint and Bianca a moment alone."

Tiger glared at the professor. "But this is why we came!" Sophie nodded vigorously, her arms crossed defiantly. Nevertheless, Chumley ushered everyone out, including the two girls, and Flint finally found himself alone with Bianca. He drifted closer to her. Now that the time had come, he felt horribly unsure. How do you even begin to tell someone you're a ghost?

I just have to bite the bullet, Flint told himself. Leaning down, he whispered in her ear: "I see you're wearing the ring, my love. It looks amazing on your finger." Bianca shot up out of her stool as if she had been poked with a pin. She glanced madly about herself only to see that she was all alone.

"I'm losing it," she muttered to herself, sitting back down and turning to meet her own gaze in the mirror.

Flint spoke again, this time in her other ear. "It's me, Flint. I'm really here. Don't be scared."

Bianca squeezed her eyes shut. "But you're not here," she said softly. "You're dead. Dead and gone."

"Dead, yes, but not quite gone."

"What are you saying? That you're a ghost?"

"I'm afraid so."

"You're not a ghost, Flint. You're just a voice in my head. I'm going crazy."

"I swear, Bianca, it's really me. I've had the most insane day."

"If you're a ghost then why can't I see you?" she asked distrustfully.

"I'm invisible to the living, but with the help of steam or mist I can be glimpsed. At least that's what the other ghosts tell me."

"I don't believe in ghosts."

"Neither did I," said Flint. "I always thought ghosts were nothing more than the grist of campfire stories and pulp fiction magazines. It turns out I was wrong. Each ghost gets to pick one mortal to communicate with. The first mortal they speak to directly is the one living cat or dog who can hear them from across the divide."

"So I'm the only one who can hear you? How convenient. You do *sound* a lot like Flint, I must admit. Why don't you tell me something only my Flint would know?"

"Do you remember when I kissed you that night sitting by the fountain in Washington Square, holding your face in my hands? Right before I told you that I loved you for the first time?"

"How do you know that?" Bianca cried. "I never told a soul!"

"It really *is* me, Bianca. I promise you."

"That's exactly what a voice in my head would say. I really am going nuts."

There were footsteps in the hallway, and Roxy poked her head in the doorway. "Did you say something, Princess?"

Bianca looked flustered. "Don't forget to pick up some sliced bread."

"It's already on the list," the alley cat assured her. "Now get into bed."

Bianca did just that, leaning back on her pillows and pulling the bedspread up over her legs.

Roxy seemed satisfied. "Sit tight. I'll be back in two shakes of a lamb's tail."

Bianca waited until she heard the front door open and close before getting up. Flint and his friends trailed her as she walked down the hallway to the living room and pulled aside the sheer drapes to reveal Roxy's ankles marching down the sidewalk in the direction of a nearby deli.

Bianca didn't bother to change. She grabbed a green raincoat off the coatrack and put it on over her pajamas.

"I called it!" said Sophie.

"Where are you going, Bianca?" Flint cried. But she made no reply. Stepping into the kitchen she grabbed a small chef's knife from the butcher block, wrapped the blade in a dish towel, and slipped it into her jacket pocket. Flint spoke urgently into her ear once more: "What are you doing with that knife, Bianca?"

This time she answered him: "I'm going to go introduce myself to Osvaldo Delgatto with it. First impressions are everything, haven't you heard?"

"Don't do this, my love."

"Well, I'm not gonna sit here crying into my pillow while the mastermind to your murder is out there feasting on a plate of linguine with clams."

"It's not worth it, Bianca!"

Her tone hardened. "They killed you, Flint. They crushed you to a pulp on a dirty city sidewalk. Don't tell me it's not worth it."

"Revenge won't bring me back."

"No it won't, but it will give me something to do now that you're gone."

"Bianca, this is crazy!"

"Crazy? Stick around and I'll show you what crazy looks like!" Bianca slipped her feet into a pair of penny loafers, clipped on her pillbox hat, and stormed out the front door, slamming it closed behind her.

11 · Junior Detective Morton Digby: The Restaurant

Mama Leone's was an unpretentious Italian chophouse on the corner of Grand Street and Mulberry, in the very heart of Little Italy. Wall sconces and shaded chandeliers cast a yellow glow on a handful of diners, while classical music played in the background through crackling speakers.

When the two detectives walked in, they were greeted by the maître d', an Italian sheepdog, who regarded them disdainfully. At Detective Puddleworth's urging they had stopped at a thrift store in search of clothing that would help them pass themselves off as dinnertime tourists. The Scottie had picked out a flowery Hawaiian shirt and dark sunglasses, adding—in a completely over-the-top move—an old camera dangling from a strap around his neck. Morton knew that the steadfast rule for undercover work was to never draw attention to yourself, but clearly the Scottie had his own ideas. Morton consoled himself with the thought that no one would ever suspect his partner of being an undercover cop in that tacky getup. For himself, Morton had opted for blue slacks, a striped short-sleeved shirt, and no tie.

The maître d' surveyed the room before grabbing two menus and leading them to a small table alongside a large mural. It showed a voluptuous cat in a peasant blouse posed with a basket of vegetables on her hip against a pastoral backdrop of olive trees. Detective Puddleworth eyeballed the garish artwork disapprovingly. A stiff waiter in a bow tie came by their table and plonked down a bread basket. The Scottie peeled back the basket's red gingham cloth, unleashing a pungent aroma of garlic. Morton watched him pull apart the gooey loaf with his fingers and wolf down a greasy slice of bread.

From where he was sitting, Morton had a straight line of sight on Osvaldo Delgatto. The large dog was ensconced in a tufted leather banquette at a table along the back wall that afforded him a broad view of the whole restaurant. Delgatto was a jowly gray Neapolitan mastiff, his face lined with deep furrows. He was wearing a black silk shirt that was unbuttoned to show off a thick gold chain medallion and tufts of white chest fur. Stationed strategically in his vicinity were three hounds in suits. Morton watched as the mob boss deftly twirled strands of linguine onto his fork and shoveled them into his mouth in a leisurely fashion.

Morton had familiarized himself with the mafia dog's lengthy rap sheet. Delgatto had been in and out of Attica Penitentiary in decades past, convicted of crimes that ranged from protection rackets, to vice, to run-of-the-mill extortion. The mafia's wall of silence had finally been cracked with the help of wiretaps that gave investigators the evidence they needed to put the mob boss behind bars. But when the war broke out, Delgatto had struck a deal with the feds in exchange for his freedom. He had ensured that the dock workers wouldn't strike, and he had introduced the government to his Sicilian mafia contacts, facilitating the Allied invasion. After the war he had been deported to Europe, but he soon made his way back stateside, with a brief sojourn in Havana, after which the feds had seemingly shrugged their shoulders and given up.

Detective Puddleworth didn't appear the least bit troubled by their proximity to one of the City's most ruthless gangsters. The Scottish terrier's attention was focused solely on the rapidly disappearing garlic bread, and on the steaming bowl of pasta carbonara the waiter had just served him. The Scottie made a spectacle of himself slurping up strands of bucatini. Their waiter, hovering nearby, eyed them with evident distaste.

For himself, Morton had ordered pasta with meatballs, which he was picking at halfheartedly. He was doing his best to appear calm, but inside he felt a gnawing sense of dread. There was no way he would be able to enjoy his meal until they had successfully executed their plan. With a simple phone call, Detective Puddleworth had procured support from the surveillance department at police HQ. They had been delighted to hear Delgatto was being investigated for dogicide, and had been quick to furnish them with support in the form of a listening device that was currently hidden in the pocket of Detective Puddleworth's pink shorts. The Vice Squad had been waiting for just such an excuse to go after the mob boss, who was as big a thorn in their side as ever. Delgatto never did business over the phone these days, having learned his lesson all too well, so HQ had suggested placing the bug near his table at the restaurant, knowing that the mob boss often broke bread with his consiglieri.

Across the table from him, the Scottie tucked his napkin into his shirt, much to their waiter's dismay, and used a clean corner of it to dab his lips. "I've gotta say, Morton, this place is a cut above the Italian ristorante my wife and I would frequent in Staten Island. This is the best meal I've had in years!"

Morton took a sip of water and pushed a meatball around on his plate. "What did you make of Miss Bianca Moon? She looked like she was about to blow her lid!"

"She's upset," replied the Scottie. "Give her some time and she'll simmer down."

"We'll see. It's always the quiet ones you have to watch out for." The restaurant was slowly filling up and the buzz of conversation grew louder as the wine began to flow in earnest. An invisible hand somewhere turned the dial up on the lively violin concerto playing over the speakers. After ensuring their waiter was out of earshot, Morton leaned in and spoke in a hushed voice. "There's a potted plant not far from Delgatto's table that looks like a promising spot for the bug."

"Roger that," replied the Scottie conspiratorially.

"Are you sure you don't want me to do this?" Morton asked. As much as it terrified him, he was even more worried that his partner would draw every eye in the room with his Hawaiian shirt.

"Nonsense! I've got it covered. This situation reminds me of a classic scene in *The Case of the Poisoned Lamb Chops* where Hercule Merlot plants a tracking device inside a sugar bowl. Of course, as I recall the villain found the device and tied Detective Merlot to a chair and set the house on fire, but I promise you I've learned a thing or two from his mistakes!"

Morton squeezed his eyes shut for a moment as he absorbed his partner's confident swagger. "So what's your plan?" he asked the Scottie.

"Plan? Improvisation is key in these situations! One must be ready to seize whatever small opportunity presents itself in the heat of the moment!"

Morton's stomach lurched sideways. "You do realize that if his goons catch you planting a surveillance device we're going to be in a real jam?"

"I'm not worried about Delgatto's thugs. We're too smart for them. And if things do get dicey, I'll put my boxing skills to good use!"

If Morton could have smacked his forehead without attracting attention, he would have. He had been harboring nagging doubts about the Scottie's mental faculties, but this latest evidence settled matters—his partner was barking mad. Morton knew he needed to do some quick thinking if he expected this operation to stay on track. "Why don't you untie one of your shoelaces," he suggested. "That will give you an excuse to kneel down by the potted plant."

Detective Puddleworth beamed at him. "That's a capital idea!" The Scottie crossed his legs and reached discreetly under the table. "Well, I reckon this is as good a moment as any. I'll be back in a few minutes." The Scottie waggled his eyebrows at Morton as he stood up. "If you'll excuse me," he declared loudly, "I need to use the little dog's room!" Morton watched his partner stroll nonchalantly toward the back of the restaurant, his short tail wagging happily. The Scottie bent down to tie his shoe right next to the potted plant. As he got back up, he put one hand on the thick ceramic pot to steady himself, and then casually went on his way. One of Delgatto's heavies eyed him with distaste, but lost interest in him moments later when the Scottie disappeared down the hallway leading to the restroom. Morton breathed a deep sigh of relief. An unmarked police wagon was parked around the corner, and hidden inside was a communications officer and a broad array of audio recording equipment. They would be privy to all of Delgatto's dinner conversations for the next few days, until the mic's transmitter battery eventually conked out.

12 · Flint Lockford: The Squareheads

A stunned Flint watched Bianca rush out the front door. Coming to his senses, he took off after her. Behind him swirled the whole gang of Ghosthall spirits—Chumley, Paco, Sophie, Tiger, Benny, and Albert. Flint knew he had to somehow stop Bianca, who had a knife in her pocket and murder in her heart.

Outside, the patches of sky visible through the clouds had turned an inky blue, while nearby streetlamps glowed yellow. Bianca was fast disappearing down the narrow sidewalk to their left, and Flint and the other ghosts set off in pursuit, mirroring Bianca's every turn as she marched east. She kept up a brisk pace and it wasn't until she hit a no-walk signal at the Sixth Avenue crosswalk that he caught up to her. He implored her to stop this madness, but got no response. He was sure she must be headed to Mama Leone's, Osvaldo Delgatto's regular dinner spot, and nothing good could come from that.

"My love, it really is me—Flint!" Bianca's ears twitched in his direction and her tail flicked back and forth, but she said nothing. When the light changed Flint reached out to grab hold of her arm but his fingers raked through thin air and Bianca took off once more.

"I've never seen her like this. How can I convince her it's really me?" Flint asked his companions.

"It often takes time to convince mortals that their mind isn't playing tricks on them," said Professor Chumley.

"Somehow I don't think she's going to listen," said Sophie. "Your sweet Bianca has gone off the rails!"

Flint marveled at how adept the ghosts were at moving through the City. They held their umbrellas in front of themselves and opened and closed them quickly in short bursts, propelling themselves forward. Alternately they used their umbrellas to catch gusts of wind or a momentary rush of air from a passing vehicle, harnessing the current to launch themselves forward. Occasionally they would even shoot high into the air and twirl gracefully back to the ground.

"I couldn't help noticing," Tiger said, landing near Flint with a nimble pirouette, "that Bianca is wearing a diamond ring. I thought you said you didn't get the chance to propose?"

"I didn't," Flint replied. "Someone must have given her the ring."

"And she put it on. That's so romantic!" cooed Sophie.

"More like tragic?" muttered Albert. "They're never going to be able to tie the knot, are they? They're trapped on different planes of existence!" His comments drew harsh glares from the other ghosts. Flint reckoned the corgi had a point.

"You know," Benny speculated, "I bet Louisa could help us convince Bianca that you're real!"

"Louisa the psychic?" asked Flint.

"Do you know her?" Benny said with surprise.

"Yes, she read my fortune just the other day. I thought she was a garden-variety charlatan."

"What? Our Louisa?" Benny gasped. "Goodness no—she's the real deal!"

"We don't have time to go ask Louisa for help," Tiger pointed out.

"Any other ideas?" asked Flint.

"You could try manifesting yourself," suggested Paco. "That would get her attention. You need to stand before her and look her in the eyes!"

"You must be joking!" cried Sophie. "Bianca already thinks she's going out of her mind and you want him to jump out at her and yell 'boo'?"

"It's a moot point anyway," said Albert. "Without any mist or fog he has no way to make himself visible!"

"Don't forget, Flint—the same rule applies for apparitions as for speaking to the living," said the professor. "Whoever gets the first glimpse of you becomes the only living cat or dog who can see you!"

"Got it," said Flint with a wry smile. "I'll be careful who I pick to scare the living daylights out of."

Up ahead of them Bianca made a left onto West 4th Street. "Guys?" said Benny in a shaky voice. "She's taking us right past Washington Square Park!"

"That's not good," said Sophie. "I bet the park is already crawling with Squareheads."

Flint shot her a quizzical look.

"The Squareheads are a rival band of ghosts based in Washington Square," the professor explained. "As you may know, the park used to be a burial ground, with up to twenty thousand souls interred there, and many of the ghosts are real old-timers. The tree in the northwest corner used to be a gallows too, so former criminals also make up a good number of their ranks. It all makes for a band of very ill-tempered and territorial spooks."

"Heads up, that church is coming up on our right," warned Paco, gesturing toward the orange-brick edifice on the south side of the street.

"That's where they like to roost," Benny informed Flint.

"Looks like they've spotted us!" cried Sophie. "They're jumping from the campanile!"

Sure enough, a flurry of ghosts was leaping from the church's bell tower and floating down to the ground with opened umbrellas, yelling insults and threats at them as they descended. One gray cat above Flint was dressed in an eerily formal turn-of-the-century-style gown, with a ruffled high collar blouse and a wide brimmed hat. Her dress fluttered in the air as she landed. She locked eyes with Flint and advanced on him menacingly.

"Intruders!" she cried out. "It's those crummy Ghosthall spooks! Get out of here, you filthy fleabags!"

"Should we be worried?" asked Flint, taken aback. "I mean, we're already dead. What could they possibly do to us?"

"Don't let them catch you," warned Tiger.

Thankfully, most of the Squareheads were touching down behind them, except for one mutt in a top hat who stepped into their path and took a swing at the professor. Paco popped him in the gut with his umbrella, causing the ghost to double over. With a clear sidewalk ahead of them the Ghosthallers raced forward. Flint was the slowest among them, but they took turns helping him along.

"Ghosts aren't invulnerable," Sophie explained as they dashed onward. "One thing that will burn a hole right through you is rock salt!"

"And if you get hit with enough of it, then you're toast," added Tiger.

"First it's sunlight and now it's salt? Any other major hazards I should be aware of?" Flint asked.

"Those are the two biggies," said Professor Chumley. "Although getting caught in a fire would be bad news too."

"How can they throw salt at us without touching it?"

"Ghosts can't go anywhere near the stuff," Chumley said. "But they *can* enlist the living to do their dirty work for them."

"Speaking of which!" cried Benny in alarm. "I think that's Bocce Ball Barry at nine o'clock! Get ready to block with your umbrellas!" Flint looked to where the tomcat was pointing and saw a scraggly living dog with matted hair. His clothes were stained and tattered, and his shoes were full of holes.

"I swear, if that groghound ruins my favorite parasol I'll be seriously cheesed off!" huffed Sophie.

"Just a little farther, Flint," Chumley said, urging him on. "Once we get past the eastern edge of the park, we should be safe."

One of the ghosts from the bell tower had floated over to Bocce Ball Barry and whispered something in his ear.

"Watch out! He's definitely got salt in his pockets!" Benny cried, swooping to the front of the pack in a panic.

Sure enough the vagrant reached into his trouser pockets and came out with a handful of coarse white granules, which he flung blindly in their direction. But his aim was off and he ended up dinging several of the Squareheads instead, causing a great commotion among their ranks. By the time their pursuers had reoriented Bocce Ball Barry in the right direction, the Ghosthallers had drifted out of range, carrying Flint along with them. The outraged yells of the Squareheads faded as they left the park behind.

"Finally a little excitement," said Sophie gleefully. "I don't mind telling you I was bored stiff before you came along, Flint."

"Well, it's not my idea of fun," said Benny, whose eyes were still round with fear. "I can't believe they set that lousy tramp loose on us!"

"Does Ghosthall have any allies among the living?" asked Flint.

"Gerald, the building custodian, keeps a bucket of salt handy in his supply closet for emergencies," Chumley replied. "You haven't met Gerald yet, he lives in the annex on the third floor. He's a tad eccentric but we are all rather fond of him."

"Does he know the place is haunted?"

"Oh, yes," Chumley assured him. "He likes having us around."

In all the commotion Bianca had nearly disappeared from sight. A slight head wind didn't help matters and Flint struggled to keep up. Jaw clenched, he redoubled his efforts, determined not to lose track of her as she zigzagged her way down city streets on her way to Little Italy.

13 · Bianca Moon: The Canal

Bianca cupped her hands around her face and pressed her nose up against the glass. Mama Leone's was in full dinner swing, its patrons chowing down on pizzas and pastas while white jacketed waiters ferried food trays back and forth from the kitchen. Bianca's eyes jumped from table to table in search of a mean-looking dog eating linguine with clams. She had no idea what Osvaldo Delgatto looked like, but she had an inkling she would recognize him when she saw him. To her surprise she spotted two familiar faces sitting at a table by the wall. Could it be the two detectives? Yes. It was definitely them. Questions flitted through her brain: Why was the Scottish terrier wearing a tacky Hawaiian shirt? Were they here to arrest Delgatto? Or was this just some weird coincidence? She decided the most plausible explanation was that they were pretending to conduct surveillance while enjoying a fancy dinner at the police department's expense. The Scottie was greedily digging into three scoops of chocolate gelato with his spoon, and for some reason the sight of this terrier gleefully eating ice cream infuriated her. *She* hadn't come here to snoop around and eat gelato. She was here to get justice for Flint, and those two detectives had better not get in her way.

Her gaze flitted toward the back of the room, and there in the distance a solitary diner jumped out at her. He was a sullen Neapolitan mastiff, with three watchful hounds hovering nearby. That had to be her dog, she was sure of it.

The problem was—she couldn't just waltz through the front door. For one thing there was a maître d' waiting there to intercept her, and it was a long walk to the back of the room. She needed to get close to Delgatto without setting off any alarms.

"Bianca, please, I beg you!" yelled the voice in her head. "Don't go in there!" She'd been doing a better job of tuning out this Flint impostor for these last few blocks, but he was back now with an added edge of raw desperation. Why would her own mind play tricks on her in this way?

A nearby door banged open and Bianca pulled back from the window. A young cat in a dirty apron emerged from the side entrance dragging a garbage bag behind him that he tossed to the curb. When he turned to go back inside, she hurried after him and slipped quietly through the back door behind him. She found herself walking through a busy kitchen. No one took any notice of her until a tubby chef with singed whiskers looked up from his chopping and glared at her. "Who are *you*?" he demanded. "And what are you doing in my kitchen?"

Bianca ignored him and quickened her pace, making a beeline for the swinging doors that led out to the dining area. A waiter kicked open the door with his foot and spun into the kitchen carrying a tray stacked high with dirty dishes. Bianca ducked around him, and as the door swung back she stepped through it, out into the restaurant proper.

She locked eyes with the border collie detective, whose name she didn't recall. He glared at her with a mix of alarm and disapproval, giving her a discreet shake of his head. She stared back at him defiantly. He whispered something to his partner and the Scottish terrier glanced over his shoulder at her, but neither detective made any move to intercept her. Bianca turned right and wove her way toward the back wall as Flint's pleas in her head grew even louder and more insistent.

The mafia dog looked up, puzzled, when she stopped in front of his table. "Can I help you?" His goons took a step in her direction, eyeing her suspiciously. Bianca smiled disarmingly as she took in the ugly mug of the Neapolitan mastiff. "Are you Delgatto?" she asked.

The gray Neapolitan patted his flabby jowls with a cloth napkin. "Who's asking?" he replied through bared teeth.

"*Osvaldo* Delgatto?" she asked, wanting to be doubly sure she had the right dog.

"You know my name. Now tell me yours."

"I'm Bianca Moon. Flint Lockford was my fiancé." Without warning she drew the knife from her pocket and lunged forward, aiming to bury it in the center of Delgatto's chest, but the unlucky thrust struck the gold medallion around the mafia dog's neck and glanced off harmlessly. Before she could regroup, the iron paw of one of Delgatto's bodyguards grasped her wrist and wrenched it until she dropped the knife with a gasp.

"Will you look at that," said Delgatto, picking up the fallen knife and delicately touching his thumb to the point. "This kitten has claws! I'll give you this, Bianca Moon, you've got guts, whoever the hell you are. You never would've gotten this close if you didn't look so completely harmless. Are you wearing pajamas under that jacket? That should've been enough to tip off my hounds." Another dog grabbed Bianca's other arm and twisted it behind her back. Delgatto regarded her coolly. "I guess I can thank Saint Christopher here for saving me and not my useless bodyguards." The mastiff examined the dented medallion on his chest. "Now, tell me, Bianca. Who sent you to kill me?"

"No one sent me. You murdered my fiancé!" she hissed in reply.

"Ahh. I think I understand. Flint Lockford, you said? He was that journalist from the *Gazette*, right? The unlucky bastard who got crushed by a falling piano earlier today?" Delgatto chuckled softly to himself. "You know, there's a bizarre rumor going around that it wasn't an accident. I'm not sure if I believe it, but then again I never know what to believe in this crazy town."

"Don't act all innocent! You hired the Queen of Spades to murder him in cold blood."

"Me? I'm afraid you have the wrong dog, Miss Moon. I'll admit your boyfriend was occasionally a thorn in our side. But he wasn't a big enough nuisance to make it onto my special list."

"Fiancé."

"What?"

"He was my fiancé."

"My apologies. *Fiancé*. I assure you, Miss Moon, I am not to blame for your *fiancé's* unfortunate death."

"I don't believe you."

"Whoever killed Flint Lockford did their best to make it look like an accident. And just between us, Miss Moon, accidents aren't really my style. I have a reputation to uphold.

My preference is always to send a message to other would-be troublemakers. So if I wanted someone dead—I'm speaking purely hypothetically, mind you—there would be nothing accidental about it. Now if you don't mind, Miss Moon, my dessert has arrived." A trembling waiter set down a plate with two large cannoli in front of the mob boss. Delgatto looked down at the cream-filled pastries and smacked his lips. He made a barely noticeable swiping gesture with his index finger to his henchmen and they dragged Bianca away from his table and through a door that led to the restaurant's supply rooms.

"Let her go!" yelled Flint's horrified voice in her head. "Somebody help her!"

In a storage room Delgatto's goons muzzled Bianca with a dish towel and trussed her up like a Thanksgiving turkey, before tossing her into a burlap sack along with two large cinder blocks. Left lying on the floor, Bianca couldn't see a thing, but she heard a door squeak open, followed by the rumble of a car engine. She did her best to break free, but Delgatto's goons clearly knew a thing or two about knots.

Moments later rough hands seized her once again, carrying her about twenty steps before chucking her into the trunk of a car, her weight making the car bounce slightly and the rank stink of motor oil assaulting her senses. When the trunk slammed shut the darkness around her became absolute. The vehicle jerked into motion, tires squealing, and in her head she heard Flint's anguished screams coming from some distance away: "Let go of me! No! I can't leave her like this!"

Between the dishcloth, the burlap sack, and the dark trunk, a sudden attack of claustrophobia hit Bianca. She focused on taking long slow breaths through her nose in an attempt to calm her racing heart. Panicking wouldn't do her any good. Her bound arms and legs grew slowly numb, and with every swerve of the car she found herself flung this way and that. In the bottom of the sack, down by her feet, she felt the rough edges of the cinder blocks. She could guess where they were taking her.

I have seven lives left. I have seven lives left, she reminded herself over and over. And she cursed her bad luck—if it hadn't been for that darn gold medallion, her knife would have hit home. Except that she found herself filled with unexpected doubts. When she had stared into that dog's unwavering eyes, she'd read only raw sincerity when she had been expecting lies and hatred. It felt absurd to think that there might be such a thing as an honest mobster, yet that was the impression she had come away with. There was no doubt Delgatto was a cold-blooded killer. A monster who had the blood of countless innocents on his paws. But did a dog like that really have any incentive to lie? It seemed more likely that he would want everyone to know if he'd orchestrated a killing, just like he said. The more she turned it over in her mind the more she became convinced that Delgatto had not killed her Flint.

The car began to climb a long incline and Bianca was thrust backward in the trunk. This was followed by an equally long decline, and the blast of a foghorn somewhere below her confirmed her suspicion that they had just passed over a bridge. Bianca felt utterly helpless.

The border collie detective had mentioned the Gowanus Canal earlier, in connection with Delgatto. That had to be their destination. Should she hold her breath when she hit the water? Or was it better to breathe in the water right away and get it over with as quickly as possible? She had yet to make up her mind when the car screeched to a halt.

I will be brave, she told herself. This was just something she had to get through. She would soon be back home no worse for the wear. The trunk clicked open and the faint glow of electric light eased the darkness. Rough hands seized her and carried her six feet from the vehicle on crunching gravel before coming to a stop. Bianca writhed in the sack, but they kept a firm grip on her. Through the sparse weave of the burlap, she could make out the shapes of the two hounds, lit by a nearby streetlamp. Then they began to swing her back and forth. Once, twice, and on the third go-around the hands released her. She flew through the air and landed in the water with a loud splash. It smelled like a sewer and felt unexpectedly warm, seeping instantly through the burlap. She instinctively held her breath as she sank under the surface. Weighed down by the concrete blocks she descended deeper and deeper into the black water.

Still holding her breath, she hit bottom, standing almost upright. She strained desperately against her bonds and felt her chest begin to ache for air, the pain growing more intense until she finally opened her lips and gasped. Her mouth and lungs filled with sewer water. It was a gruesome sensation, and while it only lasted a handful of seconds it felt like an eternity. At last she blacked out.

Bianca awoke gasping for air, the panic of drowning still gripping her. Except that it was precious oxygen now filling her lungs. She took deep breaths of air, vowing never to take such a simple pleasure as breathing for granted again.

She blinked—the world around her was a blur of yellow and blue lights. A voice in the background said: "Quick, fetch a blanket! Don't step on her tail!" Helping hands reached out to steady her, and someone wrapped a sheet around her bare shoulders. When the world finally came into focus, Bianca saw that she was sitting naked on the floor of a maternity ward. Six feet away from her a very annoyed-looking yellow Lab was lying on a cot, panting heavily as she strained to push new pups into the world. A gurney appeared beside Bianca and she was lifted up onto it. "Lie down! Relax, you're safe," another voice said, firm hands easing her gently onto her back. They wheeled her out the door and across the hall. A fluffy-haired bichon holding a clipboard asked her name.

"Bianca Moon," she replied. The nurse nodded and disappeared.

This other room was partitioned by curtains into a series of cubicles. It dawned on her that she had successfully made it back to her birthplace, just as she had all those years ago when she'd been struck by that lightning bolt on the tennis court. Her atoms had zipped through the void and reassembled themselves back at City Hospital. She felt less disoriented now, but still drained. *I'm okay*, she thought to herself, the visceral horror of drowning beginning to fade.

A sudden thought hit her and she jolted upright. Bianca pulled her hand out from under the sheet and stared at it. Her engagement ring was missing! Horrified, she realized it must be lying at the bottom of the Gowanus Canal along with all her clothes. Bianca sobbed and began to cry.

Moments later a hand pulled back a curtain and the bichon came in. Bianca was embarrassed to be caught blubbering like a kitten. The nurse smiled sweetly and said, "Welcome back to City Hospital, Bianca. My name is Nurse Bertlemina. How are you feeling?"

"A little dizzy. And I've lost my engagement ring," she replied forlornly.

"Oh no! How awful! But that will happen every time. Jewelry and other personal items never make it through the rekindling process. It must be very upsetting. Try to look at it this way—at least you're alive. Maybe you'll be able to recover it?"

"Not likely. Unless I fancy another swim in the Gowanus Canal."

"Ugh. That sounds very unpleasant. What's the last thing you remember?"

"Trying to hold my breath with black water all around me."

"I'll mark this death down as a drowning in your chart. I wouldn't be too worried. I've located you in our files and I see you still have six lives left, which is an okay number for a twenty-three-year-old. Provided you don't get careless, you should make it to your seventies with lives to spare. Dizziness is normal and should pass quickly. Here, drink this." Nurse Bertlemina handed her a glass of milk.

Bianca propped herself up and took a sip, forcing it down her dry throat. The nurse wrapped a blood pressure cuff around her arm, pumped up a small bladder, and made a note on her chart. "When you're done drinking the milk you can get dressed if you are feeling up to it. The clothes here on the chair are yours to keep. I think we got your size right for the dress. There are two streetcar tokens on the table right there to help you get home, and if you need to make a phone call just ask someone at the front desk. I'm sorry about your ring, sweetheart. Don't worry, I'm sure your fiancé will understand."

Bianca stopped herself from saying *He's dead.* Instead she mumbled: "Thank you. You've been very kind." She wiped her eyes with her hands and took another sip of milk. The nurse smiled, hooked the chart on the foot of her bed, and disappeared back through the curtain. Moments later Bianca heard Bertlemina's voice coming from the other side of the curtain as the nurse checked on a cat in the neighboring compartment.

"Mr. Ruzzo. Nice to see you again."

"Oh, please, call me Marco."

"Well, Marco, we can't keep meeting like this. What has it been? Barely six months? And this was death number seven for you, which means you're onto life eight. You're cutting it rather fine."

"What can I do? I'm a trapeze artist!"

"Have you considered working with a net?"

"Ahh, but the danger is what brings the customers into the tent!"

"Maybe just lose the blindfold, then?" suggested Nurse Bertlemina.

"But the blindfold is my signature," protested Marco.

Nurse Bertlemina sighed. "I'm writing broken neck on your form. *Again.* No surprises there. Although, if I remember correctly, last time around it was a lion that did you in."

"That was a one-time deal. I was filling in for a coworker."

"It's always something with you, Marco. Early retirement is what I'd recommend. Here's your milk. You know the drill!"

There was the sound of a curtain swishing closed, and then more distant voices farther down the line as the nurse moved on to her next patient. Bianca drank what was left of the milk and set the empty glass on the nearby cart. She swung her legs over the side of the gurney and took a deep breath. It was time to head home, where in all likelihood she would have some explaining to do to an angry alley cat.

14 · Flint Lockford: The Apparition

Now that he was a ghost, Flint felt completely powerless. Bashing Delgatto's hounds with his umbrella had been a futile gesture. The Ghosthall ghosts had held him back when he'd tried to dive into the trunk of the black Cadillac with Bianca. When the mist had finally lifted from his eyes, he'd realized they'd been right to stop him. His presence would only have made a terrible ordeal worse for her. And like all cats, Bianca would just be rekindled. Her molecules would zip across the astral plane and reconstitute themselves at her birth spot. In no time at all she would be back home good as new, albeit with one less life left to burn.

Flint and his ghostly companions made their way back to the West Village—avoiding Washington Square. He took advantage of the chance to practice his locomotion skills, improving quite literally by leaps and bounds. He even used his umbrella to catch the draft of a trolley that carried him in its wake for about thirty feet. Flint took his leave from the Ghosthall gang on the corner of Sixth Avenue and Bleecker, wanting to go wait for Bianca at her place. Professor Chumley offered to accompany him but Flint insisted he would be fine on his own. He assured the professor he would return to Ghosthall before daybreak.

"Don't worry about Bianca," Professor Chumley said

reassuringly as they parted ways. "You said she was born here in the City, right? She might even be home already!"

"She's a real spitfire, that Bianca!" said Albert. "Remind me to never get on her bad side!"

"I think you mean badass!" cried Tiger. "I can't believe she walked into that restaurant all by herself and stabbed that gangster!"

Flint smiled thinly. He was the only one who knew how out of character this whole night had been for her.

"I'll see you later at the cantina," whispered Sophie, giving his hand a quick squeeze. Tiger hooked her umbrella handle around the collie's arm and pulled her away. "Cut that out, Sophe," hissed the singer. "What part of *engaged* don't you understand?" The last thing Flint heard as the ghosts swooped away was Sophie's bemused response: "Yes, but he's dead now and she isn't!"

Invisible to passersby, Flint drifted down the sidewalk, flicking his umbrella open and closed. One advantage to being dead was that he was no longer bothered by the heat. The exorbitant temperatures were definitely taking a toll on the living. Young pups and kittens were cooling off in the spray of open fire hydrants on the street while building stoops were crowded with cats and dogs eager to escape from stifling apartments.

When he arrived at Bianca's building Flint saw that the lights were on inside her apartment. Was she home already? Flint floated through her front door, feeling even more like an intruder this time around since he was alone. The living room was empty, and the kitchen was deserted too, except for the spectral Gertrude, who gave him a nervous smile as she melted back into the pantry. Flint glided slowly in the direction of the bedroom, but stopped as he passed by the bathroom door and heard the shower running. Relief flooded over him. Bianca must've made it home safe and sound.

Flint was faced with a conundrum. He couldn't just barge through her closed bathroom door, but then again the steam from the hot shower might be his one chance to make himself visible to Bianca and prove to her that he was really a ghost. Hesitantly, and feeling more than a tinge of shame, Flint poked his head through the wooden door and took a quick peek into the bathroom interior. The yellow shower curtain was drawn across the tub and Flint glimpsed a feline silhouette on the other side. Bianca's small bathroom had a pedestal sink, a commode, and a clunky old dryer booth that was constantly breaking down. The small mirror above the sink was starting to fog over and this gave Flint an idea.

Passing into the bathroom, Flint extended his index finger and tried drawing a line through the condensation on the glass. He soon figured out that the trick was to use slow, precise movements with his finger hovering just above the surface. It still took him several minutes to write just three words on the glass: *It's me Flint.*

Clouds of steam had gathered along the ceiling and were slowly extending toward the floor. Hopefully it would be enough to render him visible. He stood facing the fogged-up mirror so that Bianca would see him when she stepped out of the shower. That would give her time to grab her towel off the back of the door before turning around. Except—what if the sight of him terrified her?

As he stood there, racked with nerves, he heard the sound of Bianca's front door slamming closed. He frowned. Had Roxy come to check on Bianca? Then Flint heard a voice he knew all too well call out. "Roxy, I'm back! Are you in the shower?" Flint's mind twisted itself into a pretzel—if Bianca was out in the hallway, then the cat in the shower must be—

"Ahhh!" A scream rang out behind him. Startled, Flint wheeled around and found himself face-to-face with Roxy, standing there wide-eyed in her bare fur, one foot in the shower and one foot out. She pulled the shower curtain across her body with one hand and raised the other to point a trembling finger in his direction. Flint turned around, covering his eyes with his hands, and blurted out an apology that she had no way of hearing.

Bianca was banging loudly on the door. "Roxy? Are you okay?"

Mortified, Flint drifted right through the wall and out into the hallway. Bianca was there, rattling the bathroom door handle. She was wearing a plain blue dress that Flint guessed the hospital must have given her. Roxy yanked open the bathroom door, and Flint was relieved to see she was wrapped in a plush pink towel.

"What is it, Roxy? What's the matter?"

"You're not going to believe this," mumbled the stricken alley cat.

"Just spit it out!"

"I . . . I . . . just saw a ghost," she stammered.

"What?"

"I must be losing my mind. I stepped out of the shower

when I heard you call my name, and he was standing there facing the mirror."

"Who? Who was standing there?"

"I can't even say it!"

"Was it Flint? Tell me, Roxy, did you see Flint's ghost?"

Roxy bit her lip and nodded. "And look, he wrote his name in the mirror."

The two cats stepped into the bathroom and Flint floated in behind them. Bianca was staring at the writing in the mirror, which was slowly fading as the steam escaped through the open door.

"I know how it looks," said Roxy. "But I swear, I didn't write that. And I really did see Flint, except he had a peculiar washed-out look to him. I mean, I thought I saw him. I'm so sorry, Bianca. I must be losing my mind."

"I wasn't going to tell you this, Roxy, because I thought I was going crazy myself, but before I left earlier I heard Flint's voice in my ear."

"Is that supposed to make me feel better?" cried the alley cat. "We're both going nuts."

"But what if he really is here?" cried Bianca. "What if he's trying to contact us?"

A speechless and bug-eyed Roxy stared at Bianca in disbelief.

"Flint?" Bianca called out in a quavering voice. "Are you there?"

Flint floated closer to her and said softly, "I *am* here. That *was* me."

Bianca wheeled around to face the direction of his voice.

Flint did his best to explain. "I thought it was you in the

shower! I mean, I just wanted *you* to see me in the steam, so that you would believe it's really me. I didn't mean to get Roxy involved."

Bianca glanced at Roxy. "Can you hear him?"

The alley cat shook her head. "I can't hear anything. Why? Do you hear something?"

"Yes! He's here. I think he may really be here. Flint, can you say something to Roxy?"

"No, Bianca, only you can hear me because I talked to you first!"

"Flint says he can only talk to me," Bianca whispered to Roxy.

"And only Roxy can see my ghost! It's the same principle, you see," Flint said with dismay.

Bianca's eyebrows knit together. "Oh no. He says only you can see him now. Quick! We need to test this! Close that door, Roxy, I'll turn on the shower!" Bianca brushed the shower curtain aside and twisted the tap back on.

"I don't know if I'm ready for this," said Roxy, securing her towel with one hand and holding Bianca's hand with the other.

"Flint, where are you?" Bianca demanded.

"I'll stand in front of the door," he replied.

"Watch the door, Roxy. That's where he'll appear."

The three of them waited for the bathroom to steam up again. The alley cat gave Bianca a sideways glance. "Bianca, what's with the blue dress? I hope that's not what I think it is."

Bianca bit her lip. "I may have gotten myself thrown into the Gowanus Canal earlier by Osvaldo Delgatto's goons."

Roxy let out an angry rumble. "I warned you that might happen!"

"You were right. And the worst part is I lost my engagement ring in the bottom of the canal. Flint, darling, I'm so sorry." Bianca stared sorrowfully at the bathroom door.

"And you're down to six lives!" grumbled Roxy.

"It was very foolish to throw away a life like that!" Flint said sharply.

"I know," she replied. "But I still have five more lives than you ever had. And for what it's worth I think Delgatto was telling the truth when he said he didn't order your murder."

"I just don't know what you were thinking," muttered Flint.

"Someone killed you, Flint," Bianca pointed out defiantly. "What would you have done if I was murdered?"

Flint grimaced. "It would have driven me insane," he admitted.

The room was slowly filling up with water vapor and Flint saw the moment the alley cat's eyes lit up with recognition. "There he is!" she yelled. "I can see him again. He's very faint, but he's getting clearer by the second, and it's definitely Flint!"

"Flint!" Bianca rushed forward to where she imagined he was standing, He tried to wrap his arms around her, but it was no use.

"Where are you?" she pleaded.

"He's trying to hug you," Roxy said. "But you keep passing right through him."

"We're trapped on different planes of existence, my love," Flint said glumly.

Bianca's face dropped, but with a big effort she forced a smile. "At least I can hear your voice. That's enough for now. Tell me—are you okay?"

"Well, I'm upset that I've bungled my big reveal. I've wasted it on Roxy! Now you will never be able to see me. It was a rookie mistake! I should have let my friend Chumley tag along, he would have stopped me from making this blunder. I feel like such a dope."

"Don't beat yourself up, darling. You know, if it was just me who could see you and hear you I don't think I would have been able to convince myself that you were real."

"But are you sure he is real?" demanded Roxy, who was listening to just one side of their conversation. "How do we know I'm not hallucinating?"

"I'll prove it," said Flint. "Watch the mirror, Bianca. You might not be able to see me, but you can see me do this!" He floated over to the sink, and underneath his previous words he wrote:

I AM A GHOST

15 · Tatiana Val:
The Bank Robber

Wednesday

Val had been coming to the Delancey Market most of her life. As a pup she'd come here daily with her mother to buy groceries and household supplies. Located on the corner of Essex and Delancey, it was one-stop shopping, with thirty odd vendors all grouped under one roof in a utilitarian cinder block building. It wasn't until after the war that Val discovered the Market was also a hub for the criminal underworld. The butcher at the Market had played an instrumental role in helping her to kick off her career as a contract killer. If she had chosen burglary instead then it would have been the cheesemonger who helped her along. For cats and dogs of the night, the greengrocer was an important intermediary for vetting new clients, while the coffee bean importer handled anything to do with catnip and other illicit substances. Of course, the mob ran the whole operation and made sure that the local authorities were well compensated for looking the other way. In as much as Val had a home away from home, the Delancey Market was it.

She spotted the butcher behind his counter along the back wall. He was a red-and-white Staffordshire terrier with a large square head. When he was done wrapping up a sirloin steak for a lone customer, she caught his eye. He wiped his hands on his bloodstained apron and turned to face her. "Nice suit," he grunted in his usual deadpan manner.

Val knew she stuck out like a sore thumb in the Delancey Market. She was wearing a high-waisted green jacket and matching boot-cut pants, a colorful ensemble she had purchased to celebrate her retirement.

"I've got some gear I need to sell," she said to the butcher, holding up an enormous canvas bag. He squinted over the counter at it. He knew without her saying so that the bag was full of guns, and that if she was selling that many weapons it could only mean one thing—she was calling it quits. The butcher did not look pleased. His cut from all the jobs he had sent her way over the years had made him a lot of dough. Grudgingly, he used his walkie-talkie to tell Lou— the one-legged mutt who managed all the hardware in the sub-basement freezer—that she was on her way down.

The transaction proceeded without a hitch. Lou knew better than to ask her any awkward questions. Of course, he only gave her a fraction of what she had shelled out for the weapons originally, but still, it felt good to be rid of them— there was no going back now.

On her way out, the butcher beckoned her over, tore off a page of his order pad, and gave it to her. She looked at him, confused. These slips of paper usually indicated a new job.

"A message just came in for you," he explained. "They said it was urgent so it's lucky you were here."

Perturbed, Val snuck a peek at the note as soon as she got outside. Her heart began to hammer. Written in the butcher's familiar scrawl were a few brief sentences: *Cops have your address. Clear out right away. Mister X.*

The third story walk-up Val shared with her mother was only a few short blocks away. She crossed Delancey and began to jog south on Essex Street, passing into the outskirts of Siamese Town. She wove her way through the cream-colored cats that were crowding the sidewalks outside the many seafood markets. Glassy-eyed fish in the open-air bins stared up at her as she hurried past.

She'd been planning to leave town either tomorrow or the next day. Now she needed to get her mom in the car and hit the road immediately. Panting heavily, Val turned the corner onto Grand Street and saw her building up ahead, with her ride parked out front. The car was a pale blue 1946 Plymouth that she had paid all cash for yesterday at a dealership in Long Island City. It had low mileage and was in tip-top shape, so she was counting on it to get her from New York to Los Angeles without any breakdowns and without drawing any unwanted attention. She would much rather fly, but the authorities were bound to get nosy if she showed up at the airport with a duffel bag stuffed with nearly five million bucks.

Val took the stairs in her building two at a time. Throwing open her front door, she yelled at her mother to grab her things. "We need to go, Mom! Now!" Her mother was an old dog, and she was confused by the sudden sense of urgency. Val dumped out the laundry basket and used it to help her mother gather up her most treasured keepsakes. "Put your shoes on, Mom, hurry!" Val urged. "Don't worry about anything else, I'll buy you new stuff in California!" Val ducked into her own bedroom and grabbed the green duffel bag from the top shelf of her closet, strapping it across her chest.

Her mother was wringing her hands and whining loudly

about leaving so many of her precious things behind. Val was unmoved. Time was all that mattered now.

"We *really* need to hurry, Mom!"

Her mother refused to leave without her prized fur coat, even though Val yelled at her to leave it. "There's no room for that thing in the trunk, Mom!" But her mother had already pulled it on and was glaring at her daughter defiantly.

Val shook her head, exasperated. "I don't think you understand Southern California weather, Mom." With plenty of cajoling, Val managed to get her mother and her mother's basket full of stuff out the door and down the stairs.

She crammed her mom's things into the trunk and slammed it shut. Then she helped her mother, who was already complaining about the heat, into the passenger seat. "Of course you're hot, Mom!" Val snapped. "You're wearing a fur coat!" Before getting into the car, Val glanced up one last time at their home, two floors up from the Heavenly Market deli, known locally for its eels and prickly fruit. It was strange to think that she might never see this place again.

Val cut off a passing vehicle as she peeled away from the curb, ignoring the other driver's angry honks. She took off down Grand Street like a shot. She still had a pit stop to make before leaving the City—the Manhattan Trust & Savings on Greenwich Avenue—where she had one last bank account to close. Her forest-green duffel bag was already loaded up with one-hundred-dollar bills from the other two accounts she had closed in the past few days, but there was still room for one last addition to her haul. She planned to guard this bag with her life until they got to Los Angeles, where she would spread her stash across various West Coast accounts.

They were only three blocks away from home when her mother grew hysterical, saying that she had forgotten to grab the photograph of her dead husband off the living room cabinet. Val's father had been in the ground going on ten years, but his presence was still palpable in their home. Val gritted her teeth as she made a right and then another right, looping back around to their Grand Street apartment. She would risk dashing upstairs to grab the photograph, because otherwise she would hear about it for the next three thousand miles.

But as they approached the building, Val's breath caught in her throat—three police cars were stopped out front, lights flashing. She rolled up her window and cruised by as calmly as she could manage. A surreptitious glance to her left revealed two plainclothes dogs barking into the building's intercom, a short Scottish terrier and a border collie, along with half a dozen uniformed officers. How on earth had they tracked her down? If happenstance hadn't found her at the Delancey Market exactly when the message came in from Mister X then the cops would've caught her for sure. Val shook her head with disgust. This was her fault. She'd been unforgivably complacent on this last job, showing an unwarranted degree of contempt for the City Police.

The flashing blue lights in her rearview mirror vanished when she turned right on Allen Street, and Val relaxed her viselike grip on the steering wheel. She wouldn't breathe easy until they crossed into Jersey. But first she needed to close that last account.

When she arrived at Greenwich Avenue, she squeezed into a spot across the street from the bank, a grandiose structure with an ornate green dome and an arched entrance. "Wait here,

Mom. Don't move! I'll be back in five minutes." Val stepped out of the car, her right arm clasped around her green duffel bag, and crossed over to the bank steps. Inside Val encountered a long line at the teller window, cats and dogs catching up on their banking during their lunch hour no doubt. Val pressed past them, moving deeper into the bank, where she was greeted by a pleasant young cat in a navy suit. "I need to speak to a bank representative about closing my account," she told him.

"Certainly, miss. Please take a seat. Someone will be with you shortly."

Val was waiting patiently in a side chair when she heard an unmistakable double click sound somewhere behind her. To her trained ears it was a sound that could only mean one thing.

"This is a stickup!" a voice yelled. Val swiveled around to see a muscular ginger tomcat in a black turtleneck standing in front of the teller window, a paisley mask tied around his face. In his right hand was a snub-nosed revolver that Val instantly recognized as a Smith and Wesson 36, a five-shot double action firearm that packed a punch. Val stared at the bank robber in dismay—this was the last thing she needed.

The ginger tom handed the teller a sack and demanded that she fill it. The nervous cat followed his instructions. Meanwhile, the ginger tom, waving his gun about madly, ordered all the customers—including Val and an unarmed security guard—to line up against the wall.

When the teller was finished, he snatched back his sack and turned to face all the lined-up cats and dogs. "Right, all of you! Add your wallets, watches, and jewelry to the bag!" he barked. The bank robber's eyes narrowed when he got to

Val, who was standing tall with her arms crossed. "What you got in the bag you're hiding behind your back, sweetheart?" he asked her.

"Nothing. Just dirty gym clothes."

"Let's have a look."

"I don't think so," she spat, staring him down. "You have enough already. You'd better hurry and get out of here, the cops are probably on their way."

"Maybe they are, maybe they're not," replied the orange cat. "Now I'm gonna ask one more time nicely, and you ain't gonna like what happens after that. What's in the bag?"

Val regarded him stiffly. The one thing she was definitely *not* going to do was hand this clown her life savings. He raised the gun to her temple. She stared into his eyes, wondering if this cat had what it took to pull the trigger, or if she could safely call his bluff. There was a gaping chasm between being a bank robber and a murderer. No one knew that better than her.

"I'm not giving you my duffel bag, so beat it!" she barked.

"I think you're forgetting about one thing," the tomcat replied.

"And what's that?"

"Curiosity. If I don't find out what's inside the bag, it's gonna keep me awake at night." He pulled back the hammer with his thumb.

Sirens sounded in the distance.

Val let out a deep-throated rumble. "Well? Don't keep everyone in suspense," she growled. "Are you gonna pull the trigger or not?"

The ginger tom unexpectedly swung the pistol and caught her on the side of the head with the butt. Dazed, she slumped to the floor, still clinging to the duffel bag. He reached down and tried to pull it off her shoulder. Val's training kicked in—she swept his legs out from under him and he fell, landing on top of her. They grappled, rolling around on the floor. She had one hand on his gun hand and the other on her bag. She was bigger than him, but he was a solid ball of muscle. She tried to get on top of him, but the security guard chose that moment to join the fray, jumping onto the bank robber's back. The ginger tom's eyes looked suddenly panicked behind his mask. He began to thrash wildly about in an attempt to break free. A loud bang rang out and Val felt a jolt in her chest. For a split second the world came to a standstill. Then the security guard let go of the bank robber and backed away, while all the other customers made a mad scramble for the door. The bank robber leapt to his feet and stared down at her with a look of horror. Val rose to her feet, still clutching her bag of money, but the bank robber seemed to have lost all interest in her, as his eyes were fixed on the floor. The gun dropped from his limp hand, clattering to the ground.

A swarm of cops poured into the bank and half a dozen rough-looking hounds grabbed hold of the tomcat. He put up no resistance, still staring at the ground, distraught. Val followed his gaze and there at her feet she saw an Afghan hound lying motionless in a puddle of blood. It didn't make any sense. Who was this dog? And why was she wearing an identical green suit to her own? The same shoes as her, even? And most bizarrely of all, why was she clutching a duffel bag to her chest? Val stared down at this dog uncomprehendingly. It wasn't until a cop stepped right through her that the truth finally sank in. She let out an anguished howl, but no one around her took any notice.

16 · Junior Detective Morton Digby: The List

Detective Puddleworth's CIA pal came through big on Wednesday morning. The Scottish terrier picked up the phone at his desk and Morton watched him jot down a name and address. Hanging up the receiver he waved the slip of paper triumphantly. "We've got her!" exclaimed the Scottie. "A dog named Tatiana Valova is the only female Afghan hound ex-operative, and it so happens she lives here in the City, over in Siamese Town!"

The two detectives raced over to the Grand Street address in their squad car, sirens blazing. Two other police vehicles followed close behind, filled with patroldogs led by a wary Sergeant Doyle. Screeching to a stop in front of the building, the detectives hopped out and buzzed the ground floor apartment marked SUPER, yelling "Police!" into the intercom. Rushing up the stairs they arrived, panting heavily, at a locked teal colored door marked 3A. Morton's pulse was pounding in his ears. There could be an armed killer lurking on the other side of that door. Feeling suddenly very warm, he took deep breaths and did his best to appear calm and collected. If he fainted in this cramped hallway, surrounded by seven patroldogs and Sergeant Doyle, he would never hear the end of it.

There was no response when they banged on the door.

A burly hound was about to put his shoulder to it when a hairless crested dog came shuffling up the stairs with a key, chattering in a foreign tongue. He unlocked the door for them, and they piled inside, ready for anything.

The place was deserted. Judging by the warm pot on the stove and the jumble of thrown-open drawers and closets, the former occupants had very recently left in a rush. The hounds all sniffed the air and pronounced that two dogs lived there, an older dog and a younger one. Discarded mail and a labored conversation with the super confirmed that Tatiana Valova lived there with her mother. Detective Puddleworth shifted into his manic clue-finding mode, sticking his nose into every corner of the apartment, a magnifying glass held up to his eye. Meanwhile, Morton, Sergeant Doyle, and the patroldogs followed the scent of the two Afghan hounds down the stairs and back outside, where it dead-ended at an empty parking space.

"Looks like your big tip was a bust!" scoffed Sergeant Doyle. "I don't know if this hound you're after is really the Queen of Spades, but whoever she is, she has slipped right through your paws!"

A crestfallen Detective Puddleworth soon joined them downstairs and reported that he too had struck out with his sleuthing. They assigned a patroldog to watch the place in case the suspect returned, and the Scottie put the word out to the local airports and transit hubs to be alert for any hounds traveling under the name of Tatiana Valova.

Dispirited, the two detectives returned to the station. At the precinct, Morton's desk was pushed right up to his partner's, such that they sat facing each other in a far corner of the bullpen. Their desktops were cluttered with the usual office paraphernalia: stacks of paperwork, a pencil holder, an electric pencil sharpener, legal notepads, and a clunky typewriter that they shared.

"This is an indisputable setback," declared Detective Puddleworth, who had yet to regain his usual good cheer. "I'm not sure where this leaves us."

"The Delgatto angle looks like a bust too," pointed out Morton. "The recordings from the restaurant seem to leave him in the clear. It may be that one of his deputies went rogue, but there's no way to pin it on him. Delgatto doesn't even seem to know who's behind it."

"Yes, I listened to the tapes earlier. I think we can safely rule Delgatto out as a suspect," mused the Scottie. "We desperately need some new leads. Did you get your paws on those newspaper articles we talked about earlier?"

"Yeah, I've got them right here." Morton picked up a stack of *Knickerbocker Gazettes* off the floor and dropped them on his desk with a thud. "These are the editions with all of Flint's articles from the past year."

"Let's split up that pile and go through them. Make a note of anyone who might have any reason to resent the murdered wolfhound."

They divvied up the newspapers and began to read through Flint's columns one by one. The constant banter among their colleagues in the bullpen made it difficult to concentrate. Vulgar jokes frequently set off rounds of sniggering, or—if a wisecrack was particularly crude—outright guffaws. Every so often someone let out a loud belch, or worse, adding to the musty feel of the air inside the station.

Propped-open windows were little help given the soaring outside temperatures.

Things got even more raucous when Buckley and Callaway strutted into the station with a handcuffed ginger tom sandwiched between them. The ragged-looking cat hung his head dejectedly as they marched him over to the booking desk, the two hounds picking up high fives and back slaps from their fellow officers along the way.

"Looks like those two finally caught up with that bank robber," Morton muttered. "This only makes our busted raid look worse."

"We were unlucky today, that's all."

"Were we, though? I can't help wondering if maybe she got some warning that we were on our way."

"No one knew we were coming," said the Scottie, "except my friend at the CIA and our colleagues here at the Sixth."

"Exactly."

"Don't be paranoid, Morton!" the Scottie chided him. "It wouldn't make any sense for my pal to tip off both sides. And I see no reason to suspect any of our colleagues."

Morton sighed. He knew the precinct hounds a lot better than Puddleworth did.

"Have you found anyone with a grudge against Lockford yet?" asked the Scottie.

"I did find this one very shady fella in my stack of papers," Morton replied. "Gustave Legrand, the sommelier at Chez Claude's."

Detective Puddleworth raised a quizzical eyebrow. "A sommelier? What did Lockford have to say about him?"

"He said the guy's nose was so bad he doubted he could

tell the difference between a Bordeaux and a box of grape juice. And he hinted that there was some funny business going on with Chez Claude's overpriced wine list. Anyone reading this article was bound to come away thinking the place was filled with cheats and swindlers, chief among them the sommelier himself."

"I see. Well, put his name at the top of the list!"

Morton printed the word *suspects* at the top of a legal pad and wrote the name *Gustave Legrand* underneath it, adding and underlining the word *sommelier*. "Done," he said.

"I'm finished with my pile also," said the Scottie. "And I have two more names for you. The first is Peggy Sneekly. She's a mutt who worked as a zookeeper for the Central Park Menagerie. Lockford wrote an exposé about the deplorable conditions some of the animals were being kept in, and Peggy Sneekly was singled out as the main culprit. I imagine she lost her job because of it."

Morton grabbed his pen. "Peggy Sneekly—zookeeper. Got it."

"And then there's this pompous pooch who goes by the name of Arthur Neverest. He's an alleged explorer, but Lockford exposed him as a fraud. This fella liked to give talks at fancy soirees around town, where he would recount his harrowing trips though the African Congo, or how he nearly froze to death on an expedition to the South Pole. Only according to Lockford he's never been anywhere more exotic than the South of France."

"Arthur Neverest—phony explorer. Got it! I've put him on the list. That gives us a grand total of three new animals of interest."

When Morton looked up, he caught sight of a white Angora sauntering into the precinct. There was no mistaking Bianca Moon, looking somber in a black long-sleeved dress with a lace collar and a matching black beret. Glued to her like a shadow was her alley cat pal Roxy, wearing the same beat-up denim and ripped jeans from the day before. Morton wasn't surprised when a brief conversation with the desk sergeant resulted in the two cats heading right for them.

"Heads up, J.B.," whispered Morton. "We've got company."

The Scottie's head swiveled around as the two cats drew close. "Lovely to see you again, Miss Moon," he said graciously, waving Bianca and Roxy into two side chairs. "How can we help you today?"

"Well, first off," Bianca said stiffly, "I want to thank you both for rushing to my rescue yesterday when Delgatto's goons grabbed me. You really stuck your necks out on that one."

Morton cocked his head at his partner. At the restaurant yesterday they had argued furiously about whether to intervene. The Scottie had been adamant that no action was required from them, since Bianca was a feline who presumably had many lives, while Morton had found it hard to just sit there and do nothing. The whole experience had left a bad taste in his mouth.

"We're terribly sorry, Miss Moon." The Scottie smiled. "But we couldn't compromise our investigation. And as you well know, you should never have been there in the first place."

"Yes, but I was there. You realize that incident cost me a life."

"That is regrettable. But let's be clear," said the Scottie firmly, "you attacked him. If we had revealed ourselves and stepped in, you would be sitting in a jail cell right now on charges of attempted dogicide."

Bianca and Roxy glowered at them, and it didn't escape Morton's notice that both cats had their claws unsheathed. He decided to try and smooth things over. "We're very sorry, Miss Moon. It was a difficult situation and I truly wish we could have done more to help."

"And you could have," she snarled. "You just chose not to! Now, tell me, have the two of you made any progress toward solving my fiancé's murder? Or have you been too busy stuffing yourselves with free dinners?"

Detective Puddleworth's lip curled up ever so slightly. "Our free dinner as you call it helped us to rule out Delgatto. It doesn't appear he was involved on any level in your fiancé's murder. I would strongly advise you to keep your distance from that dog going forward."

"Like I didn't know that already," Bianca said testily. "That mobster may be a killer, but he didn't kill my Flint."

"I'm glad to see we're on the same page," said Detective Puddleworth. "But I'm afraid that's all we have to share at the moment. We are actively investigating other suspects, but after your antics yesterday evening, Miss Moon, I think you'll understand if we play our cards closer to the vest. If we make any arrests, I'll be sure to get in touch."

Bianca's eyes narrowed. "Maybe I was a little impetuous yesterday, but that's no reason to get cagey."

"Yeah, spill it," demanded Roxy. "Who else do you think could be involved?"

Detective Puddleworth shook his head. "I'm sorry. But we really can't get into specifics at this time."

"This is baloney!" Roxy growled, crossing her arms.

A staring contest followed, with Bianca glaring at Detective Puddleworth, while Roxy locked her eyes on Morton, who felt himself squirming in his chair. Secretly he found the alley cat quite terrifying. Thankfully their standoff was interrupted when Sergeant Doyle came barreling down the aisle in their direction. "Boy, have I got news for you two fellas!" exclaimed the bulldog.

Morton gestured toward their visitors. "Sarge, you remember Miss Moon, Flint Lockford's fiancée? And this is her friend Roxy."

"Miss Moon will want to hear this too!" the bulldog proclaimed. "No, don't get your hackles up, J.B. The press has already gotten hold of this story, so it'll be all over the evening edition, which means these two will find out soon enough anyway. I take it you saw Buckley and Callaway come in with the bank robber? Well, that larcenous ginger tomcat just added murder to his rap sheet! He fatally shot a canine bystander during his latest holdup."

"Who was the victim?" asked Detective Puddleworth.

"Well, that's where things get really interesting," replied the sarge. "Her name might ring a bell for the two of you. She was an Afghan hound who went by the name Tatiana Valova!"

Morton's mind reeled.

The bulldog grinned. "You two just caught yourselves a lucky break. It seems your hitdog suspect stopped by the Manhattan Trust & Savings on her way out of town. She was shot dead by a bullet through the heart when she refused to give up a duffel bag she was carrying. A bag I have right here!" The sarge chucked a forest-green duffel bag onto Puddleworth's desk. He unzipped it slowly, savoring the moment, and then pulled open the flaps to reveal a huge stack of bundled bricks of cash. The two detectives and their visitors stared pop-eyed at the pile of one-hundred-dollar bills.

Roxy let out a low whistle. "That's a heck of a lot of dough."

The sarge grinned. "It looks like you two were right about that Afghan being the Queen of Spades. She was hightailing it out of town with her loot when she had the bad luck to run into our bank robber! Her car was parked outside with her mother strapped in the passenger seat. And guess what we found in the glove compartment?" Morton looked at the sergeant blankly. "Some detectives you two are!" The bulldog held up a deck of cards. "Blue pearl backs, just like the one you found in the piano. A full deck with only one missing card!"

Detective Puddleworth took the bait. "The queen of spades, I'd wager?"

"Well, give the Scottie in the pinstripe suit a prize! Mind you, this is gonna count as Buckley and Callaway's collar, since technically they found her while the two of you were sitting here with your feet up on your desks. But we'll be sure to credit you with an assist on the ID. Bit of a fluke if you ask me. Now you just need to figure out who hired her before the captain runs out of patience!" The bulldog zipped up the duffel bag, slung it over his shoulder, and toddled away, chortling to himself.

"Does that mean the hired killer who murdered my Flint is dead?" demanded Bianca.

Morton smoothed the hair on the top of his head. "Sure looks that way. I guess your boyfriend's killer got their just desserts."

"Fiancé."

"Sorry—*fiancé.*"

Bianca folded her hands in her lap. "I'm glad this Valova dog is dead. I hope she rots in hell! But as the sergeant pointed out, the mastermind who hired her is still out there somewhere."

"Like I said," replied Detective Puddleworth, "if we make any arrests you'll be our first call."

"Are the two of you even real detectives?" Roxy eyed them both skeptically. "How many murders have you solved?"

"It so happens this is our first dogicide," Detective Puddleworth admitted.

"That's what I thought," said the alley cat, rolling her eyes.

Morton quickly changed the subject. "While you're here, there is one other matter we need to talk to you about. I got a phone call from a dog who identified herself as Mrs. Rockwald. Do you know her?"

"She's Flint's sister," replied Bianca. "I met her this morning at the funeral home. She insisted we split the cost of a mahogany casket. Flint wouldn't have wanted anything that extravagant, but the funeral director sided with her and her husband. It was very aggravating. Flint hasn't spoken to her in years and they weren't close."

"I should warn you then that she raised some awkward

questions about your ring," Morton went on. "I think she heard rumors that it was in Flint's pocket at the time of death, and that led her to believe that she had some claim to it."

"Well, I can tell her right where to find it if she wants. Although she may want to get herself some scuba gear."

"What is that supposed to mean?" asked the Scottie.

"It's currently sitting at the bottom of the Gowanus Canal, along with my favorite pajamas," she said bitterly.

"I'm very sorry to hear that," said Morton, putting two and two together.

"Let's get the heck out of here, Princess," muttered Roxy. "We're not gonna learn anything more from these two dolts."

"You can expect to see us at the funeral later," said Detective Puddleworth when the two cats stood up to go.

Bianca looked puzzled. "Why's that?"

"Most murder victims know their killer personally."

This comment left Bianca looking stupefied. "Are you suggesting the perpetrator may show up at the church?"

"It wouldn't surprise me," said the Scottie. "Don't worry, we'll be sitting quietly in the back, keeping a close eye on things."

"C'mon, Bianca, let's beat it," Roxy said, tugging on her friend's sleeve.

"Thanks for nothing, detectives," Bianca said, and walked away.

Morton sighed. "I guess we can stop looking for the Queen of Spades."

The Scottie nodded. "But we'd better get over to the morgue to confirm the ID."

Morton's eyes had dropped to his desk and a panicked

look came over him. He began to search frantically through the loose papers on his desk.

"Did you lose something?" asked the Scottie.

"The list!" Morton cried. "It's gone! I think that alley cat must've swiped it while we were all goggling at the bag full of cash!"

"That dirty, lowdown thief!" cried the Scottie. "She's got some nerve!"

17 · Flint Lockford: The Newcomer

Flint had borrowed Paco's alarm clock and left it floating by his bedside set for half past three in the afternoon, which was the spectral equivalent of the middle of the night. It felt like he'd only just drifted off when the loud ringing woke him up. He stretched out a hand and toggled the switch. On the other side of the room Paco rolled over in his bunk—his snoring resumed with barely a hitch. Bleary-eyed, Flint floated up and out of bed. It wouldn't do to be late to his own funeral.

Grabbing his hat and his umbrella, Flint passed through the door and out into the empty hallway. Around him Ghosthall was quiet as a tomb. He proceeded groggily up the stairs, wondering if there was some spook equivalent to black coffee. That's when he heard a noise he had yet to hear inside Ghosthall—footsteps, and they were coming down the stairs. Flint stopped short and pressed himself against the wall. A living dog came around the bend in the stairs, carrying a mop and a bucket. Flint immediately pegged the mutt as Gerald, the custodian. But why did he look so familiar? He knew this dog from somewhere. Then it hit him: Gerald was also the janitor at the Calico Cat Lounge. Small world.

Upstairs, in the entrance hall, Albert was predictably passed out over the registration book. Flint drifted by him silently, heading for the front entrance, but before he could go out, Professor Chumley burst through the door with a new-comer in tow. She was a tall and svelte Afghan hound with long cream-colored locks and dark melancholy eyes, dressed conspicuously in a stylish green suit. She seemed startled to see Flint, and he guessed that she must not have met many ghosts since her passing. *Looks like I'm not the new guy around here anymore*, he thought to himself.

Chumley's umbrella was in tatters again, and he chucked what was left of it through the door, just as he'd done the day before, muttering to himself about the summer sun. "Hey there, Flint! Meet Val," said the professor. "I'm going to show her around and we'll see how she likes the place!"

"Welcome to Ghosthall," Flint said amiably.

But the Afghan just stared at him wide-eyed, clutching a forest-green duffel bag to her chest and looking as if she was ready to bolt.

"Where are you off to at this early hour?" the professor asked him.

"I've got a funeral to get to."

"Ah! So you do. Where is it being held?"

"Over at Our Lady of Sorrento on Carmine Street."

"A fine church."

The Afghan hound was eyeing the door, and sensing this, Professor Chumley hooked his arm around hers and guided her toward the registration desk, where the grumpy-looking corgi was rubbing his eyes.

Flint checked his watch. Quarter to four. Would it really matter if he was a little late? He double-checked his umbrella, making sure it was in good working order, as he planned to accompany Bianca to the cemetery afterward in Brooklyn.

Flint was just about to drift out through the doors when a row broke out at the registration table, stopping him short.

"I'm telling you, the contents of my bag are none of your business!" the Afghan hound said hotly.

"That's not the way it works, lady," Albert explained with irritation. "If you want to lodge here, we need to inspect your possessions. Don't worry, we won't confiscate anything. And I promise you I don't get my kicks by rooting through your unmentionables, if that's what you're worried about!"

"I expect Albert has seen mountains of undergarments over the years"—Chumley chuckled—"and I've never known him to bat an eye or to make so much as an inappropriate comment!"

"That's right. My interest in the contents of your bag is strictly professional!"

"I think I'd better just go," snarled the Afghan hound.

"Suit yourself," grumbled Albert, throwing his hands up in the air.

"Val, be reasonable," implored the professor. "This simple procedure helps us prevent theft and avoid squabbles between our lodgers."

"You're a bunch of good-for-nothing snoops is what you are!" she growled in reply.

"Whatever valuables you have in that bag, they are much more likely to get stolen out there than in here," the professor said pointedly. "Predatory spooks will pick you clean the moment you nod off. Take my word for it, there's safety in numbers!"

But the Afghan hound remained unconvinced. She tore herself away from Chumley's grasp and dashed right past Flint and out through the door.

Professor Chumley stared after her in dismay. "What in the world got into her?"

The large-headed corgi scratched his ear. "Just another nutty ghost roaming the city. Don't waste your time chasing after *her*."

"Tough break, Professor," Flint said to the deflated sheepdog, whose bushy tail was drooping low to the ground.

"You win some, you lose some," Professor Chumley said philosophically. "Will we see you later, Flint?"

"Hard to say," Flint replied. "I plan to trek all the way out to the Green-Wood Cemetery, in Brooklyn, for the burial. I want to be there for Bianca."

"Well, do be careful. Be sure to get out of there before nightfall. That graveyard is crawling with old phantasms. There's even some from the Civil War. And they have the groundskeepers trained to follow their commands. Hey! Why don't I come along?"

"Don't worry about me, Professor. You'd better go get some shut-eye before sundown. With luck I'll see you at the cantina later."

"I am pretty zonked," conceded the professor.

The sheepdog glided away in the direction of the stairs, tipping his hat to Albert, whose head was already beginning to droop. Flint straightened his tie and coasted through the door, out into the sunlight, popping his umbrella open as he swooped through the oncoming traffic to get to the shady side of the avenue.

Making a left, he drifted down Bleecker and before long he spotted the campanile of Our Lady of Sorrento rising up into the sky. His umbrella was taking a beating as he passed through patches of sunlight in the crosswalks, so instead of going around to the sunny front steps, Flint slipped through one of the church's green side doors. He found himself in the deserted hallway of what looked like a school. He hung a left and without a second thought passed right through a door marked PRIVATE DORMITORY. Suddenly he was surrounded by a group of living nuns sitting around on their bunks in their muslin slips and undergarments, their habits hanging on hooks along the wall. *Geez—never a dull moment in the life of a ghost,* he thought, swallowing hard. Two of the nuns were wrapped in bath towels. Flint plowed onward, determined to glide past the oblivious sisters as quickly as possible, but he was stopped in his tracks by the ghost of a thick-set brown Lab wearing a gray habit. She looked daggers at him. "And what do you think you're doing in here, you Peeping Tom!" she growled.

"I'm just trying to get to the church!" he explained. "I didn't know it was a nunnery!"

"Likely story!" snarled the brown Lab. "This church is off-limits to finders! Now scram right through that wall and back out on the street, before I tell my sisters to start throwing salt at the evil spirits in the room!"

"I'm just trying to get to the funeral ceremony," Flint protested.

"And what business do you have there?"

"It's my funeral."

"Oh." She seemed taken aback. "Why didn't you say so

in the first place? Come with me. I'll hand you off to Father Antonio and he'll take you where you need to be." Flint covered his eyes with one hand as he followed the sister right through a door and into another hallway. Her hostile manner had subsided and she even shared some advice with him: "You know, it's not unheard of for ghosts to ascend into the Almighty's embrace during their own service. The ceremony may just provide you with the comfort you're seeking."

Flint nodded noncommittally.

They passed through an open doorway into a small vestry where a black-robed priest was flipping the page of a ghostly bible. A portly pointer with a grizzled muzzle, he welcomed Flint with a benevolent smile and listened as the ghostly sister explained that it was Flint's funeral ceremony taking place in the church. When she recounted how Flint had walked in on a troop of half-dressed nuns, the priest howled with laughter.

The cleric closed his holy book and straightened his robes. "Come with me, my young friend."

The back rooms of the church were a maze of narrow passages but they soon arrived at a small door that let out to the side of the main altar. Passing through it, Flint found the church buzzing with throngs of mourners, far more than he was expecting to see. There were many faces he didn't recognize, and he guessed that news of his unusual death had drawn members of the public to his funeral. An open casket at the foot of the altar was another shock. Flint suspected he had his sister to thank for that. He noticed several ghosts roaming about in small bands along the outer aisles of the church, ducking in and out of the various alcove shrines.

The priest followed Flint's gaze. "Churches are popular haunts, but don't worry, they know better than to bother you." And sure enough, sensing that he was under the aegis of Father Antonio, the church spooks paid him no mind.

Flint thanked Father Antonio for his help and was about to head over to greet Bianca, who he had spotted in the front pew, when a murmur rippled through the room. Flint glanced over to the church doors and saw an elegant figure silhouetted there. Holy smokes! What was *she* doing here?

18 · Bianca Moon: The Funeral

Bianca sat primly in the front pew of Our Lady of Sorrento. Her gaze wandered around the cavernous space, taking in the vaulted ceilings, the marble columns, and the ornate stained glass windows, before snapping back to the open coffin at the foot of the altar. The embalmers had done an uncanny job stitching Flint up and repairing the damage caused by the piano. Lying there in his tweed jacket and brown tie, his arms crossed blissfully over his chest and a lifelike sheen on his black nose, it looked almost as if he were sleeping.

An organist concealed in the mezzanine was raining down somber chords on the gathered mourners. On Bianca's right sat Roxy, and next to her, in the aisle seat, was Tabatha. Directly behind them were alley cats Pam and Jan, along with other members of Roxy's gang, all of whom were being uncommonly kind to Bianca. Otis and Penelope were in row three, sitting with other staff from the *Knickerbocker Gazette*, including Mr. Boswell himself. The rest of the church was filling up with a mix of familiar and unfamiliar faces.

Flint's sister and her husband, both lanky wolfhounds, were sitting in the front pew on the opposite side of the aisle, surrounded by a dozen or so of Flint's cousins, aunts, and uncles. The sister had laid claim to the eulogy, which Bianca was sure would involve plenty of manufactured tears on behalf of her dearly departed brother. Bianca hadn't fought her on it. Flint's ghostly appearance yesterday had soothed her own grief, albeit with a heavy dose of added confusion. Flint was dead. But she could still talk to him. Which meant he wasn't *really* gone? And yet things were very different now. How were they supposed to build a future together when he existed in a purely disembodied state? Flint had also warned her about the ephemeral nature of a ghost's existence. At any moment he could just fade away forever. She suspected the only reason he had stuck around in the first place was to make sure she was okay, which of course she wasn't. How could she be? A moment of sudden and inexplicable violence had changed everything, and if her grief was muted, her anger was not. Around her at this very moment, all the formal trappings of civilized society were attempting to mask the ugly truth at the heart of today's ceremony: Flint had been ruthlessly murdered.

Bianca glanced over her shoulder and spotted Detectives Puddleworth and Digby lurking in the back pew of the church, keeping an eye on attendees as promised. In her purse Bianca had the shortlist of suspects that Roxy had filched from the border collie's desk. It was an odd list. The three suspects included a sommelier, a zookeeper, and an explorer. For all she knew any or all of them might be sitting here in this very church.

Bianca nudged Roxy with her elbow and whispered: "Swiping that list at the police station was a stroke of genius!"

Roxy gave her a lopsided smirk. "Just promise me you won't use it to do your own investigating. Last night's little adventure ended very badly for you."

"You worry too much, Roxy."

"I took the list to stick it to those two cops, not to help you get into more trouble."

"I'm a grown cat, Roxy. If I want to go looking for trouble there's not much you can do about it."

Roxy grunted her disapproval. "Hey, is Flint around?" she asked.

Bianca gestured to the open coffin.

The alley cat rolled her eyes. "You know what I meant, Princess."

"I haven't heard from him, but who knows where he is—he's invisible. He said something yesterday about ghosts being nocturnal and needing to avoid sunlight, but he also claimed he would come to the church today out of sheer morbid curiosity."

"That sounds like Flint. You know, I'm still pretty freaked out about seeing him yesterday."

"I know the feeling. Hearing his voice was very disturbing at first. Now that I know it really is him, it's a huge relief. I only wish I could throw my arms around him."

"When he does show up you should ask him about the names on the suspect list. I'm sure he'll know who they are. He can tell us if any of them made any recent threats."

"If I tell him about the list, he might get mad at me," Bianca replied. "He was pretty upset about me ending up in the Gowanus Canal yesterday. He doesn't really get the whole nine lives thing."

"Or *maybe* he just wants you to ditch your private eye routine."

With a few latecomers still trickling in, the church was

almost full up. Bianca waited patiently for the service to start, her fingers caressing the tip of her white tail. A sudden murmur went through the crowd behind her. Bianca and Roxy both turned to look over their shoulders, ears alert. All eyes were on an elegant Siamese cat in a strapless gown who had just walked through the doors.

"I don't believe it!" whispered Roxy. "That's Dorothy Kittlebun!"

"The Hollywood actress?" Bianca asked, puzzled. "Are you sure? What is she doing here?"

"Wow! She's even more glamorous in real life than she is on screen," Roxy gushed. "Did Flint know her? Did he ever mention her name?"

"No, never." Bianca had seen several of Kittlebun's films, many of them set in impossibly glamorous European capitals, where she always played opposite dashing leading cats and dogs. The camera adored the charismatic silver screen icon, as did her legions of fans.

"Beats me why she's here," said a voice in Bianca's ear. "I hardly knew her."

Bianca started. "Flint?" she murmured.

"Do you know any other ghosts?"

"Is he here?" hissed Roxy. "Ask him about Dorothy Kittlebun!"

"You two gals sure are doing a lot of whispering," said Tabatha, eyeing them suspiciously.

Bianca and Roxy both smiled innocently.

Flint spoke into Bianca's ear again: "You should probably just nod and shake your head to reply. That way it won't look like you're talking to yourself."

Bianca gave a subtle nod.

"I only met Kittlebun this one time," Flint went on, "at the premiere of her first feature film. But it was a memorable meeting. When she read my review in the evening edition, she flew into a rage and flung a porcelain vase at my head, missing me by a whisker. Then she cursed me out like a sailor and told me to watch my back, that when I least expected it she would get even! Can you imagine?"

Bianca covered her mouth with her hand and said quietly, "What on earth did you write in your review?"

"I was a cub reporter back then, fresh out of journalism school and working for the *Village Express*. I liked the movie well enough—*Plums of Anger* it was called—but Dorothy was terrible in it, and I didn't mince words in pointing that out. Looking back, I'm sure I was horribly unkind. She was absolutely livid. I think she must've been terrified her career would be cut short before it even began."

Flint's explanation only added to the mystery surrounding the movie star's presence as far as Bianca was concerned. She found it curious that the actress had threatened to get even with him someday. Could Dorothy Kittlebun be the kind of cat who believed revenge was a dish best served cold? Detective Puddleworth had insinuated the perpetrator would show up, and maybe she had? Bianca stole another glance over her shoulder. The glamorous Siamese had settled into a center pew, her expression unreadable behind her designer sunglasses. There was no hint of the temperamental personality that had made her famous around the world.

Flint's voice was in her ear once more. "Bianca, I'm gonna

float around. It's not every day you get to eavesdrop at your own funeral!"

She nodded her assent.

Moments later bells rang in the campanile high above them and a heavyset priest appeared out of a small side door. He was an Italian shepherd who was dressed in a simple black cassock, with wispy eyebrows and a kindly bearing. Bianca had never set eyes on him before. Back home she would attend mass with her parents every Sunday, but since she had moved to the city that custom had fallen by the wayside. As far as she knew, Flint hadn't gone in much for church stuff either. And yet here they both were.

The invisible organist fired off a few solemn notes as the priest made his way to the lectern. His raspy voice echoed throughout the church, welcoming them to Our Lady of Sorrento: ". . . to celebrate the life of someone taken from us far too soon." Bianca's eyes settled again on the nearby coffin, and she was hit by an unexpected pang of sorrow. Her eyes welled with tears, but she blinked them back, not wanting to compete with Flint's sister, who was already blubbering. Bianca reminded herself that he wasn't really gone. Not yet at least. Roxy looped an arm through hers and patted her hand.

The ceremony was blissfully short, and it wasn't long before Otis and three other dogs were shouldering the coffin down the aisle. Everyone else fell in line behind them, slowly pouring out onto the street. A black hearse was parked out front and they slid the coffin into the back. The rear doors slammed shut with great finality.

Lined up behind the hearse were three black Lincoln sedans

with gleaming white tires. Mr. Boswell had footed the bill for these cars, intended to ferry a small number of family and friends to the burial. "It's the least we can do, considering the circumstances," the newspaperdog had said. Bianca was very grateful for that, but at the same time, she couldn't help thinking that Flint had almost certainly died because of his job.

Bianca and Roxy stood on the church steps flanked by the alley cat's posse, waiting for Flint's sister, who was receiving condolences from a number of different cats and dogs. The sun was just dipping behind nearby rooftops, creating flares of golden light. Bianca looked around, wondering where Flint had disappeared to. She'd heard nothing from him since their brief conversation before the ceremony. "Flint?" she whispered. "Are you there? Are you coming with us?" But she got no reply. She hadn't even told him yet about the murdered hitdog.

Dorothy Kittlebun was still lingering on the steps outside the church, her slender tail swishing to and fro. A pair of dark-suited huskies were positioned directly behind her, casting steely-eyed stares at anyone who might think to approach her. But if there was one cat who was immune to the scowling huskies it was Roxy. "I think I'll go introduce myself," the alley cat said. "I may never get another chance."

Bianca gave her a sideways look. "I didn't have you pegged as a big Kittlebun fan."

"Are you kidding? She's my favorite actress."

Bianca wondered what Roxy would think about her theory that Dorothy Kittlebun might be the villain behind Flint's murder. She decided it was better not to share her suspicions for now. Bianca trailed Roxy as she wormed her way through a ring of gawkers surrounding the actress. The alley cat went right up to the star and blurted out: "I've seen all your movies at least five times!"

"I'm so glad you enjoyed them," replied the Siamese cat with a dazzling smile. "It's always a pleasure to meet a fan."

Bianca thought the actress sounded phony.

"How did you know Flint?" Roxy asked, having decided on the direct approach.

"Oh, we met long ago at a movie premiere he was covering, and he made a strong impression on me."

I'll bet, thought Bianca.

"I'm Roxy, and this is my friend Bianca," the alley cat said, yanking Bianca forward to meet the star. "Bianca was Flint's fiancée."

"Oh, I'm so sorry, Bianca," said Dorothy, training her hypnotic blue eyes on her. "You must be devastated."

"It hasn't been easy," Bianca replied dryly. "He was murdered, you know."

"I heard a rumor that might be the case, but I wasn't sure if it was true. How awful. Just for doing his job, I imagine? Have they caught whoever did it?"

"The police are still trying to figure out who was behind it," Bianca replied, watching the actress closely.

"They haven't exactly put their best dogs on the job," griped Roxy. The alley cat quickly changed the subject, asking Dorothy about her time filming in Paris. The actress waxed enthusiastic about the city of lights and French cuisine until they were interrupted by the arrival of a glossy red Cadillac. A very apologetic tomcat in a chauffeur hat hopped out and held the door for the movie star. Dorothy Kittlebun excused herself politely and disappeared into the gleaming vehicle with her two bodyguards.

Bianca and Roxy piled into one of the black cars, along with Tabatha. Flint's sister and her husband, and all of Flint's other relatives, commandeered the other two cars. Worryingly, there was still no sign of Flint himself.

They were just about to set off, when a nun came rushing out of the church. Roxy rolled down the car window in response to her gestures, and the nun held up an art deco aquamarine brooch.

"Does this belong to any of you gals or your friends?"

Roxy peered at the brooch and her face lit up. "Oh, yes, that's Sue's brooch. She's been desperate to find it. Don't worry, Sister, I'll get it back to her."

The overly trusting nun handed over the brooch and Roxy thanked her profusely before rolling the window back up. They pulled out into traffic, following the hearse directly ahead of them. Bianca turned to look at Roxy accusingly. "That isn't Sue's brooch, and you know it!"

"Of course not, it's Dorothy Kittlebun's. She was wearing it when she came into the church. She must've dropped it."

"And what do you plan on doing with Kittlebun's extremely expensive-looking aquamarine brooch?"

"Why, return it to her of course! And maybe get a signed photograph for my trouble!"

"How are you going to do that? Do you even know what hotel she's staying in?" Bianca asked skeptically.

"For your information, Dorothy Kittlebun has her own apartment up on Central Park West."

"And how do you know that?"

"My pal Susie does walking tours of celebrities' homes. I've taken the tour for free many times. You and I can head uptown later together and you can put your fancy manners to work charming the doordog so he lets us in."

"I don't think Bianca will be in the mood for celebrity stalking directly after the burial," Tabatha said tactfully.

"What else is she gonna do? Sit at home and mope?"

"Better than getting dragged along on your half-baked celebrity hunt." Bianca scowled, pretending to be annoyed, although the truth was she would welcome the chance for another chat with Dorothy Kittlebun. She could look that cat in the eyes and ask her if she was still bitter about Flint's movie review, after all these years.

19 · Flint Lockford: The Ex-Girlfriend

If Flint had thought showing up to his own funeral would be amusing, he was sorely mistaken. Seeing his open coffin at the foot of the altar turned out to be a jarring experience, and having to witness his sister's histrionics was no picnic either. He did his best to set aside his qualms as he roamed around the church, listening in on conversations among his friends and relatives, which mostly seemed to involve mundane matters that had nothing to do with him.

He was wandering down the right-hand aisle when he spied a Shiba Inu sitting demurely on the outer edge of a pew. He stared at her, dumbfounded. There could be no mistake, it really was her. But why was she here? Riyo Jones had short red fur, an elongated face with pointy ears, and a curly tail. She was wearing her summer stewardess uniform: a matching robin's-egg blue jacket and skirt, a white blouse with a notched collar, and a pillbox hat. The famed golden wings were pinned to her lapel.

Flint couldn't believe his ex had shown up to his funeral. They had been a serious item for a year, their relationship constituting a dizzying roller-coaster ride of epic highs and lows. Briefly, he'd been convinced she was the one, and had even made the mistake of proposing. Then, barely a week after announcing their engagement, he'd been rummaging through her suitcase in search of a bottle of flea repellent, when he'd come across a mysterious package wrapped in brown paper. Giving in to curiosity he had undone the wrapping only to find himself holding a bright-blue ceramic figurine of a monkey. Riyo had recently returned from a trip to Cairo and he'd known instantly that it was no tourist souvenir. It looked suspiciously old, like the kind of thing that might have been looted from an Egyptian burial site and smuggled out of the country by—say—an unscrupulous stewardess? When he'd confronted Riyo, the truth had come out. She had a lucrative side gig going. Being an attractive Blue Cat Airlines stewardess was the perfect cover for sneaking stolen artworks and antiquities past customs. To make matters worse, Flint had loaned her a bundle of cash before the trip. "Tell me you didn't pay for this monkey figurine with the money I gave you?" he demanded to know.

"You're such a square!" she'd snapped in response.

"And you are a crook!" he'd replied sternly. Things had only escalated from there, and their engagement had gone to pieces. He'd refused to give the figurine back to her, since she'd paid for it with his money, and she had been furious with him. He still remembered the last words she had screamed before storming out the door: "Fine! Keep the damn monkey! I'm keeping the ring! And don't even think about ever marrying anyone else! If you do, I'll *murder* you!" The thought of Riyo crossing paths with Bianca in the church made Flint deeply uneasy. A run-in with his crazy ex-girlfriend was the last thing she needed right now. Besides which, he had never told Bianca about her.

Flint followed Riyo when she got up to go pay her respects

in front of the open casket. She knelt down and crossed herself, staring at his frozen visage, a hint of a smile on her lips. When she was done she walked past the front pew, and her eyes flicked toward Bianca. Flint was terrified that she was going to stop and introduce herself, but thankfully she kept walking.

The funeral proceeded without incident. His sister regurgitated a string of misremembered childhood anecdotes for the eulogy, intended to tug at the heartstrings but falling flat. Thankfully Otis set things right by stepping up to the lectern and saying some very touching things about him. Throughout the service Flint found himself fretting over Riyo's presence. Was it possible she held some fond memories of him in spite of their ugly breakup? Or was there some more nefarious explanation for her presence?

He thought back to the Egyptian monkey statue. It was still sitting on his bookshelf in his apartment since he'd never figured out how to get rid of it without getting himself in trouble. Surely it was worth even more money on the black market now. He wondered if Riyo would try and retrieve the statue now that he was gone. Then an even more alarming thought hit him: What if Riyo had found out about his imminent engagement to Bianca and decided to make good on her threat from all those years ago?

After the funeral Flint found himself at a crossroads. The plan had been to hitch a ride to the cemetery with Bianca but he had a sudden impulse to stick close to his ex-girlfriend and find out her secrets. This was the big upside to being a ghost: he could follow her anywhere and she would never know he was there.

Riyo Jones was already strolling away down the sidewalk.

He felt terrible about leaving Bianca's side, but after the discomfort of witnessing his own funeral, he had no desire to be present at the burial. Flint considered stopping to whisper goodbye in Bianca's ear, even though she was surrounded by other cats. But what could he say? *My ex-fiancée showed up to the funeral and is acting suspicious?* Besides, he didn't want to risk setting Bianca off after the madness of last night. It was better to just leave her in the dark until he knew something definite. Flint hurried to catch up to Riyo Jones.

"I had no idea there'd be such a crowd for Lockford's funeral," said Detective Puddleworth, who was seated next to his partner in the very last pew of Our Lady of Sorrento.

"And a genuine Hollywood celebrity in attendance to boot," Morton replied in a hushed voice.

"With this many mourners it's very hard to scope out suspects," complained the Scottie. "This could be a waste of time. Maybe we should head back to the precinct?"

"Hold on, J.B.," said Morton. "Take a look at that tuxedo over there." Morton pointed with his snout to a cat about halfway up the aisle, over to their right. This cat had a bright-pink nose and a characteristic splash of white fur on his neck and chin. The oxblood velvet smoking jacket he was wearing stood out in a sea of black. "If that cat isn't Gustave Legrand, our crooked sommelier, I'll eat my hat," Morton proclaimed.

The Scottie's ears stood at attention as he scrutinized this cat. He sniffed the air inquisitively. "I can smell a trace of wine on his breath from here. You know, Morton, I do believe you're onto something."

Morton seriously doubted the Scottie's nose was that prodigious, but he kept a straight face. "I can tail him when he leaves," Morton volunteered. "See what I can find out."

"Not a chance! I'll do the tailing!" the Scottie said

enthusiastically. "I've studied all the advanced techniques for shadowing a suspect, and I'm eager to put them into practice. The secret is to move from lamppost to lamppost and throw in an occasional mailbox for cover—that way you'll remain invisible if they happen to glance over their shoulder. At the same time, you need to stick to them like glue so they don't drop out of sight!"

"Maybe we should both follow him?" Morton suggested.

Detective Puddleworth harrumphed. "Don't be ridiculous, Morton. He's much more likely to spot us if we both go after him."

Morton sighed. He had a feeling the Scottie wasn't going to budge. They kept a close eye on the tuxedo cat, and about halfway through the funeral service the tux checked his watch, slunk out of his pew during a loud hymn, and ducked out of the church early. Detective Puddleworth went out right after him, telling Morton he would rendezvous with him back at the precinct.

Morton found himself sitting alone in the back of the church, worried that his partner, who was still new to the City and unfamiliar with its many dangers, was going to get himself into a pickle. They were partners, and partners were supposed to stick together. With no one around to watch his back, things could go badly for the Scottie if he was discovered.

Morton got to his feet and slipped out of the church. Detective Puddleworth was still in sight and Morton took off after him, keeping about thirty yards behind the Scottish terrier, whose short tail was wagging back and forth with excitement. Detective Puddleworth made a right on Sixth Avenue heading south and Morton kept pace with him, employing the standard trick of stopping to tie his shoe when the gap between them narrowed. The Scottie was so intent on shadowing his own target that he never bothered to look back. In the distance Morton caught glimpses of the cat in the burgundy jacket.

Detective Puddleworth crossed Houston Street and Morton did the same. At Prince Street the Scottish terrier made a left. Peering around the corner, Morton saw his partner stopped in front of a restaurant facade. Presumably the tuxedo had disappeared into the interior. Morton hoped the Scottish terrier wouldn't be dumb enough to go inside on his own, but moments later he watched as Detective Puddleworth did just that.

Morton hurried over to the restaurant. The sign on the awning read: CHEZ CLAUDE'S. That settled the question of whether the cat was Gustave Legrand. It was also clear that the tuxedo had nursed enough of a grudge to make him show up to gloat at Flint Lockford's funeral. What kind of twisted animal did something like that?

The restaurant had a menu encased in glass outside the door and Morton pretended to study it. A well-dressed elderly couple came along and went in, joining a smattering of early diners already inside. Peeking through the front window, Morton caught a glimpse of a tux in a burgundy jacket behind the wood bar that ran along one edge of the room. Sitting at that same bar was a Scottie in a pinstripe suit.

Taking a deep breath, Morton snuck in behind another group of diners, hung his trilby on the hat rack next to the Scottie's fedora, and told the maître d' he just wanted a drink at the bar. He sat down two stools over from the Scottish terrier, with a large tan-and-black mutt seated on the stool between them. The maître d' and the waiters at the restaurant were all tuxes as well, leading Morton to believe this bistro was a family-run business.

The sommelier approached Morton. "What can I get for you, sir?"

"Just a ginger ale, thanks," Morton replied in a low voice, shielding his face behind the wine menu.

The tuxedo regarded him disdainfully, as if he had just asked for a glass of lukewarm tap water. But the cat dutifully plopped a soda on ice down in front of him before returning to check in with his more discerning guests, such as Detective Puddleworth, who was savoring a glass of red wine. Morton's ears twitched in their direction when the sommelier asked the Scottie how he liked their house wine.

"It's excellent!" the Scottie replied enthusiastically. Morton eyed the pale ruby liquid in his partner's glass dubiously.

"I'm glad you like it." The tuxedo smiled a wide toothy smile, polishing an empty glass with his bar towel.

"You seem like a fella who knows a lot about wine," the Scottish terrier inquired casually.

"I am a licensed sommelier!" the tuxedo cat replied proudly, puffing out his chest and tugging at his whiskers. "I know as much about fine wine as any cat in the City."

"Maybe you could help me, then. My cousin is getting married next week," said the Scottie, "and they've put me in charge of the refreshments. What would you recommend I pick up?"

"Well, if it's for a wedding I'd say the most important

thing is procuring champagne! You wouldn't want to disappoint the bride."

"You're right about that. She's bound to expect some bubbly for toasts."

"How large is this wedding?" asked the sommelier.

"About a hundred guests."

"And what's your budget for libations?"

"That's the thing, I would like to get my paws on the good stuff, but I'm not a wealthy dog."

"This might be your lucky day! I happen to have some extra cases of champagne. Top-of-the-line bottles of Don Chapeaux—the good stuff, as you say. I ordered too many by mistake and they're clogging up our storeroom. I'd be happy to let you have a few at a bargain price, just to free up some space."

"Don Chapeaux? That stuff is like liquid gold. I don't think my wallet will stretch that far," replied the Scottie, and Morton had to admire the way his partner was stringing the tux along.

"Take my word for it, sir, if you show up at the wedding with cases of off-brand bubbly, your cousin will never forgive you. Besides, I haven't even told you the price. Normally three cases would go around two hundred and fifty dollars. But you've caught me in a generous mood, and I'd be willing to knock a hundred bucks off that price."

"Three cases of Don Chapeaux for one fifty?"

"What do you say? Do we have a deal?"

"Oh, I don't know. I mean, can most guests even tell the difference?"

"An excellent question! Shall we do a quick taste test?

I have some open bottles of each." The sommelier reached behind the bar and pulled out two different bottles, setting them on the counter. He placed two champagne flutes in front of the Scottie.

Morton stared at the bottles from over the top of his menu. They were the same size and weight, but the one with the white and gold Don Chapeaux label announced itself to be premium brut, while the other was definitely cheap sparkling wine. Detective Puddleworth took a sip from each glass and exclaimed loudly: "Wow! The difference between these two bottles is night and day!"

Gustave Legrand beamed. "Tiny bubbles. That's the secret. They go right up your nose."

"And you say you can spare three cases?"

"If you've got the cash on you, we can load them right into the trunk of a cab for you. I mean, you'd be doing us a favor, really."

"Well, I'd have to take a look at them first—make sure this is all above board."

"Why don't you follow me to the back room, sir, and I'll show you the cases!"

Morton took a sip from his ginger ale and watched uneasily as the sommelier disappeared through a swinging door, followed by his darned fool of a partner. A more seasoned City detective would never put themselves in a dicey situation like that.

Thankfully there was a restroom sign above the doorway they had just passed through, so Morton needed no excuse to follow them. Detective Puddleworth might be furious with him when he saw him, but that was preferable to his partner getting injured or worse. Morton glimpsed the Scottie and the tux at the end of a corridor with their backs to him. The bathroom door was about halfway down the hallway, but just past it there was another door, slightly ajar, that had a mop handle sticking out. Morton's eyes lit up—a broom closet was just what he needed. He slipped silently into the darkened interior and was hit by a powerful odor of bleach. Putting his eye up to the sliver of light between the hinges, he gained a narrow view of the hallway outside. The sommelier had disappeared momentarily into a storeroom, but emerged moments later with three cases of booze loaded onto a hand truck. The white boxes were stamped with the foiled Don Chapeaux branding.

"Here you go, sir! Three cases, just as promised!" came the sommelier's oily voice.

"I don't mean to sound mistrustful," said the Scottie. "But could you open one of the boxes so I can take a look? Why don't you pull out a bottle from that bottom case?"

Through the crack in the door, Morton watched the tuxedo remove a green bottle from the bottommost case for the Scottie to inspect. Detective Puddleworth examined the label closely. "Looks like we've got a deal," he said with feigned enthusiasm. "My cousin will be thrilled!" He stuck out a hand. "J.B. Puddleworth is the name."

The beaming sommelier was quick to grip his paw. "Gustave Legrand. You're robbing me blind here!"

"I'm not sure I would go that far," said the detective, tugging his jacket open to reveal the gold police badge clipped to his belt. "City Police. I'm arresting you on charges of selling counterfeit luxury goods." The Scottie had a handcuff on the tuxedo's wrist before the stunned cat was fully aware that his deal had gone south.

"Hey! What's the big idea! You can't do this to me!" protested the aggrieved sommelier.

Detective Puddleworth twisted the cat's other arm around behind his back and cuffed his other wrist. "Anything you say can and will be used against you."

"You're making a big mistake, pal!" snarled the sommelier, his tail puffing up.

"Save it for the judge." The Scottie tucked one of the fake bottles under his arm and turned to make his way back down the hallway with the handcuffed cat, but he found his path blocked by two angry-looking tuxedos, one of them in a waiter's uniform brandishing a heavy water jug, and the other wearing a kitchen apron with a gleaming meat cleaver in his hand.

"You're not going anywhere with our cousin, copper!" the chef said threateningly. Both cats had their ears flattened back and their teeth bared. The chef hissed as he took a step toward the Scottish terrier.

"Out of my way!" Detective Puddleworth growled. "Interfering with the duties of an officer of the law is a serious offense!"

"Get him, lads!" hissed the sommelier. "Dead dogs tell no tales!"

Detective Puddleworth waved the fake bottle in front of him as the two cats advanced on him with their weapons raised.

Morton crept out of the closet and snuck up behind them,

a mop clutched in his hands. He was absolutely petrified at the prospect of a physical altercation. He had never been in a fight in his whole life, preferring to avoid confrontation whenever possible. But he hoped that the element of surprise would be enough to win the day. Gritting his teeth, Morton swung the mop handle as hard as he could. He landed a direct hit and the tuxedo in the apron dropped the meat cleaver and slumped to the floor. The startled waiter wheeled around to face him but Detective Puddleworth yanked him back by the tail and clobbered him with the champagne bottle.

The two tuxedos lay in a heap on the floor. Panting heavily, Morton looked up into the eyes of a grinning Detective Puddleworth.

"Morton! Am I ever happy to see you!" the Scottie exclaimed. "You showed up in the nick of time! It seems I got myself into a spot of trouble!"

"You should know better than to run off without your partner," Morton chastised him.

"It's a lesson I won't soon forget! How the heck did you manage to tail me here without me noticing? Did you use my lamppost technique?"

"Keep an eye on that one!" Morton warned, pointing at Gustave Legrand, who had been inching away from them while they talked.

Detective Puddleworth reached out a hand and grabbed the sommelier by his jacket collar. "No more nonsense from you, got it?" The Scottie held up his bottle menacingly. "Haven't you caused enough trouble already?"

"I take it these cases are full of fake champagne?" Morton asked his partner.

"Oh yes. The labels are real enough, but if you look closely the foil on the neck of the bottle is all wrong, as are the identification marks etched on the base. They've been peeling labels off empty bottles of the good stuff and slapping them on the cheap bottles of sparkling wine."

Morton nudged open the door to the storage room with his foot. Row after row of Don Chapeaux boxes were stacked six feet high along the wall. A tub of glue and a pile of steamed-off labels were on a small table.

Detective Puddleworth stared over his shoulder in amazement. "Whoa! This is a large-scale operation! They must be shipping cases of fake champagne to restaurants all over town. Handcuff those two cats before they wake up, would you, Morton? I'll telephone the station and get some patroldogs down here right away."

Ten minutes later there were two police cars and a police truck outside the restaurant. All the counterfeit cases were eventually loaded up into the truck, while the dazed tuxedo cats were steered into the back seat of squad cars. The sommelier let fly with a colorful tirade about the police as he was placed in the back seat, a moment that was captured on film by none other than Otis, the *Gazette* photographer.

Detective Puddleworth was only too happy to answer a few questions from Miss Penelope Flick, who was still dressed in all black. "Oh yes, this is a major fraud bust for us," declared the Scottie. "It seems these cats have been swindling citizens out of their hard-earned cash for years."

The gray tabby flipped the page in her notebook. "What tipped you off to their operation?"

"We were actually investigating the sommelier in

connection with a separate case," replied Detective Puddle-worth. "We consider him an animal of interest in the murder of Flint Lockford."

"Is that so?" Penelope Flick's pretty green eyes fixed menacingly on the tuxedo in the back of the squad car. She scribbled away furiously as the Scottie filled her in on the suspect's background.

21 · Tatiana Val: The Graveyard

After fleeing Ghosthall, Tatiana Valova found herself standing in the blazing sunlight not knowing which way to turn. The fierce heat beat down on her, seeming to increase in intensity until it began to resemble fiery pin pricks on her exposed hands, neck, and face. Desperate for shade, Val rounded the corner of the building and drifted into the deep shadows of the clocktower. The effects of the sunlight began to subside.

After a brief respite, Val drifted west along 10th Street, aiming to put some distance between herself and the ghost-filled courthouse. Val had been shocked to run into Flint Lockford moments ago. Staying under the same roof as the wolfhound's ghost was a bad idea. On top of which, they had demanded to poke through her duffel bag. There was no way that was going to happen.

As she floated down the sidewalk, Val had more questions than answers. Were there any other ghosts roaming the city whose deaths she was responsible for? Perhaps even some who were looking for payback? Was that why Flint's ghost had stuck around? But her biggest question of all was—what was *she* still doing here?

The gunshot inside the bank had obliterated her dreams of starting over in California. And now her poor mother had been left all alone in the world. She would probably live out her days in their cramped apartment, without her daughter there to help her. Everything she had worked for all those years had been snatched away in an instant. Not that she had any right to feel sorry for herself, considering how many lives she had ended with a bullet.

Val wandered aimlessly through the West Village, hurrying through sunlit intersections, but dawdling while in the shadows. She could see now why Professor Chumley had made so much use of his umbrella. She would have to get her paws on one soon. She became hopelessly lost in the maze of narrow streets, and it wasn't until she glimpsed the Hudson River up ahead that she finally oriented herself. Looking to avoid the sunny riverside esplanade, she turned around, and only then did she become aware of the two ghosts coming up behind her on the sidewalk. At a glance they looked like common street thugs, and they had their eyes fixed on her.

Val spun back around only to discover that a third spook was closing in from that side as well. He was a ghostly tomcat in a frayed baseball cap. "Where ya headed, sweet-cakes?" he asked her with a toothy grin.

"Nowhere." She made to cross to the opposite sidewalk but they swooped in to block her path.

"Nowhere? Well, then you're headed the wrong way!" said the tomcat.

"We'd be happy to point you in the right direction," sneered a mutt in a stained blue T-shirt. "For a fee!" The three ghosts hooted with laughter.

"That duffel bag looks awfully heavy for a pretty pooch like you," added the tomcat. "Why don't you let us lighten your load!"

"You're such a gentleman." The other mutt laughed. "What do you s'pose she's got stashed in there?"

"It's stuffed full of crisp one-hundred-dollar bank notes!" snarled Val. "More money than you've ever set eyes on in life or in death."

"Fine," said the mutt in the blue shirt. "You don't have to tell us if you don't want. We'll find out soon enough anyway."

"So long as you play nice," said the tomcat, "there's no need for this to end in tears!"

The third ghost made a grab for her bag, but Val pulled it out of reach. Turning, she leapt through the solid brick wall at her back. She found herself in an overgrown garden enclosed on three sides. She dashed through bushes and flowerbeds filled with towering sunflowers toward the wall on the opposite end. The three ghosts were already on her tail. The tomcat reached out and grabbed hold of her blouse, but she shook him off and darted left, plowing once more through red bricks and back out onto a side street. Judging by their smirking faces and the way they were zipping along, she soon realized the ghosts were toying with her. They knew the lay of the land and were much quicker with their movements thanks to their umbrellas. But she knew of one spot where she might be safe from them. Val dodged another outstretched hand and jumped into a patch of sunshine in the middle of the road.

"Whoa! What's the big idea, toots?" exclaimed the tomcat. "You can't stand out in the sunlight like that!" The three ghosts stopped short at the shadow line, staring at her, perplexed. "You don't even have an umbrella, you loony hound!"

The large mutt angled his patchwork umbrella between

himself and the sun and moved in her direction. He reached out a large paw and grabbed hold of her shoulder. "Gotcha!"

Val used some of the hand-to-hand combat training she'd learned in the service, twisting his arm around and putting pressure on his elbow. She snatched his umbrella from his hands and gave him a swift kick to send him tumbling away from her.

"I guess we're gonna do this the hard way!" said the smaller mutt, still standing in the shadows. They were no longer smiling.

"Time for the gloves to come off!" growled the tomcat. "Remember, you brought this on yourself!"

Val was about to turn and flee when a blue Chevy turned the corner and headed in their direction. Moments later as the car drove right through her, she dove into the trunk, yelling, "Thanks for the umbrella, jackass!" over her shoulder. Expecting darkness, she was surprised to find the trunk lit up by her own luminous figure, revealing a cluttered mess of old vacuum cleaners all around her. Filthy hands reached into the trunk to grab her, but she smacked them away and the car sped off down the street. Val squeezed through the wall of the trunk into an empty back seat and stared out through the rear window at the three angry ghosts shaking their fists at her as they receded in the distance. She'd been lucky this time—the professor was right about the dangers she would face out on the streets.

An Irish setter in a beige suit was at the wheel muttering to himself. Judging from the number of vacuum brushes, filters, and telescopic tubes strewn about the car, Val pegged him as a door-to-door salesdog. He was probably on his way to his next house call. She was content to sit back and let herself be driven around, but it wasn't long before the car stopped and backed into a parking spot. The salesdog hopped out, grabbed a vacuum cleaner from the trunk, and straightened his tie before ringing a nearby doorbell.

Left alone in blissful silence, Val slid into the front seat and stared out at the city through the windshield. The street sign on the corner read CARMINE STREET, and something jogged in her memory. She remembered what it was when her gaze landed on a church cupola down the block. Why had she ended up here of all places?

Val spent the next few minutes going over all the reasons why she couldn't go anywhere near that church. But she was experiencing an unexpected and novel emotion—shame. She had started out her career fighting bad guys overseas. When she had returned home from the war her targets became local thugs—a rogue's gallery of scoundrels and crooks. But somewhere along the line she had become the very thing she had set out to fight—a killer of innocents.

There was no way to undo what she had done. But she could confront her mistakes head-on and face the truth about the life she'd chosen. Having come to a decision, Val slipped out of the car and glided in the direction of the church, using the stolen umbrella to cross through a patch of sunlight. She arrived just in time to see Flint Lockford's coffin being carried out of the church and loaded into a hearse. She stopped on the shaded sidewalk on the opposite side of the street, struck by the large number of mourners and the genuine expressions of sorrow on many of their faces. Val hung her head, her shaggy tail drooping low to the ground.

She spotted Bianca standing in a black dress on the sun-lit steps, surrounded by alley cats. Then Val caught sight of Flint, and she shrank deeper into the shadows. She was baffled to see him disappear down the sidewalk. He must have changed his mind about going to the burial.

Val slipped into the trunk of the last black car just as the line of vehicles set off after the hearse. She needed to see this through to the end. The solemn procession drove across town and over a bridge before winding its way through the city of Brooklyn. When they eventually came to a stop, Val emerged from the vehicle and took stock of her surroundings. They were parked near a grassy hilltop, and around them graves stretched out in every direction. The hazy city skyline was visible in the distance, seemingly a world away. Val used her stolen umbrella to fend off the last ribbons of sunlight as she followed the handful of mourners threading their way past carved statues and stone obelisks as they headed up the hill. At the top Val melted into the shadows of a large tree and watched as two gravediggers used ropes to lower the coffin into an open grave. A dozen or so cats and dogs stood by with heads bowed as a somber Bianca scattered the first handful of dirt into Flint's grave.

22 · Flint Lockford: The Hotel

Flint followed Riyo Jones as she left the church and walked the short block over to Sixth Avenue. Stepping off the curb, she flagged down a taxi and he slipped in beside her onto the back seat. "The Biltmore Hotel," Riyo instructed the cabbie. Flint had occasionally conducted interviews at the Biltmore's fashionable Palm Court. It wasn't the glitziest hotel in town, but it was a world away from the typical airport crash pads that stewardesses typically stayed in. The airline wouldn't be picking up the tab for her stay at the Biltmore, that was for sure, which meant that Riyo was probably funding her high-flying lifestyle in other ways.

Flint stuck close to Riyo as she entered the hotel and strode through the carpeted lobby toward the elevator banks. But as he was stepping onto the elevator with her, he was seized roughly from behind and dragged back. "Hey! Let go of me!" he demanded, attempting to shake off the two heavy-set ghosts who had grabbed hold of him, but the pair held him firmly in their grip.

A tailless Manx in a tailored suit came up to him and stuck his snout right in Flint's face. "Thought you could just sneak in, did you?" snarled the Manx in a high-pitched voice. "This is the Biltmore, pal. You can't just waltz in like you own the place!"

"Yeah, what's the big idea!" growled one of the dogs holding him.

"What do you have to say for yourself, buddy?" demanded the Manx.

"I'm sorry," Flint replied. "I had no idea you guys ran this place."

The Manx frowned. "What are you? A newbie? Did you just kick the bucket?"

"Yesterday," admitted Flint.

"Are you looking to join up? 'Cos if that's the case—"

"I'm already a lodger at a place down in Greenwich Village."

"What's it called?"

"Ghosthall."

The Manx's scowl disappeared. "Ghosthall? Do you know Professor Chumley?"

"Chumley? Of course. The professor has been showing me the ropes."

"That squares," said one of the dogs. "He's got a Ghosthall patch on his jacket!"

"Well, why didn't you say you were a friend of the professor!" cried the Manx. "Let go of him, lads!" The hands released him and smoothed his jacket apologetically. "Any friend of Chumley's is a friend of mine! The professor and I go way back. What's your name?" The Manx was all smiles.

"Lockford. Flint Lockford."

"What brings you to the Biltmore, Flint, if you don't mind me asking?"

"I was following this dog I used to know. An ex-girlfriend of mine."

One of the mutts snorted. "He's just some perv, peeping on an old flame!"

Flint glared at him. "That's not it at all! I think she may be connected to my murder."

"So you're haunting this Shiba Inu, then, are ya?" asked the Manx.

"No, that's not it either. I'm not a haunter. I just had this feeling she's up to no good."

"Wait a second!" cried one of the dogs, peering excitedly at Flint. "Did you say 'Lockford'? Aren't you the guy who got crushed by a piano? The journalist?"

They were all staring at him now.

"Yep, that was me."

"No way! Best death ever, man!" said the Manx. "And you think it was murder?"

"Pretty sure, yeah. And like I said, I think that Shiba I was following might be involved somehow."

"I see." The Manx tugged on his whiskers thoughtfully. "Well, that's your business. You're the talk of the town these past two days, Flint! I want you to make yourself at home. Anything you need, just ask."

"Thanks. But all I really want is to find out her room number. I have no idea where she went."

"What's her name? We can just ask Stanley at the front desk. Easiest thing in the world."

Riyo was staying in room 945. Flint rode the elevator up to the ninth floor along with a half dozen living tourists. He followed the arrows as he stepped out, drifting down a long carpeted hallway. When he found her room he pushed right through the door, and it didn't occur to him until he was already inside that he was starting to think of closed doors differently than he used to.

Riyo's room was comfortably furnished with a plush queen-sized bed, a smooth walnut coffee table, a dresser, and a desk. Riyo had kicked off her shoes and was sprawled on the bed flipping through a glossy magazine. Flint floated around the room looking to see if any items lying in plain sight might offer up any useful clues to her life, but all he saw was a receipt for her dinner from the night before, and a recent boarding pass from an incoming flight originating in Athens.

Flint made a hasty retreat back out to the hallway when Riyo began unbuttoning her blouse. He might be the only ghost in the city who had qualms about spying on the living in the buff, but he had no intention of changing who he was just because he was dead.

Killing time outside her room it occurred to him that Riyo might be showering, in which case he would be stuck out here for a while. But just then the door opened and Riyo appeared, wrapped in a green and orange striped cover-up, the outlines of a white one-piece bathing suit visible underneath. She marched boldly over to the elevator bank.

Two middle-aged Airedale terriers were standing in the back of the elevator when the doors opened, a married couple from the looks of it. The husband gawked at Riyo when she stepped on, earning him an elbow in the ribs from his spouse. Riyo took no notice of either of them. She got off on the second floor and followed signs for the Turkish baths. This turned out to be a lavish blue-tiled pool bordered by an ornate gold railing. Steaming water cascaded into the pool from gold spouts set high in the wall. Flint let out a low whistle. He had no clue this little oasis existed smack dab in the center of the humming metropolis.

A spotted dog in a white jacket was circling the pool, bringing fresh towels and taking drink orders for the half dozen lounging guests. Riyo started off with a quick dip in the pool, and then spent the better part of an hour relaxing on a slatted wooden lounge chair while she tackled the *Gazette*'s crossword puzzle. As the minutes ticked by, Flint began to wonder what he was doing there. Poor Bianca was probably standing by his grave at this very moment. And yet he couldn't bring himself to leave. His gut was telling him that Riyo's presence at his funeral spelled trouble.

After successfully completing the puzzle she took another short swim. Climbing out of the pool, Riyo shook herself before stepping into a nearby dryer booth. Then she put on her cover-up and made her way back upstairs. Flint stopped short at the door to her room and waited a few minutes. When he heard the phone ring on the other side of the door, he decided to risk it, passing into the room. Thankfully she was fully clothed, looking set for a night out on the town in a strapless purple silk dress. She had always looked good in purple, a color that set off her orange fur perfectly.

Riyo was speaking into the receiver: "You're on your way? Great. I'll see you in twenty minutes down in the tea room. Yes, under the clock." She hung up. Flint wondered who it was she was meeting. Some underworld contact perhaps? Or could it be some hapless paramour who had no idea what he was getting himself into?

A short while later the phone rang again. This time Riyo's

tone was sharper. "Yes, it's me! Of course I have something for you. I leave for Rome tomorrow night so I'll stop by your gallery in the afternoon. What do I have for you? Classical Athenian coins, magnificent pieces, three silver and three gold. One of them has a depiction of the goddess Athena with an owl on the flip side. You'd better have cash on hand. What? No, I don't have anything else! Well I'm sorry you're disappointed! Haven't you heard? There's a crackdown on looted antiquities. Getting anything bigger than coins through customs is risky right now." Flint heard the sound of squawking from the receiver and outrage was written all over Riyo's face. "That's it? That barely covers what I paid for them in Athens!" She switched the receiver to her other ear. "Okay, look. What if I told you I could get my hands on an ancient Egyptian figurine. A blue glazed ceramic monkey. About four inches tall and in excellent condition. You could easily move a piece like that for seven figures in today's market." Flint heard more chirping from the receiver and Riyo's face lit up. "Now you're talking. No, I don't have my paws on it yet, but I know just where to find it. I'll see you tomorrow."

She hung up.

Flint felt vindicated that his suspicions had been justified. It sounded like she was planning to break into his apartment and steal back the statuette. Had this been her plan all along? Bump him off and grab the monkey? Flint knew of cats and dogs who'd been killed for a lot less, but he still wasn't convinced Riyo was that kind of pooch.

But moments later he revised his opinion of her as he watched her dump the contents of her black purse on the bed. There amidst the pile of hair pins, combs, lipstick, crumpled dollar bills, and loose change was a small gun. She picked up the pocket pistol and weighed it in the palm of her hand before dropping it and all her other junk into a gold purse that better matched her dress.

A stunned Flint muttered: "Yowza! I really dodged a bullet when we split up."

Riyo rode the elevator down to the Palm Court, a purple beret and purple pumps completing her outfit. She cut through the busy tea room and cats and dogs alike moved aside to let her by, their heads turning to follow her as she sashayed over to the clock.

Looking up at the iconic timepiece, Flint saw that it was already seven thirty. He needed to go check on Bianca, but before he left he wanted to see who Riyo was meeting up with. He expected it would be a downtown businesscat, or some Madison Avenue ad guy, or perhaps even a gullible doctor. Flint certainly wasn't expecting to see the familiar face that sauntered up and touched noses with Riyo. He recognized this wire fox terrier. Arthur Neverest was a stocky white dog with ratty eyes, a long muzzle, and folded ears. Flint had written an exposé about him after learning that Neverest was passing himself off as an intrepid explorer among the jet set, when in reality he had never traveled anywhere truly exotic. His tales of exploring the heart of the African continent were pure fabrications extrapolated from a brief day trip to Tangiers from the south of Spain. Flint peered at him curiously. It made a strange sort of sense that his crooked ex-girlfriend and this upper-crust con artist had found each other. And for all he knew they might *both* be in on his murder.

"How was the track today?" Riyo asked the wiry terrier.

"My horse placed first in the fifth race! Twenty to one odds. I made a tidy sum!" Arthur beamed. "Take my word for it—inside information is the key to a successful gambling operation!"

"Sounds like you can afford to treat me to a nice dinner."

"What do you have in mind?" asked the fox terrier with some trepidation.

She hung a finger from her lips, carefully considering her reply. "I bet we can snag a table at Lutece if we hurry."

Some things never changed, Flint thought wryly. Leave it to Riyo to pick one of the most expensive restaurants in town. For his part, the fox terrier managed to turn his grimace into something that passed for a smile.

23 · Tatiana Val: The Shotgun

The black car rolled over the Manhattan Bridge and eased to a stop at a traffic light. Val poked her head up through the trunk and immediately recognized the familiar landmarks of Delancey Street. She shimmied up and out of the car. Twilight was enveloping the city as she floated south toward Grand Street, instinctively heading for home. Part of her wanted to check in on her mother and maybe whisper some reassuring words in her ear. But by now her mom was sure to have learned all about her daughter's criminal history, a secret Val had guarded diligently for years. The cat was out of the bag. Her mother was a deeply religious dog and the news that her only child was a professional assassin was sure to have filled her with a deep sense of shame, perhaps even revulsion.

When Val reached the intersection with Grand Street she hesitated for a moment before turning right, away from her old home. She needed to find somewhere to stash her duffel bag full of ghostly cash before she ran into another troublesome gang. Briefly she considered hiding it in one of the many nearby tenements, but there were too many hollow-eyed ghosts lurking in the doorways and windows of these old buildings, timid and barefoot shades dressed in smocks and bowler hats that harkened back to an earlier time.

Val's next thought was to conceal the duffel bag under a

manhole cover on a dark side street, but she quickly dismissed this notion too, worried that someone would see her. Inspiration finally struck as she walked past the Bowery Savings Bank, a palatial building with soaring Roman columns framing the entrance. Was it crazy to hide her money in a bank? She went around to the back of the building and saw nothing but solid stone walls. When she was sure no one was watching she sunk back into the wall, the green duffel bag tucked under her arm. It took an uncomfortably long time to push her way through dense layers of stone, rock, and cement. Making it through to the other side, she arrived at an empty hallway lit by fluorescent lamps. It was quiet, with no hint of either the living or the dead. A preliminary inspection showed no signs of a vault. Maybe it was underground?

Following her hunch, Val dove into the floor, a move she had never attempted before. She passed right through it no differently than a wall and her head poked through the ceiling of an enormous vault. She pulled herself the rest of the way down and dropped slowly to the floor. All around her were piles of cash and coins stacked on rolling shelves. She tried to grab a solid gold bar but her hands went right through it. Only ghost money meant anything anymore. Val unzipped her bag and put one brick of ghostly cash in her left jacket pocket and another brick of cash in her right jacket pocket. Then she tucked the duffel bag into a nook up on a high shelf, far from prying eyes.

Val's next stop was the Delancey Market. She knew that the only way to make amends was to help Bianca, and the best way to help Bianca was to uncover the identity of the mysterious Mister X. With any luck, the Delancey Market butcher would have some idea who he was. A day ago Val would have regarded this line of inquiry into her client's background as a breach of her professional code, but her views had shifted dramatically now that she was dead.

It was just past eight o'clock when she arrived at the corner of Delancey and Essex. The Market had only just closed to the public. Val pushed boldly through the locked doors and into the gloomy interior. A bored-looking feline in a dirty apron was pushing a mop and bucket around on grimy tile floors. A few other stragglers among the living were still wiping down counters and bundling up their stock for the night.

But the place was crawling with ghosts. Sketchy-looking phantasms who eyed her with crooked grins and beady eyes. Val made her way along the Market's familiar aisles. Most of these ghosts were fellas, but there were a few hard-edged gals peppered among them. Val wasn't surprised. She had been expecting the Market to be teeming with former criminals like herself.

Mutterings from this rabble trailed her as she strolled deeper into the Market. Val overheard one hound say: "What's with this crazy dame in the green suit?" But none of them challenged her directly, they were content to simply follow her as she made her way to the butcher shop along the back wall, in the very heart of the Market. When she got there she saw the stall was all packed up, and there was no sign of the Staffordshire terrier anywhere. But the ghosts were closing in to form a circle around her in the open space in front of the meat-monger's counter. A figure stepped out from under an awning into her path.

"Hey, I know you," said an enormous Siberian cat with a tipped ear. He had a folded bandana tied around his head and a knife tucked into his belt. "But you had a pulse last time I saw you, and you weren't wearing some fancy Madison Avenue getup! Are you looking to join the Delancey Market ghosts? Because you seem a tad highfalutin for the likes of us!"

"I'm not here to sign on to your little band for two-bit thugs," she replied coolly. "I'm just looking for information."

The Siberian let out a hearty laugh. "I bet you're nothing but a run-of-the-mill haunter with a score to settle. Well, here's the thing, sweet-cheeks. Information ain't free."

A smug-looking black-and-white cat sitting on a metal barrel in the corner spoke up: "Where does she get off? Waltzing in here like she owns the place! I say we toss her out on her keister. Or maybe use her for target practice!" This suggestion drew cackles of laughter from the feral band of cats and dogs gathered around her. The black-and-white cat smiled craftily and preened his misshapen whiskers.

"Can it, Charlie!" snapped the Siberian. "We don't need any of your dumbass suggestions."

"All I'm saying," the black-and-white cat insisted, "is that someone's gonna take her wallet off her, so it might as well be us." Another approving murmur rippled through the crowd of ghosts.

"I said zip it!" yelled the Siberian, yanking the knife from his belt and pointing it at the black-and-white cat.

"What?" Charlie replied, spreading his hands. "Are you the only one allowed to have an opinion around here? I don't care for this uppity dame! I say we shake her down and introduce her to Rocko."

With a flick of the wrist the Siberian cat whipped his knife at the black-and-white cat. Val saw Charlie jump into the air, puffing up to twice his size, but he moved too slowly to dodge the blade, which lodged deep into his shoulder. With a look of cold fury Charlie grasped the knife by the hilt and slowly drew it out. He massaged the gap left behind in his shoulder until it had disappeared. The sniggering from the other ghosts was at his expense this time. Charlie let out a low rumble of displeasure.

Val took deep, slow breaths to still her racing heart. Short of dragging her into the sunlight during daylight hours she wasn't clear what kind of threat these ghosts posed. The ghost knife's effect seemed to confirm the notion that spirits were basically invulnerable. But who was this Rocko guy that Charlie had mentioned? And why did they all think her meeting him would be amusing?

The Siberian's tail twitched back and forth and he bared his teeth. "Come to think of it, Charlie does have a point. There's nothing to stop us from just taking whatever you're hiding in those silk-lined pockets of yours."

"I'm gonna level with you clowns," Val spoke brazenly. "I've got more money in my pockets than I know what to do with." She reached into her right pocket and pulled out one of the bricks of cash, drawing gasps from the ghosts encircling her. She slid off the paper tie and tossed the stack of hundreds into the air with a flourish. Hooting with glee, the ghosts swooped in to scoop up the fluttering bills. The swarming spooks reminded Val of a shark-feeding scene she'd seen in a pirate flick. The Siberian was the one ghost in the room who didn't move a muscle. He stood still in front of her, looking at her through hooded eyes. She winked at him and gave her other pocket a subtle pat. His eyebrows shot up.

"You know how to make an entrance, lady. I'll give you that! Maybe we can do business together after all. You got a name, dollface?"

"Tatiana Valova. But everyone just calls me Val."

The other ghosts had all gathered up the scattered money and retreated back to their circle to count their spoils and compare notes with their pals. One cat who seemed to have got the short end of the stick was Charlie, who had only managed to pick up two stray bills. He was grumbling unhappily as he eyed grinning cats and dogs around him thumbing five or six Benjamins apiece.

Settling back down on the steel barrel, Charlie turned his sullen gaze back on Val. "Let's see what else she has on her!"

The Siberian growled furiously and puffed out his chest. "Now, now, lads," he shouted. "Settle down. I think we may have misjudged our guest. She's got moxie and she's got cash, which makes her okay in my book." The Siberian turned to face her once more. "I have a feeling you're gonna fit right in around here, Val. Only problem is we're all full up. Not a single open bunk left!" This comment drew sly nods of agreement from the other ghosts. "But no matter," the Siberian went on, "perhaps Rocko can solve that problem for us." He gestured to a lone living mutt who was wiping down the nearby fish counter. "Our pal Rocko keeps a shotgun behind the counter loaded up with rock salt for just such a situation." The other ghosts in the room looked suddenly nervous and a few began to back away. Before they could get very far, the Siberian whistled sharply through his fingers. "Hey, Rocko!" he boomed. "Spook at three o'clock!"

In the blink of an eye the fishmonger pulled the shotgun out from under the bar, wheeled ninety degrees to his right and pulled the trigger. The blast echoed through the empty market. The ghosts around them all ducked for cover, except for the one directly in the sights of the shotgun. Charlie, perched on his barrel, had once again been slow to react. He looked down incredulously at the dozens of tiny holes in his chest made by the shotgun blast. As Val watched, the holes began to sizzle and grow larger. Charlie let out a shriek that soon fizzled into silence as he evaporated into thin air.

The other ghosts who had taken cover risked a peek at the Siberian, no doubt wondering if the shooting was over.

"Stand down, Rocko. Good shot! You hit the bullseye," yelled the Siberian. Then he shook his fist at all the cowering ghosts. "Buck up, you witless morons! Charlie had it coming! All that cat ever did was cause trouble. Someone fetch me my knife!" The shock of what had just happened seemed to dissipate as quickly as Charlie himself and the ghosts swiftly returned to celebrating their recent windfall. The Siberian put an arm around Val's shoulders and drew her to one side. "Let's you and me step into the back room for a little chat. I'm happy to report that a bunk has recently opened up, and you're welcome to it. I think you'll like it here. As you can see, things get pretty lively!"

Val followed the Siberian down a gray corridor. She'd managed to keep her features frozen and unexpressive, but inside she was in shock. She had been clueless that annihilating a ghost was so easily accomplished. Only luck had prevented her from being the target.

"I just might take you up on that bunk offer," Val replied, thinking to herself that she would have to sleep with one eye open. But she liked the prospect of sleeping out on the streets even less, and she had no desire to go back to Ghosthall. Flint and Professor Chumley could soon discover her identity if her name and photo hit the papers.

The Siberian slipped through a closed door and she passed through behind him only to find herself alone with him in a small back room with an industrial desk. "Now, tell me," purred the Siberian. "What kind of information are you looking for?"

"I need to talk to the butcher."

"You mean like you, personally?"

"Yes. Why not?" Val asked, perplexed.

"Well, sure, if you like. But you *do* know that every ghost gets only one mortal to communicate with. For me it's Rocko. He comes in real handy, but the downside is no other living cats or dogs can hear a word I say."

Val blinked slowly. "I admit I didn't know that."

"I had a feeling you were a real greenhorn. Don't worry, you'll learn all the ins and outs soon enough. But there are a few ghosts around here who can talk to the butcher, so if you tell me your questions I'll get you some answers."

"I need to find out the identity of a client I had when I was alive. I only ever knew him as Mister X."

The Siberian smiled. "Sure. We can look into that. The butcher might still be puttering about in the basement. I'll send someone down to talk to him right away! Of course, there is the small matter of my fee." The Siberian looked at her expectantly.

Val reached into her pocket and drew out the second brick of money. She snagged three bills to keep for herself and chucked the rest of the wad at the Siberian. Holding that much cash in his hands rendered him momentarily speechless. She thought she saw tears in his eyes. He stuffed a bunch of bills into his various pockets, and then crammed the rest into the top of his boots. "I won't lie to you, Val. Times have been tough lately. Getting these lazy spooks to do anything around here is an uphill battle. But that doesn't stop them from demanding a mug of Spume at the end of the day! Your donation to our general funds is going to raise morale around here, and that makes my job a heck of a lot easier. Things are looking up. I even got rid of that rat fink Charlie. Did you catch the look on his face after he got shot!" The Siberian let out a raucous laugh.

"What's Spume?" Val asked him.

"Oh, brother, you really are fresh from the gallows. I'll buy you a pint later and you'll find out."

"One more thing?" said Val. "How do I get my paws on a decent umbrella?" She placed the battered umbrella she'd pulled off the street thug on the desk and pushed it away disdainfully.

The Siberian flashed a toothy grin. "You're in luck. I've got a box of British imports stashed in a storage room. They've got hardwood handles, steel frames, and a forty-one-inch canopy, which is just the thing for propelling yourself and catching drafts. We'll get you one right away and I'll send someone down to have that chat with the butcher."

24 · Bianca Moon: The Party Crashers

Bianca sat wedged between Roxy and Tabatha as they drove back across the bridge, the car's bright headlights cutting through the surrounding dusk. She could only muster monosyllabic responses to her companions' attempts to draw her into conversation. She hadn't heard from Flint for hours now and was worried he might be gone for good.

Roxy was prattling on about paying Dorothy Kittlebun a visit to return that brooch. "You *have* to come with me, Princess!"

Bianca wrinkled her nose but said nothing.

"What?" Roxy exclaimed. "You know alley cats are still looked down on in certain circles, right? I'm much more likely to be allowed in if I have you with me. You have this special way about you, a certain—" She paused as she searched for the right word.

"Social grace?" Tabatha suggested helpfully.

"Yes, that's it! Social grace! You have boatloads of social grace! It must be something in the water up in Scatsdale!"

"That's exactly why I can't imagine showing up unannounced and uninvited to this movie star's home," Bianca replied.

"Well it beats lying in bed crying your eyes out. C'mon, Princess! It will be a quick little detour to drop off the brooch, and I'll get you home in a jiffy right after!" Roxy was nothing if not persistent.

Bianca sighed. "Fine. I'll go. But I don't promise to talk to anyone."

Roxy gave her hand a squeeze. "I knew I could count on you, Princess!"

Twenty minutes later they dropped off Tabatha outside the Calico Cat Lounge and Roxy asked the driver to take them up to 81st Street and Central Park West. She was counting on arriving at Dorothy Kittlebun's building in style.

They soon pulled up in front of a massive turreted building and a beagle in a crisp gold trimmed uniform and white gloves trotted over to open the car door for them. He ushered them into a marbled lobby and eyed them expectantly, his expression taking on a note of skepticism when they mentioned Dorothy Kittlebun's name. Bianca was sure he was going to send them packing, but the doordog picked up the intercom receiver and dialed an apartment number. A brief back and forth followed, where he repeated their names twice.

"From the church earlier!" Roxy chimed in.

The beagle hung up and, to Bianca's surprise, pointed over to an elevator bank. "Marvin will see you up to the sixteenth floor."

Breathing a sigh of relief, Roxy and Bianca strolled nonchalantly toward the elevator, where they found a wiry affenpinscher at the controls. They told him the floor number and he gave a nod, pulling the elevator doors and the scissor gate closed. With a flick of the wrist he sent them lurching upward. The numbers above the door lit up one by one. When they approached sixteen, the elevator slowed. Roxy fished the art deco brooch from her purse, squeezing it in her fist. She seemed suddenly skittish.

The elevator doors opened directly into the foyer of Dorothy's apartment. Standing there stiffly with their backs to the wall were the two black-suited huskies from the church earlier. The dogs' heads swiveled toward them, their expressions unreadable behind tinted glasses. Conga music was blasting out from an arched doorway, beyond which Bianca glimpsed a crowd of nattily dressed cats and dogs. They were snaking around a spacious room in a conga line, shuffling three steps forward and then kicking out a foot in time with the music. Bianca and Roxy exchanged a sideways glance—they were not expecting a party. Dorothy Kittlebun herself was at the head of the line of dancers, but when she caught sight of them she broke free and hurried over to greet them. The Siamese cat had changed into a tropical print hostess gown paired with purple cigarette pants. She had a silk scarf tied around her forehead. From her movements and speech it was clear she was tipsy.

Roxy immediately held up the brooch. "Miss Kittlebun, hello! We found this on the floor of the church and I thought it might belong to you?"

The actress took the bauble from her gleefully. "Thank heavens! I thought I'd lost it for good! It's so very sweet of you to come all the way uptown to return it to me. Most animals would've pocketed it. Just between us, this brooch was on loan from Zartier and they would have charged me a small fortune for losing it."

Unaccustomed to praise, Roxy seemed to have gone suddenly tongue tied. Bianca spoke up: "It was our pleasure."

"You *must* stay for a drink," said the actress.

Bianca eyed the frenzied partiers dubiously and shook her head. "Thanks, Miss Kittlebun, but we aren't exactly in a party mood tonight."

"Please—call me Dorothy. And I understand completely. How thoughtless of me. Maybe we could have a quick toast to Flint out on the terrace where it's quieter?" Roxy nodded giddily. Dorothy latched on to the alley cat's arm and pulled her through the living room toward sliding patio doors. Bianca followed, dodging the conga line revelers.

Stepping out onto a yellow brick terrace, Bianca and Roxy were met with a sparkling view of the City skyline bordering the park. The night air, which had been oppressively rank and humid down at street level, felt cleaner and cooler standing there, high above the din of the City.

A black Labrador in a gray suit was sitting alone at one of two small metal breakfast tables, reading a newspaper. "That's Louis, my agent," said Dorothy with a dismissive wave. "He's here to make sure my little soiree doesn't get out of hand. Aren't you, Louis? At my last party we got a little overzealous and may have lost some patio furniture and a vase over the balcony railing, which caused a big hubbub with the building management." The Labrador lowered the paper long enough to give them a perfunctory nod.

Dorothy leaned in to whisper: "That's one thing they don't tell you when you become a star: they're always watching you to make sure you don't screw things up. You can forget about having a private life, the studios basically own you!"

A tuxedo cat in a black bow tie came out onto the patio and offered them champagne flutes from a tray. They each took one. "To Flint," declared the actress, raising her glass. "A wonderful dog and a fine journalist."

They clinked glasses, and Bianca took a polite sip. Their host set her glass down on a ledge and leaned against the railing of the balcony, striking a pose with arms outstretched. A mischievous look stole into her clear blue eyes and she addressed the two cats in a hushed voice: "Are you gals up for a little catnip?" Right on cue the tux reappeared carrying a small silver box, which she presented to the actress. "It's imported from the far east. Prepare to have your minds blown."

A hollow cough sounded from the direction of Louis, her agent. He was staring at them disapprovingly.

"Ignore him," whispered the actress, dipping a tiny mother-of-pearl spoon into the catnip powder and then snorting it through her nose. "A little catnip never hurt anyone."

Roxy politely helped herself to a small pinch of the stuff, her eyes glazing over as it took immediate effect. Bianca demurred, saying she would stick to champagne.

Almost instantly Roxy's nerves around her celebrity crush seemed to evaporate. She spent the next few minutes gushing about her favorite Kittlebun flicks. The Siamese cat soaked up the compliments with obvious pleasure, and before long the two of them were chatting like friends. Dorothy, in her hopped-up state, shared several behind-the-scenes stories involving her leading men, complete with amusing impressions and dramatic hand gestures. "There was this one scene where I was supposed to be furious with Gregory Fleck and I improvised my anger by crushing his favorite fedora into a ball. I don't think he ever forgave me. His head was so big he had all his hats custom-made, you see, and I wrecked his favorite one!"

Bianca wasn't sure how long it would be before the actress was whisked away, so when a brief lull in the conversation presented itself she said: "Dorothy, can I ask you something? What made you come to Flint's funeral today?"

The actress blinked repeatedly. "Like I said earlier, we met at one of my movie premieres. I didn't know him that well, I confess, but he made a strong impression on me."

"You know, Flint mentioned meeting you," said Bianca. "The way he told it you hurled a vase at his head and vowed to get even with him someday. Is that true?"

A sideways glance at the alley cat showed her standing frozen, open-mouthed.

"Flint told you that?" Dorothy looked momentarily flustered. "Well, it's possible I might have lost my temper in the heat of the moment, but that was an awfully long time ago. I certainly didn't mean anything by it, and I have no hard feelings toward him, I assure you."

"Is that so?" Bianca scowled, pleased to have caught the actress off guard. "Because Flint said you told him to watch his back. That when he least expected it, you would get even."

Roxy's mouth opened and closed like a goldfish's. Dorothy's expression grew suddenly wary. "Oh, for Pete's sake! Don't tell me you crashed my party to accuse me of wanting to kill him?"

Bianca had come too far to back down now. "The possibility had crossed my mind. Admit it! You hated Flint for what he wrote about you!"

"Yes. Of course I was furious about what he wrote!"

"And you've held on to that grudge all these years!" Out of the corner of her eye, Bianca saw Louis put down his paper and disappear through the balcony doors.

"That's not true!" exclaimed the actress. "I was mad at him, sure. But when I cooled off I realized he was right. My performance in *Plums of Anger* was terrible. I ruined that movie with my cheap melodrama. I can't bear to watch it to this day. But you know what I did after that? I framed Flint's review and hung it in my dressing room so I could look at it every time I'm on set. It became a good luck token of sorts. So as you can see, in a way, I owe everything I've accomplished to Flint Lockford. *That's* why I went to his funeral today."

Bianca stared deep into the Siamese cat's almond-shaped eyes. The actress was telling the truth. Bianca bit her lip— this was awkward. "I'm sorry, Dorothy. I had to ask. I'm determined to track down Flint's killers, and when I saw you at the church today I got suspicious."

"Sorry? That's what you have to say for yourself. Sorry? I invite you into my home, give you some of the world's finest champagne, and you practically accuse me of dogicide?"

"It sounds bad when you put it like that," Bianca conceded.

"Do you have any idea what would happen to my career if the press got so much as a whiff of this story?"

"But it isn't true."

"The tabloids don't care about that! They would splash it all over the front page in ten-foot type! Then, six months later, after they've milked it for all it's worth, they would print a tiny two-sentence retraction buried in the back."

Bianca didn't know what to say.

The actress advanced on her menacingly, and Bianca retreated until the balcony railing hit her in the small of the back. "Bianca Moon," hissed the actress, "I never want to see your face again." Turning on her heels, the star stormed back inside, rushing past Louis and the two huskies, who had dashed out onto the terrace.

"We'll show ourselves out," said Roxy with a nervous smile. They made for the exit, but the huskies blocked their path. The Labrador slid the balcony door shut.

"What you two lasses need to understand," the agent said coldly, "is that nobody messes with Dorothy Kittlebun's reputation and gets away with it. Not if I have anything to say about it!" He nodded to the huskies. The two dogs had grabbed hold of Bianca. Roxy launched herself at them, tearing at their suits with her claws, but they paid her no mind. They lifted Bianca up and heaved her right off the balcony. Bianca's arms flailed as she flew backward. She hung in the air for a brief instant, then she began to fall, the air billowing her black dress.

Bianca had always wondered if falling from a great height would feel a bit like flying. This turned out not to be the case. Each millisecond she plummeted toward the ground filled her with terror, as she anticipated her imminent impact with the pavement below. The city lights streaked by around her and the world was reduced to sky and ground. Then she heard a scream above her and Bianca's heart caught in her throat. Looking up, she saw the silhouette of a cat being launched off the balcony. *Oh no—not Roxy too!* Bianca momentarily forgot about her own plight as she was filled with anguish for her friend. Bianca hated to think that her idiocy would end up costing the alley cat a life as well.

The air rushed past her and the sidewalk raced up to meet her. Bianca closed her eyes.

The molecules that made up Bianca Moon disentangled themselves from one another for the time it took to zip through the void on a path back to her birthplace, where they promptly reconstituted themselves.

"Make room for a *rekindler*!" called out a voice. Everything around her was fuzzy and cold. A figure in green scrubs stepped up and draped a blanket over her bare shoulders. Bianca stared down at the vinyl floors of the City Hospital maternity ward. Her pulse was still racing, the memory of her last moments still fresh in her mind. She forced herself to take long, slow breaths as they wheeled her across the hall in a gurney, depositing her once more in a small cubicle with blue curtains.

A few minutes passed before the same frizzy-haired bichon Bianca had met the night before appeared. "Miss Moon! Back already?" said the nurse. "That's two days in a row. Should I be worried about you?"

Bianca shook her head.

"What happened this time?" asked the nurse.

"Someone just threw me off a balcony."

"No kidding? You didn't jump, did you?"

"It was entirely involuntary, I assure you." Bianca glanced at the nurse's name tag—Nurse Bertlemina, that was it.

"How are you feeling?"

"Like I just got taken apart and then put back together. But grateful to be alive."

"No one ever said dying was fun. Here you go, Bianca. Drink your milk." Nurse Bertlemina pressed a glass into her hands. "Thrown in the Gowanus Canal. Thrown off a balcony. I get the feeling you're hanging out with the wrong crowd."

"It was a different pair of thugs tonight, if that makes you feel any better."

"Well, I can contact the police if you like. But just between us, when it comes to killings, all they really care about is dogs."

"No need to trouble the cops on my account."

"Well, you've got five lives left. That's still a good number. But I don't want to see you back here anytime soon. Got it? Your dress is on the chair for you. Did yesterday's dress fit you okay?"

"Yes, it was just right. Thank you." Bianca took another sip of milk. She wondered where Roxy was. Was the alley cat sitting in a similar maternity ward somewhere sipping milk just like her? She had to find Roxy and tell her how sorry she was. Hopefully the alley cat could find it in her heart to forgive her.

When Bianca arrived home, all she wanted to do was take a shower and crawl into bed, but Flint was waiting for her there. He was hopping mad when he saw her wearing another blue dress. She told him about Dorothy Kittlebun and the events leading up to her and Roxy being thrown off the balcony.

"For Pete's sake! Is it open season on cats in this city? Are you okay?"

"It was a horrible sensation, falling helplessly through the air like that. But the worst part is that I cost Roxy a life."

Now it was her turn to confront Flint about his disappearing act. She listened, incredulous, as Flint came clean about Riyo and their whirlwind romance. He explained how he'd asked Riyo to marry him, and how it had all gone to pieces when he'd uncovered Riyo's secret life of crime.

"She put me in an impossible position," Flint lamented. "I expose criminals for a living and there was no way I could just look the other way. So I called the whole thing off. She didn't take it well. She even kept the ring—a family heirloom."

"Why am I only hearing about this now?" she asked, feeling miffed.

"She didn't mean anything to me anymore. And to be honest, I didn't want you to know I'd been engaged once before."

"Death threats? A crooked ex-fiancée? What's going on, Flint? I'm beginning to think I never really knew you."

"I'll admit I play my cards a bit too close to the vest sometimes."

"Where did this Riyo dog go after the funeral?"

"She took a cab to the Biltmore Hotel, up by Grand Central."

"So you spied on your ex in her hotel room? Flint Lockford, you ought to be ashamed of yourself!"

"It wasn't like that, Bianca, I swear."

"What *was* it like, then? And why were you gone for so long?"

"She spent a big chunk of time lounging by the hotel's indoor pool."

"I see. So you spent the afternoon poolside with your

ex-fiancée while I was at a cemetery watching your casket being lowered into the ground."

"But Riyo's up to no good. I'm sure of it! I needed to find out what she was scheming."

"And what did you discover?"

"She's still smuggling antiquities. And she's intent on recovering the monkey figurine that's still sitting on my cabinet shelf."

"Nothing you've said suggests she might be a murderer."

"Did I mention she keeps a handgun in her purse?"

"You sure can pick 'em."

"After I called off our engagement, Riyo threatened to kill me if I ever tried to marry anyone else. She was always intensely jealous. Now I'm wondering if maybe it was Riyo who I glimpsed on the rooftop with the knife. She could have planted that playing card just to mess with the cops."

"That wasn't her." Bianca told a dumbfounded Flint all about Tatiana Valova, the deadly bank heist, and the duffel bag full of money. "There's even a photo of this hitdog in the *Gazette*'s evening edition. I picked up a copy on my way home from the hospital. Here, take a look." She grabbed the newspaper off the lowboy in the hallway and opened it to page nine, holding it up for him to see the headshot of Tatiana Valova.

"Wait a darn second—I know that dog!" cried Flint. "Professor Chumley brought her into Ghosthall earlier today. No wonder she gave me such an odd look."

"You already ran into your own murderer?" Bianca said, shocked.

"I'm sure it was her."

"I guess this leaves your ex-girlfriend in the clear," Bianca said acidly.

"I wouldn't be so sure. She might've hired this hitdog. I wouldn't be shocked to learn Riyo has mob connections. She really hated me in the end. I want you to stay clear of my apartment, Bianca. We wouldn't want you running into her when she does go looking for the figurine."

Bianca decided not to tell him that she had already agreed to clean out his stuff from his apartment in the morning. If she did run into this Riyo character she planned to ask her about Flint's death. But that was all a problem for another day. Suddenly bone weary, she didn't have it in her to argue any further with Flint. "Well, I'm going to call it a night. You've given me a lot to think about."

"Please don't be mad at me, my love."

Bianca faced his voice. "I'm not mad because you turned out to have a crazy ex-fiancée, or because of your disappearing act. It's the secrets that really get to me. You have to promise me, Flint—*no more secrets.*"

"I promise," Flint said earnestly.

"You're welcome to stay in my living room tonight if you like," she said in a conciliatory tone.

"Thanks, but I told the Ghosthall gang I'd meet them at the cantina. But before I go, there's one more thing I should tell you."

Bianca's frown deepened. She wasn't sure she could cope with any more revelations.

"You have a ghost living in your kitchen," he said.

"Excuse me?"

"Well, not *living*, but you know what I mean."

Bianca was stunned. "A ghost in my kitchen?"

"She's a springer spaniel named Gertrude. A harmless old lady," he said breezily. "She was murdered in your kitchen by her niece, ages ago. The best thing for you to do is just pretend she's not even there."

"Okay. Let me get this straight," said Bianca. "Just as I'm going off to bed you tell me my apartment is haunted?" Bianca stamped her foot. "One of these days, Flint Lockford, you and I are going to have a long chat about your timing."

25 · Junior Detective Morton Digby: The Milk

Detectives Digby and Puddleworth were working late. They'd spent the last hour and a half interrogating Gustave Legrand about Flint Lockford's murder, without managing to connect him to the crime in any way. This was not good news vis-à-vis their imminent briefing with Captain Maddox, who it turned out was in a lousy mood.

Outside his office, Shirley held up a hand for them to wait. "He's having a little chat with Kenneth," she said. Morton stole a glance through the captain's open doorway and saw the large mastiff glowering at a uniformed mutt cowering in the middle of the room. "Our station has ten squad cars!" the captain roared. "Now you've gone and bent one of our cars around a lamppost, that leaves us with—" Captain Maddox glared at the poor patroldog expectantly.

"Nine patrol cars?"

"Nine patrol cars! Which is one vehicle less than we had before you got behind the wheel!"

"But, sir! A young pup rode his skateboard into the street!"

"Are you so sure he wasn't just a kitten? Never mind. Don't answer that. I'm not interested in your excuses. Excuses aren't gonna buy us a new cruiser, are they?" The captain raised his eyebrows. "Answer the question!"

"No, sir."

"No is right! I'd take the expense right out of your salary if they let me. But they don't, so I gotta comb through the budget and figure out where we're gonna come up with the cash. Shirley?" he yelled through the open door to his secretary. "Do we have three thousand dollars lying around in our budget this summer?"

The papillon's plumed ears swiveled in his direction. "No we don't, Captain!" she yelled back.

"Did you hear that? We don't have the cash. Which means we have to limp by with nine cars for the foreseeable future!" Captain Maddox slammed his fist down on his desk.

"Sorry, sir," said the patroldog, eyes downcast.

The two detectives watched, horrified, as the captain grabbed the phone off his desk and hurled it at the poor mutt's head. Kenneth ducked, and the phone crashed into the wall.

"Get outta my sight!" yelled the captain. The patroldog scurried from the room. "Shirley! Get the phone repair guy in here as soon as you can!"

"I've already got him on the line!" she said, anticipating her boss's needs. This was true—Shirley had started dialing the repair cat's number before the phone had even left the captain's hand. The patroldog shot past them, head bowed, and Shirley waved them in. "You're up!" She cast them a pitying look, as if she was throwing them to the lions.

Stepping into the captain's office, Detective Puddleworth laid out the details of their arrests. The beetle-browed mastiff sat in silence with his feet up on his desk. The Scottish terrier explained that they had come to suspect the sommelier after reading Lockford's article in the *Gazette*. "And when we saw him at the funeral our suspicions grew stronger."

"But . . ." said the captain.

"But so far we've been unable to tie him directly to the crime," the Scottie admitted. "Legrand denies having anything to do with the killing. He claims the article blew over pretty quick."

"There's no way we can charge him with dogicide, then."

"No, there isn't," Detective Puddleworth answered.

The captain swung his chair around so that he was staring out the darkened windows behind his desk. His fingers drummed on the arms of his chair. "I doubt the district attorney will be chomping at the bit to prosecute anyone for wine label fraud. Bit of a victimless crime, isn't it? Bilking rich dimwits out of their cash?"

"This was a large-scale criminal operation," Detective Puddleworth clarified. "Turns out they were shipping cases up and down the East Coast. Based on the numbers in their off-the-record books, we've estimated this fake bubbly scheme may have netted Chez Claude's around a couple million bucks in fraudulent charges over the years."

The mastiff swiveled back around. "What a racket! Well, nail that cat's butt to the wall for fraud, then, and let's hope he doesn't skip town when he posts bail. As far as the other two tuxedos go, don't be surprised when those charges get knocked down to resisting arrest."

"But they attacked Detective Puddleworth!" protested Morton.

"Seems like they were *thinking* about jumping Detective Puddleworth. Then you came along and clobbered them. You can't chuck cats in jail for thinking things, can you? Now, as far as the murder case goes, you whiffed with Delgatto, and whiffed with this wine guy. That's two strikes by my count. I'm sure you know what that means."

They both nodded.

"Dismissed!"

Morton was relieved. All things considered, they'd gotten off easy. Clearly the captain had spent his anger on the patroldog. The two detectives grabbed their hats and exited the precinct together. Outside, on the narrow sidewalk, Detective Puddleworth broke the silence: "Time to draw a line through Gustave Legrand and move on to the next name on the list. We'll start fresh tomorrow morning!"

Morton was glad to see the Scottie recover some of his usual good cheer. "I'm gonna grab a bite from my favorite deli down on Houston. You interested?"

"You want to walk down there in this heat? I don't know how you manage to stay cool, Morton! I'll probably melt before we get there, but sure, I'll tag along. I'll consider it part of your tour of the City's culinary underbelly!"

"Hey, I know how to eat on a budget."

"When we solve this case, Morton, I'm gonna take you out for a three-course meal at the best steakhouse in town!"

At the deli, Detective Puddleworth ordered himself an egg salad sandwich with extra paprika, while Morton opted for the chicken soup. When they went to pay, they stumbled onto a scene unfolding at the register. A red-and-black tortoiseshell cat was arguing furiously with the tan dog behind the counter. "Look, I swear I'll come back with cash tomorrow morning," said the tortie. "I'll pay you triple what this one bottle of milk is worth. I just don't have it on me right now." The exasperated alley cat waved the bottle of milk at the cashier. She was dressed in rags and scraps from paper bags haphazardly taped together. Morton peered at her curiously. There was something oddly familiar about her.

The dog at the register was having none of it. "Pay for the milk or I'm calling the cops!" he snapped.

"Over a lousy bottle of milk?" cried the alley cat in disbelief.

"Please get out of line. I've got actual customers waiting."

By now Morton had placed this bizarrely attired alley cat. He stepped up and put fifteen cents on the counter. "*I'll* pay for her milk." The mutt behind the counter shrugged and snatched up the money. The alley cat tore the cap off the milk and chugged half the bottle in one go. Then, wiping her lips with the back of her hand, she turned to thank him. That is to say, she started to thank him but petered out halfway through. "You! If I'd known it was your fifteen cents I would've told you to keep your money!"

"You're welcome," said Morton, digging a quarter out of his pocket to pay for his soup. "Roxy, right? Nice outfit!"

"Yeah. Ha ha. I must look pretty funny to you."

"Why don't you tell us what happened?" Morton suggested.

"What happened? What happened is I got thrown off a building terrace. I fell sixteen stories and smashed into the cement sidewalk!"

"I see," said Detective Puddleworth. "Then you got rekindled in a nearby alley."

"Nothing gets past you," smirked the alley cat.

"Let me guess," said Morton. "Our friend Bianca was

poking around in things she has no business sticking her nose into?"

Roxy nodded. "She's obsessed with finding Flint's killer. She cost both of us a life. I'm so mad at her I could spit!"

"I don't blame you," said Morton. "How many lives do you have left?"

"I'm down to four now. And Bianca's got one more than that, although at the rate she's going it won't take her long to catch up." Roxy made for the door.

The two detectives scooped their brown bags off the counter and caught up to her on the sidewalk outside, where the alley cat had stopped to guzzle the rest of the milk. She flung the empty bottle into a nearby trash can.

"Where are you headed?" Morton asked her.

"The Lower East Side. Not that it's any of your business."

"That's a long walk in this muggy weather," said the Scottie. "How about you let us treat you to a cab?"

Roxy shook her head. "I don't want any more favors from the two of you. I can find my own way home." She turned to go.

"Horsefeathers!" Detective Puddleworth whistled at a yellow taxi and it screeched to a stop in front of them. The Scottish terrier pulled two singles from his wallet and pressed them into the alley cat's hands.

She protested at first, but they overcame her reluctance and helped her into the cab. "You know, for cops, you two ain't half-bad," she admitted grudgingly as she slid into the back seat. They slammed the door shut and watched the taxi speed away.

26 · Flint Lockford: The Raid

Flint took a slow meandering route back to Ghosthall, his head drooping low, rankled by a rat's nest of troubled thoughts. He found Professor Chumley and Benny sitting on the steps outside the abandoned courthouse when he arrived.

"Look who turned up!" said the tomcat with a grin.

"Flint! We were just debating whether to come look for you," said the professor.

"Hey there, fellas." Flint did his best to sound cheerful, but they weren't fooled.

The professor peered at him closely. "What's with the long face, my friend?"

"Yeah, what gives?" asked Benny "You look a little off-color, even for a ghost!"

"Oh, I'm okay. It's been a trying day. Bianca is upset with me, and I'm not too pleased with her either." He proceeded to tell them all about his long afternoon with Riyo Jones and about Bianca's own misadventures.

The professor put his hand on his shoulder. "Just going to your own funeral is a lot to deal with, never mind all that other stuff. For some, they provide necessary closure. For others, it just makes a bad situation worse. Let's go inside, the cantina is in full swing! We'll see if a mug of Spume will lift your spirits."

Benny nodded vigorously and said: "We can watch the end of the umbrella ball match!" Flint's brow furrowed, but he imagined he'd find out soon enough what umbrella ball was.

A ghostly net had been strung up in the open space behind the benches and all eyes were focused on the four players batting furiously at a ghostly basketball with their umbrellas, in a bizarre mixed doubles competition. A throng of spectators was loudly cheering after each point. Flint grabbed himself a mug of Spume and joined Professor Chumley and the rest of the gang, who were lined up along the back of a bench watching the game.

"Flint, you made it!" cried Sophie, hopping up to give him a long hug, broken up only when Tiger grabbed hold of the collie's blouse and pulled her away.

"Sophie's had one too many mugs of Spume," said the marmalade cat, "and they've gone right to her head."

"Don't be ridiculous!" protested Sophie. "I'm just excited to see our new friend!"

"Is this game anything like tennis?" Flint asked, squeezing into a spot between Benny and Albert.

"It's closer to volleyball," Paco explained. "Except you can only hit the ball with your umbrella!"

Flint watched as one of the players, a spindly borzoi in goggles, used his umbrella handle to bash the basketball over the net. One of his opponents, a tall feline, flicked open her umbrella and used the canopy to deflect his shot. Back and forth went the ghostly basketball, hanging in the air after every hit in a manner reminiscent of a beach ball.

Five minutes later the borzoi and terrier team had earned themselves a match point. The crowd leaned forward in their seats as the limber terrier with a pink umbrella set the ball high above the net and her teammate soared into the air to spike it with a fierce windup swing. The ball went streaking down in a gap between two open umbrellas and hit the ground, eliciting a mixture of cheers and groans from the crowd. Coins changed hands among many of the ghosts.

"I'm buying the next round," declared Chumley. "But I'm leaving you out, Sophie. You've hit your limit!"

"If you don't come back with a mug for me then you'd better not come back at all," the collie snapped peevishly.

Chumley was just turning to leave when a ghost came streaking into the cantina shrieking: "Fire! Fire! The bushes along the south wall are on fire!"

"Someone go find Gerald!" yelled Albert, jumping to his feet. A bunch of nearby ghosts paired up, with one ghost giving the other a boost to launch them up in the air and right through the ceiling. Still others rushed toward the south wall, wanting to see the blaze for themselves.

"Let's go see if we can help!" cried Sophie. Flint wondered what exactly a ghost could do about a fire.

"Hold on, guys. Let's not be hasty," Professor Chumley said warily. "This may turn out to be a diversion."

Sophie let out a squeal of delight. "You think this could be the start of a raid?"

"You know, Professor, I think you're onto something," said Albert, looking suddenly suspicious himself. "Something doesn't smell right!"

Just then, Gerald the mutt came rushing down the stairs carrying two empty buckets, keys jangling from his belt. He rushed past them in the direction of the back door. A large contingent of Ghosthallers cheered and chased after him, including Tiger and Sophie. Flint hung back with Chumley, Albert, Paco, and Benny.

"What exactly is a raid?" asked Flint.

"It's when a rival band of ghosts storms the place to try to steal anything valuable," Benny explained. "Raids happen a couple times a year when a neighboring band of ghosts gets greedy. They can lead to some nasty fights. A few of our more thuggishly inclined lodgers seem to relish the occasional brawl, but not me!" Benny looked around nervously.

Not ten seconds later, a swarm of unfamiliar ghosts burst through the walls, howling like banshees.

Benny let out a yelp.

"It's those damn Squareheads!" yelled Albert. "I bet they're after our Spume!"

Sure enough, the intruders headed straight for the barrels stacked in the back of the courtroom and began to roll them down the aisle toward the exit. Utter chaos ensued as the few remaining Ghosthallers in the cantina began to grapple with the intruders. Paco stuck out his umbrella and managed to trip a much larger dog, who went sprawling, dropping his loot. Albert leapt into the air and jabbed the tip of his umbrella right in the eye of another ghost. The larger dogs like Chumley swung their umbrellas about like clubs. Flint took his cue from his companions and moved to intercept a trespasser who had drifted down through the ceiling clutching half a dozen stolen umbrellas in his arms. Flint hooked his own umbrella handle around the ghost's neck, yanking him back, but was immediately forced to duck as one of the raiders came up behind him and aimed a savage blow at his head.

The Squareheads' diversion had worked like a charm, as the handful of Ghosthallers left in the cantina were severely outnumbered. A few Ghosthallers were beginning to trickle back into the room, but word of the raid wasn't spreading quickly enough to stop the theft of the barrels. For every raider they grappled with, there were always two more roaming free and ransacking the place. Sophie and Tiger were among the first to come rushing back in. "These lowdown dirty bastards!" shouted the collie indignantly. "We won't let them get away with this!"

"How's the fire?" asked Chumley.

"Fire's out!" Tiger replied. "Gerald's gone to grab a bag of salt from the storage room, but I don't know if he'll make it back in time."

Leading the raid were two huge Alsatians with thick ruffs of fur around their necks. They fought fiercely, clearing a path for their comrades to escape with the looted Spume. It was clear that the Ghosthallers were on the losing end of the struggle when suddenly a dark figure loomed on the tower steps behind the intruders. The Ghosthallers gasped as they caught sight of him, including Flint, who had never before seen such a huge dog—if he was even a dog. This gargantuan canine towered over the other ghosts. He was dressed only in dungarees, his bare chest a mass of shaggy gray fur, and his bulging biceps encircled with rings of iron.

"It's Moose! They've woken up Moose!" the Ghosthallers cheered while the raiders looked around in confusion. Then they caught sight of the hulking beast standing behind them. Moose had paws the size of sledge hammers, tipped with long, raking claws. With a roar of fury he set about the intruders, lashing out left and right, ripping right through the heart of the raiding party, sending ghosts flying in all directions.

"Who the heck is *that?*" Flint exclaimed, staring in amazement as chaos broke out in the ranks of the Squareheads.

"That's Moose," replied Professor Chumley with a grin. "He lives up in the tower. What a stroke of luck! You almost never see Moose up and about. I haven't set eyes on him in over a year!" Moose's fury had sent the raiders into a panic and almost single-handedly put a stop to the raid. The Squareheads dropped their stolen goods and fled in terror. One of the Alsatians snuck up behind Moose and delivered a nasty blow with a baseball bat to the back of the giant dog's head, but the bat just splintered into pieces. Moose turned around and grabbed the Alsatian by the throat. He shook the large dog like a rat and then tossed him into a stone wall, where he crumpled to the floor. The Alsatian's twin dropped the crow bar he was holding and dove out through the door with the rest of his band. The fight was over.

Everyone watched, awestruck, as Moose stomped over to one of the barrels of Spume lying abandoned in the entry hall. He held it up with two hands, twisted the tap with his teeth, and emptied the barrel contents down his throat. Dropping the empty casket, Moose wiped his mouth with the back of his paw and belched loudly. Only then did Moose look around at all the Ghosthallers who had begun giddily chanting his name: "Moose! Moose! Moose!"

"Me. Sleep. Now," grunted the brute. He turned around and clomped back up the tower steps.

"How remarkable!" exclaimed Flint. "Is he some sort of timber wolf?"

"No, not a timber wolf exactly," replied Professor Chumley. "We think he may be more of a missing link between modern-day dogs and some primitive canine ancestor. He has been haunting this patch of land for thousands of years, long before the City was even built. His vocabulary is strictly monosyllabic."

"Is he safe to be around?" Flint asked. "I don't think you mentioned him on the tour."

"Moose is harmless enough unless he's provoked! We don't talk about him much because ghosts inevitably become curious and want to go take a peek in the tower, and as you can see, he gets grumpy when he gets woken up. But he sure turned the tide of the fight in our favor today!"

"You're not kidding! Moose is like a one-dog army!" Tiger cooed admiringly.

Gerald had returned with a bag of salt, and he was guided around the room to where knocked-out Squareheads were strewn about. The mutt scattered salt on the spots he was told to do so and Flint watched in horror as the unconscious ghosts began to sizzle and evaporate into thin air.

"Is that really necessary?" Flint said, aghast. "It seems rather cold-blooded."

"Cold-blooded!" growled Paco indignantly. "We are ghosts, my friend. We are cold-blooded by nature. And that is no better treatment than they deserve!"

"That's right," exclaimed a suddenly courageous Benny. "We need to send those Squareheads a message. This is what they get when they mess with us!"

"I know it seems rather ruthless," Professor Chumley said contritely. "But what you need to understand, Flint, is that the spirit world doesn't have proper laws, or courts, or jails. If we just tossed these comatose ghosts out on the street, they would soon be back, and they might do a better job of setting fire to the place next time. So instead we help them cross over, and who knows, maybe they will end up in a better place."

27 · Bianca Moon:
The Monkey

Thursday

Bianca lit the stovetop and added coffee grounds and water to the percolator. She was counting on her morning brew to help clear away some of her mental cobwebs. She glanced around nervously at the seemingly empty kitchen, wondering where Gertrude, the springer spaniel ghost, might be. With a slight shudder, Bianca went back to making her coffee. Flint was right—it was better not to think about it. She had lain awake in bed for an hour last night, thinking about how her apartment was haunted, and it had gotten her nowhere.

Unhampered by any encounters with supernatural apparitions, Bianca emerged from the kitchen five minutes later with a precious cup of hot java, which she set down on the coffee table in the parlor. Sunlight was seeping through purple curtains, filling the room with a nebulous radiance. Bianca switched on the oscillating fan on the bookcase, hoping it would help ease the parlor's warm and heavy air. Then she let Rupert out of his cage so he could stretch his wings. The parrot had his favorite perches around the room but as always, he ended up on her shoulder. He liked to rub his beak on her neck fur, which she loved, but she had to scold him when he tried nipping at her whiskers.

Bianca savored a few gulps of her coffee. At the top of her to-do list for the day was apologizing to Roxy, but the Calico Cat Lounge wouldn't open until noon and Bianca had no idea where the alley cat lived. Bianca decided she would stick with her original plan to clear out Flint's apartment this morning. Otis and Penelope had kindly offered to meet her there at eleven a.m. to help her with any heavy lifting. After hearing Flint's story last night, Bianca was determined to get her hands on that monkey figurine before Flint's ex showed up and made a grab for it.

Bianca picked out a gray dress with a V neckline and bow-tie waistband as her outfit for the day. She took a quick shower, then brushed her teeth, combed her fur, and was out the door by ten a.m. Flint lived over on Sullivan Street in a white brick eleven-story building above a local chess studio. Newly constructed, it had a mix of swanky apartments and more modest units. Bianca picked up the keys for apartment 7H from the super, who told her to leave anything to be tossed down in the basement.

Bianca rode the elevator up to the seventh floor. Flint's unit was a tiny alcove studio with a Murphy bed. The air was musty inside the closed-up apartment, and the first thing she did was pull back the drapes and open the windows wide. A quick survey of the place confirmed that all the electronics—his record player, toaster, and window fan—had vanished. She was especially sorry to see that a brass ship's lamp that Flint had prized had fallen prey to his sister's treasure hunt. All that was left were clothes, papers, books, and various knickknacks that Flint's sister had not deemed valuable. Bianca went straight to the glass-paned cabinet by the window. Inside were odds and ends from Flint's travels. There were a few empty spots where a dust footprint betrayed a missing object, but most of these souvenirs had escaped the purge, including a blue monkey figurine tucked away in the back.

Bianca fished it out and turned it over in her hands, wondering what Flint's sister would think if she knew she had left behind the one thing of real value in her brother's apartment. The monkey was sitting on a small pedestal with his large hands resting on his feet. He had a round head with pitcher ears poking out on either side and a mischievous grin on his face. Bianca wrapped the figurine in one of Flint's handkerchiefs and placed it in a cardboard box along with the remaining souvenirs.

Flint's apartment needed to be broom clean by the end of the day. She got to work cleaning out Flint's closet and his chest of drawers, making piles of clothes and other items that could be donated to Goodwill. She dumped all the books from his small bookcase into a flat-top trunk that she planned to take home.

As the morning wore on, there was no sign of a crazy Shiba Inu attempting to burgle the place. Bianca tried calling Otis and Penelope to warn them about Flint's ex—she had a gun after all—but Flint's phone line had already been disconnected.

Bianca had just finished boxing up the silverware when she heard the muted ding of the elevator doors opening, followed by the click of high heels coming down the hallway. Bianca smoothed her dress and stood casually by the box with the monkey statuette.

The doorknob rattled and the front door swung open to

reveal a foxy orange dog in a blue stewardess uniform. She stepped into the apartment and set the blue suitcase she was carrying down at her feet. "Miss Bianca Moon, I presume?" she said, smiling as she met Bianca's gaze.

"You must be Riyo," Bianca replied, trying her best to quiet her pounding heart.

Astonishment registered on the Shiba's face. "You know who I am?"

Bianca nodded.

"Does that mean you also know that Flint and I were once engaged?"

"So I've heard," Bianca replied frostily.

"Like actually engaged, not just pretend engaged."

Bianca scowled—she'd known Riyo for all of ten seconds and she already hated this dog. "Whatever you're insinuating—"

"Simmer down! It was just a little joke," Riyo said with a hollow laugh. "I must say I'm surprised Flint told you about me. He was always so tightlipped when I knew him."

"And I'm surprised that you would turn up at his funeral and then at his apartment the next day, considering how long ago the two of you broke up."

"I'm looking for something Flint was holding on to for me. It's a small, worthless trinket, but it has great sentimental value."

Bianca reached down and plucked the statuette from the box, pulling back the folds of the handkerchief and holding up the monkey. "Is this what you're after?"

Riyo's smile faded. "I don't know how you're doing it, Bianca Moon, but I get the distinct feeling you're a step ahead of me. And I don't like it one bit. But yes, that happens to be my monkey, so if you don't mind handing it over—"

"Not so fast," Bianca replied. "Call me crazy but something tells me this little monkey might not be the trifling knickknack you make it out to be."

"Knickknack or not, I assure you it's mine. I purchased it on a trip to Egypt."

"According to Flint, you paid for it with money he loaned you."

"What else did Flint tell you, little miss know-it-all?"

"He said you were a common crook."

The Shiba's lip curled back in a snarl. "A crook maybe, but a common one, certainly not! I see you suffer from the same puritanical streak that bedeviled Flint. Just so you know, most of the items I smuggled would have been lost or destroyed if they'd remained in their country of origin. In the hands of wealthy collectors, they are preserved for posterity. Now, if you don't mind, Bianca, I have a pressing engagement." The Shiba held out her hand for the statuette, but Bianca made no move to relinquish it.

"I'm going to ask you nicely one more time," Riyo growled. "Hand over that monkey!"

When Bianca made no move to comply, she suddenly found herself staring down the barrel of a tiny revolver that the Shiba had whipped out of her purse.

"I'm not a dog to be trifled with. Now put the figurine down on the table right there and take three steps back!"

Bianca let out a low growl. She held the figurine aloft with just her thumb and forefinger. "I'm guessing you wouldn't want me to drop it."

A look of alarm flashed across the Shiba's face.

"Tell you what, Riyo," said Bianca. "I'll make you a deal. I'll put the statue on the table for you, but first you need to answer one little question for me."

Riyo said nothing, but her eyes were locked on the blue monkey.

"Did you have Flint killed?" Bianca demanded to know.

Riyo's eyes flicked to Bianca's face. "What? You think I'm behind Flint's murder? Are you nuts?"

"You showed up at his funeral unexpectedly. You have criminal connections and you walk around with a concealed firearm. Flint also mentioned that you threatened to kill him if he ever married anyone else."

"So I went a little crazy when he called off the engagement. Can you blame me? I was an absolute wreck. But it's ancient history. Sure, we had a messy breakup, but Flint was right—it never would've worked between us. He was too much of a stuffed shirt, and I'm too much of a maverick. Neither one of us was going to change to suit the other."

"Still, you hated him," Bianca pointed out.

"Hated? Loved? It's the same difference if you ask me. The truth is my feelings for Flint ran a lot deeper than even I realized. When I heard he'd been killed I was devastated. I was at the funeral yesterday because the part of me that still loves him needed to say goodbye."

Bianca held Riyo's gaze for a long moment, looking deeper and deeper into the Shiba's pained eyes. Bianca sighed as she realized this dog was telling the truth. "I'm sorry, Riyo. But I had to ask. I'm trying to track down the mastermind behind Flint's killing, and for a moment there you looked the part."

Riyo gestured toward the table with the gun. "Well, I answered your nasty little question. It's time for you to keep your end of the bargain."

Reluctantly Bianca put the ceramic monkey down on the square folding table and stepped back. The Shiba Inu crept forward and scooped it up with her free hand. "Thanks, doll. The market for these figurines has gone through the roof. If you know the right buyer it's worth a bundle, and I know the right buyer. Now, I want your word you won't call the cops the minute I'm out the door. Tying you up seems like an awful lot of trouble for us both, and like I said—I'm in a rush."

Bianca stared back at the Shiba coolly. "Tell you what, I'll count to thirty and then yell, 'ready or not here I come.'"

The Shiba Inu's eyes narrowed. "Wrong answer, Bianca."

Three loud pops rang out in quick succession, the sounds sharp and dry in the small space. Bianca felt a stabbing pain in her chest and looked down in shock to see three red spots spreading on her gray dress. She tried to say something but a strange gurgling sound came from her throat. She couldn't believe this dog had just shot her. Bianca tottered backward until her back hit the wall. Her legs buckled beneath her and she slumped to the floor. The world around her blurred, and the last thing she heard was Riyo's voice as if from a great distance away: "It's been a real pleasure. See you never, Bianca Moon."

Bianca sat on the City Hospital cot, propped up by a bulky pillow, calmly sipping her requisite glass of milk. There was a different nurse on duty this morning, a wire-haired terrier who seemed by turns impressed and distressed that Bianca had lost three lives in as many days.

Downing the last of the milk, Bianca swung her legs over the side of the bed. She was still woozy, but she knew from experience that once she stood up and got moving she would feel a heck of a lot better. She slipped on the now-familiar blue dress and did up the buttons along the front. The gray dress she had been wearing earlier was now lying on the floor of Flint's apartment with three bloodstained holes in it. It had been one of her favorite summer dresses. She'd lost her black dress last night in a similar fashion, and her favorite silk pajamas the day before that. Safe to say her wardrobe had taken a hit in the past couple of days.

A half hour later, Bianca found herself staring at her reflection in the dressing room mirror of an Eighth Street vintage clothing store. She was experimenting with a new look, something better suited for the rough and tumble world she'd been plunged into. She had on a pair of used black jeans that were already beginning to wear thin in places, a simple T-shirt, black-and-white saddle shoes, and a black leather jacket that fit her just right and boasted some striking diagonal zippers. The store clerk had deemed it a motorcycle jacket, which sounded about right to Bianca.

She paid at the register and told the clerk to keep the blue dress she'd come in with. On her way out the door, her eye snagged on a flyer pinned to a bulletin board. It advertised a used motorcycle for sale. Bianca peered closely at a grainy photo of a sleek Matchless G80. Perhaps it was her new leather jacket that put the thought in her head, but whatever the reason, owning a motorcycle suddenly seemed like just the ticket. Two days ago she would have dismissed the idea out of hand. Bianca tore off one of the notched squares with a phone number for someone named Kevin.

It was past one o'clock when she finally arrived at the Calico Cat Lounge. The back door was on the latch and Bianca pushed her way in. She was surprised to see Roxy's friend Jan standing behind the bar.

"Bianca? Is that you?" asked Jan. "I love the new look! You could easily pass for one of us!"

"That's the idea," Bianca replied with a grin.

"Tabatha asked me to help out until you get back on your feet, but don't worry, I'm just here to keep things going until you're ready to take over again."

"Thanks for stepping in. I'm sure you will do a great job. Hey, have you seen Roxy?"

"Yeah, she's downstairs restocking shelves in the pantry."

Sure enough, Bianca found the alley cat down on her knees stacking cans of baked beans on a low shelf. Hearing the pantry door swing open, Roxy looked up and gave Bianca a cold look.

Bianca launched into her apology. "Roxy. I'm *so* sorry about last night. I should never have gotten you mixed up in my crazy theories. I don't know what I was thinking."

The alley cat snorted. "Crazy is right! That's another life gone for me, Bianca. You know I don't have that many left."

"I know. And I'll never forgive myself. If I could give you one of mine I would."

"I've never fallen to my death before either. It was horrible."

"So awful. Dropping through the air and not being able to grab on to anything. And then—"

"Splat! You're toast!"

"I won't blame you if you hate me now, Roxy. I just wanted you to know how awful I feel about it."

The alley cat stood up. "I could never hate you, Bianca. Let's just put that whole ugly business behind us. Although I really can't forgive you for ruining Dorothy Kittlebun movies for me. She was my favorite actress!"

"What a mess she was yesterday! Can you believe she sniffs catnip?"

"That didn't surprise me at all. Half of Tinseltown's biggest names are addicted to the stuff."

"I suppose that's how they cope with the stress of celebrity life," said Bianca.

"But never mind about Dorothy. What's with this new look?"

"Do you like it? My wardrobe has a few gaps in it after the past few days, so I went shopping."

"You're down that dress you wore to the funeral and a pair of pajamas, right? That's hardly what I'd call a wardrobe emergency."

"Actually, I've lost two dresses. Don't be mad at me, Roxy, but I had a run-in this morning with Flint's ex-fiancée, who it turns out is using her stewardess job as a cover to smuggle stolen artifacts into the country. Flint had this notion she might have been involved in his murder."

"Hold on. Flint has an ex-fiancée? And what do you mean you had a run-in with her?"

"I only found out she existed yesterday. She came to the funeral, which freaked Flint out. Then she turned up at his apartment this morning just as I was cleaning it out, and we got into a spat over an Egyptian monkey figurine. I took the opportunity to ask her a few pertinent questions about Flint's death, which it turns out she had nothing to do with, but—"

"But what, Bianca?" Roxy snapped, her hands on her hips.

"She was worried I'd call the cops on her for taking the statuette, so she shot me with a small revolver she had in her bag."

"Holy smokes! Are you telling me you've lost yet another life since yesterday?"

Bianca nodded sheepishly.

"That makes us even, doesn't it? We've each got four left."

"Yep."

"Bianca, you can't keep going on this way."

"I know. I know. You were right all along. I've been reckless. But at least I keep ruling out suspects left and right, and that counts for something in my book."

Their conversation was interrupted by Tabatha yelling for Roxy to come and help her in the kitchen. "We'll talk more about this later," Roxy said, giving her a hug. A wave of relief washed over Bianca—their fledgling friendship was still intact.

"What time do you get off?" Bianca asked.

"I'm only working until six today."

"Want to come over afterward? I can cook us dinner."

"Sure thing," Roxy said over her shoulder as she took off in the direction of the kitchen. "And until then—stay out of trouble!"

"Don't worry. I've had enough excitement for one day!"

* * *

Feeling peckish, Bianca stopped at a nearby deli and bought herself an egg-and-cheese sandwich on a bagel for lunch. She walked over to the small park on Christopher Street and found a spot on an empty bench in the shade. Opening up the brown bag, she peeled back the warm tinfoil and took a big bite of the gooey sandwich. Farther along the bench an abandoned newspaper rustled in the breeze. She picked it up and flipped through the pages absently as she ate. Usually she would search the *Gazette* for Flint's byline, but those days were over. Then a headline in the Metro section caught her eye and she stared at it in amazement: "Police Make Arrest in Murdered Journalist Case." Abandoning her sandwich, Bianca gripped the paper with both hands. She recognized the name of the suspect in the article from the list Roxy had swiped—it was that sommelier! Bianca's eyes flew across the page as she read all about Gustave Legrand and his fraudulent wine scheme. The short article ended with a paragraph about how detectives considered him a feline of interest in Flint Lockford's murder. As a possible motive they mentioned a restaurant review from nearly a year ago where Flint Lockford had exposed the tuxedo cat as a swindler.

Stunned, Bianca stared out into the distance, letting the paper fall to the ground. Why hadn't the two detectives let her know about the arrest? It was infuriating! She should have been their first phone call. Springing to her feet, Bianca tossed her half-eaten sandwich into a nearby trash can and took off at a fast clip in the direction of the 6th Precinct.

When she got there, she demanded to speak to Detectives Puddleworth and Digby, but was told at the front desk that they were currently out investigating a case. When she insisted on talking to someone in charge, Sergeant Doyle, the boorish bulldog who had given her the ring the other day, trundled over.

Sergeant Doyle sympathized with her complaints about being left out of the loop. "I'm not surprised you're not happy," he said. "I wouldn't be happy if I was you either. I'll level with you, Miss Moon, Detectives Digby and Puddleworth aren't exactly the shining stars on our detectives team. I'm still scratching my head trying to figure out why the captain put them on this case. They arrested this sommelier fella, but they couldn't make the murder charge stick for lack of evidence. Legrand posted bail this morning and is already back out on the street!"

Bianca felt the outrage building up inside of her. She had suspected incompetence on the part of the two rookie detectives, but she found it unfathomable that Flint's murder suspect would be released on bail. She wanted to scream at the top of her lungs, but instead she took a deep breath, thanked the sergeant for his time, and marched back out of the precinct. If she couldn't rely on the law for justice, then she would just have to take matters into her own hands.

Bianca stopped at the phone booth on the corner, pushing through the accordion doors and dropping a dime in the slot. She dug the crumpled phone number out of her pocket and dialed the number.

"Hello, is this Kevin? Do you still have that motorcycle?"

28 · Junior Detective Morton Digby: The Diner

Detective Puddleworth was delighted to see his photo in the *Knickerbocker Gazette* on Thursday morning. "Take a look at this, Morton! Penelope Flick reported on our arrest and there's even a picture of me in action!" Morton looked over the Scottie's shoulder and read the headline: "Police Make Arrest in Murdered Journalist Case."

And sure enough, alongside the article was a snapshot of a handcuffed Gustave Legrand being ushered into the squad car by Detective Puddleworth. The Scottie's confidence in the arrest had rubbed off on the reporter, who portrayed the tuxedo cat as a promising suspect in Flint's murder. "The thing is, J.B.," said Morton, "this article is problematic now that Legrand has been cleared of murder charges."

The Scottie stroked his beard thoughtfully. "You're right, Morton. I think we'd better update Penelope Flick on the latest developments. We don't want the public to think we released a murderer on bail. I don't have much sympathy for Gustave Legrand but we should probably clear his name when it comes to these particular charges. Give Penelope Flick a call and set up a lunchtime meeting. It'll be smart for us to cultivate good relations with the press. Many of the finest detectives had the ear of a helpful journalist!"

"Do you mean in mystery stories?" Morton asked.

"Yes, books, Morton! I'll lend you a few choice titles one of these days so you can brush up on your reading."

The two detectives agreed to meet Penelope Flick and her photographer colleague at the West Village Coffee Shop for lunch. This turned out to be a dingy little diner on Greenwich Street that served up cheap fare for locals. Standing outside, Detective Puddleworth looked at the storefront and shook his head disapprovingly. "I hope we don't end up with food poisoning."

"Penelope Flick picked this spot. Stick to the coffee if you're worried about the food."

"But it's lunchtime!" protested the Scottie. "I'm famished!"

Morton held open the door.

The reporters were already sitting in a booth in the back, with Otis Hubbard, the massive Saint Bernard, taking up the bulk of a striped red and white leather bench. The two detectives squeezed in across from them and accepted paper menus from the curly-haired waitress. The Scottie peered studiously at the menu and settled on a broccoli omelet with hash browns as his choice, while Otis went with the flapjacks, and Morton and Penelope both ordered eggs over easy on toast with home fries.

Penelope was all business. She took a notebook out of her purse and flipped it open. "I take it you fellas saw my piece in the paper this morning?"

"We sure did!" said the Scottie, beaming. "I can't believe I got my photo in the *Gazette* on my very first week at the precinct!"

"First week? No kidding." Penelope made a note in her little book.

Morton sighed. "As it turns out," he said, "we didn't charge Gustave Legrand with murder due to a lack of evidence tying him to the case. He's already out on bail for the fraud charges."

"Is that so?" Penelope scribbled a few more lines in her notebook. "Does that mean you have ruled him out as a suspect?"

"That tux is certainly guilty of fraud, we're sure about that," Detective Puddleworth clarified.

"You were pretty gung-ho about this tuxedo cat's role in the murder case yesterday," said Otis. "Seems like you're changing your tune."

Penelope nodded. "So are you certain Legrand didn't kill Flint? Or do you just lack the evidence to prove it?"

"At this time we have no reason to believe he's connected to the killing in any way," Morton stated clearly. "He was always simply a feline of interest in the investigation."

"I see." Penelope's ballpoint pen hovered above the notepad. "Do you have any official suspects, then?"

"We have a couple promising leads," said the Scottie. "But we can't reveal any names at this time."

"Just to be clear," said Morton, "Gustave Legrand's posting bail doesn't mean there is a murderer on the loose. We wouldn't want the public to get the wrong idea."

"That's where we could use your help," added Detective Puddleworth. "We need to get the word out that Legrand is no longer a murder suspect."

"No problem," said Penelope. "I'll write a short follow-up piece when I get back to the office. But if you make any new arrests I expect to be your first phone call."

"Oh, absolutely!" the Scottie assured her. "You'll be the first to know."

"And don't expect me to go easy on you. There's a murderer out there somewhere," the reporter said pointedly. "And it's your job to find them."

The Saint Bernard's large brown eyes turned serious as he said: "This isn't just another story for us. Flint was our friend."

The detectives nodded gravely.

Detective Puddleworth inclined his head. "Don't worry. Using the process of elimination we will soon put our paws on the mastermind behind Flint's murder!"

Otis gave a skeptical harumph.

Detective Puddleworth launched into a lengthy monologue about modern criminology methods, talking about the overreliance on olfactory evidence, and how adept criminals had become at masking their scent. "The nose is no longer the most important tool in an investigator's toolbox. It's what's between your ears that really matters! You will either outfox a professional criminal or they will outfox you. And like a chess match, it's important to think five moves ahead!"

The two reporters seemed puzzled by the Scottie's impromptu lecture on criminal theory. Morton smiled uneasily and was grateful when the food's arrival cut his partner's speech short. Detective Puddleworth wiped his knife fastidiously with his napkin and eyed his plate hungrily.

Otis dumped a pool of maple syrup over his short stack. Penelope eyed her colleague askance. "Try not to get syrup all over your fur like you did last time, Otis." Then she speared a potato cube with her fork and waved it in the air before the two detectives. "You know, we were supposed to meet Bianca at Flint's apartment this morning to help her clear out his stuff, but she wasn't there. We thought she was a no-show until we spotted a bloodstained dress on the floor with bullet holes in it."

"Bullet holes?" Detective Puddleworth mumbled, his mouth full of hash browns. "How do you know they were bullet holes?"

The gray tabby reached into her purse, her hand emerging in a closed fist. She dropped three crumpled bullets onto the tabletop with hollow clinks. "These were mixed in with her clothes. We put two and two together and figured Bianca was the most likely victim. We went to check on her but she wasn't home."

"We need to have a little chat with Miss Moon," Morton said irritably.

Detective Puddleworth grunted in agreement. "Darned straight! We can't have her running around doing her own investigating and getting herself knocked off left and right. Our job is hard enough already without her constant interference!"

The Scottie picked up the check when they were done, and the two detectives made their way back to their parked cruiser. Morton got behind the wheel but didn't start her up right away. "Listen, J.B., are you sure we're on the right track? What if we went back to the drawing board and looked for new suspects? You know—widen the net!"

"Horsefeathers!" cried the Scottie. "We have a list of suspects and we need to pursue them doggedly! They all had a reason to hate Lockford because of what he wrote. Legrand didn't pan out so it's time to move on to the next name on the list. It's gotta be either Peggy Sneekly, the disgraced zookeeper, or Arthur Neverest, the self-proclaimed explorer. Deduction tells us that Arthur Neverest, with his deep pockets, is the more likely of the two. Hiring a hitdog is an expensive proposition. Did you find his address?"

"Yep, he lives up on Park Avenue."

"Let's not waste another second. It's high time we introduced ourselves to this terrier."

Morton turned the key in the ignition. "If you say so, J.B."

They drove uptown with the windows rolled all the way down. Detective Puddleworth stuck his head out of the car, his tongue lolling to one side, his expression joyful. Morton wished he knew his partner's secret for remaining unaffected by all the pressure. Their careers hinged on successfully closing this case. Morton knew that failure would prove that Buckley and Callaway had been right all along—that he wasn't City detective material.

Traffic was light and they soon found themselves cruising along the wide expanse of Park Avenue, its sidewalks swept clean by doordogs lurking under hunter-green awnings. Imposing brick buildings rose up on either side of them, home to the City's movers and shakers and their old money neighbors.

The doordog at 457 Park Avenue was polishing a gleaming brass pole when they arrived. He did not look pleased to see a squad car pull up in front of his building. He quickly informed them that Mr. Neverest had just stepped out.

"Any idea where he was headed?" Detective Puddleworth asked gruffly.

"I'm sure I couldn't say," replied the mutt in the trimmed gray uniform.

"Perhaps this will help jog your memory?" The Scottie plucked a dollar bill from his wallet.

"Discretion isn't everything," conceded the doordog, pocketing the cash. "You didn't hear it from me, but my understanding is that Mr. Neverest often heads over to the Explorer's League in the afternoons. It's a private club."

The two detectives radioed dispatch for the address. It turned out to be only a few short blocks away and they were soon double-parked outside. The Explorer's League was a narrow stone building with elaborate flags hanging out front. Walking into the lobby, Morton felt transported back in time. It had red leather chairs, a marble fireplace flanked by standing iron lamps, and a tiger skin rug by the hearth. A mounted warthog head on the wall eyed them warily with its glassy eyes.

A Cornish rex in a black suit was seated behind a reception desk. Her welcoming smile turned sour when she saw their police badges.

"We have reason to believe that a Mr. Arthur Neverest is on the premises," said Detective Puddleworth.

"If you take a seat I'll send word to Mr. Neverest that you wish to speak with him." She waved them in the direction of the tall leather chairs.

"Hate to break it to you, lady," growled Detective Puddleworth. "But that's not how this works. Just tell us where we can find him."

The Cornish rex pursed her lips and said ruefully: "You can check the second-floor terrace and the library on the third floor."

The two detectives wound their way up a carpeted stair-case with wood-paneled walls, oil portraits of famous explorers staring down at them. On the second-floor landing they encountered an enormous stuffed polar bear rearing up on its hind legs, its paws frozen in perpetual attack.

They walked through a large drawing room and into the adjoining terrace without spotting a wire fox terrier among the various members loafing about. Morton and the Scottie proceeded up one more flight of stairs, where they discovered a huge library with a massive fireplace at the far end. Floor-to-ceiling bookshelves lined the space, each shelf packed with worn leather-bound volumes. On the walls above the fireplace hung framed maps charting the paths of famous expeditions, while in each corner of the room huge elephant tusk sculptures added an exotic note to the decor. Sitting in an armchair facing the fireplace, his head barely visible above an outstretched newspaper, the detectives spied a wire fox terrier with a neatly trimmed beard.

"Mr. Neverest, I presume? We have a few questions for you," said Detective Puddleworth.

Brow furrowed, the wiry terrier looked up from his paper at the two detectives. Detective Puddleworth tugged open his jacket to reveal the gold badge clipped to his belt.

Arthur Neverest swallowed hard. "What is this about?"

Before Detective Puddleworth could start grilling him, they were interrupted by a fidgety retriever in a green blazer. A small tag on his breast pocket identified him as the League's executive director. "Good afternoon, sirs. Perhaps you would prefer to conduct this interview in private. I'd be happy to give you access to the study on the first floor."

Detective Puddleworth seemed annoyed but he grudgingly agreed.

Arthur Neverest folded his paper and stood up, showing himself to be marginally shorter than the Scottie. The fox terrier's initial alarm at seeing the police badge had quickly turned to irritation. "Don't the police in this city have better things to do than harass upstanding citizens?" For a brief moment Morton wondered if there was going to be trouble, but Arthur Neverest tucked his paper under his arm and followed them meekly out of the room.

They went down the stairs in single file with the director leading the way, followed by Morton, Neverest, and Detective Puddleworth pulling up the rear. When they got to the second-floor landing, the Scottie's yelp alerted Morton that something was amiss. He turned on his heel and was startled by the sight of his partner being tackled by a ten-foot polar bear. It took him a second to realize that the fox terrier must have toppled the giant stuffed bear and that instant of confusion was all Arthur Neverest needed to bolt past him down the stairs. Morton gave chase, reaching out to grab hold of the fox terrier's jacket collar, but Neverest wiggled out of his jacket, snatched a wooden snow sled off the wall, and cracked Morton on the head with it. Morton staggered backward and then tumbled down the stairs, landing in a heap at the bottom. The world spun madly around him, a white blur raced by him, headed for the exit, then everything went black.

29 · Flint Lockford: The Message

At around four p.m. Flint finally gave up on sleep, having spent the past hour tossing and turning in his bunk, besieged with worry over Bianca. Mid-afternoon was prime sleeping time for ghosts, but he rolled out of bed, grabbed his hat and umbrella, and set off for Bianca's apartment. Dark clouds were gathering overhead, bearing down on the City with the promise of long overdue rain.

Predictably, Bianca was not home when he arrived. Gertrude was quietly snoring inside the kitchen pantry but Rupert was wide awake. The parrot squawked repeatedly when Flint walked into the parlor, and Flint was convinced the bird was somehow aware of his presence. He would have to ask Professor Chumley about this later.

Flint settled down to wait on Bianca's small sofa and as the minutes ticked by his eyelids grew heavy. Without intending to, he drifted off to sleep. He woke up with a start to the growl of a motorcycle on the street outside. The rumble of the bike grew louder, coming right up to Bianca's building, where it sputtered to a stop. Flint rubbed his eyes, stretched, and floated over to the window, poking his head through the sheer drapes. Droplets of rain were splattering the sidewalk outside, and there at the curb was the motorbike, a sleek machine with a red fuel tank and polished silver fenders. Seated astride the bike was a white cat in a black motorcycle jacket, black jeans, and a silver helmet. It wasn't until she turned in his direction and flipped up her goggles that he recognized Bianca. Only she looked nothing like her usual self. He blinked in astonishment, watching as she dismounted and propped the bike up on its kickstand. Moments later she was inside the apartment, striding purposefully into the kitchen.

The first words out of his mouth were: "You bought a motorbike!"

"Flint?" she said, startled, turning to face the sound of his voice. "I didn't think you'd be here at this hour."

"I couldn't sleep so I came to check on you."

"That's very sweet of you, darling. But I'm afraid your timing isn't great. I'm just making a quick pit stop and heading right back out!" As she said this she pulled a short knife from the butcher block, wrapped a cloth napkin around the blade, and tucked it inside her jacket.

"You stopped home to grab a kitchen knife?" His voice faltered.

"Yes. Very useful things, knives. Never know when one might come in handy. By the way, I met your old flame this morning. That Riyo is something else. I have no idea what you ever saw in her. She put bullet holes in one of my best summer dresses!"

"Bullet holes!" he cried in disbelief.

"Long story short is she got away with the monkey and we didn't hit it off. I'll tell you all the details later, but I can't talk now. I gotta run!"

"What are you planning to do with that knife?" he demanded.

"I've got a few questions for Gustave Legrand, the sommelier. Remember him? Turns out he was released on bail even though he was arrested for your murder. Go figure. I'll see you later, darling!" Saying this, she bolted out the door, not bothering to lock it behind her.

Flint stood there, stunned, trying to make sense of everything she had just said. Coming to his senses, he rushed through the door and out onto the rain-spattered sidewalk, fighting a strong gust of wind. He was surprised to discover that the downpour felt strangely invigorating. It had the opposite effect on him to sunlight, somehow making him feel more substantial, the raindrops passing right through him with no need for his umbrella. Holding on to his hat with his free hand, he steadied himself and hurried to catch up to Bianca, who was already straddling the motorbike, snapping her goggles back into place over her bright green eyes, and giving the starter a swift kick. The engine growled to life.

Flint stood directly in front of the motorcycle. "Bianca! Stop this madness! You can't just mention a suspect has been arrested and then run off. And you can't stuff a kitchen knife in your jacket and pretend like it's nothing. And you most definitely can't ride that blasted bike in the rain!"

"It's just a little rain, darling. What's the harm?"

"When did you even learn to ride a motorcycle?"

"Earlier today. I bought it off a dog named Kevin, and he gave me a quick lesson. I just need a little practice and I'm sure I'll get the hang of it. No more trolley fares for me!"

"Don't you need a license for that thing?"

"Could be. But I'm not worried about that right now." She stuck out her hand, palm up. "Wow! It's really coming down! I'd better go or I'll be completely drenched. I'll catch you later." With a flick of her wrist the motorbike let out a roar, the wheel spinning on the wet tarmac before catching and sending the bike surging forward, right through him. He spun around and watched as the bike skidded frighteningly for a moment before Bianca regained control and zoomed off down the street, carving a trail of bubbles in the wet roadway. Flint watched, horrified, as the rumbling bike receded in the distance.

Someone tugged at his jacket sleeve and a bright young voice said: "Excuse me, mister. Are you Flint Lockford?"

Flint looked down to see the ghost of a young beagle pup looking up at him questioningly.

"Who wants to know?" Flint asked him.

"It's a simple question," the beagle pup said petulantly. "Either you are or you're not! I reckon you are, though. Give it to the wolfhound in the tweed jacket, she said. Is that a tweed jacket you're wearing?"

"It is, and I am Flint Lockford. What do you want?"

"Here. Take this." The beagle pup gave Flint a small white envelope.

Intrigued, Flint took it from the lad. "What is it?" he asked.

"No idea. She paid me ten bucks to put it in your hands, so that's what I'm doing, and I got another ten coming my way once the job is done!" The chipper pup scampered off.

Flint tore open the envelope and read the folded note:

Tell Bianca the contract on your life was taken out by a Mister X at the 6th Precinct.

Flint stared at the letter, mystified. The rain pelted down on him, passing right through the translucent paper in his hands. Still grasping the note, Flint took off in the direction the beagle pup had disappeared, determined to get to the bottom of this new mystery right away. Rounding the corner, there was no sign of the pup, so he swooped up to the next intersection with the help of his umbrella. In the distance to his right, he saw the young beagle standing next to a tall Afghan hound in a green suit, who was handing him a banknote. Flint did a double take—it was none other than Tatiana Valova, the Queen of Spades! Flint popped open his umbrella. The powerful wind was at his back and he closed the distance between them in a few giant leaps.

"You!" he barked as he drew near, lunging at the hound and waving the letter in her face. "What is this supposed to mean?"

She stood still, unflinching. "I needed to get a message to you. To Bianca, really. I only want to help."

Flint's nostrils flared. He was shaking with rage. "It's because of you that we're trapped in this nightmare to begin with!"

"I know," replied Valova in a hollow voice. "If I could go back and undo my actions I would. Just tell Bianca that the order and the payment for the contract on your life came from inside the Sixth Precinct. I can't narrow it down any further yet, but she shouldn't be wasting her time or precious lives investigating any other suspects."

"The Sixth Precinct?" A light bulb went off in Flint's head. In the weeks before his death he'd been working on a story dealing with the mob's infiltration of their local precinct.

The story had been triggered by an anonymous tip he'd received suggesting that someone at the station house was using their position to make evidence disappear and further the interests of organized crime. Flint had gone right to the top, calling up the precinct captain and questioning him sharply. At the mere suggestion that the mob had wormed their way into the precinct, the captain had cursed him out in unprintable language and hung up on him. Now, Flint couldn't help but wonder if that one phone call had triggered a chain of events leading to his own death. He stood there shell-shocked for a moment, then he glared at the Afghan hound. "How do you know this?"

"The butcher at the Delancey Market was the intermediary for the contract. I made contact with him and he claims the call came from someone with significant clout at the Greenwich Village Precinct."

"Let's say I believe you. What then? If I tell Bianca, she will just confront them and cause even more trouble. They would be as ruthless with her as they were with me."

"They are not to be trifled with," Valova conceded. "We could try and unmask the culprit first."

"Do you think the order came from the very top? From the captain himself?"

"I don't know. But sixteen thousand dollars isn't chump change. If we can find out who signed off on that payment it might tell us who was behind it."

Flint grunted.

The Afghan hound looked him dead in the eye. "I know nothing I say will ever make up for what I've done, but I want you to know I deeply regret my role. My targets are always real scumbags, and I assumed you were no different. I thought you must be some corrupt journalist in the mob's pocket. It was my last job and I just wanted to get it over and done with. Now that I'm dead I feel compelled to make up for my crime however I can, and I won't find peace until I do."

"You're only saying that because you got a taste of your own medicine," Flint said bitterly.

30 · Bianca Moon: The Wine Cellar

Bianca sped along slick city streets, the single cylinder engine humming between her legs. It was lucky Kevin had thrown in a pair of goggles for free because without them she would have been blinded by the rain. Puddles were beginning to build up on the sides of the road and every time she rode through one, the bike sent a wave of water splashing to both sides, making her feel a bit unsteady. Yet she was completely unafraid. She knew this had something to do with the anger raging inside of her, which didn't leave any room for fear.

She arrived at Chez Claude's in no time at all and backed the bike in between two parked cars. Hopping off, she unbuckled the helmet and hung it from the handlebars. Thankfully the rain had begun to let up.

A CLOSED sign hung on the back of the restaurant's door. Bianca tried the handle and, finding it unlocked, she pushed in without hesitation. She startled a tuxedo cat on the other side of the door who had been busy sweeping the floors with a broom, a toothpick hanging from his mouth and an untied bow tie dangling around his collar. "Can I help you?" he snapped.

"I need to talk to Gustave Legrand."

"Regarding?"

"I have a message for him from his lawyer." The lie came

smoothly and easily to mind. She held the cat's gaze and saw boredom replace his initial inquisitiveness as he pointed to a door on the right. "Go through that door there and down the stairs. You'll find Gustave in the cellar, drowning his sorrows in bottles of merlot."

Normally, descending a dark and narrow stairwell in a strange building would have scared her witless, but Bianca felt perfectly calm. The air in the basement was cool and damp. Someone close by was singing a mopey ballad in an off-key voice, and the sound led her to a large chamber stacked on all sides, from floor to ceiling, with wine racks. Seated at a table in the middle of the room was a tuxedo cat who she recognized from the photograph in the paper. In front of him was an open bottle of wine and a stemmed glass.

"Gustave Legrand?" she asked, just to be sure. These tuxedos could be notoriously difficult to tell apart.

He looked up, surprised to hear her voice.

"My name is Bianca. Bianca Moon."

"Do I know you?"

"I'm Flint Lockford's fiancée."

"That bastard!" he snarled. "That muckraker was a real son of a bitch! You've got a lot of nerve showing your face here. What the hell do you want?"

"I want to know if you had him killed because of that article he wrote about you."

The tuxedo cat tilted back his head and cackled like a hyena. "That's rich. You're here because of that damn article in the paper this morning, aren't you? As if I didn't have enough problems already, now the whole city thinks I'm a murderer!" The tux shook his head. "Do you really think I'd be sitting here a free cat if I'd killed a dog?"

"You tell me."

"Well, I didn't murder him!" snarled the tuxedo. "Wine is my avocation, not dropping pianos off of rooftops! Which isn't to say that the thought of strangling that wolfhound with my bare paws never crossed my mind."

"So you did hate him?" Bianca wasn't sure she believed Gustave. On the one hand he was inebriated, which made it less likely he was lying. Then again, you wouldn't expect a murderer to just openly confess to their crime.

"Of course I hated him!" he cried. "He made up all those lies about me in the *Gazette*. And if it weren't for Flint Lockford, those undercover cops would never have come sniffing around yesterday to bust up my side hustle. Do you have any idea how much money that cost me? Not to mention the stain on my reputation. There's even a good chance I'll end up behind bars. Yeah, you'd better believe I loathed that darn wolfhound, and I doubt I was the only one who felt that way. Your boyfriend was always digging up dirt on hardworking cats and dogs."

"Fiancé."

"Excuse me?"

"Not boyfriend. Fiancé."

"You know what, Bianca? You are one nutty cat! Anyone ever tell you that?"

"Yes, I've been getting that a lot lately."

"Well, here's a crazy idea for you. Now that you have your answer, why don't you pull up a chair and join me for a drink? I hate drinking alone and I promise you this chateau Mondrian grand reserve is like nothing you've ever tasted. I've been saving this bottle for a special occasion. Turns out posting bail was it!"

Bianca regarded the tux with disgust. "No offense but I can't think of anything I'd enjoy less."

"We could drink to Flint Lockford's health!" The tuxedo cat guffawed. He stood up on wobbly legs and toddled over to a cabinet in the corner, returning with a second glass. Back at the table he poured her three fingers worth of wine from the bottle and held it out to her. She accepted it reluctantly, more than anything as an excuse to hang around until she had made up her mind definitively. She was almost convinced he was telling the truth, but there was something shifty about this cat that made him hard to read.

The tux raised his glass. "To life on the outside!" He sniggered. She reflexively brought the glass to her lips and gave it a sniff. Notes of oak and cherry filled her nose. She took a small sip. It wasn't the worst wine she'd ever had. Bianca put the glass down and pulled the knife from the inside pocket of her jacket. In a swift motion, she swung her arm down and drove the blade into the center of the wooden table. Then she leaned forward and looked Gustave Legrand straight in the eyes. "Do you swear on your mother's grave that you didn't kill Flint?"

He shot her a venomous look. "You are one vindictive kitty. No! For the last time, I swear I didn't kill him. But if I ever meet whoever did I'll be sure to shake their hand and congratulate them on a job well done!"

Bianca unsheathed her claws. She detested this lowlife.

But she was finally sure he was telling the truth. Gustave wasn't Flint's killer. She would have to move on to the next name on the list. Footsteps sounded on the stairs and Bianca swiveled to see a young tux in an apron poke his head into the cellar. "Everything okay here, Boss?"

"Fine and dandy." The sommelier beamed. "Our guest was just leaving."

Bianca hissed at the tux as she worked her knife out of the table and tucked it back inside her jacket. Then she drained what was left of her wine and, turning on her heels, she strode out the door.

She made it about halfway up the stairs before they began to sway under her feet. In her ears she heard the sommelier's cackling laugh. That underhanded cat! What had he done to her? She toppled backward, clattering down the steps and landing sprawled at the foot of the stairs. She stared up at the hideously distorted countenance of Gustave Legrand, horns sprouting from his head and his tail becoming strangely pointed, like the devil himself.

She tried moving her limbs but it was as if she was frozen in amber. The simple act of breathing became a struggle.

Gustave Legrand sneered down at her. "An excellent vintage, don't you agree? My own special blend! I slipped some deadly nightshade into your glass when your back was turned. If there's one thing I've learned as a sommelier, it's that no one ever turns down a free glass of wine! This evens the score a little with your rumormonger of a boyfriend. And if you dare to show your face around here again I'll even the score some more."

Bianca took a tiny breath, staring up at the monstrous

sommelier. Her heart was pounding but she struggled to remain conscious. The tightness in her throat was growing more intense and she closed her eyes, gasping for air. With her last breath she managed to whisper one solitary word. "Fiancé." The next thing she felt was the strange sensation of her life force leaving her body and projecting itself through the ether.

Before long Bianca found herself sitting in a curtained-off cubicle at City Hospital. Nurse Bertlemina was back on duty, and was currently staring at Bianca's chart, stupefied. "This can't be right, can it? It says here this is your second death today! Bianca, tell me this is a mistake?"

"I've had a rough day."

"And that's four deaths in the past three days, leaving you with only three lives. Bianca, what's going on? Talk to me."

"My fiancé was murdered, and I'm doing my best to find whoever was responsible for his death."

"How was he killed?"

"Someone dropped a piano on his head."

Nurse Bertlemina's surprise was transformed to amazement. "Hold on a darn second. Your fiancé was that poor journalist who got crushed by the piano?"

"Yep. That's him."

"Oh, I am so sorry, Bianca. How dreadful. But this vendetta you're on clearly isn't getting you anywhere."

"Don't worry, I'm running out of suspects fast. I've just had a run of bad luck is all."

Another nurse, a mixed breed dog, poked her head in through the curtain. "Is this her?" she whispered to her colleague, who nodded.

"Wow, you got your ticket punched four times in three days?" exclaimed this new nurse. "It's hard to fathom! Here, let me see that chart!" Nurse Bertlemina looked at her colleague reproachfully and held on to the chart.

"I'll save you the trouble," said Bianca. "Let's see, on Tuesday night I was tossed into the Gowanus Canal by two mafia thugs, on Wednesday I was thrown off a terrace by a celebrity's bodyguards and fell sixteen stories to the pavement below, then this morning I was shot by a vindictive art smuggler, and most recently I was poisoned by an embittered sommelier who slipped deadly nightshade into my wineglass."

The nurse's jaw dropped. "Hold on, I'm gonna go grab Nancy and Joanne."

Bianca took a sip of milk. She soon found herself surrounded by a gaggle of medical personnel, all of whom wanted to hear the story of her dead fiancé and her multiple fatalities straight from her own mouth.

By the time they all left to get back to their duties Bianca was feeling better. She got up and slipped on the blue dress. Flint and Roxy were going to be furious with her, but she would just have to head home and face the music. She also needed to retrieve her leather jacket from Chez Claude's, in the pocket of which were the keys to her motorcycle. Gustave Legrand had warned her not to come back, but there was no way she was going to let that creep keep her bike.

31 · Junior Detective Morton Digby: The Pool Shark

Morton opened his eyes and squinted up at the ceiling of the Explorer's League, feeling like he'd just had a pile of bricks dropped on his head. Reaching up, he gingerly touched the goose egg forming on his forehead and decided this probably accounted for his splitting headache. He sat up and then struggled to his feet, helped by a very concerned-looking Scottish terrier.

"I'm okay," Morton muttered woozily.

"Well, you don't look it. Here, sit down in this armchair while I radio in a description of Arthur Neverest. Then I'll drive you to a hospital!"

"I don't need medical attention," Morton protested. "It's just a little bump. But I'm surprised to see you on your feet, seeing as how you were attacked by a polar bear."

The Scottie chuckled halfheartedly. "That villain caught me off guard! I suppose you can't be feeling too bad if you're still cracking jokes. Your head isn't bleeding either, thank goodness. Still, you took a nasty knock, and at the very least you should take the rest of the day off. Come on, I'll drive you home."

Morton lived in a five-story walk-up on the corner of Wooster and Prince. His apartment took up the entire fifth floor, which sounded amazing when he told friends, but was always a disappointment when they discovered that the building's footprint was miniscule.

Detective Puddleworth helped Morton up the stairs and into his apartment, setting him down on the ratty couch in his living room. The Scottie brought him ice wrapped in a dish towel for the bump on his head and proceeded to heat up a can of chicken soup on Morton's small stovetop, all the while rambling about what he planned to do to Arthur Neverest when they caught him. "I'm gonna toss that weasel into the dingiest holding cell in the precinct! The one with the rat infestation!"

"We have to catch him first," Morton pointed out. He was not feeling optimistic about corralling Arthur Neverest. According to dispatch, patroldogs had looked for the fox terrier at his residence and his place of business without success. The pseudo-explorer had gone to ground.

"Oh, we'll sniff him out, don't you worry about that!" Detective Puddleworth tapped his nose meaningfully.

They ate off of TV tray tables while watching the nightly news on Morton's small television set. After dinner, Morton began to feel almost doglike again. Tired of getting concerned looks from his partner, Morton said: "Relax, J.B. I feel a lot better now that I've got some food inside me, and this bump seems to be shrinking."

"Still, it would be a good idea for you to hit the hay early."

"It's barely seven o'clock!" Morton objected. "I'm not ready to call it a night."

"Well, it's too late in the day for us to pick up the trail of our fugitive."

Morton thought about this. There had to be something

useful they could still accomplish. "How about we get ahold of Penelope and Otis," he suggested. "An article in the *Gazette* might flush out our runaway explorer."

"Hmm. That's not a bad idea," admitted the Scottie. "We did promise to keep them up to date on the investigation."

As luck would have it their phone call caught Penelope right as she was leaving the office. After consulting with Otis she suggested they rendezvous at the Calico Cat Lounge. Twenty minutes later, when they arrived at the lounge, the two journalists had already staked out a pool table. Detective Puddleworth was quick to challenge them to a game of eight ball. "I don't mind telling you that back in school I was considered something of a whiz at billiards!" boasted the Scottie, preening his whiskers. "It all boils down to good old-fashioned physics and geometry!"

The gray tabby listened with an arched eyebrow as the Scottie rambled on about angles and sidespin. "Why don't we make things interesting," she suggested in an offhand manner. "Shall we say ten cents for every ball pocketed and a dollar to the winning team?" Morton couldn't help noticing the way the Saint Bernard's face lit up at her suggestion.

"I would like nothing more than to take your money, Miss Flick!" replied Detective Puddleworth. "But regrettably, as officers of the law, we are barred from participating in gambling of any sort."

Hearing this, the Saint Bernard's face sunk back to its usual shape and he muttered something unintelligible under his breath.

Morton racked up the balls and Penelope broke with a thundering crack that sent them crashing all over the felt table.

The number two ball dropped and Penelope gave Detective Puddleworth a mock innocent smile and said: "Lucky break, I guess." Penelope lined up a shot off the rail that sent the four ball rolling slowly down the length of the table until it fell neatly in a corner pocket. "So why did you guys want to meet?" she asked, steering the conversation to business.

In hushed tones Detective Puddleworth brought the journalists up to date on their uptown misadventure with the runaway fox terrier. On cue, Morton showed off the big lump on his head.

"I don't know, fellas," mused Penelope. "A lot of cats and dogs run from the police. You can't assume guilt from that."

"Alley cats and street pups may run for no reason," said Detective Puddleworth. "But not high-society gentledogs like Arthur Neverest!"

Penelope Flick chalked her cue stick and walked around the table, sizing up her next move. "Let's not forget about that sommelier you went and arrested who turned out to have nothing to do with the crime. I'm not sure I'm ready to bite on this one. What do you think, Otis?"

The Saint Bernard shrugged his wide shoulders. "I bet that dog hated Flint, and it sounds like he had the money to pay for the hit job. This explorer might be our guy."

"Tell you what," said Penelope, sinking yet another shot, "I can do a brief write-up with the headline 'Police Detective Assaulted' and describe how this upper-cruster attacked Junior Detective Digby. Then I'll tack on something at the end about how Arthur Neverest is wanted for questioning regarding the Flint Lockford murder. The public can put two and two together if they want."

Detective Puddleworth looked pleased. "That should do the trick!"

"We'll get you a photo of Neverest first thing in the morning," Morton promised. He was wondering if Penelope was ever going to miss a shot as he watched the cue ball kiss gently off the five ball, which dropped into the side pocket with a clunk. Morton leaned on his cue stick and sighed as she sank two more shots. Glancing around the game room he spotted a familiar alley cat lurking within earshot. He elbowed his partner and whispered: "Look, J.B. It's our old friend Roxy."

The Scottie's thick eyebrows met in the middle. "Keep your eyes open for Bianca. Those two cats are never very far apart."

"Speak of the devil!" Morton said. Bianca had just appeared at the top of the stairs, dressed in a plain-looking blue dress. Roxy ran over to greet her as she came down, the alley cat's expression one of alarm. "Bianca, please tell me that's not another City Hospital dress!"

Everyone around the pool table pricked their ears and edged a little closer to the two cats.

Bianca took a twirl, holding the hem of her dress. "Why? Don't you like it, Roxy? This is my fourth blue dress. I've got quite the collection!"

The alley cat's eyes flashed angrily.

Bianca turned apologetic. "I'm sorry, Roxy. A treacherous sommelier slipped me a poisoned glass of wine."

Penelope abandoned the pool game and went up to Bianca. "I couldn't help overhearing what you just said. How many times have you died in the past few days exactly?" the reporter asked in disbelief.

"Oh, hi, Penelope!" Bianca replied. "I've died four times, including twice today. I've been drowned in the Gowanus Canal by mafia thugs, thrown off a sixteenth-floor terrace by a Hollywood celebrity's bodyguards, shot by a crazy antiquities smuggler, and poisoned by an aggrieved sommelier." Bianca rattled off her now-familiar spiel.

Penelope looked astonished. "Bianca, you have to let me interview you. The *Gazette*'s readers are going to want to hear all about the ordeals you've been through."

"Oh, I don't know about that," replied Bianca. "I think I would come across as terribly foolish."

Morton could tell from Penelope's expression that she wasn't about to take no for an answer. The reporter crossed her arms and squared her shoulders. "Please reconsider, Bianca. An article like this would help draw attention to the pervasive violence against cats in this city. Aren't you tired of everyone treating us as fair game just because we have nine lives? With your help we can draw attention to this barbarity!"

Bianca's brow knit together. "When you put it like that, how can I say no? But first I need to retrieve my motorbike from Chez Claude's before those slimeballs sell it off for parts. My keys were in my leather jacket when I died, so that horrid sommelier must have them!"

Roxy unsheathed her claws. "Me and the gals will go down there with you. If we threaten to make a big scene in their fancy restaurant, I bet they'll cough up your things right away!"

Morton cleared his throat. "Perhaps it would be best if you enlisted our help to retrieve your personal property, Miss Moon. And while we're at it, we can question Mr. Legrand about cat poisoning."

"Taking a feline's life is a clear violation of his bail provisions," Detective Puddleworth chimed in. "That alone is enough to justify hauling him back to the pokey."

"Are you sure I won't be interrupting your game?" Bianca asked, casting them a cutting look.

Penelope Flick came to their defense. "The detectives are still on the clock, Bianca. They met us here to talk about the case. They need the *Gazette*'s help to locate an animal of interest."

"Let me guess," said Roxy. "Arthur Neverest or Peggy Sneekly?"

"Arthur Neverest. That's right!" Penelope was taken aback. "You seem very up to date on the ins and outs of the investigation."

"No thanks to these two fleabags." Bianca jerked her thumb derisively in the direction of the two detectives.

To Morton's surprise, Roxy also stood up for them. "Don't be so hard on them, Bianca," said the alley cat. "As coppers go, these two ain't half-bad."

32 · Flint Lockford: The Menagerie

Friday

Flint couldn't believe Bianca had lost two more lives yesterday. It made him want to tear his fur out. His new plan was to shadow her everywhere she went, even if it meant staying awake all day. This was a daunting task now that Bianca had recovered her Matchless G80. She had hopped on her motorbike and roared off down the street, with Roxy clinging precariously to her back. Flint had done his best to climb on but had been blown off seconds later.

Chagrined, he'd had to catch a trolley instead. Professor Chumley had volunteered to tag along, and they were both rattling their way up Sixth Avenue in a standard army-green streetcar. The two ghosts were sitting together on a rattan bench, while above them wooden ceiling fans did their best to stir up the stifling hot air. Flint's gaze wandered over the row of ads above the windows that cheerfully extolled the virtues of cleaning products and popular snacks. There were only a few living passengers scattered about, as well as a solitary ghost passed out in the back row, a translucent newspaper tented over his face.

The professor parted the wooly hair hanging down over his eyes and, turning to Flint, he said: "I had a chat with

Louisa the psychic last night. She's been troubled by your untimely death. Especially since she read you your fortune only a few days earlier. Glimpsing the future is often a burden for clairvoyants. Almost no one takes her warnings seriously, and even when they do it's not clear that fate can be changed. Louisa offered to help out by using her network of spooks to track down the suspects Bianca is looking for. This Arthur Neverest character may be the easier of the two to locate since he worked at the Natural History Museum. There's a huge ghost lodge in that museum, and it would be a snap for them to find out if this Arthur fella is hiding there."

Flint gave a wry smile. "You know, Professor, I have a feeling both Bianca and the detectives are wasting their time. I recently learned that it was someone at our local precinct who orchestrated my death."

"Is that so?" Chumley's fuzzy eyebrows shot up. "Then why haven't you pointed Bianca in the right direction?"

"I don't like keeping the truth from her," Flint replied ruefully. "But I'm worried she would stir up a hornet's nest at the police station if she found out, and then they would inevitably come down hard on her. It's much safer for her to be off chasing red herrings."

The professor regarded him thoughtfully. "It's too bad you and Bianca are working at cross purposes lately."

"I just don't know what's gotten into her," said Flint. "She shouldn't be getting herself mixed up in the sordid details of my murder."

"I'm not sure she can help it," replied Chumley. "Her grief is pushing her on a quest for justice."

"Yes, but what's done is done! She can't let herself become

consumed by this thinly veiled thirst for vengeance." Flint shook his head. "I just hope those two detectives solve the case before she lands in any more dicey situations."

Chumley looked puzzled. "If the hit was masterminded by someone from the precinct, can you really trust these detectives?"

"I've watched those two dogs in action. Neither of them is exactly the pick of the litter, but they genuinely seem to be doing their best to solve the case. My guess is someone made sure the investigation was handed off to these unseasoned detectives knowing they wouldn't be up to scratch."

Every few blocks the trolley pulled over to the curb and the doors squeaked open to let passengers on and off. When it pulled back out into traffic the trolley's bell rang intermittently, warning pedestrians and vehicles to steer clear. A brief silence fell between the two ghosts as they listened to the bell clang and watched the metropolis streak by through the windows.

"It's a big city out there, Flint," said the professor. "I hope you have some idea where Bianca and Roxy were headed?"

Flint nodded. "I overheard Bianca say she wanted to go up to the Central Park Menagerie to try to locate Peggy Sneekly, the disgraced zookeeper. The two detectives are focused on the phony explorer, but Bianca reckons they're probably going after the wrong suspect given their track record so far."

"I see. The Central Park Menagerie, you say?"

"Hang on a minute, Professor! Didn't you say you kicked the bucket up at the menagerie?"

"I did, and I haven't been back since. But I suppose today is as good a day as any for a trip down memory lane."

"Look, if you'd rather not go back there, I understand. Don't worry about me, I'll manage just fine on my own."

"Nonsense!" cried the sheepdog. "A visit to the zoo is long overdue. It will do me good to face down some old demons."

Flint cocked his head. "You never told me what happened to you that day."

Professor Chumley took a long moment to collect his thoughts. "Much like you, I had an unusual death. It all went down nearly twenty years ago when I was working as a chemistry teacher at the Beekdog Hill Middle School, over on East Fifty-Fifth Street. We were out on our yearly field trip to the Central Park Menagerie and I was chaperoning a class of rambunctious seventh graders. One of the highlights of the trip was the lion enclosure. They had about half a dozen big cats on display, with the meanest among them being the famous Charles the Tiglon, a half-Siberian tiger, half-lion hybrid. He was larger than the other big cats and he had a thick black mane and faint stripes on his tawny hide. He was as ferocious as they come. My class was watching the beasts prowl about in their cage when one of my students, a mischievous young cat, swiped my hat and tossed it over the railing. It was a felted wool fedora that I was awfully fond of—this very hat I'm wearing right now as a matter of fact. So I leaned over the rail, stretching down to try to grab it, when suddenly that same student gave me a shove and I tumbled into the narrow ditch separating the railing from the caged lions. Dazed, I sat up and grabbed my hat. Then I looked up right into the menacing jaws of Charles the Tiglon himself. I sat there hypnotized by the beast's amber eyes. In a flash, Charles reached one of his huge paws through the bars of the cage and swiped me right in the throat with his razor-sharp talons. I bled out within minutes."

"What a story! And you say one of your students pushed you?"

"I'm afraid so."

"Do you know who did it?"

"It was a snively little tabby named Cuthbert who was always causing trouble."

"So why haven't you been haunting him ever since?"

"I couldn't bring myself to haunt a twelve-year-old, no matter how horribly he had behaved. Which probably explains why I'm still floating around the city twenty years later."

"What happened to that vile little Cuthbert? Did he end up in the slammer? Or at least get kicked out of school?"

"I don't think anything happened to him. As I recall the newspapers all reported that a gust of wind took my hat and that I lost my balance trying to retrieve it. His classmates all kept his secret, not wanting to get in trouble themselves."

"So no one ever found out you were pushed?"

"Nope. And in all fairness, it's unlikely Cuthbert was actually trying to kill me. He was just looking to get a laugh from his classmates."

Flint shook his head sadly. "That is so messed up!"

"It was a long time ago," the professor said philosophically.

The two ghosts rode in silence for the rest of the way and hopped off at the Central Park South stop. They drifted into the park and up to the menagerie entrance, flitting from one patch of shade to the next. Inside, Flint soon spotted Bianca and Roxy standing over by the sea lion exhibit, smack-dab in the middle of the small zoo. The two cats were out in the open, chatting with a zookeeper who was holding an empty pail. The midday sun was bearing down in full force so Flint and the professor had no choice but to take cover under a set of arches by the gorilla enclosure, for fear that they would burn through their umbrellas.

"I can't hear a word they're saying from here," grumbled Flint.

"Me neither," replied the professor. "But it looks like they may have struck out." Sure enough, the zookeeper with the bucket had shrugged his shoulders, and the two cats were on the move again, now heading for the wolves exhibit. Flint and Chumley homed in on them there, finding cover in the shade of two soaring elm trees.

"Hello, Bianca," whispered Flint. "What did you find out about Peggy Sneekly?"

Bianca wheeled around. "Oh, hello, Flint," she whispered. "Fancy running into you all the way up here at the menagerie! What a coincidence." She pursed her lips and shot a dirty look in the direction of his voice.

"I thought you might benefit from an extra pair of eyes and ears," Flint said sheepishly. "My friend Professor Chumley came with me and we had a pleasant trolley ride uptown together."

"Is Flint here?" asked Roxy. "Say hello to him for me! How is he doing?"

"Yes, he's here with his new pal Chumley. They're determined to keep an eye on me today and make sure I don't get myself into trouble."

"I thought that was my job?" Roxy smirked. "I can't say I

blame him, really, seeing as how you've been chasing trouble all over town. Hey! Ask Flint if he remembers the day I set the high score on Lighting Ball?"

Flint whispered his reply in Bianca's ear and she repeated his words. "He says, 'You mean the night you drank three Pink Squirrels in a row and started singing along to Count Basset Hound's "Fly Me to the Moon" on the jukebox?'"

Roxy's mouth fell open. "Sorry, I promise I'm not doubting this whole ghost business again. It's just that sometimes it helps to get some fresh evidence I'm not going crazy!"

"I know exactly how you feel," Bianca replied. "I'm the one hearing voices, remember?"

Flint and Chumley listened in as the two cats struck up a conversation with a zookeeper outside the wolf enclosure. This pooch said he remembered Peggy, but he had no idea where she had disappeared to after being fired. Their next stop was the lion exhibit, where a pudgy tabby zookeeper in gray overalls was keeping a sharp eye on the visitors crowded around the railing. "Careful there, sonny," the zookeeper cried when a young pup placed a foot on the lowest bar to get a better view. "You don't want to get close to hungry lions like these!"

Flint glanced at Professor Chumley. "I guess this was the scene of the crime."

"I remember it like it was yesterday. It's almost like nothing's changed," said Chumley, gazing intently at the caged beasts. "Except, of course, that Charles the Tiglon died years ago."

"Excuse me, sir," said Bianca, catching the zookeeper's attention. "We're looking for someone who used to work here. Peggy Sneekly. Do you know her?"

The tabby shot them a curious look. "Been a long time since I heard that name. You two friends of hers?"

"Not exactly. We just need to talk to her about an urgent matter."

"You reporters?" he asked.

"No. It's more of a personal matter."

The tabby scratched himself absently behind his ear. "Peggy never had many friends around here. Kept to herself mostly. But I got to know her better than most over the years and eventually we became pals of sorts. She had a way with animals and she certainly didn't deserve what happened to her."

Bianca's brow furrowed. "How do you mean?"

"Well, it's more than my job's worth to talk about it with two strangers, but I've always regretted not speaking up at the time, and I can't bring myself to hold my tongue any longer. The truth is that when that article got published and everyone started asking questions about the deplorable conditions some of the animals were being kept in, management decided they needed a scapegoat. The menagerie director singled out Peggy since she kept to herself and had few friends—loners make good fall guys. So they pinned the whole thing on Peggy and told her to clear out her locker. The poor dog was crushed. She never wanted anything more than to spend her days working with animals. After that, well, she couldn't make rent and ended up on the streets with her pets. I wanted to put her up until she got back on her feet, but my missus put her foot down." The tabby stared at his feet.

"Have you seen or heard anything from her recently?" asked Bianca.

"Not for ages. Last I heard she took shelter in the abandoned freight train terminal down on Eleventh Avenue. Somewhere around Twenty-Seventh Street, I think it is." The zookeeper's whiskers drooped. "It's a sad business. If you do manage to get ahold of Peggy, please tell her that Cuthbert Turner sends his warmest regards."

Flint saw Professor Chumley give a start. The sheepdog swooped closer and scrutinized the zookeeper's face. "What did he say his name was?"

Flint whispered in Bianca's ear: "Ask this cat to repeat his name!"

"Did you say 'Cuthbert Turner'?" Bianca asked the zookeeper.

"That's right."

Professor Chumley stared at the zookeeper, astounded. "I can't believe it. That skinny little tabby has become a full-grown cat. Yes, now that I look closely at the markings on his cheeks, I see it's actually him. This is the cat who pushed me into the lions' enclosure. And here he is, spending his days making sure no one else ever becomes a victim to one of these wild creatures. I daresay he has redeemed himself. Why—he has turned out to be a kind and decent cat!"

"Bianca," whispered Flint, "ask him if he remembers a sheepdog named Professor Augustus Chumley."

Bianca did as he asked, and the zookeeper looked suddenly stricken. "How do you know that name?" he demanded. "Poor Professor Chumley. He was such an amazing teacher. I think about him every single day. I'm still haunted by his awful death."

"Tell him," said Professor Chumley. "Tell him that it's okay. That I know he didn't mean for any of it to happen the way it did."

Flint relayed the message, explaining quickly to Bianca that as a young lad this zookeeper had pushed his friend over the railing—with deadly consequences.

Bianca was outraged and it was all Flint could do to calm her down. "It was twenty years ago, Bianca. This cat was just a kitten back then! It was just a stupid prank gone horribly wrong."

With an effort, Bianca managed to get ahold of herself. "Well, Mr. Turner. I think it was a beastly thing that you did that day, and if it were me, I'd hold you accountable for your actions. But I have a message for you. A message from Professor Chumley himself. He says to tell you that it's okay. That he knows you didn't mean for it to happen that way. And that he's glad to see you've grown up to be an honest and respectable cat."

The poor zookeeper gave a shudder. "Are you in touch with the spirit of Professor Chumley?"

She nodded. "He's right here with us."

Cuthbert Turner went wide-eyed. "Please tell him that I am dreadful sorry to this day. That I will never forgive myself for it."

Bianca repeated the words that Flint whispered in her ear. "Chumley says it's all water under the bridge. An unfortunate accident, and that you shouldn't beat yourself up about it anymore. And he says he knows you cheated on your chemistry test the day before, but he won't hold that against you either."

"Oh, miss. That's such a relief to hear. Twenty years it's

been weighing on my conscience. That's how I ended up working here at the menagerie. I made it my mission in life to prevent anything like that from happening again. Every chance I get, I argue for higher railings, wider moats, and better locks!"

Flint was watching Professor Chumley with alarm. "Professor? Are you all right?" The sheepdog had begun to fade in and out of sight, and when he was visible, his ghostly form had a peculiar shimmer to it.

"This is it, Flint!" cried the professor. "It's finally my time to cross over. I can't believe it! I feel so light and free. Say goodbye to the Ghosthall gang for me. I'll catch you on the flip side, my friend!" With these words, the sheepdog dissolved into little motes of dust that were caught by the breeze and scattered upward into the sunlight. Flint watched, astonished, as his friend and mentor dissipated into nothingness. Flint's anguish was diminished by the expression of sheer joy he'd glimpsed on Professor Chumley's face as he finally crossed over. The affable professor would be deeply missed, but he had surely gone on to a better place.

33 · Junior Detective Morton Digby: The Psychic

Morton exchanged worried looks with Detective Puddleworth. The captain was in a foul mood. There was no hint of sympathy for Morton getting clobbered by a suspect the day before. At the 6th, short of being stabbed or shot, you were expected to pull up your socks and get on with it.

The testy mastiff pounded on his desk and barked: "This Angora should not be meddling in your case! We can't have civilians taking the law into their own paws! Not in my precinct! I expect the two of you to rein in this rogue cat! Lock her up if you have to! And it beats me how you let this Arthur Neverest dog run off, or why you still haven't tracked him down!" The mastiff's right hand twitched in the vicinity of his phone. Morton braced himself, getting ready to dodge. Thankfully, the ever-attentive Shirley spoke up, reminding the captain that he was expecting a call from the commissioner. The captain scowled and dismissed them.

The two detectives returned to their desks with their tails between their legs. They busied themselves with examining a trove of suspicious documents and letters they had confiscated from Arthur Neverest's study. Detective Puddleworth's keen eyes soon spotted something dodgy. "Cast an eyeball on this, Morton!" said the Scottie, handing him a letter. "You recall Bianca telling us all about Riyo Jones yesterday? Well, this document is signed by her!"

Morton certainly remembered hearing all about Lockford's ex, the stewardess with a fondness for pocket revolvers. He examined the letter. "That's strange. This letter shows Riyo Jones and Arthur Neverest are selling artifacts to the City Museum of Natural History. I'm guessing with cooked-up records of provenance."

"Exactly!" cried the Scottie. "Those two scoundrels are in cahoots! And probably making out like bandits!"

"I bet Neverest gets a big kickback from Riyo's profits."

"They would never get away with this garbage if the museum curators didn't look the other way. I suppose it doesn't pay for the museum to look too closely at where their display pieces are coming from."

This new development set Morton's mind racing. He knew that swindles involving stolen antiquities could sometimes have international repercussions and draw the attention of the feds. "This makes me wonder," he said, "whether Arthur Neverest bashed me over the head and bolted for reasons that had nothing to do with Flint's murder."

"Horsefeathers!" exclaimed Detective Puddleworth. "What you need to understand about criminal masterminds, Morton, is that they have a finger in every pie. This sideline Neverest has selling stolen artifacts is probably just one of many criminal operations he has running. Our job is to trace back the various tendrils of his criminal web until we find the fiendish monster lurking at the center of it all! When I

looked into that terrier's eyes yesterday I knew he was a ruthless character fully capable of murder. If he's not our dog then
my name isn't J.B. Puddleworth!"

Morton scratched his chin. He was reluctant to point out
to his partner that he had been wrong every step of the way so
far. "So what's our next move?" asked Morton. "We may get
some tips called in when Penelope Flick's article hits news-
stands this evening, but we can't sit around until then."

The Scottie tapped his fountain pen on his desk. "There
is that one lead we haven't followed up on yet."

Morton grunted. Roxy had given them a wacky suggestion the night before, urging them to pay a visit to Louisa's
Psychic Parlor on Christopher Street for help finding the fugitive terrier. "Trust me on this one. Just go talk to her," the
alley cat had said cryptically.

Morton had no idea how talking to a psychic was supposed to help. "I hope you're not suggesting we should take
Roxy's advice seriously."

"Leave no stone unturned, that's what I always say! And
that includes kooky psychics." Detective Puddleworth pushed
back his chair. "C'mon, Morton, let's motor."

"If Buckley and Callaway find out about this we'll never
live it down," Morton muttered, getting up and grabbing his
hat off the peg.

"Then let's hope they never do," replied the Scottish terrier, who had keen hearing.

The two detectives walked out of the precinct and into
the blinding summer sun. The heatwave gripping the city
had, if anything, tightened its vise in the past few days, with
the mercury hitting record-busting temperatures. "This city

seems determined to cook us all," groaned the Scottie. "The squad car is going to be like an oven."

"Why don't we hoof it?" suggested Morton. "It's not far and we'll draw less attention to our visit that way."

The Scottie reluctantly agreed.

Louisa's Psychic Parlor turned out to be a little hole-in-the-wall storefront. A colorful window display featured a flashing neon sign in the shape of a cat's eye. The two detectives pressed the buzzer by a small red door and it was quickly thrown open by a plump middle-aged Russian blue. She was wearing a silk robe and had a gold turban wrapped around her head. The egg-sized pendant dangling around her neck played peekaboo with her ample décolletage. "Ah, detectives, I've been expecting you," she cooed, ushering them in.

Detective Puddleworth frowned, disconcerted. "You were?"

"Yes, of course! You are investigating the Flint Lockford murder."

"Er. Yes. That's correct. I am Detective Puddleworth, and this is my partner, Junior Detective Digby. Your name was mentioned to us by an alley cat named Roxy. We were hoping you might be able to help us with our investigation."

"Step right this way, detectives," replied Louisa. "A brief session with the spirits may provide us with some answers."

"Is a session strictly necessary?" asked Morton. "Couldn't you just answer our questions?"

"Ah Detective, it is not I who have the answers you are looking for. I am merely a conduit for those who have traveled beyond the veil."

She led them to a small windowless parlor. In the center of

the room was a round table covered in a velvet tablecloth and encircled by richly upholstered chairs. Sitting on the tabletop was a quartz crystal ball on a silver stand, flanked by two tall candles. Louisa struck a match, lit the tapers, and sat down in front of the crystal ball, waving them into seats opposite her.

"Kindly state the question you seek to answer," she said in a rich theatrical tone of voice.

"Do you know where we can find a wire fox terrier by the name of Arthur Neverest?" Detective Puddleworth asked matter-of-factly.

"Allow me a minute to get in touch with the spirits." Louisa put her hands on the crystal ball, which began to glow a seafoam-green color. She closed her eyes and began to chant: "Spirits of the great beyond, come to me. Spirits of the great beyond, come to me."

Detective Puddleworth watched the fortune teller with keen interest. Morton rolled his eyes. This wasn't proper police work. Not by a longshot.

Suddenly, Louisa sat bolt upright, her mouth forming a perfect O. "Hello, Frankie! Hello, Leo! I haven't talked to you fellas in forever. Still floating around, I see? It's been so long I could've sworn you'd both crossed over. What's that? You just moved uptown to the Natural History Museum? How do you like it up there? Drafty, you say? Well, I would imagine so. Now, tell me, have you perchance caught sight of a wire fox terrier by the name of Arthur Neverest? Yes, I realize you have serious reservations about helping coppers. I don't blame you. But take a look at these two detectives. Do they look like your usual thuggish hounds? Of course not. They are doing their best to solve the cold-blooded murder of a *Gazette* journalist.

Yes, the piano guy! Now, what can you tell me about this fugitive terrier . . . ? I see, so he *is* holed up in the museum, then! Good work, lads."

"But we've already searched the museum top to bottom!" exclaimed Detective Puddleworth.

Louisa opened one eye. "Please don't interrupt me when I'm conversing with the spirits of the dead!" she said sternly. "It's a vast building, and these shades know every nook and cranny. They tell me that this fox terrier wandered the deserted halls last night in the vicinity of the hall of Ancient Canine Cultures. A friendly security guard brought him dinner, and another friend, an attractive dog in a blue stewardess uniform, slipped him a cinnamon roll and a daily newspaper this morning. He has constructed a small hideaway behind a stack of crates in the Specimen Archives room. That's where you will find him." Saying this, Louisa opened her eyes and removed her hands from the luminous crystal ball. The light in the glowing sphere faded and went out.

"There is no way you could know all of that!" Morton scoffed.

"Everything I've told you is true," the Russian blue assured them stiffly. "Whether you believe me or not is entirely up to you. I don't blame you for being skeptical, Junior Detective Digby—there are a lot of charlatans out there." She reached out and took Morton's hand. "If you will permit me, I have noticed a peculiar tinge to your aura and I'm curious to see what the future has in store for you. She turned Morton's hand over and examined his palm. "How curious! I daresay your skepticism will be short-lived, and that you and I will be meeting again soon."

"Sorry, Louisa, but I'm just not buying any of your mumbo jumbo," grumbled Morton, retrieving his hand from the psychic's grip.

"Well, this has been a very singular experience," declared Detective Puddleworth, pushing back his chair. "Your intel should be easy enough to verify!"

"Thank you for stopping by, detectives." Louisa smiled broadly. "Four dollars will do nicely to cover my fee."

Morton stared at her, open-mouthed. "We are City detectives conducting a criminal investigation. You can't charge us for answering our questions!" But the Scottie had already pulled a few bills from his wallet. He slid them over to the Russian blue, who rolled them up and tucked them deftly into the cleft of her bosom.

34 · Bianca Moon: The Spear

Bianca pulled up outside the Calico Cat Lounge on her Matchless G80, and Roxy hopped off the back of the bike, hurrying up the steps and disappearing through the back door. Bianca's next stop was the Siamese restaurant around the corner from her apartment, where she picked up an order of fried rice with shrimp to go, before walking home.

Flint was waiting for her there.

"Hello, darling," she said cheerily. "I'm just stopping for a late lunch and then I'm going right back out to look for that zookeeper."

"Of course you are," he replied, sounding none too pleased.

Bianca set an Andrew Sisters record on the turntable and placed the needle on the outer edge. The crackle of static came over the speaker and then a jazzy tune kicked in. Bianca plopped down on the settee, split her chopsticks apart, and pried open the fried rice carton. Flint was yakking on about the many reasons she should abandon her search, raising his voice to be heard above the music. Bianca alternated between shoveling fried rice into her mouth and countering his points in their never-ending quarrel. An agitated Rupert hopped about in his cage, bopping his head to the beat.

"I heard you promise Roxy that you wouldn't go searching for Peggy Sneekly on your own!" Flint ranted.

"I lied," Bianca replied unashamedly, snagging a pink shrimp with her chopsticks. "I've already cost Roxy a life and I refuse to put her in danger again. I'm sorry, darling, but this is just something I have to do."

"Why don't you go looking for Arthur Neverest instead?"

"Because I have no idea where to find him!" snapped Bianca.

"I may be able to point you in the right direction," Flint confessed.

Bianca glared at him. "Spit it out, Flint! No more secrets, remember?"

Flint grumbled something she didn't catch and then said: "My friend Sophie talked to Louisa the psychic and found out that Neverest has been spotted at the Natural History Museum. He's hiding out in a storage area for fossils and other specimens in an employees-only section on the second floor. Near the hall of Ancient Canine Cultures."

Bianca scowled. "Why do I get the feeling the only reason I'm hearing this is because you think the museum is less dangerous than an abandoned train station?"

"Neverest clobbered our detective friend yesterday. I'm not sure how much less dangerous that makes him. In all honesty, I doubt either suspect had anything to do with my murder."

"I'll soon get the truth out of Neverest if I find him," said Bianca. "I guess I'll stop by the Natural History Museum first. I hope you're right about this tip."

Their conversation drifted to less contentious topics.

Flint was forlorn after losing his new friend Chumley at the menagerie, and Bianca did her best to console him. "So he just disappeared into nothingness?" she asked.

"Yep."

"Is that it or does he end up someplace else?"

"Nobody really knows. I'm sure I'll find out someday."

"It better not be anytime soon," Bianca said sharply. "I know we've been arguing a lot lately, but having you around means everything to me right now."

"Don't worry, my love. I'm not going anywhere."

A few minutes later she set the empty container on the table and stood up. "Time for me to get going."

"Keep an eye open for Riyo Jones," warned Flint. "I think she may be helping Arthur Neverest. We don't want a repeat of the other day."

"Riyo had better keep an eye open for me!" snarled Bianca. "I've got a bone to pick with that trigger-happy pooch." She zipped up her black leather jacket and tucked her helmet under her arm. "I'd offer you a ride but I know you'll just get blown off. I'll tell you everything when I get back."

"I hate being a ghost."

"I know, darling. But you do have a few new talents. You're invisible, you can walk through walls, and you can eavesdrop on your fiancée at all times!"

"A lot of good that does me." Flint sighed. "Try not to get yourself killed."

"You make it sound like I have a death wish. I promise I'll be extra careful. No one is catching me off guard today!" She blew him a kiss and dashed out the door.

* * *

Bianca's motorcycle-riding skills were improving steadily. Her rides were a lot smoother, and she had gotten the hang of using the two round mirrors to check her blind spots when turning. If a vehicle got too close, she wasn't afraid to give the throttle a twist and speed out of harm's way.

In spite of heavy traffic around Times Square, she made it uptown in under twenty minutes, parking the motorbike between two cars on 77th Street, along the south side of the museum. A police car was double-parked down the street and she wondered if that meant Detectives Puddleworth and Digby were close by.

Bianca went up the main steps and into the cavernous lobby. Long-necked dinosaur skeletons soared high above the throng of patrons. She purchased a ticket—suggested admission meant it only cost her a nickel—and grabbed a trifold museum map. Flint had said the fox terrier was hiding in a storage area near the hall of Ancient Canine Cultures on the second floor. She pinpointed the location on the map and walked briskly through the African Mammals gallery with its troop of enormous elephants grouped in the center of the room.

She passed through a colorful exhibit of exotic birds from all over the world and ended up in a central corridor that led her straight to the hall of Ancient Canine Cultures. This far-flung gallery was practically deserted. Dimmed ceiling lights cast the room in darkness. Bianca stopped for a moment to admire an intricate diorama of primitive dogs dressed in animal skins, poised mid-hunt with bows drawn. The next display over depicted the arctic precursors of the malamute, giant dogs with thick, furry coats. If this scene was to be believed, these dogs had been fervent seal hunters.

Bianca soon spotted a small door over to her right with an EMPLOYEES ONLY sign on it. Looking around, she made sure no one was nearby and took a step toward the door. Suddenly, the door flew open and a figure burst through it, running at a full sprint. He was a short, bearded white terrier with frantic eyes. He ran right toward Bianca, glancing back desperately over his shoulder. About ten paces behind him came another sprinting pooch—none other than Riyo Jones herself—and close on Riyo's heels were the two detectives. Puddleworth, with his short legs, was falling behind, but Junior Detective Digby closed in on the Shiba Inu with a burst of speed.

Bianca quickly put two and two together and figured the detectives had flushed Arthur Neverest and Riyo Jones from their hiding place. As Arthur Neverest ran by her, Bianca stuck out a foot and tripped the fleeing fox terrier, sending him sprawling to the museum floor.

Riyo Jones bared her teeth. "You again! You meddlesome fleabag!" she growled. Reaching into her purse, the Shiba Inu whipped out a familiar-looking pocket pistol. *Oh no, not again,* thought Bianca, distraught to find herself staring down the barrel of the gun for the second time in as many days. The Shiba Inu took aim at her and fired off a shot right as Junior Detective Digby knocked the gun from her hand. The bullet ricocheted harmlessly off the marble floor and shattered the glass of a nearby diorama. The border collie quickly slapped a handcuff on Riyo's wrist and wrenched her other arm behind her back to lock the other restraint in place.

"Arthur! Help!" Riyo cried out. Scrambling to his feet, the fox terrier glanced in her direction before turning to make a break for it. He was clearly more focused on saving his own fur. Bianca went after him, prepared to tackle him if necessary. Hearing her footsteps, Arthur Neverest whirled around and let out a guttural snarl. Spying a carved narwhal tusk hanging on the wall, he wrenched it free of its bracket. Drawing his arm back, he launched it through the air aimed right at Bianca's chest. Diving to the floor, Bianca heard the spear whistle right over her head. That was a close one.

Bianca sprang back to her feet, determined to go after the murderous terrier. To her surprise, he was just standing there—frozen—with a look of horror written on his features. Bianca heard a whimper behind her and she turned to see Riyo Jones gasping for air about ten feet away. Shock was written on the Shiba Inu's features as she gaped at the narwhal tusk protruding from her chest.

Junior Detective Digby caught Riyo Jones as she fell.

Arthur Neverest's eyes went wide. Something seemed to click in his mind and he turned to flee once more, but before he could escape, he was tackled ferociously by Detective Puddleworth, who quickly subdued the terrier.

Bianca rushed over to see if she could help Riyo in any way. The collapsed Shiba Inu was staring straight into Junior Detective Digby's panicked eyes. Bianca was close enough to hear the words she hissed up at the border collie: "This was your fault." Then her eyes glazed over and she went limp.

* * *

Ten minutes later the hall of Ancient Canine Cultures was a mob scene of security guards and cops. Bianca had to give her statement three separate times. It was only when witnesses confirmed that she'd played only a minor role in the whole incident that she was permitted to leave.

She wanted to go over and thank Junior Detective Digby for saving her life, but he seemed so overwhelmed that Bianca decided it could wait until the next day. She exited the museum, hopped on her G80, and took off down Central Park West. Her mind was whirling. Was Arthur Neverest the mastermind behind Flint's murder? He had certainly proven beyond any doubt that he was capable of dogicide. The phony explorer was looking at serious jail time for killing Riyo Jones, even if she wasn't who he'd been aiming for. The grisly scene of the Shiba Inu's death was etched in Bianca's mind. When emergency personnel had arrived, they'd pulled out the narwhal tusk and blood had spurted three feet up into the air, causing Riyo's corpse to give a final shudder. Bianca had despised Flint's ex after their earlier run-in, but she hadn't wished her dead. Not when she had only one life to lose.

Bianca sped south on her Matchless G80 through light traffic on Seventh Avenue. Her sweet spot was the middle lane, keeping the trolleys directly to her right. She didn't have to worry about the streetcars making any unexpected turns, as they followed a fixed path along their rails, bells dinging at intersections. Another trick she'd learned was to keep up with the flow of traffic, even if that meant going a little faster. This way she avoided having to deal with any yahoos coming up behind her and honking their horns. Meanwhile, the left

lane, favored by yellow cabs, was often clogged with stopped
vehicles. A taxi roared past her on her left just then, screeching to a stop up ahead to drop off a fare. Passengers always
exited curbside, so Bianca was caught completely off guard
when the cab door suddenly flew open on the traffic side, and
a gray-haired old tom staggered out with the help of a cane.
Bianca gritted her teeth in frustration. The door was blocking a big chunk of her lane. She hit the brakes, but it was
too late to stop, so she aimed to squeeze by the wide-open
door. Of course a trolley would choose that very moment to
wall off the lane on her right side. Bianca's eyes went round
and her tail puffed up as she neared the narrow gap. For a
second she was sure she would just slip through, but then
the tip of her motorbike's handlebar clipped the cab door.
Suddenly she was flying through the air, the world around
her a slow-motion blur of moving pieces. She hit the pavement hard and everything sped up again as her momentum
carried her right under the wheels of the neighboring trolley.
The screech of brakes filled the air and sparks flew as metal
scraped on metal—but it was too late. The last thing she
heard was the mad clang of the trolley's bell.

Bianca's consciousness zipped across the ether, a moment in
time that felt somehow both fleeting and infinite. All her
physical sensations were wiped away and her raw panic was
replaced by a feeling of serenity.

    She landed in the hospital room gasping for breath, her
heart hammering in her chest. The nursing staff quickly
wheeled her into the recovery room and placed her in a blue
curtained cubicle. Bianca's strength slowly returned and she

managed to prop herself up on her pillow by the time the curtain parted and a nurse stepped in to check on her. She was a Maltese with a blue ribbon in her long white hair and she was carrying a glass of milk.

"Is Nurse Bertlemina working today?" Bianca asked hopefully.

"It's her day off," the nurse replied in a raspy voice. "Here, drink this." She handed Bianca the glass. "Let's take a look at your chart." The Maltese stared at the clipboard. First she frowned and then her eyes got big. "Wait a second. You're that cat! The one who keeps cashing in her chips. I read about you in the *Gazette*!"

Bianca had forgotten about Penelope's interview. It must've been published today. "Yep, that's me."

"And you're back again! You certainly lead exciting lives, Miss Moon. What was it this time?"

"I wiped out on my motorbike and got run over by a trolley."

"Oh. You mean like a traffic accident?" The Maltese sounded disappointed. "Well, Miss Moon, you know the drill by now—your dress is on the chair and your trolley token is right here on the table." She gestured to them both. "You've only got two lives left so you might want to start playing it safe. I'd certainly steer clear of any motorcycles if I was you! Those blasted contraptions are nothing but two-wheeled death traps."

"I'm pretty sure my bike got totaled."

"Probably for the best." The Maltese hung the clipboard on the foot of the bed and disappeared back through the blue curtain.

35 · Tatiana Val: The Thief

Since making her big entrance two days ago, Val had become a popular figure among the ragtag spooks at the Delancey Market. The Siberian had been right in predicting that the mood among the querulous ghosts would improve following an influx of cash. Half a dozen barrels of Spume had been procured and the ghosts had whooped it up every night since. Val didn't get the fascination with Spume, but she'd been told that in time she would come to relish the stuff. Considering how many ghosts kept treating her to pints, that moment might not take long to arrive.

Val had made another trip to the bank vault to restock her pockets with stacks of C-notes, making sure she wasn't followed by any of her fellow lodgers. It wouldn't do to lead this lot straight to her stash.

The Siberian ran the Market with an iron fist, which Val knew was the only way to keep this band of troublemakers in line. She'd hit it off with the rakish cat, and their alliance ensured none of the other ghosts messed with her. Her money had even earned her a certain deference from the other ghosts, who were quick to offer their help with anything she needed. She didn't trust the Siberian yet, or any of the other ghosts for that matter, but the strange beauty of a place like the Delancey Market was that trust didn't really come into it.

Val's sleeping quarters were in storage cubicle number 57 down in the second basement. It was one of a hundred padlocked wire cages that market businesses used to store old equipment. Narrow corridors crisscrossed the lower basement, lit by hanging fluorescent lamps with dangling pull chains.

With nothing but wire cages separating the sleeping comrades, there was no escaping the loud snores of the rest of the crew during daylight hours. This didn't bother Val much, even though she had always been a light sleeper. More annoying was having to sleep in her tight-fitting jacket—its pockets stuffed with lumpy bundles of cash. Considering how many of the Market ghosts were former burglars, she dared not take it off. But she soon discovered that even this precaution was not enough to deter one light-fingered ghost. On her third day's sleep, she was woken up by a slight tug on her jacket pocket. She cracked open an eyelid and saw a mangy tabby floating beside her cot. His glowing green figure was hunched, his manner was furtive, and one of his paws was digging delicately in her right pocket.

The cat's eyes lit up with delight as he came away with a fat stack of one-hundred-dollar bills. The money quickly vanished into his pants pocket.

"Find what you were looking for?" Val asked, yanking her jacket out of his grasp. She sat up and glowered at him.

The ghost smiled weakly. "You're awake! I'm so sorry to bother you. I misplaced my umbrella and I thought it might have floated down here!"

"Into my jacket pocket? I'm pretty sure you couldn't fit an umbrella in there!" She held out her hand. "Hand over the money and we can avoid any unpleasantries."

"I have no idea what you're talking about!" replied the mangy cat, backing slowly away. With a few feet of buffer between them, he turned and made a break for it, dashing through the wire cage.

Val took off in pursuit, chasing him down the dark hallway. The tabby had almost reached the elevator shaft when she dove and tackled him, sending him crashing to the floor. A tussle followed and Val used her military training to pin him down to the vinyl tile flooring. Only then did Val become aware of the various sets of boots that had appeared around them. She looked up to see the Siberian and several other ghosts eyeing them, perplexed.

The mangy cat was quick to appeal to the audience. "This lunatic attacked me! I think she may be rabid!"

"What? He stole money right out of my pocket!" growled Val. "I caught him in the act!"

"That's a filthy lie!" yelled the mangy tabby.

Val released him and stood up. Ignoring the cat's pleas, the Siberian yanked him to his feet. Pulling his pockets inside out, he retrieved the stack of Benjamins. He ran a thumb through the wad of bills before handing them back to Val. The Siberian shook his head from side to side, a look of great disappointment on his face. "Oh, Jerry, Jerry, Jerry. You just couldn't help yourself, could you? Once a pickpocket, always a pickpocket."

The cat trembled in fear. "Please, you don't understand. I needed the cash to pay off my bookie!"

"I'm gonna need a chair and some rope!" yelled the Siberian.

The pickpocket squirmed, arching his back in an effort to break free, but by now several rough hands held him tight. Val watched with interest as the hysterical cat was tied to a wooden chair. His desperate yowls were silenced when a dirty rag was shoved into his mouth.

"What's going to happen to him?" Val asked the Siberian.

"Stick around and find out. We have little patience for thieving in the Market. Otherwise this place would quickly descend into chaos."

The ghosts carried the cat into the waiting elevator. A mortal pooch was at the controls and at the urging of one of the ghosts, he punched the button for the third floor. As word spread around the Market, they were joined by more sleepy-eyed ghosts, until practically the whole band had gathered around them on the third floor. Val joined the procession as the trussed-up thief was carried up the stairs to the rooftop exit. They all piled out through the door and into the brilliant sunshine. Umbrellas popped open in unison to create an unbroken shield blocking the sun's rays. It was a whisker past five p.m. and the midsummer sun had lost some of its potency, but the ghosts still pressed themselves into the few meager shadows the roof afforded. The four ghosts carrying the cat deposited the chair in the middle of the rooftop and retreated back to the shaded hut entrance.

Val positioned herself next to the Siberian in the partial shade of a water tower. He extended his umbrella to cover her, his teeth bared in a frozen grimace. They all watched as the thief, sitting in direct sunlight, began to writhe desperately in his chair. His gag disintegrated before the rest of him did and his arms broke free from dissolving ropes. He clawed at the ties around his ankles but it was too late. Val watched in horror as pinprick holes appeared all over the cat, expanding quickly and eating away at him, until, with a last high-pitched yelp, he broke up into glittering motes of dust.

"And *that's* how we deal with thieves at the Delancey Market!" growled the Siberian, twirling his whiskers. They all piled back inside. On their way back down to the basement, the ruthless feline pulled Val to one side for a confidential chat. "We've been keeping close tabs on the butcher's business, just like you asked."

"And . . ." She looked at him expectantly.

"He got another call today from Mister X," said the Siberian. "They've put a hit out on some cat called Bianca Moon. Does that name mean anything to you?"

"Does it ever! She's Flint Lockford's fiancée. This is just what I was dreading. She's gone and made herself a target with all her snooping around!"

"She's a cat, right?"

"Yes."

"Well, my guess is Bianca's life count is about to head south in a big way."

"Do you know who took the job?"

"A hitcat who goes by the name of the West Side Cowboy picked up the contract. We see him every so often. He's a pretty slick customer."

Val was familiar with the name. She had crossed paths with the West Side Cowboy once or twice. He was a gray British shorthair who was fond of old-fashioned single action revolvers, and had a reputation for deadly efficiency. Val had always considered herself the number one hired killer in town, but the West Side Cowboy had stolen the occasional job right out from under her. If this cat had Bianca in his sights, it spelled trouble with a capital T.

36 · Flint Lockford: The Barrel

Flint pushed his way through the red wooden door that barred the entrance to Ghosthall. Albert was passed out in his usual spot at the register desk. With a heavy heart, Flint rapped softly on the tabletop. The corgi lifted his large head, opened his eyes, and stared quizzically at Flint. "What's the big idea, pal? Don't you have enough sense to let sleeping dogs lie?"

"Sorry, Albert. I'm afraid I bring unhappy news." Flint spit it out cold: "Professor Chumley crossed over this morning when we were up at the menagerie."

The corgi stared at him, uncomprehending, as the words slowly sank in. "Not the professor," he croaked. "Chumley is the glue that holds this place together. What happened?" Flint recounted everything that went down at the Central Park Menagerie. Much like Flint, the corgi took some consolation in the thought that the professor had finally found peace.

Word of Chumley's crossing circulated quickly through Ghosthall, before spreading out into Greenwich Village proper, and then farther corners of the city. Old friends of Chumley's from all over town dropped by that evening, and Flint was repeatedly called on to share his account of their menagerie adventure. This was followed each time by the hollow clink of pint glasses as they toasted the professor's memory.

Benny and Tiger ditched their usual playlist and launched into a string of melancholy ballads. The portly tom's moving trumpet solos combined with the ginger cat's wistful crooning had ghosts all over the cantina tearing up. When they were done with their set, Tiger and Benny joined Flint and the rest of the gang on a bench in a quiet corner of the room, where they sat in subdued silence, cradling mugs of Spume.

Looking around at all the heavyhearted ghosts, Flint was struck by how much the professor had touched them all. That woolly sheepdog was proof that ghosts were capable of good deeds and needn't give in to darkness or despair. Without Chumley's help, Flint knew he might never have overcome the dark lure of Claudette's Bakery, or found new friends, or reconnected with Bianca.

He glanced at his watch. If the professor were here, he would tell him to quit moping. Flint drained his mug and got to his feet. "Right, I'm off," he said to the group. "I'll see you all later."

Eyeing him suspiciously, Tiger caught hold of his sleeve as he made to walk away. "Where do you think you're rushing off to?"

"I've got some business to attend to," he replied vaguely.

"What kind of business?" Paco asked him. "You have a look in your eye, like you're up to no good. I think you'd better tell us exactly where you're headed, Flint. Now that Chumley is gone, it's our job to look out for you."

"Look, I appreciate the sentiment. I really do," Flint protested. "But I'm a grown dog and this is completely unnecessary."

"Just tell us where you're sneaking off to!" Albert barked.

Flint blinked and decided to level with them. "I've learned that the contract on my life was taken out by someone from the Sixth Precinct. I need to unmask the culprit before Bianca gets into any more trouble. I'm heading over there to do a little snooping."

"Are you serious?" growled Tiger. "You were going to run off to the Sixth Precinct all on your own?"

"Are you looking to join Chumley in the hereafter?" Benny laughed. "Don't you know that police station is chock full of some of the meanest spooks in the city?"

Flint blinked. "Is there a ghost lodge there? I had no idea."

Tiger let out an exasperated sigh. "Picture the worst murderers and cutthroats this neighborhood has seen in the past fifty years," she said, "then sprinkle in some of the most ruthless and brutal cops that ever walked a beat, and that's who you'll be surrounded by the moment you set foot in that hellhole. Did you even have a plan?"

"I was going to look for some sort of paper trail. Hitdogs aren't cheap."

"Follow the money," mused Albert. "Not a bad place to start. We just need to figure out how to get in there without getting torn to shreds by those thugs."

"I don't want anyone taking any risks on my behalf," said Flint. "I can do this alone."

"No way, my friend!" cried Paco. "Besides, you're gonna need our help to have any hope of success."

"He's right," said Benny. "We're your pals now, Flint. If you're set on going, then so are we."

Flint ran a hand over the fur on the top of his head. He was touched. Even Benny, who everyone knew was a real scaredy-cat, was willing to put it all on the line for him.

An hour later Flint and his five friends were rolling a barrel of Spume down the sidewalk. Albert had used his pull to get them a good price, and they had all chipped in to pay for it, with Sophie, who seemed to have the deepest pockets, contributing the lion's share.

"I swear I'm gonna pay all of you back," Flint promised.

"Don't sweat it!" said Benny. "Let's just hope this barrel does the trick! I still say we should've woken up Moose. I'd feel a lot better if we had him along on this little outing."

When they arrived at the steps of the police precinct, Albert told them to wait outside while he went in to test the waters. As a respected Ghosthall spook, the corgi felt he had the best chance of opening a dialogue.

The rest of them hovered nervously outside. Flint was greatly relieved when Albert stuck his large head through the door and waved them in. They carried the barrel up the stairs and through the doors. They were met by a horde of ghosts, about half of them in police uniform, while the other half were wearing black and white scrubs. They were a mean-looking bunch, but to Flint's relief they all had big grins plastered on their faces. "We'll take that!" they said, and several hands reached out to take the barrel from them.

Albert gave them an update in a hushed voice. "I had a chat with their leader. He's that chunky rottweiler with the gold-trimmed cap over there. I told him we are investigating a murder and he grudgingly gave us permission to poke around for a few minutes when I mentioned our little gift. We need to keep our paws off any ghost items, and stick to things from the mortal world. He was very emphatic about that."

Flint looked around at the chaotic precinct. A living Maine coon sat behind the front desk, oblivious to all the ghosts before him. To his right in the bullpen, Flint glimpsed a handful of living cops and detectives sitting at their desks, chewing the fat. The precinct ghosts had rolled the Spume barrel into an open area in the middle of the room and were already filling their mugs.

A hound in a dark suit peeled off from the group and floated over to greet them, a pint of freshly poured Spume in his fist, his tail wagging back and forth. "I appreciate the drink, fellas. I hear you lot are working a murder investigation? I'd be happy to lend you a paw. I was a senior detective here for decades and I know where all the bodies are buried!"

This kind offer set tails wagging among the Ghosthall spooks. "We'd be glad for any help you can give us," said Flint. "We're looking for evidence that someone from the precinct recently paid for a hit job."

"I can't say I'm shocked! You can't swing a dead cat in here without hitting a crooked cop!" The hound let out a hollow laugh. "There's always been a ton of bad apples at the Sixth."

"The one I'm looking for goes by the handle Mister X."

"Doesn't ring any bells," said the ghostly detective.

"We figured we'd look for a paper trail. The expense may have been disguised in some way. Sixteen thousand, five hundred dollars is a big price tag."

"Lucky for you fellas I've got the ear of Gary, the night

sergeant," said the hound. "He's a good buddy of mine who hasn't kicked the bucket yet. Right this way!"

The night sergeant turned out to be a sleepy basset hound with long gray-flecked ears and a droopy face. The detective explained what Flint and his friends were after, and the basset hound mulled over their request. Then in hushed tones he told them: "All that financial stuff ends up in the file cabinets downstairs. Nobody's gonna care if I go down and take a look."

They all followed the night sergeant downstairs into the empty basement. Judging from the number of ghostly blankets and sleeping pads lying around, the space doubled as a dormitory for ghosts. The basset hound turned on the overhead lights as he crept down a long hallway, at the end of which was a row of filing cabinets. He slid open the heavy metal drawers and rooted around for a few minutes before finally emerging with a document.

"Is this what you're looking for?" he asked. "This invoice is for sixteen thousand, five hundred, the exact sum you mentioned. It's marked for 'capital improvements' but I haven't heard anything about any big projects in the precinct. Nothing around here would cost this much to fix. Let's see. Yep, it was signed by Captain Maddox himself, and it's got the official Sixth Precinct PAID stamp here in the corner. What should I do with it? A cooked-up document like this could be radioactive around here!"

A worried look crept across Flint's face. If the top dog at the precinct was implicated, that was bad news. Flint had no idea what to do with the invoice. They couldn't take it with them. There was only one thing he could think of. He quickly explained his idea to the ghostly detective, who relayed the message. The night sergeant wrote out a short note that read:

Mister X payment to Tatiana Valova? Share with Penelope?

The basset hound put the invoice and the note in an envelope marked urgent and left it on Detective Puddleworth's desk. Flint knew that was all they could do. With any luck, this clue would be enough to put the two detectives on the right trail.

37 · Junior Detective Morton Digby: The Roommate

The narrow staircase in Morton's building had a tenebrous feel to it, with tattered carpeting, a rickety wooden banister, and weakly glowing wall sconces. Morton wound his way up the five flights leading to his front door. The air on the stairs was warm and musty, except for a patch of icy cool air on the third floor that seemed to come out of nowhere. He shivered as he passed through it, guessing that his neighbor must have installed an air conditioner.

Inside his apartment, he kicked off his shoes and flipped his hat onto the peg on the wall. A glance at the clock above the sink showed that it was almost midnight. Morton threw open the windows and turned on the fan, hoping to get some air moving in the soupy apartment. Grabbing two cans of Rheingold lager from the fridge, he plunked himself down on the couch.

The deadly events of the afternoon kept replaying themselves in his head. At least the culprit had been apprehended on the spot. And no one had thought to pin any blame on him for Riyo's death—apart from Riyo Jones herself, that is. Morton kept reminding himself that he'd only been carrying out his sworn duty. Arthur Neverest was the one who had launched that primitive spear in their direction. Still, Morton couldn't help but feel partly responsible. If he hadn't restrained

Riyo, she might still be alive. An image of the bloodied tip of the narwhal tusk sticking out of the Shiba Inu's back flashed through his mind.

A half hour later Morton got up and chucked the empty beer cans in the kitchen bin. He stepped into the bedroom and stripped down to his white boxer shorts, tossing his blood-spattered clothes into the hamper. Plodding over to the bathroom he ran the hot water in the tub. A fistful of bath salts turned the water a cloudy white and filled the air with the warm scent of cedar. The smell always took him back to his childhood on the family farm, where he used to take long soaks in a wood-burning outdoor tub after a long day's work.

Morton slipped into the steaming water, sinking in up to his neck. Bit by bit the tension in his muscles eased. He reminded himself that this was the life of a City cop. There were good days, there were bad days, and there were days that were so awful that your only hope was to try and forget them.

Easier said than done. He couldn't get the moment Riyo took her last breath out of his head. She had placed the blame for her death squarely on his shoulders. He kept hearing her voice even afterward, recriminating him for her demise. The Shiba Inu's tone had been crisp and clear, as if she'd been standing there in the museum beside him.

Closing his eyes, Morton pushed these thoughts from his mind and focused his attention on the water dripping slowly from the spout. He exhaled. "It really wasn't my fault," he murmured.

A voice hissed in his ear. "Don't kid yourself, Detective. If it weren't for you, I'd still be alive." A chill ran along the length of Morton's spine, his eyes shot open, and he sat up in the tub, only to find he was completely alone in the small bathroom. He quickly decided his mind must be playing tricks on him. Morton settled back down in the tub. But moments later the voice was back: "If you hadn't handcuffed me, I wouldn't have died!"

"Who said that?" Morton cried, looking this way and that, his eyes panicked.

"Who do you think, you dope? It's me, Riyo. I'm here to make sure you don't ever have a moment's peace after what you've done. Arthur was partly to blame, of course—that dog has lousy aim—but I can't begrudge him for trying to skewer that meddlesome Bianca. Ultimately the fault lies with you coppers. You had to come looking for him, sticking your pesky noses into our affairs. Then you had the nerve to hand-cuff me in public, as if I were some common criminal!"

Morton clapped his hands over his ears to try and shut out the voice.

"Yeah. Cover your ears, you louse! It won't help now that I'm a ghost. This apartment of yours is a real dump, by the way. What do they pay you that you're forced to live in this hovel? That PH sign on your door is a cruel joke!"

Morton sat still in the tub. He had no idea what to do. Maybe hearing voices was par for the course after what he'd been through. Or maybe yesterday's bump on the head had rattled his brains a lot worse than he thought.

Morton stood up and stepped out of the tub.

"A little warning would be nice," muttered the voice. "And if you're trying to scare me away, I'll have you know that I had three brothers and I've seen it all before."

Morton yanked his towel off the back of the door,

wrapping it about his waist and scowling at thin air in the empty bathroom. The voice sounded just like Riyo Jones. Brash, with a distinctive smoky quality, her register low, yet unmistakably feminine. They had spotted the foxy stewardess immediately upon arriving at the museum and followed her from a safe distance as she'd gone downstairs to the cafeteria and purchased a sandwich and a bottle of soda. From there she led them directly to Arthur Neverest's hideaway.

Still jittery, Morton stepped into his dryer booth and pushed the button activating the jets of warm air all around him. In the few minutes it took him to dry his fur, he neither saw nor heard anything out of the ordinary. But on his way to the bedroom, the pages of the newspaper on the counter fluttered loudly, as if a fan were blowing directly on them.

Morton pulled on a white T-shirt and a pair of sleeping shorts. He brushed his teeth and turned off the kitchen lights. The living room lamp proved more difficult. He stepped on the pedal switch, but as soon as he turned around, he heard a click and the room lit up again. Frowning, he stepped on the switch a second time, but once again the lamp lit up the moment his back was turned. A deep sense of unease overtook him. Morton hurried into his bedroom and banged the door closed, throwing the latch for good measure.

"Seriously? You think a locked door is going to keep me out?" said the voice. "Newsflash! I can walk through walls. There isn't anywhere for you to hide."

Morton refused to talk back to this figment of his imagination. Instead, he switched on the small transistor radio on his bedside table and spun the dial until a popular song by the Five Knights blared from the speaker. He sank down into his pillow and tried to still his racing pulse. Suddenly the music was replaced by static. Frowning, he dialed into the station once more, but yet again it refused to stick. With trembling fingers, he switched off the radio and slunk down under his sheets.

"Nighty-night, Detective. I hope you don't have nightmares!" The voice let out a nasty laugh.

Morton rolled on his side and pulled his pillow over his head.

The voice whispered in his ear, crisp and clear. "Nice try. But you won't get off that easy. I'm dead because of you. Dead-dead. Cut down in my prime. I had big plans, you know. I was going to set the world on fire. Now my corpse is sitting in the City morgue waiting to be claimed. From here on out, I'm going to make your life a living hell."

38 · Flint Lockford: The Warning

Flint sat in Bianca's parlor drumming his fingers on the arm of the settee. Across from him, sitting cross-legged in the armchair, was Roxy. The alley cat was eating sardines straight from a can with greedy fingers. Needless to say, she had no clue he was there. Flint ran his hand through the lightbulb in the floor lamp next to him, causing it to flicker. The alley cat looked up and frowned, but quickly went back to slurping down sardines. Flint sighed. Being invisible was a curse.

The jingle of keys in the front door came as a great relief for Flint. Roxy jumped up and hugged Bianca as she walked in. "Hey, Princess! Where the heck have you been?" Then Roxy winced.

Flint followed her gaze and to his dismay he saw Bianca was wearing a blue dress. "Is that another hospital dress?" he exclaimed.

"Oh, hello, darling," Bianca said, looking in his direction. "I didn't realize you were here too."

"Flint's here?" Roxy said with surprise.

"He's standing right next to you from the sound of it. And yes, I've come straight from City Hospital—again. Nurse Bertlemina wasn't on duty tonight and this other nurse was kind of a dud if I'm being honest."

"Bianca!" growled Roxy. "Don't tell me you kicked the bucket again!"

"Yep. I'm down to two lives."

"Was it Arthur Neverest?" Flint asked in a strangled voice.

"No, it wasn't Neverest, although he did give it the good old college try."

"What happened, then?" Roxy demanded.

Bianca looked abashed. "I got into a motorcycle accident on the way home."

Flint gritted his ghostly teeth. "I knew that bike was a big mistake!"

"But how?" asked Roxy. "I thought you were getting the hang of that thing."

Bianca explained about her motorbike hitting the taxicab door, and the resulting trolley accident. Then she told them all about her close calls at the museum earlier, and about the Shiba Inu's tragic death.

This news came as a second shock for Flint. "I can't believe Riyo's dead," he mumbled. "I just saw her two days ago. I was furious when I heard she shot you, but—"

"She didn't deserve to die. I know," Bianca said ruefully. "It was an awful thing to witness."

Roxy was perplexed. "Is this the same Riyo who shot you with a pistol the other day?"

Bianca nodded.

"Well, don't expect me to shed any tears over her," spat the alley cat.

Bianca went to wash up and change into her pajamas. She said she was starving so Roxy disappeared into the kitchen to make a tuna salad sandwich for her friend. Left alone in the parlor, Flint sat stewing over these latest calamities. Each day seemed to bring fresh trouble with it. After his own death, Bianca had begun losing lives left and right, then this morning Chumley had crossed over, and now Riyo had been killed in a grisly fashion. It was all too much.

He was startled out of his thoughts by the appearance of a ghost in a green suit floating down the corridor and into the parlor. His ears drew back and his lip curled when he recognized Tatiana Valova. "What are *you* doing here?" he barked. "You can't come in here!"

"I have some news that you need to hear," she said, locking her steely eyes on him.

"Who are you talking to, darling?" came Bianca's voice from the hallway. She stepped back into the parlor wearing silky black pajamas with white piping. "Is one of your ghost friends here with us?"

Flint did his best to keep his voice steady. "Yes. It's a ghost. You don't know her, but she needs to talk to me about something."

"Why were you barking at her?" Bianca asked suspiciously. "You sounded furious."

"I was just surprised to see her is all."

Bianca crossed her arms and stamped her foot. "Flint Lockford, even when you're invisible I can read you like a book. There's something you aren't telling me. Out with it this minute!"

Flint groaned.

"You promised no secrets, remember?" she reminded him.

"Her name is Tatiana Valova. There—are you happy?"

Bianca drew in a sharp breath. "Hold on a darn second! You mean you're sitting here in my apartment talking to the Queen of Spades? The hitdog who murdered you?"

"The very same," he replied coolly. "But we're gonna step outside now for a quick chat."

"Why are you even talking to that beastly hound?" Bianca demanded. "Throw her out of here right this minute!"

"Look, Bianca, I don't like her any more than you do, but I need to hear what she has to say. Now that Valova is a ghost, she regrets everything that happened and says she wants to help. She is doing her best to figure out the identity of the individual who hired her."

"And you believe that?" cried Bianca. "How gullible can you be? She's not on our side, Flint! Can't you see that? I would scratch her eyes out right now if I could." Bianca's needle-sharp claws were unsheathed and ready.

"And you wonder why I don't tell you things," Flint said huffily.

"Is this the first time you're speaking to her?"

"No. She showed up yesterday afternoon after you left."

"And you didn't think to mention it? Something like—hey, Bianca, you'll never guess who I ran into. The dog who dropped a three-hundred-pound piano on my head! Flint Lockford, I just can't believe this!" Bianca was shaking with rage.

"Don't worry, we're leaving right now. But I'll be right back, okay?"

"Don't bother!" she growled. Turning on her heels, Bianca stormed out of the parlor.

Flint's shoulders drooped as he followed the Afghan hound out onto the street

Valova faced him and said: "She's right, you know. I wouldn't forgive myself either if I were her."

"Just say what you came to say," grumbled Flint.

Valova told him how she'd signed on with a band of ghosts at the Delancey Market, over on the Lower East Side. She explained that it was one of the biggest criminal hubs in the city and that she used to go there to get her hitdog assignments back when she was alive. "The butcher who works there is the middledog who gives out the contracts. I've been keeping tabs on him for the past couple days."

"So what?" Flint asked impatiently.

"Another job came in this morning from Mister X. The intended target is Bianca."

A knot of fear twisted in Flint's stomach. "What? Why would they want to bump off Bianca?"

"She keeps drawing attention to your case in the press, which puts pressure on the cops to solve it. And she doesn't look like giving up anytime soon. Someone's had it with all her meddling and is looking to silence her permanently."

"What does this mean?" asked Flint. "How long do we have to figure this out?"

"The contract has already been picked up by the nefarious West Side Cowboy," she replied. "He's a sharpshooting hitcat with a penchant for old-fashioned revolvers. This cat is a cold-blooded killer who always gets the job done."

Flint did his best to fight the feeling of panic rising in his chest.

39 · Junior Detective Morton Digby: The Polygraph

Saturday

A technician wheeled the futuristic machine into the interrogation room. He was a skinny old greyhound with wire-rim glasses. When Morton referred to the contraption as a lie detector, the technician became indignant. "The Fibutron 5000 is not just some lie detector," he said brusquely. "It is a state-of-the-art polygraph device with a guaranteed ninety-five percent accuracy rate."

Detective Puddleworth was delighted to be on the technological cutting edge. He had read about the Fibutron 5000 in a law enforcement trade magazine and he assured Morton it represented a huge leap forward for interrogation methods. The Scottie gave a nod to the polygraph operator, who started hooking up the wire fox terrier to his device. Arthur Neverest looked miserable as wires running from the apparatus were strapped around his arm and his midsection. The greyhound took his time calibrating the machine, asking Neverest a series of test questions and ticking off his answers on the graph paper with a mechanical pencil. When he was satisfied that everything was working smoothly, he moved on to the set of questions the detectives had supplied him with.

"Did you know a dog named Riyo Jones?"

"Yes."

"Were you working with her to defraud the City Museum of Natural History?"

"*Defraud* is a strong word!" objected the terrier.

"Please answer yes or no." The operator repeated the question.

"No," Neverest replied.

"Did you conspire with Riyo Jones to sell stolen artifacts to the museum?"

"No."

"Did you stab Riyo Jones with a narwhal tusk yesterday?"

"I wasn't aiming for her!" yelled the wire fox terrier.

"Please confine your responses to a yes or no format," cautioned the technician once more. He repeated the question.

The terrier hung his head. "Yes."

"Did you know a dog by the name of Flint Lockford?"

"Yes."

"Did Flint Lockford interview you for an article about a year ago?"

"Yes." A dark cloud passed over Arthur Neverest's face.

"Did you hire a contract killer by the name of Tatiana Valova?"

"No."

"Did you arrange to have a hired killer murder Flint Lockford?"

"No."

"Were you involved in any capacity in Flint Lockford's death?"

"No."

Five minutes later, after many follow-up questions, the technician turned off the machine and tore off the chart. The two detectives stepped outside with him to confer. "The results are very clear," the greyhound declared. "The subject is telling the truth about the murder case, but he is lying through his teeth when it comes to the fraud charges."

Back in the bullpen, Morton rested his head on his desk just for a moment. Riyo Jones had been relentless in her efforts to keep him awake the night before. Then at dawn she had complained about the early-morning sunlight stealing through the cracks in the blinds, and Morton, in a fit of pique, had thrown the shades wide open, after which Riyo had disappeared in a huff and Morton had managed to snatch a couple hours of shut-eye before his alarm went off.

"Look alive, Morton! We have work to do!" cried Detective Puddleworth. "Grab a cup of joe if you need a pick-me-up!"

"I've had three already," Morton replied, stifling a yawn. He wished he could tell his partner that Riyo's ghost had kept him up most of the night with her inane chatter. But the Scottie would think he had lost his mind. And perhaps he *had* lost his mind? It was either that or start believing in ghosts. He wasn't sure which of the two options was preferable.

Detective Puddleworth plucked a fresh pen from his desk drawer. "We'd better draw a line through Arthur Neverest's name and move on. It's extremely disappointing—I was certain he was our dog."

"I agree that he doesn't seem to have had anything to do with the murder," said Morton. "Clearly he only ran from us because he thought we were going to bust him for trafficking stolen artifacts." Riyo had told Morton as much last night during her long ramblings. She had also found the notion that Arthur Neverest might be involved in Flint's murder quite ludicrous. Not that the opinion of a voice in his head merited much weight.

"Well there's only one name left on our suspect list!" exclaimed Detective Puddleworth. "So the question we are faced with now is—how do we find Peggy Sneekly?"

"Or we could look for other possible suspects." Morton shot his partner a pointed look.

"We don't have time to widen the investigation, Morton! If it wasn't Arthur Neverest then it must be Peggy Sneekly! We've exhausted the other possibilities, so whatever remains must be the answer, however improbable."

Morton sighed. Once the Scottie got an idea in his head he went after it with a one-track mind, with his partner along for the ride. Morton couldn't escape the feeling that there was something big about the case they were missing. But for now Detective Puddleworth was the only one with a real lead, and that meant Morton would have to humor him again. He just hoped they wouldn't waste too much time tracking down this missing zookeeper. "Well, I have no idea how to find her," Morton admitted.

"Let me think," replied Detective Puddleworth. "It's not like a clue is going to just land in our laps!" The Scottie mopped his brow with his pocket square and reached over to flick on his desk fan. As the blades picked up speed, a stack of papers on his desk began to flutter. The Scottie hurriedly placed the photo of his wife on top of them, but not before an envelope on top of the stack went airborne. It did a loop-the-loop in the air and landed flat on the desk in front of him. J.B. picked up the envelope and peered at it curiously. "What's this?" he muttered, reaching for a letter opener. He was interrupted in his task when the telephone rang.

"Senior Detective Puddleworth speaking," he said crisply into the receiver. Morton could hear a faint voice on the other end. The Scottish terrier mouthed the word *Bianca* to him. Detective Puddleworth switched the phone to his other ear and updated the Angora on the latest developments in the case: "We hooked Neverest up to a lie detector," said the Scottie, "and put some tough questions to him. Actually, I shouldn't call it a lie detector, it was a state-of-the-art Fibutron 5000, but you get the idea. Unfortunately, Neverest passed the test with flying colors, which means we have no evidence linking him to Flint's murder at this point. I'm sorry."

The voice emanating from the other end of the phone went up a few decibels.

"Well, by my reckoning it must be Peggy Sneekly! It's a simple process of elimination. Unfortunately we are still endeavoring to track down this zookeeper, but we will be sure to let you know when we find her." The Scottie frowned and stared at the beeping receiver. "She hung up on me. How rude!"

"Knowing Miss Moon, she's about to stick her nose right back in the case no matter what we tell her. Hey! You don't suppose Bianca has a lead on the missing zookeeper?"

The Scottie seemed intrigued by this notion. "So far that Angora has shown an unerring instinct for locating suspects."

"You know, Bianca was on the local news last night," said Morton, who had only happened to hear the report because

Riyo Jones kept turning his radio on and off in an effort to drive him up the wall.

"Really? What on earth for?"

"She has lost a large number of lives in a very short time span, and that has gained her some notoriety. According to last night's news report, she crashed her motorcycle on her way home from the museum yesterday and got run over by a trolley."

"Poor cat. And after dodging that narwhal tusk too. How many lives is she down to now?"

"She has two left."

Detective Puddleworth let out a low whistle. "That's it? How extraordinary! But I don't suppose that will stop her from mucking about in our case." The Scottie stroked his beard. Then he pushed back his chair and said: "Grab your hat, Morton. Let's go stake out Miss Moon. It's high time we started using that meddlesome feline to our advantage!"

40 · Bianca Moon: The Terminal

When she woke up on Saturday morning, Bianca felt pangs of guilt for snapping at Flint the night before. She had always admired how forgiving he was, and it didn't seem fair to hold that quality against him now. She called out to him in the parlor, but got no response. With a sigh she resigned herself to waiting until later to put things right.

A brief phone call to Puddleworth left her determined to track down Peggy Sneekly, the wayward zookeeper. Bianca chose a red plaid dress for the day, with a matching pillbox hat, and filled a saddle bag purse with a few essentials—a handkerchief, a small mirror, sunglasses, a comb, and a flashlight—before setting out.

When she got to Eleventh Avenue, she saw that the old railway tracks were still embedded in the roadway. Bianca knew that if she just followed them north she would arrive at the abandoned freight train terminal. With any luck, the tip she'd received from the tabby zookeeper would pan out and she'd find Peggy Sneekly holed up there.

A half an hour later, the tracks curved and disappeared under the arched metal doors of a forbidding brick building. It took up an entire city block and had fortress-style towers on each corner and shuttered windows, giving the structure an air of impregnability.

Bianca walked west on 27th Street, along the length of the building, discreetly testing the handles of any side doors that she passed and finding them all firmly locked. A short ways down the block, there was a long sidewalk shed that looked like it had been put up and forgotten about. Above this scaffolding, up on the second floor, Bianca spotted a shutter dangling askew on its hinges. Her eyes narrowed as she zeroed in on this chink in the building's armor.

She waited for a quiet moment, then she pulled herself up the scaffolding's bars and shinnied up a second pole to get to the plywood barrier. Placing a foot on a narrow ledge, she clambered over it and onto the surface of the shed. It was littered with construction debris: rubble, metal poles, and warped planks of wood. Bianca picked her way over a pile of bricks until she got to the window with the busted shutter. A broken pane of glass hinted that she might not be the first to find her way in this way. She stuck her arm through the missing pane and felt around for the latch. *Click*—the window swung open in front of her. The interior was pitch black, and Bianca was glad she had thought to put the flashlight in her purse. Eyeing the murky interior, she regretted not bringing a knife too.

Even with the flashlight Bianca had to steel her nerves before going in. The old her would never have dared to set foot inside this derelict building. But all she had to do was think of Flint's death and let that anger bubble up within her. If the answers she was looking for were hiding inside this old warehouse, then so be it. Bianca's pulse quickened as she slipped through the window. Her plaid dress snagged on a nail jutting out from the sill, tearing a long gash, and she spat out a swear. That was another of her favorite outfits ruined.

Bianca swept the light around the room, revealing rows of dusty metal shelves that held a jumble of odd-looking trinkets. Were they theatrical props? If so, that would make this some kind of theater storage room. Lending weight to this theory was an old marquee resting along the floor and racks of dusty period clothing. Under different circumstances curiosity would have driven her to explore the secret treasures hidden in this room.

Passing through a half-open doorway, she found herself in a narrow corridor. Turning left, she soon encountered a staircase that presented her with a choice. She decided to go down and explore the main level first, knowing she could always double back. The stairs deposited her in a wide passageway that stretched endlessly in either direction. At her feet the flashlight reflected off train tracks flush with the cobblestones. Platforms on both sides of the tracks called to mind the loading and unloading areas for the now defunct railroad. Bianca turned left and crept down the gloomy tunnel. This place was big enough that she could easily stumble onto a whole gang of delinquents and not know it until it was too late.

A scurrying sound made her swing the flashlight to her right. In the darkness a pair of red eyes reflected back at her. The rat skittered along the ground and its pink tail disappeared behind a barrel. Bianca paused. She really hated rats. The light in her hand wavered slightly as she continued down the interminable passageway. Flint and Roxy had both warned her not to come here alone, and she was beginning to see their point.

The space soon opened up into a cavernous train station. High above her, grime-covered skylights let in a faint radiant glow. She switched off the flashlight and let her eyes adjust to the weak ambient light. If Peggy Sneekly had been forced to find shelter in this bleak spot, then Bianca felt sorry for her. She couldn't imagine anyone making a home in this grim place. "I bet there isn't a soul in this whole building," she muttered. But just as these words escaped her lips, she heard what sounded like distant footsteps—coming from somewhere behind her. Bianca stopped cold and looked over her shoulder, her tail twitching back and forth. Was it her imagination or was there a light flickering in the distance? A moment ago she had been the pursuer, but no longer. Bianca couldn't bring herself to turn around and confront whoever was behind her so she pressed on, her heart in her throat. About a hundred steps farther down the passageway she saw large black silhouettes looming ahead. As she drew closer, they revealed themselves to be old freight train wagons, sitting abandoned on the tracks since the day the terminal closed its doors.

It soon became clear that several of these box cars were inhabited. Yellow light seeped out through cracks and vents, and the unmistakable odor of grilled fish hit her nostrils. As she approached the first wagon, she heard the sound of a radio announcer dedicating a song to a listener. Bianca stopped in front of the sliding freight door. After coming all this way, her nerves were finally starting to fray, but she hadn't trekked over here just to chicken out at the last minute.

Bianca rapped gently on the door with her knuckles. Heavy footsteps sounded, then the door slid open. Standing there was a gap-toothed tomcat holding a lantern, the sudden brightness of it blinding her. The tomcat looked her up and down.

"Ain't never seen the likes of you around here!" he growled. "What happened? Did you take a wrong turn at Baylor and Bowman?" He slapped his own thigh as he let out a guffaw. He was dressed in filthy long johns, and Bianca desperately wanted to take two steps back just to put some distance between herself and the rank odor.

"Good afternoon, sir," she said, standing her ground. "I was wondering if you could help me. I'm looking for a dog named Peggy Sneekly."

The gray-muzzled cat peered at her curiously. His left ear was all chewed up and the tip was missing. "And what would you be wanting with Peggy?" he asked in a scratchy voice. "I'm not saying she's here and I'm not saying she's not, mind you. You're not a copper, that's for darned sure. Are you one of them pesky counselors determined to save us from life on the streets?" Before she could answer, the gray cat broke out into a fit of coughing that ended with him spitting out a gob of phlegm to one side.

Bianca decided to take a step back after all. "I am neither of those. I just need to talk to Peggy about a personal matter."

He scratched his behind with his free hand. "Well, you look harmless enough. I reckon our Peggy can handle the likes of you. If she's home you'll find her in the fourth box car down. The green one. A word to the wise—most of us terminal dwellers don't take kindly to strangers poking their noses into our business." With that, he banged the wagon door shut in her face, leaving her alone once more in the darkness.

Their conversation had drawn the attention of some of

the old cat's neighbors and Bianca was conscious of several faces peering out of hatches and peeking through slits as she made her way along the line of wagon cars. Encouragingly, the fourth car had a soft glow emanating from behind the door. Bianca reminded herself to be ready for anything and not let her guard down.

She knocked and moments later the door slid open a crack. "Who the heck are you?" an eyeball asked her from behind the door.

"My name is Bianca Moon. Are you Peggy Sneekly? I would like to speak with you if I may."

"About what?" came the curt reply through the crack.

"I bring greetings from an old friend. Cuthbert Turner? From the Central Park Menagerie? He sends his warmest wishes."

The crack widened considerably. "You know Cuthbert? How is that tubby cat doing these days? I haven't seen him in ages! I can't go back to the menagerie, you see. It holds too many awful memories for me."

"He seemed well," Bianca replied. "Still diligently guarding that lion exhibit. He's worried about you."

"Seeing as how we have a friend in common, you may as well come in. Do you think you could pass along a message to him from me? I don't like to think of him fretting about little old me." Peggy Sneekly threw open her door, revealing herself to be an overweight mutt with patchy brown fur. She was wearing only a pink slip and fuzzy slippers.

"I'd be happy to pass along a message," Bianca assured her as she grabbed onto a metal bar and pulled herself up the tall steps.

"I'll make us some tea, shall I? Gosh, I don't often get visitors. Close the door behind you and sit yourself down on that crate right over there. Don't touch nothing. My little pets are all hiding. They don't like strangers any better than I do." Looking around, Bianca caught sight of a dark shape flitting around along the ceiling of the box car. It disappeared into the deep shadows of a corner. She thought it might be a crow, but then it hit her that its jerky flight pattern was more suggestive of a bat.

Peggy Sneekly traipsed over to a camper stove, the mismatched slippers on her feet slapping against the planks on the floor. Bianca settled herself awkwardly onto the crate. *Little pets? Plural? What else was hiding nearby?* Her unease over any hidden critters competed with her concern about the tea her host was brewing. The funky-smelling box car was in shambles, and needless to say there was no sign of indoor plumbing anywhere. "Oh, no tea for me, thank you," she said. "I don't want to impose."

"Nonsense!" Peggy scratched vigorously at the ruff of her neck, sending tiny specks flying off of her. "It's not often I get company, and I plan to do right by you. That way you can give Cuthbert a glowing report! Such a kind dog he is. Just between us, his wife doesn't know how good she has it! If I was married to that cat, I wouldn't be nagging him night and day the way she does. I would treat him like a king!" Peggy ladled water from a bucket into a rusty kettle and set it on the brass camping stove. She pulled two mugs from a cardboard box and wiped each one diligently with a dirty rag.

A piercing screech almost made Bianca jump out of her

skin. She looked up at the ceiling of the wagon where a small animal was hanging from a hook. It had a black face framed by a shock of white hair, and a long thin tail. Bianca gasped—it was a monkey.

"Nutmeg, mind your manners! She's our guest!" Peggy berated the angry creature. "If you keep up that racket, I'll put you outside!" Turning to Bianca, she said, "Best not to be scared of him, he can sense fear. Don't make the mistake of trying to pet him neither. He's sweet-natured, but only with me."

"Did you take him from the menagerie?" Bianca asked nervously.

"I *liberated* him from that awful place! He was cooped up in a cramped cage little bigger than a hatbox. Here he has room to climb and jump around, which is what he loves to do."

"Cuthbert told me that you were unfairly blamed for that bad press the menagerie got?"

"Darn right I was. My scuzzball of a boss decided I was going to take the rap. Why, I've never mistreated an animal in my life! I get along better with wild creatures than I do with most cats and dogs." Peggy frowned. "No offense to present company intended."

Bianca smiled genially.

Her host filled a chipped ceramic mug with the boiling water and plopped what looked to be a used tea bag into it. She handed the mug to Bianca, who blew softly on the dirty brown liquid, prepared to pretend it was too hot to drink for a long while. She needed to find a way to bring the conversation around to Flint. "That article was published in the

Knickerbocker Gazette, wasn't it? What was the journalist's name, Flint something or other I think?" Bianca probed. "Did you blame the *Gazette* at all for what happened to you?"

Peggy's face took on a guarded expression. "Well, aren't you nosy?" said the mutt. "You seem to know a lot about what happened. Are you a reporter? I bet you are! Full of prying questions. Wasn't it enough to ruin my life once already?"

"No, no, Peggy. I promise you I'm not a reporter!"

The mutt had grabbed hold of a cast-iron frying pan and looked ready to chase Bianca out of her wagon car.

"I'll be straight with you, Peggy. I'm Flint Lockford's fiancée. You probably haven't heard, but he was murdered the other day. I'm just looking for answers."

"What? You think I mighta killed your dog? Is that it? Why, I wouldn't know that pooch from a hole in the ground. I never blamed that Flint fella. He was just trying to make life better for the poor creatures in the menagerie. Same as me."

"You really didn't hold a grudge against him?" Bianca fixed the mutt with a penetrating stare.

"No. Not one bit. Oh my stars! And they say *I'm* crazy. You're as loony as they come! Why don't you run along, Miss Whoever-You-Are. Never mind the tea."

Bianca put the mug down on the floor and stood up. Once again, that stupid list Roxy had swiped from the detectives had led her nowhere. "I'm sorry to have troubled you, Peggy. I believe you. I just needed to know."

"Enough with the sweet-talking already!" shouted her host. "You pretended to be a friend of Cuthbert's when you were really just snooping around, waiting to accuse me of being a dog killer! Get out of my wagon before Nutmeg decides to show you how sharp his teeth are."

Bianca slid open the box car door and was startled to see two figures standing directly outside. They shone their flashlights in her face and she took a step back, shielding her eyes. Then she recognized the detectives. "What are you two doing here?" she exclaimed. "Were you following me?"

"Never mind that," snapped Detective Puddleworth, shining his light deeper into the wagon. "Peggy Sneekly? We're detectives with the City Police!" He flashed his badge. "We need you to come down to the station with us to answer some questions."

"Coppers!" cried Peggy. "You went and led the fuzz straight to my door?" She glared spitefully at Bianca. "I'll teach you not to poke around in my business!"

"Don't do anything foolish," growled Junior Detective Digby, climbing into the box car. "All we want is a little of your time."

"Sure you do!" yelled Peggy. "The two of you are here for the same reason as her. You're trying to pin a murder on me! I'm not dumb, you know. They framed me once with no evidence at all and now the two of you are looking for someone to take the blame for an unsolved dogicide! Well, I won't be your patsy!"

"Put down that frying pan!" Detective Puddleworth barked. Junior Detective Digby was eyeing the frying pan uneasily, but to his credit he stepped into the space between Bianca and the angry mutt. The dark little monkey was leaping around the car, shrieking at the top of his lungs.

Peggy Sneekly scowled at the two detectives during the standoff. Then she slowly backed away, hung the pan from a hook, and held up her hands. "I don't want any trouble. Just give me a minute to put a dress on over my slip."

Detective Puddleworth nodded at her warily. "Get that monkey under control!"

"Nutmeg! Come here, Nutmeg!" Peggy stretched out an arm and the creature leapt onto her from about ten feet away, scrambling up around her neck. She carried him over to a tin box sitting on a shelf along the back wall and dropped him inside. The monkey poked his head out just enough to glare at the intruders. Peggy Sneekly slipped what looked like a burlap sack with holes for arms over her head and exchanged her furry slippers for slip-on sandals. Then she wrapped a tattered scarf around her neck in a woeful attempt to dress up her outfit.

Once again, Bianca couldn't help but feel sorry for Peggy. Bianca reached out and put a hand on Morton's arm. "Hey, fellas! I've already asked her about Flint's murder. She had nothing to do with it!"

"This is police business, Bianca," snapped Detective Puddleworth. "Don't interfere."

Bianca rolled her eyes.

"Don't pretend like you're on my side!" griped Peggy, pointing an accusatory finger at Bianca. "I'm not falling for your innocent act again! This was your doing!"

Peggy Sneekly was attempting to cinch a belt around her waist, but it wasn't quite meeting in the middle.

"Let's go!" barked Detective Puddleworth.

"Hold your horses. I've got another belt in here

somewhere." Peggy Sneekly bustled over to a basket in the corner and reached inside, coming away with a long leathery band. She took a few steps toward them and threw the belt right at Bianca.

As it flew through the air, the belt writhed and twisted and sprouted a fanged head. By reflex, Bianca found herself catching what turned out to be a sleek brown snake. In a flash it struck out, clamping down on her hand. Bianca screamed and flung it away from her. The snake darted its tongue in and out as it slithered into a corner of the wagon. Bianca stared at the two red dots on her white fur. "It bit me!"

Peggy Sneekly smiled wickedly. "Ziggy is an inland tai-pan, one of the most venomous snakes in the world. One little bite has enough venom to kill a hundred cats!" She walked over to the snake and picked him up. "There, there, snoo-kums. Did the mean lady scare you?" She eased him back into his basket and placed the lid over him

"You shouldn't have done that," snarled Detective Pud-dleworth as he clasped a handcuff around one of the mutt's wrists, locking the other end on a metal grab bar.

"That prissy Angora had it coming!" screeched Peggy. "I made her tea! Welcomed her as a friend! No good deed goes unpunished is what my papa used to say."

The room began to go in and out of focus, and Bianca teetered on her feet. Junior Detective Digby reached out to steady her and she collapsed in his arms. He guided her gently to the floor. "Hold on, Bianca," he said. "We're gonna get you outside and call an ambulance from our squad car. You're gonna be fine!"

But even as he spoke she felt her muscles begin to freeze

up and a wave of nausea swept over her. Her body arched as an intense spasm passed through her. "It's too late. I'm not going to make it," she said weakly.

Peggy Sneekly let out a rattling laugh and the monkey hopped up and down in his box, shrieking with glee. Bianca closed her eyes as Junior Detective Digby picked her up and threw her over his shoulder. He carried her out of the wagon and down the darkened passageway, with the Scottie right behind them. They barely made it a hundred feet before Bianca felt herself dissolving into nothingness.

Disoriented and nauseous, Bianca awoke in City Hospital's maternity ward once again. The obstetric nurses wrapped a sheet around her, plopped her onto a gurney, and wheeled her into the recovery area. Shortly afterward, Nurse Bertlemina strode into her little cubicle and pressed a glass of cold milk into her hands. "Oh, Bianca! What are we going to do with you?" the frizzy-haired bichon said despairingly. "What was it this time?"

"I got bit by a venomous snake," Bianca replied, staring at the back of her hand where the two red spots had been. Her white fur was now smooth and unbroken.

"A poisonous snake! In the City? How on earth did you manage that?"

Bianca shrugged. "It's a long story involving a stolen snake, a nutty homeless mutt, and a troublesome Angora."

"Oh my. Listen, Bianca, I should warn you. I think Linda in reception has already alerted the press that you're here. She can be a real blabbermouth sometimes. I have a feeling you may be ambushed by reporters on your way out. I can sneak you out a back door if you like."

"That's okay, I don't mind talking to them. It keeps Flint's case in the spotlight." She took another sip of milk.

"You do realize you've run out of spares?" Bertlemina admonished her. "You're down to your very last life!"

"I know. Just like every single dog walking around the City right now. I'll be fine."

"I hope so, because if there is a next time, you won't end up here—you'll wind up down in the basement. In the *morgue.*" Nurse Bertlemina fixed Bianca with a meaningful stare, dropped fresh clothes on the chair, and slipped back out through the curtain.

41 · Flint Lockford: The Dance

A severe lack of sleep had finally caught up with Flint and he spent most of the daylight hours on Saturday passed out in his cot at Ghosthall. When the sun went down and the old courthouse descended into the usual nightly bedlam, Flint ducked out and set off in search of Bianca. Not finding her at home, and seeing as how it was a Saturday evening, he decided to try his luck at the Calico Cat Lounge.

He hadn't spoken to Bianca since their argument the night before. Which meant she didn't yet know about the danger she was in. He had no choice now but to come clean and tell her everything. Hopefully he could convince her to leave town.

But first he had to track her down.

Drifting through the open doors of the lounge, he found it hopping with the usual mix of West Village oddballs, cats and dogs united in their desire to kick up their heels. Flint found it nearly impossible to move around without passing through living cats and dogs, a sensation he still deemed markedly unpleasant.

Flint turned and went up the stairs to Bianca's old stomping grounds—the bar area on the mezzanine level. Two alley cats behind the counter were slinging drinks as fast as they could throw them together, surrounded by a throng of thirsty revelers. The Wurlitzer next to the bar was blaring a peppy doo-wop tune, inspiring a handful of cats and dogs to bust out their dance moves in the open space by the railing. Flint looked everywhere, including the bathrooms, but there was no sign of Bianca.

Back on the bustling main floor, diners were eagerly chowing down on hot sandwiches with french fries. The cacophony of voices—shouting, laughing, whispering—felt disorienting to Flint. It occurred to him that places crowded with the living were not meant for ghosts. He floated into the kitchen, where the staff were busy chopping pickles, peeling potatoes, and tending to a sizzling griddle. Tabatha was there and she ran right through Flint, carrying a hot plate piled with food in each hand. The calico stopped cold for a second, shuddered, then resumed her mad dash to the counter to deposit her orders and ring the bell.

Flint checked the stockroom next and found it empty.

Lastly, Flint made his way down the stairs to the basement game room. The two bowling lanes on the left side of the room were both packed. The bowlers let out whoops of delight and exchanged high fives whenever someone scored a strike. The soda counter along the near wall was standing-room only, with the usual cluster of sport fans hunched around the radio in the corner listening to the Brooklyn Bolters game.

Flint spied a familiar figure by the row of pinball machines—Roxy, flanked by two of her gal pals. Flint recognized several other familiar faces among the cats and dogs around him, but there was no sign of Bianca. He could scarcely believe that less than a week ago he'd been down here in the game room shooting pool with Otis and Penelope, laughing and joking like all these other fools, thinking he had his whole life ahead of him. Now he felt like an invisible intruder.

He decided he might as well hang around for a bit to see if Bianca showed up. It was preferable to waiting by himself in Bianca's parlor. Flint drifted over to the pinball machines and amused himself by making the pinball lights go haywire in Roxy's game. He experimented with nudging the silver balls helpfully at critical moments to keep the round alive. Then he did his best to knock the pool chalk off the side of the billiards tables, with mixed results. Being a ghost was an invitation to mischief.

Tired of bumping into the living, he passed through the soda counter and settled into a low-traffic spot in the corner by the radio. From there he could survey the room and listen to the ball game, which was already in the bottom of the ninth. The inning concluded with a tough loss for the local team and the dejected Bolters fans dispersed, commiserating with one another over their team's shortcomings. The programming on the wireless switched over to the local news.

Flint wasn't paying any attention to the radio broadcast, but his ears pricked up when he heard an unexpected name on the newscaster's lips: "And when we return we'll have an exclusive interview with Bianca Moon, the cat who has lost six lives in the past five days. But first, a message from our sponsor." One of Roxy's alley cat pals was sitting on a nearby stool, sucking down a cola and batting her eyes at a dog she was sweet on, and she too heard Bianca's name. She ran over to where Roxy was still nursing her nickel. "Roxy, come quick!"

she cried. "You'll never believe it! They just mentioned Bianca on the news!"

Roxy used a wad of gum to park a ball on a pinball flipper and hurried over to the wireless. Flint hovered impatiently on the other side of the counter from them, listening as a cheery voice extolled the virtues of Tip Top Toothpaste. Chimes announced the return of the news program. Roxy reached out and cranked up the volume.

"We're at City Hospital right now with Bianca Moon, girlfriend to the allegedly murdered Gazette reporter Flint Lockford. Miss Moon has been searching for answers in her boyfriend's death, and has bravely taken matters into her own paws by attempting to track down suspects, with often fatal consequences to herself."

Flint leaned toward the radio, slack-jawed.

"We have Bianca with us right here," said the reporter. "Miss Moon, please tell our listeners how many lives you've lost in the past few days?"

"Well, first I wanted to clarify that I am Flint's fiancée," Bianca's voice came through the speaker, clear as day. She sounded moderately peeved.

"What did I say?" the interviewer asked, taken aback.

"You said girlfriend."

"My apologies, Miss Moon. But please, tell us, how many lives have you lost?"

"Including today, that would be six lives in the past five days."

"And none of these deaths were by your own hand?"

"No. Certainly not. Not even in my darkest moments did that occur to me."

"Would you mind telling our listeners how you died today?"

"A homeless zookeeper threw a venomous snake at me, and it bit my hand. An inland taipan, she said it was. Turns out that's one of the deadliest snakes in the world."

"Oh my! And how else have you died recently?"

"I was tied up in a sack and tossed into the Gowanus Canal by mob goons, I was shot by an antiquities smuggler, I was tossed off a balcony by a celebrity's bodyguards, I was poisoned by a despicable sommelier, and I got into an unfortunate motorcycle accident where I was run over by a trolley."

"That's terrible! So how many lives do you have left?"

"Well, I died twice in childhood, so I have just the one life left now."

"A cat down to her very last life! Does this mean that you are done investigating your fiancé's killing?"

"No, absolutely not. I won't stop until whoever took out the contract on my Flint lands behind bars."

"You heard it here first, folks! Bianca refuses to throw in the towel! This is Gene Riley, signing off for the City Broadcasting Service."

Flint stood there, stunned, not caring that one of the soda jerks had just stepped through him. Roxy too was incredulous. "I can't believe it!" she exclaimed. "Bianca is down to her ninth life! That cat is going to have a lot of explaining to do when I catch up with her!"

Flint couldn't have put it any better himself. Down to one life and with a hired killer on her tail. Bianca had done half the hitcat's job for him.

* * *

It didn't take long for Bianca to appear at the top of the stairs. Flint reckoned she must've splurged on a cab. As she came down, she was quickly surrounded by Roxy and her alley cat pals, as well as Tabatha, who by now had heard the news. They all demanded to hear her story. Flint listened closely, not wanting to announce his presence in the midst of all this commotion. Bianca recounted her misadventures at the abandoned railway terminal, with Roxy glaring at her furiously the whole time.

"Weren't you terrified to go there by yourself?" asked one of the alley cats in amazement.

"My skin was crawling by the end of it," Bianca admitted.

"But you did it anyway, because that's how much you love Flint!" gushed another of the alley cats.

Tabatha, at least, didn't seem impressed. She gave her former bartender a disapproving frown. "We're going to talk about this later," she said, and hurried back to her kitchen. One by one the other alley cats drifted off, until it was just Bianca and Roxy left. Flint was about to whisper a sharp remark in the Angora's ear, but Roxy, who had clearly been holding her fire, beat him to it. She began to berate Bianca angrily. "You lied to me, Princess!" the alley cat growled. "I'm never going to believe another word out of your mouth!"

Bianca reached out and put her hands on her friend's shoulders. "I'm sorry, Roxy," she said. "I really am. And it turns out the whole thing was just another wild-goose chase. Peggy Sneekly had nothing to do with Flint's death. Every single suspect on the detectives' list was a bust."

"Color me surprised. Those jackass coppers don't have a clue what they're doing. But that doesn't mean you get to run off on dangerous expeditions all on your own. An abandoned freight train terminal? I always thought you were a smart cat. Didn't you go to college and everything?"

"You knew about that?" Bianca said, surprised.

"Sure."

"You never teased me about it."

"I was saving that little tidbit for a rainy day. But don't change the subject. What were you thinking?"

"I already cost you a life, Roxy, and there was no way I was going to put you in danger again."

"It's not up to you to decide how I risk my lives, you idiot!"

"Well, it's over and done with now. I hope you're not planning on staying cross with me all evening? Being down to my last life is a strange feeling—it's as if the world were suddenly fraught with danger. I can't believe this is what it's like for dogs from the moment they're born."

The longer Flint waited to break in and announce his presence, the harder it became. Bianca would think he'd been eavesdropping again, which was kind of true. He was mad at her too, not just for burning up another life, but also for stopping here first to talk to her friends, rather than rushing home to see if her dead fiancé was tearing his ghostly fur out waiting to hear from her. But at the same time, he didn't relish the thought of another big blowout.

"I need a drink!" Roxy declared, grabbing Bianca's hand and leading her up the stairs. Flint trailed them silently.

"I have to go," Bianca protested. "I'm sure Flint is waiting for me back home. I only stopped here first because it's on the way."

"You have time for one drink. Flint isn't going anywhere."

"One drink. But only if you promise to forgive me," said Bianca as they climbed the stairs to the mezzanine level, the swinging beat of the jukebox growing louder.

"Fine," Roxy grunted. "I forgive you."

The alley cat put in an order for two ginger fizzes, and it wasn't long before the icy drinks were in their hands. An up-tempo rock-and-roll song hit the jukebox and Roxy hopped off her stool. "Ooh, I love this one," she cried. "C'mon, let's dance. If I don't let off some steam tonight, I'm going to burst!"

Bianca reluctantly let herself be dragged to the small dance arca. The two cats began to hop around, with Bianca moving shyly at first, but loosening up when they began to playfully mimic one another's moves. Flint hovered nearby, watching them. Bianca's silky white fur looked luminous. She was as pretty tonight as he had ever seen her, even if she was wearing a hospital-issue dress. He was struck by how uninhibited she seemed. So fearless and full of confidence, not caring who was watching her now, just content to grab a moment of joy where she could.

The next song was the popular "Splish Splash," and Bianca and Roxy pranced around the dance floor goofily, spinning around in circles, their skirts ballooning in the air. They were both grinning now, and Flint realized suddenly that it had been ages since he'd seen Bianca smile. As the song rose to a climax, the two cats twirled with utter abandon, drawing cheers of approval from the surrounding bar patrons. When the song was finally over, they collapsed into empty chairs, out of breath, tears in their eyes. A slow ballad was the next record to drop in place inside the Wurlitzer. The alley cat stood up and held out a hand to her friend. Bianca hesitated before taking it. Roxy pulled her close and the two cats clung to one another, dancing cheek to cheek, winding their way round and round in small circles, one of several couples swaying on the dance floor.

Flint wasn't surprised to see that one drink had turned into two, followed by dancing. That was the way of bars. A part of him found it unbearable to watch her, knowing he was trapped on the outside looking in. But another part of him was relieved to see Bianca enjoying herself. Just because he was stuck in a strange limbo didn't mean she should be too. It made him wonder if the best thing he could do for her would be to simply vanish forever. To stop haunting her and just let her be free to live her life.

But there was no way he could do that when there was a hired killer out there somewhere with his sights set on Bianca. He debated when to tell her about the hitcat. Breaking the news to her now was sure to ruin her night. If he stuck close by and watched over her carefully, then the bad news could wait until morning.

42 · Junior Detective Morton Digby: The Villain

Sunday

Morton took some sensible precautions before going to bed on Saturday night in an attempt to ghost-proof his apartment. He unplugged his radio, he tied back the curtains, he threw out all the old newspapers, and most importantly he stuffed cotton balls in his ears. He could still hear the ghostly voice of Riyo Jones berating him as he fell asleep, and she managed to make the lamp on his bedside table flicker, as he'd forgotten to unscrew the light bulb, but he was so exhausted that he soon drifted off, ghost or no ghost.

He slept soundly, and in the morning he heard not a peep from Riyo in his sun-kissed bedroom. To give the hot water time to reach his apartment, he let the shower run while he made himself breakfast. Grabbing the *Gazette* from his door-mat, he sat down at his small kitchen table to skim the day's headlines while he ate two slices of toast, washing them down with black coffee.

By the time he was done, he was running late. He tossed his pajamas onto his bed, wrapped a terry cloth towel around his waist, and stepped into the now-steamy bathroom. He stopped short, his fur standing on end—someone had drawn the outline of a skull in the steamed-up mirror above the pedestal sink. With a low growl he snatched the hand towel from the rack and wiped the mirror clean. That's when he saw the reflection of a glowing figure standing directly behind him.

"Riyo?" he cried, whirling around. "Is that you?"

She glared at him. "Who else would it be, you nimrod? Do you have any other ghosts haunting you?" Only then did her brow furrow as she exclaimed: "Hold on. Can you see me?"

"I sure can. You're transparent, but I can definitely see you in the steam."

"Fascinating. I guess you'd better say goodbye to hot showers."

"Riyo. Enough already! A dog needs his space. We need to set some boundaries."

"Don't tell me how to haunt, Detective. That's my job! And what do you have to complain about? I'm the one who is dead. Two days ago I was a glamorous stewardess with a suite at the Biltmore and the whole world as my sandbox. Now I'm stuck in this rat hole with a second-rate cop for a roommate."

"There's a whole wide world out there for you to haunt," Morton observed dryly.

"You don't get it!" she moaned. "You're the only one who can hear me." The glowing figure that was Riyo slumped down onto the lid of the commode and put her face in her hands. "All the other cats and dogs I've tried talking to act like I'm not even there. Being a ghost is a real nightmare." Her shoulders began to shake.

Morton was taken aback. "Wait, are you crying?"

"So what if I am! Did you know there's another spirit

In the apartment downstairs? He's this pesky tomcat with horrible manners. He keeps poking his head up through the floor and jumping out at me when I least expect it. Then he disappears, howling with laughter. I don't know how much more of it I can take. I went up to the roof yesterday to get away from him and I nearly fried myself when I stepped out into the sunlight. Turns out I don't know the first thing about being a ghost."

Morton took a deep breath and perched on the edge of the tub. He tried putting a paw on her shoulder but it passed right through her. "Riyo. I'm truly sorry this awful thing happened to you. How about I go ask Louisa for advice—she's a local psychic, and something of an expert on the spirit world. I bet she'll have some good pointers."

"You mean you would actually help me? Even after I decided to haunt you?" Riyo looked up at him with big watery eyes.

"Of course! Now, do you think you could give me a little privacy so I can get ready for work?"

Riyo sniffed. "Why are you even working on a Sunday? Don't you get any time off?"

"Not when we're working a murder investigation. It's an around-the-clock commitment. Now, if you don't mind . . ." He pointed to the door.

"Fine. But first you have to close the blinds in the living room."

Morton was only too happy to make his apartment a little more accommodating for the light-sensitive ghost. If they were going to be stuck with each other, then he much preferred to be on good terms. He managed to shower, comb his fur, and brush his teeth in record time, but he was still running late by the time he shot out the door.

His conversation with Riyo had given him food for thought. If she could only talk to *him*, then it was like she was his very own ghost, which made him feel strangely responsible for her well-being. It also meant it would be difficult to prove to anyone else that she was real. The thought that there were other ghosts in the building that were invisible to *him* was also unsettling. Hopefully popping in to see Louisa at lunchtime would bring some answers.

Detective Puddleworth was already at his desk when Morton arrived at the precinct. The Scottie greeted him with a wordless nod. At first glance, Morton was struck by the fact that his partner didn't seem like his usual exuberant self. Plopping down in his desk chair, Morton peered curiously at the senior detective. Yes, there was definitely something off about him. "What's got you looking so down in the mouth, J.B.?"

Detective Puddleworth started. "I'm sorry, Morton. I have a lot on my mind." The Scottie stroked his beard thoughtfully. "Listen, Morton, perhaps you wouldn't mind showing me how the coffee machine works in the break room?"

"It's not that hard," Morton replied. "You add water, you push the button, and the coffee practically makes itself."

"All the same, I'd appreciate a quick tutorial." The Scottie raised his bushy eyebrows meaningfully. Morton shrugged and followed his partner into the break room. Once there, away from prying eyes, J.B. showed no interest in the coffee machine. Instead, he pulled a white envelope from the inside pocket of his suit jacket. "Do you remember that mystery envelope that flew onto my desk the other day? I finally got around to opening it this morning. It has no postage on it, so clearly someone from the precinct left it for me." The Scottie removed the enclosed sheet of paper and handed it to Morton.

"What exactly am I looking at?" Morton asked, staring at the invoice in confusion. The eye-popping sum listed on the sheet seemed somehow familiar.

"Check out the note clipped behind it."

Morton read the attached note and his eyes went wide. "Mister X payment to Tatiana Valova? What the heck? This means—"

"Keep your voice down," the Scottie said sharply. "But yes, it means that Mister X might be someone from our very own precinct."

"But who left this for you?"

"No idea, but whoever it is, they might be trying to help us get this investigation back on track."

"It could be a Buckley and Callaway prank."

The Scottie stuffed the papers back in the envelope. "It's a tad sophisticated for a Buckley and Callaway gag, don't you think?"

"Yeah, you're right. I don't think they would forge the captain's signature, or mess with the precinct stamp."

"If it is legitimate," said the Scottish terrier, "that would put us in a real bind. I mean, are we really prepared to treat Captain Maddox as a suspect?"

Morton swallowed hard. "Yikes! This is the perfect recipe for getting drummed out of the force. You know, it's funny, all along I've had a peculiar feeling that the answers were hiding right under my nose."

"Well, our job is to follow wherever the investigation leads us," said the Scottie. "I hope we are in agreement about that."

Morton nodded gravely. "We owe that much to Flint Lockford, to Bianca, and to ourselves. I just hope it doesn't blow up in our faces."

Footsteps sounded in the hall outside and Sergeant Doyle's ugly mug poked into the break room. "Why are you two fellas hiding in here? I've been looking all over for you. The captain wants an update on your investigation. Immediately! I'm guessing he finally ran out of patience. Hop to it, fellas!"

With the sergeant looming over them, Morton knew they had no way of dodging this briefing. The two detectives reluctantly followed the bulldog up the stairs to the second floor. Shirley was sitting at her desk outside the captain's office and she gave them a pitying look.

Morton followed his partner and the sergeant into the captain's office. The mastiff leaned back in his chair and glared at them. "Well, detectives? Sergeant Doyle tells me that polygraph test with your latest suspect was a bust. I've lost track of how many cats and dogs you've brought in for questioning on this case. It's time to raise the white flag! Unless you've made some big breakthrough that I don't know about?" This last comment from the captain drew a derisive snort from the bulldog.

Morton stared down at his feet. They were in a real pickle. They had a major clue that could transform the case, but they couldn't share it with the captain. But apparently Detective Puddleworth thought otherwise. The Scottie drew himself up to his full height, which wasn't much to speak of, and reached into his jacket for the incriminating invoice. "As a matter of fact, sir, we've gotten our hands on a remarkable piece of evidence." He handed the mastiff the document.

The police captain groped around for his reading glasses.

"They're on your head, sir," Sergeant Doyle said helpfully.

Captain Maddox reached up and settled the specs over his wide muzzle. He stared at the document, his jaw set in a hard line. "Is this invoice real? Sixteen thousand five hundred bucks? And what does it mean by capital improvements? I would never have approved this! We don't have this kind of cash to throw around! Shirley, do you know anything about this invoice?" He waved it in the air as he yelled through the open doorway.

For once there was no reply.

They all turned and stared at the secretary's empty desk. "Where has Shirley run off to?" groused the captain. "Somebody had better explain the meaning of this document to me right now or heads are gonna roll! Who signed off on this?"

"You did, sir," said Detective Puddleworth.

"What?" The captain's nostrils flared, and Morton cringed, afraid for his partner's life.

But the Scottie himself was fearless as always. He pointed to the bottom of the page. "I believe that's your signature right there. And it has the precinct stamp as well."

The captain's barrel chest let out a deep rumble that seemed to shake the floor under their feet. Morton gritted his teeth as he desperately searched his mind for some way out of this jam. Something was off about this whole situation, and in a flash he realized what it was. The captain seemed genuinely outraged. That meant he was either a remarkable actor, or this was his first time seeing this invoice. Morton took a deep breath and in a shaky voice he said: "Captain, the figure shown on this invoice matches the sum of money the Queen of Spades was paid for her hit job, and we think there may be a connection."

The giant mastiff blinked at him uncomprehendingly. Then slowly his features were transformed by rage. "Are you suggesting I'm a suspect?" he bellowed.

Detective Puddleworth, to his credit, did not flinch. Morton's legs were trembling, but he told himself he would stand shoulder to shoulder with his partner no matter what. For once in his life, the sergeant had been struck speechless. A blob of drool dripped from his jowls onto the carpet.

"I take it you don't remember signing this document?" Detective Puddleworth inquired delicately.

"No, of course not!" yelled the captain. "But Shirley gives me so many papers to sign every day, and I can't always find my glasses, so I couldn't swear to it. But—" Once again they all looked over at the papillon's empty desk.

The Scottie stroked his thick beard. "Then might I suggest that we locate your personal secretary immediately? It seems that right now she is the only dog who can shed some light on this situation, and I find her sudden absence troubling."

Morton could see the wheels turning behind the captain's eyes. Then the mastiff thumped his desk with his fist. "Find Shirley right away! Get her in here! We need to get to the bottom of this mess immediately!" The two detectives and the shocked sergeant took off in search of the vanished papillon.

They turned the precinct upside down but Shirley was nowhere to be found. Eventually they wandered outside and looked up and down the empty sidewalk. "I can't believe it," said Morton. "I don't think it was the captain after all! It was Shirley this whole time!"

The Scottie bobbed his head in agreement. "The pieces of the puzzle all fit together perfectly."

"I bet it was Shirley who put us on the Lockford case in the first place," Morton spluttered, "thinking we wouldn't get anywhere with it."

"We still have time to make her regret that decision."

Back inside the precinct the detectives had dispatch put out an APB with a description of the papillon. Sergeant Doyle picked out a team of patroldogs to accompany him to Shirley's home address and they sped away, sirens blaring. Meanwhile, the two detectives set about going through Shirley's desk and files. Buried in the papillon's rolodex they found the phone numbers for several known mafia dons, including a circled number for Osvaldo Delgatto at Mama Leone's. They also uncovered a suspicious list of officers and detectives with black dots next to their names.

They shared both discoveries with the captain, who let out a low rumble as he mulled over the implications. Smashing his fist on the desk, he asked them: "But if Shirley was a mob plant, why would she take it on herself to have that reporter bumped off?"

"I think I can answer that," said Detective Puddleworth. "Mr. Boswell at the *Gazette* had mentioned Flint was working on an article about the mob infiltrating law enforcement at the time of his death. We didn't think it was a factor because it hadn't been published yet, but what if Shirley got word of it somehow?"

Captain Maddox looked suddenly sheepish. "You know, fellas, a *Gazette* reporter called me a couple weeks back. He was asking for comments on an article he was writing. Shirley put the call through. I thought this corruption business was a bogus story so I just yelled at him and hung up. Now I'm wondering if it could've been that Lockford fella."

The two detectives exchanged a wide-eyed glance. "If it was Lockford," exclaimed Detective Puddleworth, "that would explain why Shirley got spooked and decided to hire a hitdog. It's like the last piece of the puzzle falling into place!"

Morton's head was spinning. He could scarcely believe that everything fit together perfectly.

"That Shirley sure had me fooled." The captain looked suddenly dismayed. "I'm not too big a dog to admit it. I've failed miserably. Likely as not this will cost me the job."

"Don't beat yourself up, Captain," Morton said sympathetically. "Shirley had all of us fooled. There is one last thing. We found this in Shirley's outbox." Morton handed the captain a new document. "It's another invoice. Very similar to the first one, but this one is dated only two days ago. It also has your signature."

The captain stared at it in disbelief. "Do you think this means . . ." He trailed off.

"Yes, we were wondering the same thing," said Detective Puddleworth. "It could be a payment for another hit job."

"If that's the case, we need to figure out quickly who that might be," cried the captain.

"We've been racking our brains," Morton replied. "Without success so far."

"Who is the biggest thorn in Shirley's side right now?"

asked Detective Puddleworth. "That's the million-dollar question at the moment."

Junior Detective Morton scratched his chin as he mulled this over. Then the penny dropped. Eyes wide, he turned to face his partner and saw the Scottie's eyes light up at the same time.

"Bianca Moon!" they both exclaimed in unison.

43 · Bianca Moon: The Telegram

Bianca stepped into the parlor carrying a small tray loaded with a pot of tea, two teacups, sugar, and milk. Roxy was curled up on the settee, where she had spent the night. The alley cat sat up, rubbed her sleepy eyes, and smoothed her ruffled fur. Bianca poured out the tea through a silver strainer. Roxy sniffed the air, taking in the aroma of freshly brewed Darjeeling, and said: "I'm guessing this won't taste anything like the swill I made the other day."

Bianca smiled. "Let's hope not." She added a lump of sugar and a splash of milk to each cup. "The trick is to be gentle with the tea leaves and not scald them or over-brew them. Do you mind if I let Rupert out of his cage?"

"Go right ahead!" Roxy replied enthusiastically.

Bianca opened the cage door and Rupert was soon fluttering around the room, squawking happily and landing on all his favorite perches. Roxy watched him with obvious delight. Bianca sat down in the armchair opposite the alley cat, stirred her cup, and took a sip. Perfect, as usual. Her thoughts drifted to the night before. She'd actually had fun at the lounge with Roxy last night. *Fun.* It seemed like such an alien concept. She hadn't realized how badly she needed to laugh and to dance.

Of course, she'd nearly burst into tears when they arrived

home and she'd realized Flint wasn't there waiting for her. Or was he? She'd had a funny feeling all night that he was close by, keeping an eye on her and brooding over her sharp words from the night before. Or was that just her imagination—there was that invisible fiancé problem rearing its ugly head once again.

The doorbell rang, and Rupert screeched with alarm. Bianca frowned. She wasn't expecting anyone at this early hour.

"Don't answer that!" Flint's fearful voice came from a spot to her right.

"So you are here!" Bianca cried accusingly, staring beetle-browed in the direction of his voice. She fired off a few questions: "Has anyone ever told you it's not polite to lurk? Where did you disappear to yesterday? Or have you been here this whole time? And why exactly can't I answer my own door?"

"Because you are in grave danger, that's why," he said sternly, ignoring all her other queries.

Oblivious to Flint's warning, Roxy had sprung to her feet and was on her way to the door. "Roxy, wait!" Bianca called out, chasing after her. "Flint says not to open the door!"

"Hiya, Flint!" Roxy called out. "And why the heck shouldn't we answer the door?"

"That's what I asked him!" said Bianca. "So far he hasn't offered any explanations, but he seems adamant."

"Telegram for a Miss Bianca Moon!" came a voice from the other side.

"I'll go take a look," Flint said. "Do *not* open that door unless I give you the all-clear."

"Okey dokey," answered Bianca, putting her eye to the peephole. She could make out the blurry figure of a young dog in a red uniform with a round cap on his head.

Flint was back seconds later. "False alarm," he said. "It's a genuine telegraph dog."

"As opposed to a telegraph dog impersonator?" Bianca asked, perplexed. "I'm not sure why you felt the need to scare us like that." Bianca tightened the knot in her robe and cracked open the door.

"Telegram for Miss Bianca Moon?" repeated the pup, waving a yellow envelope in his paws.

"That would be me," she said, taking it from him and thanking him.

He tipped his hat and scurried away.

"A telegram, how exciting!" exclaimed the alley cat. "Let's see who it's from!"

Bianca slid a razor-sharp nail under the edge of the envelope as they made their way back to the living room. Roxy peered eagerly over her shoulder as she unfolded a slip of paper with the well-known Western Transmit letterhead at the top. The message read:

```
I know who hired the Queen of
Spades STOP Meet me at pier 42 at
1PM today for answers STOP Come
alone STOP
```

"How very mysterious," said Bianca.

"It's downright suspicious is what it is," hissed Roxy. "I'm sure I don't even need to tell you that you're not going."

Bianca's whiskers quivered. "What if the sender is someone who genuinely wants to help?"

"You can't be serious," grumbled the alley cat. "Snap out of it, Bianca! You have to stop putting yourself in the crosshairs! Flint? Are you there? What do you think of the message?"

"Tell Roxy I'm right here," came Flint's voice to her right. "It's definitely a trap. And trust me, I have good reasons for thinking that. We need to talk, Bianca."

"I'm all ears," she replied. "But this better not have anything to do with that loathsome hitdog you were chatting with the other night. I haven't forgotten about that, you know."

"That loathsome dog, as you call her, came here to warn us!" He paused, as if gathering the courage to say something. Finally, he said: "There's a contract out on your life now, Bianca."

Her green eyes went wide. "What do you mean there's a contract out on my lives?"

"Yes. Well, it's just the one life now, isn't it?" Flint said icily. "Which only makes the job that much easier for them. Someone out there has decided they've had enough of your meddling and they've hired a hitcat to take you out."

Bianca wondered in passing how Flint knew she was down to one life. Had he heard it on the radio? She filled Roxy in on Flint's bombshell revelation. The alley cat made a sour face and said: "Really? Flint thinks there's a contract out on your life? How could he possibly know that?"

"That hitdog told him as much the other night," Bianca explained. "Though why he would believe a word out of her mouth is a mystery to me."

"I believe Valova," grumbled Flint, "because everything she has told me adds up. Someone called Mister X hired her, and she'd been keeping tabs on their go-between, which is how she heard about this latest development."

"And she can't tell us who this nebulous Mister X is?" asked Bianca.

"No, but we've narrowed it down some," said Flint. "It turns out Mister X is someone at the Sixth Precinct."

Bianca gasped. "Do you have any proof?" she asked sharply.

"I went looking for proof the other night and I found a bogus invoice for sixteen thousand and five hundred dollars in the precinct files. The exact amount that Valova was paid. This phony invoice was approved by none other than the precinct captain, so in all likelihood he is implicated."

"I don't understand," Bianca said, puzzled. "Why would they want to murder a *Gazette* reporter?"

"I got a tip that the mob had infiltrated the Sixth Precinct, and I was putting together an article about it. I made the mistake of calling the police captain directly. He yelled a bunch of expletives at me and hung up. I probably became a target at that very moment."

Bianca's brow furrowed. It all made sense, but they needed hard proof. "How sure are you that the precinct captain is the dog behind this?" she asked.

Flint hesitated. "Not a hundred percent. But he's the most likely suspect, that's for sure."

Bianca relayed everything Flint had told her to Roxy. The alley cat snarled in disgust. "How about that? The very dogs we were relying on to solve the case turn out to be the bad guys! I shoulda known better than to trust coppers!"

"I doubt the two detectives are involved," Flint clarified. "At least, I hope not, because I'm counting on them to do their jobs. In the meantime, Bianca, your apartment isn't safe. You need to get dressed and pack a bag while we figure out somewhere for you to lie low."

"I'm not letting these thugs chase me out of my own home!" Bianca said, outraged.

"What did he say?" asked Roxy.

"Flint doesn't think my apartment is safe anymore."

"Well, he's got a point!" said the alley cat. "The next time you answer the door it could be a hired assassin! You're welcome to hide out at my place if you like, but I've got six roommates and none of them can keep a secret. Hey, I bet Tabatha would let you stay at her apartment uptown. I lived there with her for a few weeks when I was between places. You should see her pad. It's in a luxury building with twenty-four-hour doordogs posted at the entrance. You'd be safe there. Hey, Flint? Who should we be on the lookout for?"

"The killer who took on the job is a cat known as the West Side Cowboy. Valova says he's a nasty customer."

"Flint says he's a cat called the West Side Cowboy?" Bianca repeated. "What a weird name."

"I've heard it before," said Roxy. "Didn't they used to work for the railroad, riding on horseback in front of the freight trains back when the tracks were at street level? I guess this cat turned to a life of crime when he lost his job. Do we know what he looks like?"

"He's a lanky black tomcat who wears all black from boots to hat," said Flint. "His weapons of choice are two single-action revolvers."

"Yikes! This is serious," said Roxy when she was clued in.

Bianca stared down at the telegram in her hands, the tip of her white tail twitching restlessly. This message could be a trap, but what if it wasn't? The thought of going into hiding like some frightened rabbit didn't sit well with her, even if she was down to her last life. If these murderous thugs had any notion of the white-hot anger that still consumed her, they would be the ones quaking in their boots. And there was no way she could rely on Puddleworth and Digby to solve the case. The detectives' track record so far had been an uninterrupted string of blunders, each one worse than the last.

44 · Tatiana Val: The Cowboy

Sleep eluded Val in the early-morning hours. The thought that there was a hitcat out there stalking Bianca Moon at this very moment had her on edge. Val knew all too well how these jobs typically unfolded. There was a brief period of reconnaissance, but once the best time and location were decided on, the job unfolded in a flash. She had heard Bianca's interview on the radio last night and the thought that the Angora had only one life left had sent a shudder down Val's ghostly spine.

Giving up on rest, Val slipped out of her bunk and grabbed her umbrella. She drifted through the locked cage door and along the basement passageway. Around her the space resonated with the bullfrog-like snores of her fellow ghosts. Winding her way up the stairs to the ground floor, she found the Delancey Market bustling with the living. Passing out into the street, she was momentarily blinded by the bright light. The morning sun was well on its way into a clear blue sky, compelling her to put her umbrella up to cross over into the shade. From there it was a matter of hopscotching from one patch of shade to the next, with the broad expanse of Houston Street being her biggest stretch of exposed sunlight. Val's umbrella began to smoke as she traversed the wide crosstown street, but she plowed onward, knowing that if she burned through this umbrella, the Siberian would just replace it with a new one.

The night before, Val had slipped some twenty-dollar bills to a few handpicked Market ghosts and put them to work. One of her scouts had reported back to her just before sunrise. The West Side Cowboy had been spotted drinking at a bar on the Lower East Side, not far from the Market, as it happened. Her scouts had tailed him back to his pad down on Rivington, which was where Val was headed now. The plan was to keep an eye on this hitcat's movements so she could warn Bianca before he got her in the crosshairs.

Arriving at the Rivington Street address, Val proceeded upstairs to apartment 4K, where she found the lanky tomcat snoring in bed with some scantily clad floozy curled up next to him. His cowboy hat was on a hook by the door, and his gun belt was slung over the nearby bedpost, the revolvers' pearl handles glinting in the morning sunlight.

His place was in disarray, with empty beer bottles and broken glass scattered about the floor. Clearly this cat liked to blow all his loot on hussies and booze. She spotted two ghosts cowering in the living room, a young couple dressed in turn-of-the-century-style clothing. The cat in the billowing dress was clutching a bundle in a blanket to her chest. The family hid in a closet once they realized they'd been spotted, terrified looks on their faces.

Val soon grew bored listening to the two snoring cats. Clearly this lout wasn't going anywhere anytime soon. Then the phone rang in the other room. With a loud snort the bedraggled tomcat sat bolt upright, blinking in confusion. When he realized it was his telephone that had woken him up, he cursed and spat into a corner of the room. Swinging his legs over the side of the bed, he pulled on his boots and tottered over to a utility sink, where he drank long and hard from the faucet. Then he ducked his head under the stream and let the cool water run over him. The phone had stopped ringing, but it started up again a minute later. Letting fly with another curse, he stomped over to the living room and picked up the receiver.

"Who the hell is this?" he growled into the phone.

Val wasn't near enough to make out the voice on the other end of the line so she drifted closer, standing cheek to cheek with the black cat. "Why are you calling me at this ungodly hour!" he demanded angrily.

This time Val heard the reply, and she recognized the gruff voice on the other end—it was the Delancey Market butcher. "Hey, I'm just the messenger, pal. But you'd better listen up. Mister X isn't happy. Says you're dragging your heels on this job when it needs to be done quick. This Angora is getting a lot of press, and that spells trouble for your client. The target is down to her last life, so that should make your job simple and quick. Mister X just sent the Angora a telegram, luring her to pier 42 at one p.m. today. All you gotta do is show up and make good on your contract."

"Today? Mister X wants it done today? That's not how this works!" protested the black cat.

"Well, that's the way it's gonna work this time if you wanna get paid!"

The West Side Cowboy complained bitterly, but in the end, he jotted down the pier number and the time on a torn bit of newspaper and said he would be there. "This better not turn out to be a setup!" he griped, before hanging up the receiver.

The disgruntled tomcat stretched and walked stiffly back into the bedroom, where he poked the sleeping tortie in his bed with a boot toe until she stirred and opened one eye. "Time to clear outta here, baby. I've got a job to do."

While his nighttime companion got dressed and gathered her things, the West Side Cowboy sat down at a small table with his guns. He dismantled each weapon one at a time, cleaning them meticulously. Val approved of his work. This guy might be a slob in daily life, but he took good care of his weapons. When he was done, he loaded each six-shooter with 45-caliber bullets and spun the cylinder. Pulling back the hammer, he looked down the barrel and sighted on an empty can across the room. "Bang!" he said, before lowering the hammer gingerly with his thumb.

Val hurried back down the stairs and out onto the street. The sun had risen still farther in the sky and she popped open her black umbrella for cover as she made her way west along Rivington. She needed to track down Flint right away.

45 · Junior Detective Morton Digby: The Milk Truck

The two detectives got no response when they rang Bianca's doorbell. Morton jammed his thumb on the buzzer a second time and finally the door opened to reveal Roxy, blocking their way and glowering at them in a decidedly hostile manner.

"Hey there, Roxy," said Detective Puddleworth. "We need to speak to Miss Moon about an urgent matter."

"Bianca's pretty busy right now," replied the alley cat, not moving.

"Oh, just let them in already!" came Bianca's voice from somewhere distant.

The two detectives stepped into the parlor, where they found the Angora surrounded by cats. Tabatha, the lounge owner, was there, along with a handful of alley cats who all seemed to take their cues from Roxy. Bianca was sitting in the armchair, dressed in black pants and a teal blouse, with a pirate-like scarf wrapped around her head. It seemed to Morton like they were attempting to disguise her. Bianca was complaining that she was hot, doing her best to argue her way out of the opera gloves Roxy was pushing on her.

Detective Puddleworth cleared his throat. "Bianca, could we have a word with you alone?"

Roxy bristled. "Alone? You two birdbrains are lucky I let you through the door! Just say what you came to say and get out!"

Bianca slipped on a pair of oversized sunglasses and peered at her reflection in a hand mirror. "Let me guess," she said, addressing the detectives. "You finally figured out that Peggy Sneekly had nothing to do with Flint's murder?"

Detective Puddleworth looked hurt. "It didn't take us long to realize she wasn't involved, and *no*, that's not why we're here. We're concerned that your continued interest in the case has made you a target of sinister forces."

The Angora shot them a quizzical look. "Sinister forces? Do you mean that Mister X is out to kill me?"

This comment caught Morton and his partner off guard. The Scottie exclaimed: "How on earth do you know about Mister X?"

"I have my sources," Bianca replied coyly.

"Did you think we were playing dress-up?" snarled Roxy. "We need to make sure no one can recognize her! We also know that Mister X is someone from your very own precinct. He's been hiding under your noses this whole time!"

"She," corrected Detective Puddleworth.

Bianca pushed the sunglasses to the top of her head and looked at them squarely for the first time. "She? Let me guess, you have another suspect."

"We do," replied Detective Puddleworth. "And we're quite certain this time. It turns out the captain's personal secretary—a papillon named Shirley—was a plant for the mob. She took advantage of the captain's poor eyesight and faulty memory to further the mafia's interests. When she

found out Flint was doing a story about organized crime infiltrating their precinct, she decided to eliminate the threat."

Bianca's frown deepened. "Have you arrested her?"

"Unfortunately, the suspect fled before we could appre-
hend her," an abashed Morton confessed. "We have patroldogs
all over the city looking for her as we speak, and I have no
doubt we will soon track her down."

Bianca shook her head in disgust.

Tabatha stood up and handed Detective Puddleworth a yellow envelope. "You should take a look at this, detectives. We're
worried someone is trying to lure Bianca out into the open."

The two detectives scrutinized the short message with
interest. "You are right to be suspicious," cried the Scottie.
"Don't go anywhere near that pier, Bianca!"

"Of course she's not going!" snapped Roxy. "We're planning to whisk her off somewhere safe and keep her there until
you two put this hitcat behind bars."

Morton fixed the alley cat with a piercing stare. "What
makes you think it's a hitcat this time?"

"Have you two heard of the West Side Cowboy?" asked
Roxy.

"Sure," said Morton. "His name is on a wanted poster at
the precinct."

"Well he's the hired gun this time," the alley cat assured
them.

"What makes you think he's involved?" asked the Scottie.

"Just trust us, it's him," Roxy replied, exchanging a knowing look with the Angora.

"So where are you planning to hide out?" asked Detective
Puddleworth.

"We're going to take her up to my apartment in Yorkieville," said Tabatha.

"We can drive you up there in a squad car and post a patroldog at your door," offered the Scottie.

"No squad cars!" growled Roxy. "And no cops. We're going for speed and secrecy. And I already got her a ride." The alley cat smirked. "My friend Cliff has a milk truck, and once he's done with his deliveries he's going to pick us up and motor us uptown before he heads back to the warehouse with the empties!"

Just then a horn beeped outside. Roxy ran over to the window and peeked through the curtains. "Here he is now! Let's go, Bianca! No time to waste!"

"Morton, why don't you help escort Bianca uptown?" suggested the Scottie. "I'll head back to the precinct and put together a team to catch this West Side Cowboy character if he shows up at the pier."

Morton pulled Detective Puddleworth to one side. "We're partners, J.B. We need to stick together, remember?"

"Yes, but someone needs to keep Bianca safe now that we know she's the target. She only has the one life left. We don't have a choice—we need to split up!"

"Why don't I take pier duty?" The thought of confronting an armed killer scared Morton witless, but it was also his chance to show he had what it took to be a big-city detective, to prove hounds like Callahan and Buckley wrong, and to finally dispel the doubts that had plagued him since joining the force.

But the Scottie shook his head disapprovingly. "Sorry,

Morton. We both know Sergeant Doyle will expect me to take the lead on this."

"Fine," Morton grumbled. "But once Bianca is installed uptown, I'm going to hightail it down to the pier!" Morton checked his watch and frowned—it was nearly noon already.

Out on the street, Morton examined the small white truck parked at the curb. It had a rounded hood and wide accordion doors so the milkdog could hop in and out with ease. TWO FIELD FARMS was painted on the side in wavy red letters. Roxy's friend Cliff was leaning against the vehicle chewing on a toothpick. He was a skinny whippet in an all-white uniform with a black bow tie and a peaked cap. Morton looked up and down the street warily before signaling to Roxy that the coast was clear. There wasn't enough room for all of them to ride up front so Bianca volunteered to ride in the back, pointing out that no one would see her that way. They cleared a narrow space for her among the stacks of crates and she climbed in. Cliff got behind the wheel, and Morton, Tabatha, and Roxy piled onto the front seat beside him. Even so, Roxy was forced to sit on Morton's lap, which she was none too pleased about.

"You really didn't have to come, Detective," griped the alley cat.

"I for one feel better knowing the detective is along," Tabatha said kindly.

Roxy rolled her eyes. "Yeah, if the bad guy shows up, maybe Detective Digby can herd him into a phone booth."

Morton gritted his teeth but decided to let this dig slide.

Cliff zipped through traffic, making good time on their

drive uptown. Barely twenty minutes had passed before they pulled up in front of a staid residential building with a red awning on East 72nd Street, a stone's throw from the East River. It was a sedate neighborhood in Yorkieville with neatly planted trees and clean sidewalks dotted with parents pushing strollers. They all piled out of the truck, but they were in for a rude shock when they threw open the milk truck's back doors—Bianca had vanished.

"That sneaky, two-faced furball!" howled Roxy. "I can't believe she gave us the slip! How the heck did she get out?"

"She must've just opened the door and snuck out at a stoplight," said Morton. He couldn't believe it. His partner had given him a simple task—keep Bianca safe—and he'd lost track of her mere minutes later.

"I bet she was planning this all along," fumed Roxy. "Cliff! You need to turn this truck around and take us back downtown!"

"I would if I could, Roxy," lamented the whippet, "but I gotta go drop off the empties and return the truck or I can kiss my job goodbye!"

"Hurry!" cried Tabatha. "If you take the Second Avenue trolley you might still be able to catch her!"

46 · Bianca Moon: The Boat

Bianca moseyed past the colorful storefronts and quaint restaurants on Christopher Street, its narrow sidewalks and tree-shaded blocks brimming with West Village charm. She was still wearing her teal blouse and her black pants but had ditched the scarf and the gloves in the truck. Dark sunglasses hid her eyes. The wind picked up and the streets grew quieter as she neared the river. Bianca's pulse began to race when she got her first glimpse of the Hudson River up ahead and the Hoboken shoreline in the distance. Her watch showed ten to one—she was right on time.

Slipping out of the milk truck at a traffic light had been child's play. It had amused her to watch the truck start up again, carrying Roxy, Tabatha, and Junior Detective Digby uptown without her. It was better this way. The message had said to come alone, and surely that meant not having a temperamental alley cat glued to her side.

This mysterious telegram could be a trap—she knew that. But there was also a chance it might be a genuine tip, one she risked losing out on forever if she didn't show. Detective Puddleworth was convinced that the precinct secretary was behind Flint's murder, but he'd demonstrated that same conviction with all the previous suspects. She had long since concluded that the Scottish terrier and his partner were both hopeless, even if they meant well.

Reaching West Street, Bianca came to a stop in a shady spot and took in the wide cobblestone thoroughfare standing between her and the waterfront. A chaotic mix of automobiles, bicycles, and trolleys streamed back and forth, with pedestrians exploiting the gaps between vehicles to cross. To her right, farther uptown, Bianca spotted the Chelsea Piers Terminal, with its impressive stone facade. A line of four black smokestacks hinted at the large ship docked there. Directly across from her, the five-finger piers were built on a more modest scale, jutting out from the City's shoreline like jagged teeth. Most of them had narrow ferry terminals erected along the length of the pier, but Pier 42 had only a small boxy structure street-side, with a large sign that read DAY LINE FERRY bolted to the flat rooftop. An untidy line of local families and out-of-town tourists were queued up at the ferry's outside ticket window, doubtless looking to board a cruise up the scenic Hudson. Bianca had caught the Day Line ferry once herself, many years ago, when her adoptive parents had taken her on a cruise up the river to Wolf Mountain Park for a day spent picnicking.

Bianca knew that Flint must be sulking close by. Her escape from the milk truck had rendered him apoplectic. For blocks he had badgered her nonstop to turn around. Eventually, she'd snapped at him and told him to *zip it*, just so she could hear herself think. But now it was time to extend an olive branch. She stared up at the cloudless sky and said: "There isn't much shade by the piers, darling, so please be careful."

"There isn't a lick of shade out here," came his surly response. "And my umbrella is already wearing thin."

"You know you don't have to tag along," she said in as kindly a manner as she could manage.

"Do you expect me to just sit back and twiddle my thumbs while you tempt fate on the pier?"

Bianca shrugged. "There's a pedestrian bridge down there," she said, pointing to a covered structure spanning the roadway a few blocks to the south. "You could cross in its shadow."

"Fine."

"I'll look for you in that patch of shade on the north side of the ferry building when I'm done." Saying this, she stepped off the curb, but was forced to jump back when a sedan whizzed by, honking loudly.

"Please don't do this, my love!" he begged her.

"I have to see this through to the end, darling. It's the only way forward for me."

He made no reply.

Bianca waited for a group of bicycles to go by and then stepped out into the bright sunlight of the roadway. Halfway across she had to break into a jog to get clear of a taxi, but she reached the other side without incident. She zigzagged her way past the ferry line and the vendor carts selling shaved ice, before finally stepping out onto the wooden planks of Pier 42 itself. Her eye was drawn to a massive ocean liner being towed up the river toward newly built midtown docks. The ship's decks were crowded with transatlantic passengers waving cheerfully to indifferent locals.

Scanning the crowd around her, Bianca saw that almost

everybody was wearing a lid of some sort. There was a dizzying medley of caps, cloches, fedoras, berets, trilbies, porkpie hats, and pillbox hats. But not a single cowboy hat in sight.

Bianca pushed her sunglasses up onto her forehead. Removing the yellow telegram envelope from her purse, she held it prominently in her hand as she wandered down the long pier. A spiffy day tripper boat was docked to her right, its crew busy checking tickets for the line of passengers filing on board. The number of cats and dogs on the pier thinned the farther along she went, whereas the seagulls flapping overhead grew in number, the noisy white birds jockeying for coveted spots on top of the wooden pylons anchoring the pier.

She came upon an old steamboat docked on the southward side. The name on the bow identified it as the *Langhorne*. She realized with delight that it was the very same boat she had traveled on with her family years ago. In decades past the *Langhorne* had been the crown jewel of the Hudson. Painted white, it had long, elegant lines, four stacked decks, and two slender funnels poking up into the sky. Bianca moved in to get a closer look at the now-derelict vessel. Peeling paint and patches of rust made it clear that the boat's glory days were well behind it. The fading wake from the ocean liner made the *Langhorne* rock back and forth with a rhythmic clanking sound as it bumped up against the truck tires hung along the side of the pier. Bianca had read that old boats like this one were often towed out to sea and sunk, and she wondered if the *Langhorne* was fated to end up in the ocean's depths, a prospect that made her wistful. She was standing there lost in thought when she was startled by a strange voice in her ear. "Watch out, Bianca! He's here!"

Ears flattened and tail puffed, she spun around. There was no one there. "Who is this?" she asked, suddenly suspicious.

"It's Val. Tatiana Valova, that is."

"How is it that I can hear you?" Bianca asked, bewildered. "And why are you speaking to me?"

"You're the first mortal I've talked to. But we don't have time for explanations! You need to run, Bianca! He's been shadowing you from the moment you set foot on the pier."

"I don't see anyone!" Bianca said irritably.

"He's hiding behind the flagpole," said the voice of Flint's killer. "Don't look directly at him!"

Bianca stole a sideways glance at the large flagpole erected in the middle of the pier about twenty yards away. Sure enough, she glimpsed a shoulder poking out from behind it, along with the brim of a hat. Someone skinny was pressed right up against it.

A head peeked out and looked in her direction, and stony eyes met her own. Bianca's breath quickened. Realizing he'd been spotted, the figure stepped out from behind the flagpole, a malevolent sneer on his face. He was a black cat dressed all in black from his boots to the top of his cowboy hat. He brushed open his jacket in a practiced movement and drew a revolver from a belt holster. Bianca cast about frantically for somewhere—anywhere—to take cover, but there was nowhere to hide on the wide-open pier. Moving on instinct, she whirled around and leapt onto the old steamboat, clawing her way over the side railing. Her sunglasses were knocked off her head and they bounced off the rail before dropping into the water below. A shot pinged above her and lodged in the boat's metal siding. Bianca raced along the deck with her head ducked down. Four more pops sounded behind her. She dove behind a metal bench, her heart pounding, and stayed crouched down, listening intently for any movement. *It was a trap after all,* she thought. Coming here had not been her brightest idea. If not for that ghost's unexpected warning, this guncat would have easily picked her off. But she would have plenty of time to beat herself up about it later—if she survived.

The black cat cursed loudly. She risked a peek over the top of the bench and saw that he had closed the distance between them. He holstered his weapon, took a few steps forward, and jumped onto the boat's railing.

Bianca crawled away on her hands and knees until she encountered a door. Tugging on the brass handle, she opened it just wide enough to squirm through into the dull gray interior of the vessel. A bullet cracked the door's rounded glass window above her, sending a shower of broken glass raining down on her head. Scrambling to her feet, she made a mad dash up a flight of stairs to her left. She took them two at a time and had only just turned the bend onto the landing when she heard the metal door being wrenched open below.

Heavy boots clomped on the iron flooring, the sound echoing throughout the empty ship. A raspy voice cut through the air, not ten feet away: "Here, kitty kitty! You're only making this harder for yourself!"

Bianca crept silently up toward the second level, one hand on the metal banister, as her pursuer's footsteps passed the staircase and grew more distant. Then her metal watch band pinged brightly against the railing and she froze. Below her, the black cat stopped, then his footsteps turned back in her direction and he started up the stairs.

She scrambled up the remaining steps, flung open a side door, and rushed back out into the light. There was a commotion on the pier and she saw three figures sprinting along it in her direction. Her heart leapt: it was Roxy and the two detectives! On their heels was a whole squad of patroldogs.

She just needed to buy herself a little time.

"Gotcha!" A rough hand seized her from behind and she felt the hard barrel of a gun pressed against her temple. "Say your prayers, Bianca Moon," he hissed through bared teeth.

This was followed by a hollow click.

And then another.

"Rats!" he swore. Hope rekindled in her chest. She elbowed him hard in the gut and he grunted, releasing her. She gave him a shove and ran down the deck. A glance over her shoulder showed him pulling a second revolver from his belt. He leveled it in her direction. Breaking left, she clambered onto the top bar of the railing and sprang out toward the pier, ten feet below. She landed hard on the wooden planks, feeling a sharp pain in her ankle and scraping a gash in her forearm. Terrified, she turned onto her back, only to see the West Side Cowboy looming above her as he stretched over the railing. His gun was aimed right at her, a twisted smile playing on his lips.

The shot rang out across the pier just as Roxy flung herself on top of her—a frantic ball of denim and mottled red-and-black fur. The alley cat shielded Bianca with her own body as the gun rang out five more times. To Bianca's horror, her friend flinched each time.

"Roxy!" she shrieked. "What have you done!"

"Don't worry, Princess," gasped the alley cat. "I've still got three lives left, remember?" As she said this, Bianca felt the weight of her friend's body slowly lift off her. Right before her eyes, Roxy vanished into nothingness, leaving Bianca clinging desperately to a denim jacket.

Bianca limped to her feet, hot tears streaming down her face. Above her, the West Side Cowboy had cracked open his revolver and was rapidly slotting gold bullets into the cylinder. Out of the corner of her eye she saw the blur that was Junior Detective Digby scrambling onto the *Langhorne*. The border collie shinnied his way up a pole to get to the second level, then he tackled the black cat, sending the gun skittering across the deck. A fierce struggle ensued as the two animals traded punches. Junior Detective Digby had the last word when he landed a right hook that left the black cat dazed. In a flash, Digby slipped a handcuff onto the cat's wrist and latched the other loop around the railing. At the stern of the ship, the patroldogs had lowered a gangplank onto the old steamboat and were streaming aboard.

Detective Puddleworth rushed over to where Bianca was still sprawled on the dock. "Are you okay, Miss Moon? Are you hit? Do you need an ambulance?"

That's when Bianca noticed that her teal blouse was covered in blood. She had to pat herself down to be sure. "I'm okay, just a twisted ankle," she assured the detective. "It's not my blood," she added in a strangled voice.

"Roxy is the hero of the hour!" the Scottie said admiringly. "She raced up the pier like a bat out of hell, leaving the rest of us in the dust!"

Bianca struggled to her feet and the detective helped her over to a nearby wooden beam. She sat down on it gingerly. "Did you catch that crooked secretary yet?" she asked Detective Puddleworth.

"I'm afraid Shirley is still at large. But it's only a matter of time before we get our paws on her. And once we do, she'll spend the rest of her days in a prison cell, I assure you!"

From her seat Bianca had a good view of Junior Detective Digby and the half a dozen patroldogs as they escorted the snarling hitcat back onto the pier. Spotting her, the West Side Cowboy shot a venomous look in her direction until a police hound prodded him in the back with his baton. Detective Puddleworth was called over to brief Sergeant Doyle, who had just arrived on the scene, panting heavily. Bianca was left alone, staring at the stained denim jacket in her hands.

A figure stepped between her and the sun.

Bianca squinted up at the backlit silhouette. The dog staring down at her was hard to make out, her face hidden behind a floppy sun hat and bug-eyed sunglasses. It was her distinctive ears and tail that gave her away—she was a papillon. Alarm bells went off in some dim corner of Bianca's mind. Hadn't Detective Puddleworth said that the captain's secretary was a papillon? The dog's raised arm came down swiftly, catching Bianca off guard. The crowbar gripped in her paws hit Bianca squarely on the side of her head.

"You just couldn't leave well enough alone, could you!" screeched the papillon. "You meddlesome busybody!"

Bianca collapsed onto the pier. For a brief moment, her world was all pain and confusion and a ringing sound that felt as if it would consume her. Just as suddenly as it had arrived, it all went away. She rose to her feet, her mind miraculously clear. Even her ankle felt fine. The logic behind these medical marvels became instantly and horrifyingly evident as she gazed down at the white cat in the teal blouse sprawled bleeding at her feet. Bianca gasped. Was she a ghost now too? She raised a luminous white paw and stared through it at the *Langhorne* still bobbing in the water sloshing under the pier.

She looked around herself as if in a dream. Detective Puddleworth was sprinting furiously in their direction, his features twisted with a look of horror. He tackled the papillon, wrenching the crowbar from her grip. With Sergeant Doyle's help, they soon had her attacker restrained. The Scottish terrier then dropped to his knees. "Bianca!" he cried. "Talk to me, Bianca!"

"I'm right here, Detective," she blurted out, but it was useless—he couldn't hear her.

Bianca suddenly became aware of the sizzling heat from the sun beating down on her. The light was blinding.

"This way, my love, hurry!" It was Flint. He held a patchy umbrella over her head as they ran. The umbrella began to smoke and disintegrated into nothingness halfway through their mad dash toward the sliver of shade afforded by the ferry terminal. Bianca dove into the building's shadow and the stinging on her exposed arms and face quickly subsided. Her blouse was smoldering but intact.

"Let's get you inside!" Flint took hold of her elbow, and to her astonishment, pulled her right through the wall and into the ferry terminal itself. They drifted over to an empty bench in the waiting area. It was the strangest sensation—hovering a half inch above the wooden slats of the bench.

"Are you okay, my love?" Flint asked, concern etched on his face.

"Yes, I think so," she replied. "Now that I'm out of the sun I feel fine. Light as a feather, though. It's as if I didn't weigh anything at all!" There was a slight tremor in her voice.

"Oh, Bianca, why did you have to throw all your lives away?"

"What's done is done, Flint."

He sighed, his amber eyes filled with sadness.

"Hey, Flint! I can see you!" she cried.

"We're both ghosts now, Bianca. We can see other ghosts. That's how it works."

She reached out, caressing the fur on his scraggly face and scratching him under his chin. "And I can feel you too!"

Flint leaned forward and kissed her softly on the lips. "Yes, we are on the same plane once again. But at what terrible cost."

"At least we're together once more. Being ghosts can't be all bad, so long as we're together, right?" She searched his eyes for some small kernel of joy. "Hey, did you know that Val came and warned me when I was out on the pier?"

"Val, is it? You two are on a first-name basis now? But, yes, she was already halfway to you by the time I spotted that devil in the cowboy hat. Her umbrella burned up and she barely managed to dive through the side of that other day-tripper boat."

Bianca thought about this for a long moment and then said: "You may be right about giving her a second chance."

"There's no point in holding on to grudges in the afterlife. A good friend of mine taught me that. I think you're gonna like it at Ghosthall, Bianca. It makes me feel wretched to think you ended up the same way I did, but I can't wait to spend the afterlife with you."

"And I can't wait to meet all your new friends," Bianca replied excitedly. She looked the wolfhound up and down. He was as handsome as ever with those bushy eyebrows of his.

Next thing she knew, Flint was down on one knee. "I want to do this properly this time!" He reached into his side pocket and pulled out a ring box. Bianca's eyes went wide. "How?" she cried. "How do you have the ring?"

"I'll explain later. First you need to answer my question." He gazed up at her earnestly. "Bianca Moon—my sweet pretty—will you marry me?"

"Yes, darling, I will," she purred, her heart flooding with joy as he slipped the ring onto her finger. Springing to his feet, he took her in his arms and tipped her back for a long and wondrous kiss.

47 · Junior Detective Morton Digby: The Aftermath

Monday

Monday morning found the usual hurly-burly of the 6th Precinct in full swing. Morton was at his desk typing up the case report. Sitting opposite him, just a few feet away, Detective Puddleworth was fielding phone calls from the press. It wasn't the best moment for Buckley and Callaway to mosey over, but this had never stopped the two hounds before.

"Howzit going, Digby?" said Buckley. "We heard about your case! Did Shirley really clock that poor Angora on the head with a crowbar?"

Morton nodded grimly.

"And it was the unlucky cat's ninth life too!" cried Callaway. "What a waste."

"Who would've believed it?" said Buckley. "Our little Shirley, a murderer *and* a plant for the mob!"

"I hope she rots in jail," muttered Morton.

"She sure gave the precinct a black eye," said Callaway.

"It's too bad that hitcat didn't stick around in jail," said Buckley. "He burned a life the first chance he got. Could be anywhere by now."

"It's hard to hold on to feline crooks." Callaway shook his head ruefully. "Our bank robber pulled up stakes too."

"But we'll catch him again once he goes back to his old tricks," growled Buckley. "And someday he'll run out of lives!"

"That's a copper's life for ya," Callaway said philosophically. "It's a bit like that famous cat who has to push that rock up a hill over and over."

"I think you mean Sisypuss," said Buckley.

"Yes, that's it! Us cops are like Sisypuss."

"Hey, Digby," said Buckley. "We heard you tackled that armed killer single-handedly yesterday. Nice work!"

"Thanks." Morton blinked uncertainly, caught off guard by the note of genuine approval in the hound's voice.

"Sergeant Doyle claims you fellas are in the captain's good books," said Callaway, grinning and punching Morton in the shoulder. "I guess that means you're rolling with the big dawgs now!"

"Yep, you're one of us now, Digby," said Buckley. "And that means we've got your back!"

"Darn straight we do," added Callaway. "You can count on us!"

The two hounds wandered off, tails wagging. Before they passed out of earshot, Morton overheard a snickering Callaway revert to form: "Who'd have thunk it? A herding dog as a detective in the City Police force!"

The Scottie had hung up the phone and caught the tail end of their conversation. "Looks like you've got two new pals to lean on around here." He chortled.

"Yeah, that's a real hoot," Morton replied, straight-faced.

"All kidding aside," said the Scottie, "they're right, you know. You showed great courage in the face of danger yesterday. I'm proud to have you as my partner."

"Thanks, J.B.," Morton said. "I was just doing my job."

"Horsefeathers! Not many cops would have jumped on that boat and tackled an armed guncat single-handedly!"

"*You* would have," said Morton. "If only you could run a little faster."

The Scottie threw his head back and laughed. "Not much chance of that with these pint-sized legs."

Detective Puddleworth's phone rang again and he spent the next five minutes being interviewed by another reporter about Bianca's death.

Morton couldn't help wondering if Bianca's ghost had stuck around, just like Riyo's, and he decided to add that to his list of questions for Louisa later today. Riyo had been disappointed to hear that he hadn't had time to talk to the psychic yesterday, but when he had explained about Bianca losing her last life, the Shiba Inu had broken down in tears. She had blamed herself for callously taking one of the Angora's lives. Like a lot of dogs, she had fooled herself into thinking cats never ran out of lives.

When Puddleworth hung up, he said: "Who could have imagined our first case together would turn out to be so newsworthy!"

"Not me, that's for sure," Morton replied. "But I just can't feel good about it considering how it all ended."

"I know what you mean, Morton. This one is going to sting for a long time. The only thing we can do is show up to work the next day and keep plugging away."

Morton supposed the Scottie was right. In this crazy city the main thing was to keep moving forward.

Sergeant Doyle came whistling down the aisle a short

while later, just as Morton was putting the finishing touches on the report. "Hey, fellas! All done with the paperwork? Great. I'll take that!" He snatched the typed document from Morton's hands. "Why the long faces? You two should be walking on air! You unmasked that double-dealing Shirley, and the captain won't be forgetting that anytime soon."

Faced with two stubbornly down-in-the-mouth detectives, the bulldog realized his message wasn't getting through. "Look, I get it," he exclaimed. "It's the dead cat, isn't it? You two are gonna need thicker skins if you want to last at this job. But this oughta cheer you up! I've got a real gem of an assignment for the two of you. Someone broke into a brownstone on Ninth Street overnight and cracked into a prominent jeweler's private safe." The sergeant dropped a dispatch ticket onto Detective Puddleworth's desk. "Better get to work, lads!"

The bulldog sauntered back up the aisle. Detective Puddleworth reached for the slip of paper and examined it intently, eyebrows raised. "Grab your hat, Morton. We'd better get our tails over to Ninth Street before the trail goes cold! We've got a jewel thief to catch!"

DELAS HERAS was born in Los Angeles, grew up in England and Spain, and moved back to the United States as a teenager. Heras has worked as a book editor, a stay-at-home parent, a dance photographer, and most recently as a museum security guard. He lives in New York City.

Made in United States
Troutdale, OR
12/15/2024

26573796R00230